ENTITLED

A novel by Carlie Yates

This is a work of fiction. Names, characters, businesses, places, events, locales, and incidents are either the products of the author's imagination or used in a fictitious manner. Any resemblance to actual persons, living or dead, or actual events is purely coincidental.

ISBN: 978-1-7332649-0-7

Cardinal Moon
Clayton, OH

CONTENT WARNING!!

This book contains emotionally sensitive subjects and situations.

To my boys. Zachary, Marcus, Jacob… You're my whole heart. You've taught me love, patience, joy, and acceptance. When I want to be a better person, I look to all of you as examples. Each of you makes this world a better, brighter place, and I couldn't be prouder if I tried.

PROLOGUE

This Wasn't Supposed to Happen

Catherine could feel the blood draining from her face, her stomach dipping uncomfortably, her heart momentarily stopping before taking off soaring, making her feel lightheaded.

No… no, this wasn't what was supposed to happen.

Not at all.

She'd planned everything so carefully, each move meticulously calculated, timed almost to the minute. How… how was it all falling apart?

This wasn't supposed to happen.

She was Catherine Garner. Everything she demanded came to be.

So why… *why* had this… this stroke of brilliance that she'd masterminded fallen apart?

But she already knew the answer to that, as the thud of fist on skin, the dotting of blood against her shirt were reminding her of the reality of her life now.

The reality of her life ever since Brody Harris had entered it.

Her mind was a whirlwind, thinking up something…anything to get this under control, to get the end result that had to happen.

It had to.

CHAPTER 1

Lady Catherine

Catherine Garner's charmed life was, for the very first time, disrupted.

"No… no, no, no."

That one simple word had been the catalyst for over sixteen years' worth of Catherine getting her way. When her mother replied with, "It's merely temporary, Catherine," she could only stare with a mixture of anger and disbelief.

She hadn't been denied anything her entire life.

Here, in this home—in her domain, the coveted house on the hill that only those she deemed worthy would enter—Catherine Garner always got her way.

Until that day, when she stood in the middle of the room filled with her trophies and pictures from her various cheerleading and gymnastics teams with her hands on her trim waist, her green eyes hard as she stared at her mother. "I'm not giving up this room."

"You have your own bedroom, and Sam needs a place to sleep."

"Sam?!" Catherine's tone was incredulous. She shot a glare to the small, frail girl with the stringy, mousy brown hair, who stood in the doorway, her dull gray eyes full of fear. "She couldn't even have a feminine name."

"Catherine Denise Garner, I did not raise you to be rude."

Catherine crossed her arms, raising her perfectly sculpted eyebrow at her mother's blatant lie. Theresa Garner was rude to any and all beneath her, turning up her tanned nose at those unworthy to be in her presence.

"That... girl is *not* taking over my room."

"Of course not, dear," Theresa said, placing her manicured hand on her daughter's arm before leaning in. "Hush now, it's only temporary."

"I don't care how temporary it is. I don't want my things moved to the basement. I entertain my friends down there, Mother, and you know that."

"For now, you can entertain them elsewhere." Theresa's smile was forced as she stepped back. "And Tyler will be in the game room."

"Seriously? Another one? And why *my* rooms? What about one of your never-used libraries?" Catherine's voice was shrill as she pushed past her mother and the small girl in the doorway, this time her glare settling on a young boy, no more than nine, who was carrying a bag far too big for his frame down the hallway. In a huff, she turned back to her mother.

"Stand up straight, Catherine."

"What am I supposed to tell Mitch when he wants to play Xbox now?"

"Well, dear, I'd say we could put it in your room, but your boyfriend isn't exactly permitted there, is he?" Theresa asked coolly.

"I suppose that's going in the basement, too?"

Catherine didn't wait for her mother's reply, choosing instead to go in search of Frank Harris, the one and only smooth-talking formerly on-the-side boyfriend of her mother's. She descended the stairs to the main floor of the house, walking past the steps that led down to the entryway and pausing to glance into the living room, which hardly looked lived in. No one was in there, its pristine furniture which she was certain the younger children would ruin looking as if the housekeeper had just finished cleaning. She turned then, passing the formal dining room on her way to the kitchen.

"Greta?" It wasn't necessary for Catherine to speak as loudly as she did when she entered, but the way her voice startled the older woman would always make her smirk. For as long as the housekeeper had been employed by her mother, Catherine still didn't know which country she came from, or if she was even legally permitted to be there.

Greta turned towards Catherine as she wiped her hands on her apron, her smile as welcoming as always. "Si, sweet girl?"

With a huff, Catherine gestured as if Greta should automatically know why she was in the room. "Frank?"

Greta gave one quick nod. "Basement, Ms. Catherine."

Catherine's smile was neither pleasant nor genuine. "Basement. Thank you. Did you know about this?"

"Isn't it wonderful? Small children here again. Sam is so much like you."

"Nothing like me. Nothing." Catherine's hands were on her hips. "And no, it's not wonderful. Did you see them? Have they even bathed recently?"

"Oh, I bet little Sam would love a bubble bath, like I used to draw for you."

A bubble bath.

Loads of bubbles and giggles, carefree fun. Greta piling bubbles on top of her hair, saying it was her crown.

But Catherine was sixteen now, and just growing used to her father no longer being there.

How dare any of them think that *this* was okay.

"Is this what has you in a mood, sweet girl?"

Catherine refrained from rolling her eyes as she turned from her housekeeper and walked back towards the stairwell leading to the entryway, where another open stairway led to the fully finished basement, feeling as if Greta had turned on her, too.

The stomping on the stairs sounded more like a herd of buffalo were running down them rather than a slender, irate sixteen-year-old girl. Strands of her blonde hair were coming loose from her messy bun, settling around her face. Under other circumstances it would have looked endearing, but today it only angered her more.

"Great. Just great. I'm supposed to be getting ready to go out with my boyfriend, and…"

"I thought you had cheerleading practice today," she heard Frank Harris, her mother's now-live-in boyfriend, say from the basement.

She inhaled sharply, refraining from reminding him that he was not her father and didn't need to start acting the part.

"Catherine?"

She proceeded down the second set of stairs, ready to instruct Frank on how to set her things up and muttered a curse as someone pushed past her on his way up.

"Do you mind?" she snapped at someone who must have been helping Frank and his children move in. The man—boy?—continued up the stairs, his hat and baggy clothes leaving it impossible for her to tell.

"Now, now… someone's in a mood."

Catherine was now at the bottom of the steps, her hand on her hip, facing her mother's boyfriend. She surmised that whomever had passed her on the stairs was the one doing all of the work; Frank stood before her in a tailored suit, his dark hair perfectly combed, the slight lines around his light gray eyes showing as he smiled at her. "Well, Frank, I wasn't even aware you had children. You never spoke of them." She purposefully left out the 'or your wife,' but the jump in her eyebrow seemed to say it for her.

"Well, Lady Catherine, I do."

She didn't even crack a smile for the nickname he'd given her, the one that made her friends swoon with envy over her mother's charming, handsome boyfriend. "Mother says it's merely temporary."

"Perhaps." His smile widened. "Why? Are you that opposed to sharing your space?"

She opened her mouth to exclaim that yes… emphatically yes, she *was* opposed to sharing her space, when she spied another suitcase and duffel bag by the large pullout couch.

"*Another* one?"

"Brody's your age; when I get them enrolled, you can show him around school." Again, Frank flashed his million-dollar smile in her direction. "I'm sure you won't mind."

She couldn't be bothered to suppress the rolling of her eyes at Frank's suggestion. And Brody? What kind of name was that? If he was expecting her to show his son around school, then by all things holy he better be as good looking, as well groomed, as…

"Excuse me," she heard the soft mumble come from behind her as that same boy that had pushed past her on the stairs was coming back into the room, another bag and a tattered book in his hands. He had sweat dripping from the ends of his dark hair that was partially covering his pale face, and his baggy clothes were hanging unattractively from his slender frame. Catherine felt the bile creep into her throat at the mere thought of having to be seen with this boy, let alone having to share her home with him when he and his siblings were so far beneath her stature.

"Catherine, this is Brody. And Brody, this is Theresa's daughter, Catherine."

Brody pushed his baseball cap back, briefly showing his blue eyes and what Catherine considered average features before pulling his cap back down over his eyes and returning his attention to his bag, which also seemed full of old, tattered books. To Catherine, not only was he ordinary, not only was he beneath her, but he had the nerve to be rude to her in her own home.

This was not going to go well.

"Well, now that that's settled, I need to help the other two," Frank said, stepping past Catherine and making his way up the stairs.

"If you don't mind," Catherine spoke up, "you might want to keep your things together, not all spread out. My trophies and such have to be moved down here."

Brody remained silent, choosing instead to sit on the couch, sinking into its plush cushions before opening a book and holding it in front of his face.

"Are you serious? Or are you just mute?"

He lowered the book, his expression one of indifference before he resumed reading.

"Whatever," Catherine huffed before stomping up two flights of stairs to her room, slamming her door so hard that the windows rattled.

Outside, the bustling in the hallway told her that her mother, her mother's boyfriend, and his never-before-mentioned children were settling in to their new rooms, beginning their new routines.

In her room, flopped on her bed, she opened her laptop, her Twitter page with its thousand-plus followers lighting up before her eyes, and she said the words aloud as she typed in her latest update.

"My life is officially over."

CHAPTER 2

So Ordinary

Catherine was lying in the middle of her plush Queen Size bed, one of her over-sized pillows covering her face. While her Twitter timeline flooded with her friends' concern, some speculating what could possibly be wrong, her cell phone began to ring. With a resigned sigh, she moved the pillow, glancing briefly at the screen before she answered.

"Just kill me now," was her plea.

"What happened?" Chelsea Reeves—her best friend and worst enemy since grade school—asked, her voice dripping with syrupy concern. "Is it Mitch? Did he break up with you?"

"Puh-lease." Catherine dismissed the question with a wave of her hand, as if she could be seen. "Look up the word 'worship', and the boy's picture is beside it, okay?"

"Then why is your life over?"

"Oh my god, so you know… Mother's been dating that guy, Frank Harris, right?" Catherine asked as she rolled to her stomach and propped up on her elbows.

"Yeah, so?"

"So she just moved him in here."

"Wouldn't that keep her out of your hair more?"

Catherine rolled her eyes at Chelsea's question. "If it were that easy, would my life be over?"

"What would be,"

"He has kids," Catherine cut her off. "Three of them. And he brought the brats with him."

"Oh, you poor thing. Do you have to share a room?"

Catherine reached over and grabbed a nail file from her nightstand, carefully working it around a tiny imperfection in her nail that she noticed. "Um, no."

"A bathroom?"

Again, Catherine rolled her eyes, as Chelsea already knew the answer. "The bathroom is part of my room; they have to use the one down the hall."

"So, what's the problem?"

"Are you kidding me, Chelsea?" Catherine stopped filing her nail, her hand outstretched as an exasperated expression filled her face. "Three brats. Three of them. My trophy room is gone, the game room is gone, and… and the basement is…" She shuddered, unable to finish the sentence.

"Is that the storage place?"

"No, one of them is staying down there. And their names? They scream white trash. Sam? For a girl? And… Tyler… that's so late 80's. And the oldest? The one who's taken over the basement? Get this… Brody. Ugh!"

"Oooo, like…"

"Hell no." Catherine cut Chelsea off before she could even finish. "He's this… this… he's this…"

"This what?" Chelsea asked.

"He's so ordinary," Catherine said, unable to even say the word without shuddering again and wrinkling her nose in disgust. "So plain, so ordinary. They all are. And that Brody kid? Frank seems to think I'm going to show him around the school. Like I'd be seen with someone like him."

"Could he be our pet project?"

Catherine shook her head at Chelsea's audacity. Did she just not get it? "Don't even think about it. He isn't even someone I would think of trying to give a makeover to. One would think someone who came from Frank would at least be halfway decent looking."

"Is he really that bad?"

"He was carrying a copy of *Catcher in the Rye,* Chels. He's probably a future serial killer."

Chelsea let out a short, harsh laugh. "Oh, Catherine, that is cold."

"I swear I'm going to have to… spend more time at Dad's or something."

"For some alone time with Mitch?"

"Yeah, something like that." Catherine squinted at the clock, her scowl deepening. "If I get so stressed that I break out, someone is going to die."

"Did you get the email from Bethany?"

Was she kidding? "In the middle of this mess?"

"Phoebe has officially resigned from the squad."

Catherine let out a short huff of air at the news. Finally, something she wanted to hear. "Good."

"Rumor has it her mother is sending her to Brighton."

"The boarding school?" A smile almost threatened to break through.

"The all-girls boarding school. Mother said that her parents were bragging about it, acting like it had been planned all along and they were just waiting for a spot to come up. We all know she wasn't about to face us."

"There's no way that troll could face *me*." Catherine sat upright, anger renewed. "Suggesting that Mitch would be interested in her? Using words like 'predatory'? Mitch… predatory?" She rolled her eyes for roughly the millionth time that day and flopped back on the bed.

"None of us believed her."

"Why would she think anyone would?" Catherine snapped. Mitch wouldn't dare cheat on her, not when being with her had done wonders for his social status at school. She'd fought her way to the top, to be the best, just like her mother had engrained in her, and she would only date someone her equal.

Never settle, her mother had said.

"Your car still out of commission?"

"I made sure I got it back with a quickness."

"It was just a scratch, Catherine," Chelsea said with a quick laugh.

"A scratch on a custom painted pearl white convertible, and I was *not* going to drive it around like that. Especially not after making sure my father got me exactly what I wanted."

Because Catherine never settled.

Not with friends, not with clothes, not with phones, or cars, or even having her home invaded by the children's laughter as they dismantled rooms' worth of her accomplishments.

She would never settle for this.

Never.

Her mood continued to darken as she prepared for her date, growling out loud at her hair that, to her, didn't want to cooperate, but to others would look flawless. She wiped at her eyeliner, swearing it was smudging even though the line was perfectly straight. And when she turned in her full-length mirror after changing clothes for the fifth time, she decided that a pair of her designer jeans and a cute summery top would have to do.

Six o'clock on the dot she received the text from Mitch, letting her know he was about to knock on the door. Catherine was not a girl to be kept waiting, nor was she a girl who liked surprises.

Not in the least.

"Lady Catherine," she heard Frank call up the staircase, and she rolled her eyes, as had done quite often that day. He was so going to pay for not telling her he had children, almost as much as he was going to pay for bringing them to her home. "Your chariot awaits."

She let out a short, soft snort before bounding down the stairs. Chariot? Try a Dodge Charger, cherry red, leather seats, and a custom stereo to die for. The car was part of the draw Catherine felt to Mitch, a fullback on the championship football team. He was hardly the sharpest knife in the drawer, but he worshiped her… as much as his brain could comprehend.

On the definite plus side for Catherine, his dark good looks more than made up for it, and his tan made his white shirt look as if it were glowing. Said shirt's seams protested at the tight fit around his muscular shoulders. His pants weren't as tight, as he claimed he needed extra room in the front to accommodate him. This wasn't something Catherine knew for a fact, as their physical intimacy hadn't progressed to that level. Mitch, however, would brag of his endowment to anyone who would listen.

Thanks to his association with her, everyone did.

He was smiling at her before she reached the bottom step. His eyes were raking over her showing exactly what he wanted from her that evening, and it certainly wasn't dinner. She smiled slyly, making a mental note, and yet knowing that he would still go home without.

"Catherine," Mitch said, his deep voice filling the entry way, "you look absolutely…"

"Aaarrhhhh!"

His words were cut off as Sam came running in, bumping into Catherine and spilling her cherry red drink down the front of Catherine's designer jeans and onto her boots, setting off the already temperamental girl.

"Are you kidding me?!" Catherine shrieked. "My jeans… my boots…"

"Samantha, why do you have that drink out of the kitchen?" her father scolded, his tone hard and cold.

"I just wanted to see."

"Well, you see what you did," Catherine snapped, her face red with anger.

"I didn't mean to." Sam's voice was small and quivering, prompting another eye roll from Catherine.

"These jeans cost over a hundred dollars," she said, as if the child would understand. "These boots? These boots were close to three hundred, and they're ruined!"

"We can replace the clothing, Lady Catherine," Frank said soothingly.

"It isn't like you don't have several other pairs of jeans… or boots, either," Mitch offered, completely missing the glare his girlfriend shot him.

"I had this wardrobe planned for weeks, Mitch." It was so easy to use her anger to justify her lie.

"I'm sorry."

Catherine turned her glare to the small girl. "Nah, you think?"

"Hey, Sammi," Brody said as he came into the entryway.

"C'mon, let's get you cleaned up."

"Her cleaned up? What about me?" Catherine asked, her eyes narrowed.

"Go on up and change, Lady Catherine," Frank said with a smile. "I'm sure we can keep Mick occupied."

"Mitch," the bulky football player said, correcting him.

"Sure thing."

Catherine was infuriated. "That's it?! You send her to get cleaned up, and usher me off to get changed?"

"She'll be dealt with appropriately," Frank replied smoothly before turning his gaze up the stairs for a moment.

"You'll have to compensate Greta for having to clean that crap off the floor," Catherine added.

"Noted."

"And… um… hello." She held her hand out. "My compensation."

"I'll take you shopping tomorrow," he said, and Catherine's eyebrow shot up.

"Or you could hand me your card and I can do my own shopping," she countered, scowling when he merely laughed as he walked down the hallway with his hand on Mitch's shoulder.

Once again, her heavy steps echoed as she stomped her way up the stairs in her stained jeans and ruined boots, muttering under her breath at the atrocity of it all. Down the hallway, another door opened, and she spotted Tyler sticking his head out trying to see what was going on.

"What?" she snapped at him, feeling vindicated when he quickly disappeared and the door shut again.

Within a matter of minutes, she'd grabbed another fabulous pair of jeans, thrown on another pair of boots, and was bounding down the stairs, scowling at the young girl who was sobbing in her big brother's arms as he carried her up. Again, Brody failed to even acknowledge her presence, and under any other circumstances she would have demanded an apology from him as well.

But not tonight.

Tonight, she couldn't wait to escape and vent for hours on end, even if Mitch didn't always seem to comprehend what she was talking about. They headed out into the muggy evening air, the Charger looking even more fabulous when parked to a rusted-out vehicle that now sat in the sprawling drive way.

"What is that?" Catherine asked, turning her nose up.

"Um… a Ford… Escort," Mitch replied, looking at the writing on the back.

"A Ford Escort?" she scoffed. "In my driveway?"

"Yeah, I think that other kid was driving it," Mitch said, opening her door for her as he always did, lest he be berated for forgetting. "They don't even make these anymore."

"And it fits here as much as they do," she muttered, checking her appearance as Mitch walked around to the other side of his car and folded into the driver's seat. "You know you have nothing to worry about," she added, turning down the radio when it came roaring to life.

"What do you mean?"

"Brody," she replied, as if he should have read her mind.

"Who's that?"

"Frank's son, the one with that… Escort."

Mitch let out a short laugh. "Ah, babe, that pipsqueak is the last thing I'd worry about." He grinned as he winked at her. "He's so far beneath your standards. Besides, he probably gets all hot for those brainy chicks or something."

"So, what, I don't have a brain? I could hardly get the grades I do if I didn't."

"And you could hardly help me get the grades I do if you didn't," he joked, still smiling even as she glared. "Is it that time of the month, Catherine?"

"No, and it's rather rude of you to ask," she replied, her arms folded defiantly in front of her.

"Then lighten up." He grinned, raising his eyebrows. "We'll hit the movies after dinner, and by the time I get you home, none of those kids will be up to give you any kind of hell."

"They better not be," she muttered, sinking further into the seat, her scowl deepening. "By the time I'm done, they'll all be wishing they hadn't come with him."

Mitch laughed at her statement. "Knowing you, I have a feeling they already do."

CHAPTER 3

Bet Me

The windows of the Dodge Charger were fogged over, the sounds of a man's heavy breathing echoing within. The young woman he was with struggled briefly against his pawing hands and probing tongue before she pushed roughly on his shoulders.

"Geez, Mitch, there's no reason to devour me." Catherine sat up as she wiped the wetness from around her mouth.

"Yeah there is," he replied, turning his attention to her neck where he proceeded to leave wet kisses. She rolled her eyes, sighing at his insistent attempts to go further than she wanted to.

"You know, I thought we were coming here to talk."

Mitch sat back with a sigh of his own, as if he knew exactly what her translation of 'talk' was. She'd complain, he'd listen. He would agree with her, and eventually pick up where they left off—until she'd put the brakes on. Again.

"Go on," he said, with his best reassuring smile.

She crossed her arms in front of herself. "Forget it."

"No, seriously… say what's on your mind." It wasn't as if she hadn't already. She'd complained at the restaurant, growing more agitated as he just didn't seem to understand why she would possibly be upset. She kept a cold, indifferent distance from him at the movie after he'd told her she should just relax because at least she was going to go shopping the following day. The only way he'd been able to appease her at all was to agree to find a place to park. And 'talk'.

"You know what's on my mind?" she asked, her arms still crossed. "What's on my mind is how my feelings are never taken into consideration."

"How do you figure?" Mitch asked, returning his attention to her neck.

"How do I… really? No one asked me what I thought about mom's boyfriend moving in to begin with! And then… then he brings these… brats with him, and do they ask me? No! No, I find out when my things are being moved out of my trophy room, when the game room all of a sudden has an occupant, when the basement is now someone else's domain!"

"Whoa, the basement?" Mitch asked, sitting back.

"Oh, suddenly when your sacred place to do this to me is invaded, you care to listen."

"Look, Chels…"

"Chels?!" She shoved him as hard as she could, although he barely moved. "You're calling me by my best friend's name? Does she have blonde hair? No. And last time I checked, *my* eyes weren't brown. Now get off me!"

"Easy mistake, you act just alike."

"Please," Catherine scoffed with a flip of her hair. "Chelsea only wishes she could come close to being me. Now why did you call me by her name?"

"You're inseparable most of the time; it's a simple mistake."

"Nooooo no no no you don't," Catherine said, her hands on his shoulders when he tried to lean in for another kiss. "No, you need to take me home. Right this instant."

He let out a short huff. "Right now?"

"No, I'm lying to you. Yes, right now." She straightened her top before she flipped the visor down, checking her makeup in the mirror. "Maybe you'll think twice before you call me by another girl's name."

"Fine," was all he said, and Catherine bit back a satisfied smirk. Perhaps she'd taught him well enough to know to not test her when she was angry.

"I don't suggest walking me to the door," she added as she fixed her lip gloss. "I don't know how Mother's boyfriend will be, and I'm so not in the mood for another scene."

"Of course."

She peered at him through her lashes, smiling softly. "In a couple of weekends, I'll be going to Father's condo. Come visit me?"

Mitch was grinning as he glanced over at her. "Will Father approve?"

"I'm sure he'll check in on me… by phone, of course. What do you say?"

His grin widened as he started the engine. "Oh, yeah. I'll be there."

It was five past midnight—one hour and five minutes past the time she'd told her mother she'd be home—when Catherine walked through the front door. She punched in the code for the alarm and pulled her boots off wiggling her toes in the carpeting of the stairs as she ascended.

"So."

She screeched slightly, turning towards the living room at the sound of Frank's voice. "Do you mind?"

"You're late, young lady." He was sitting in what once was her father's chair, glaring disapprovingly in her direction. Had she been raised any different, perhaps she would have cowered, even slightly.

"Yeah, and?" she said instead. "Save it for your kids. My mother and I have an understanding."

"You're certain you rule the roost here, Lady Catherine?" Again, his tone was even and dark, and had her friends been there, they probably would have laughed at his seeming attempts to sound like something from a horror movie, or worse… like a parent.

"No doubt," she replied, her chin lifting in defiance.

"As punishment for your disobedience, the trip to the mall tomorrow is out of the question."

Catherine stared blankly at him for a moment before she laughed—a genuine laugh, regardless of how unfriendly. "Bet me."

"Young lady,"

"As I told you, you have children of your own who are in obvious need of your parental skills. I have parents of my own, got it?" And with that, she turned and walked down the hallway, her blonde hair swaying with every step. She wasn't surprised when she didn't hear him follow her, so she entered her room, crossing to her large walk-in closet before she flipped her lamp on.

And she stared.

She stared at the several bottles of expensive scented lotions that had been moved from her private bathroom and laid scattered across her bed.

"What?!" she exclaimed loudly, not caring of the hour or who she would wake. "Who has been in my room?!" She threw her bedroom door open, stomping loudly as she marched down the hall. "You!" she snapped at Frank, who glanced up from his paper. "You keep your brats out of my room, do you hear me? And now you owe me more than just jeans and boots!" She threw the half-empty bottles on the floor at Frank's feet, and he stared down at them for a moment, one eyebrow raised. "You're replacing every single one of these, do you hear me?"

"Samantha?" Frank asked, his voice booming as he glanced past Catherine. She promptly noticed his line of vision and turned on her heels.

"You," Catherine said, her voice full of venom as she pointed at the small child, "need to learn a thing or two, like not touching things that don't belong to you!"

The young girl stood in the hallway, trembling as she looked up at Catherine's glaring face. "I'm sorry."

"Sorry?" Catherine snapped, unaware at how the child seemed to cower as her father neared. "You think that just wipes everything away? You think that it makes it okay to go into my room, get into my things?!"

"Catherine," her mother's tired voice came from down the hallway, "we will deal with this tomorrow."

"I want a lock on my door!" Catherine demanded, placing her hands on her hips.

"Of course, dear," her mother replied, shuffling back into her room and closing the door. Catherine smirked down at the small child, who still looked homely despite the fact she'd obviously been bathed. Someone else was behind her, claiming it was their fault for not watching her, although Catherine paid it no mind.

"Try getting in my room after that, you little snot," she snapped, not even blinking an eyelash when the little girl rushed past her, narrowly missing her father's grasp. Catherine heard a soft, soothing male voice, calming the child, and she glanced over her shoulder, seeing the child's oldest brother gather her into his arms. She opened her mouth to make what was sure to be a sarcastic comment, until Brody looked up at her, his blue eyes so very cold.

And she remembered he'd been carrying a copy of *Catcher in the Rye.*

And she decided he most definitely must be a serial killer in the making.

She moved quickly into her room, shutting the door and placing a chair in front of it. With one sweep of her hand, the remaining bottles of lotion scattered across her floor, and she dramatically laid across her bed.

There was no way she was going to live under the same roof with that boy. She was going to demand that he be removed from her home the first chance she got.

And this time no one was going to tell her 'no.'

CHAPTER 4

The Gauntlet

The great art of compromise was not in Catherine's repertoire. Never in her charmed life had she found the need, nor the desire, to bend to someone else's wishes. Perhaps she could be seen as spoiled; perhaps her parents as well as others in her life were to blame. But for Catherine, compromise was a non-issue. It simply didn't happen.

She wouldn't let it happen.

Even if her once-doting mother insisted upon it.

"I have yet to see the new jeans and boots to replace those that girl ruined," she said, her arms crossed, a look of disdain on her face. Said look was automatic when it came to all things regarding Frank Harris's children.

"You have yet to apologize for being late," her mother countered, her voice cool as she turned the page of her morning paper.

"It happens all the time! What makes this time any different from all the others?"

"Frank believes that you need some discipline in your life."

"Well, Frank needs to concentrate on teaching that to his own brats. He's not my father." Catherine's eyebrow raised as she challenged her mother to come up with an acceptable reply.

"This is a learning process, Catherine. We all need to learn to get along with one another."

Catherine let out a short laugh. "Right. That's going to happen."

"At least you have the lock on your door."

"And I practically had to starve myself to get that!" Catherine said as she walked away in a huff.

Time was running short that day, and the rest of her cheerleading squad would soon be over to practice before the scheduled afternoon lounging around the pool. The sprawling lawn to the left side of the pool was the same spot they'd practiced nearly every day this past week, and had some way managed to do so uninterrupted by Frank's unsightly children.

Today, it seemed, she wouldn't be so lucky.

She perched her hands on her hips as she watched Brody toss a baseball into the air before hitting it with the bat he held in his right hand, sending it sailing high and deep. Off towards the back of the lawn was the middle pest, Tyler, squinting up into the sun, wearing a mitt, and failing miserably at catching.

"Don't sweat it, don't sweat it," Brody called out to him. "Toss it back. Let's do it again."

Catherine rolled her eyes at Tyler's feeble attempt to throw the ball back to his brother, who ran forward to scoop it off the ground. Again, Brody tossed the ball into the air and swung his bat, dropping said bat beside him as he kept his eye on the ball. The loud crack resonated on Catherine's grated nerves, snapping her from her daze and sending her stomping towards them.

"I have practice out here in a half hour," she stated loudly, seething when once again Brody failed to even acknowledge her presence. Instead, he clapped with vigor as Tyler struggled, falling backwards, still ending up with the ball in his mitt.

"Good job!"

"Did you hear me?" Catherine demanded, hands on her hips as again he ignored her. He ran forward to catch the ball that Tyler tossed back to him.

"You ready?" he asked, and his little brother nodded. Once more, he tossed the ball into the air, hit it with the bat, and sent it soaring.

"Are you deaf?" Catherine asked, stomping her way towards Brody. When again he failed to answer, she stepped in front of him, her cheeks flushed from her anger. "I said… are you deaf?"

Brody barely glanced at her before moving aside, his eyes again trained on his little brother. "Good try. Toss it back, let's go."

"What is wrong with you?" Catherine asked, stepping in front of him again. She shrieked as he roughly pushed her aside, the ball missing her by a mere fraction of an inch. "Don't you ever lay another hand on me, do you hear me?" she shouted, pushing him roughly. He barely budged, but his blue eyes were now focused on her.

"Sure thing, Lady Cath-er-ine," he said, drawing out each syllable of her name. "Next time I'll let it hit you."

His voice was low, an unmistakable hint of anger in it. His jaw was set as he silently challenged her to come back with another scathing remark. When he concluded by her slacked jaw that she was stunned silent, he returned his attention to his little brother and their task at hand. He motioned for Tyler to go deeper as he hit the next ball with considerable force.

Catherine stomped after him. "You act as if I'm not even here! You know we have practice back here, right at this time." Which wasn't entirely true; it was a half hour before the other girls were scheduled to show up, and the first few minutes was normally spent catching up on gossip and showing off whatever new trinkets they'd bought the day before.

Brody's jaw was set as he ran forward, catching the ball that Tyler tossed back to him. "That's what you gotta do, Ty. Keep it up." He took a few steps back, pointing for Tyler to go deeper before he set the ball in motion again.

"Honestly, you are the most…" She faltered as he glared at her, the pure anger in his gaze suddenly reminding her of why she'd avoided him whenever she could. How could she have forgotten about the book, about the potential serial killer she had living under the same roof as her? And now she'd pissed him off… she was sure to be hacked to bits in her sleep. No, no… she had a lock for her door now. She was safe.

Wasn't she?

"Catherine," her mother called out, "Chelsea's here."

"Looks like your time's up," Catherine snapped at Brody before turning on her heels and heading back towards the house. Chelsea, dressed in her tiny shorts and spaghetti strap tank top along with her stylish dark glasses, slowly made her way to the patio furniture, sitting in a cushioned chair before Catherine had made her way up there. "They won't be out there much longer."

"Hmm," Chelsea said, pulling her glasses down a fraction, her dark brown eyes looking at the scene before her. Brody sent another ball flying in Tyler's direction, shouting out his instructions as Tyler lost sight of the ball. "Charming."

"Tell me about it," Catherine muttered with a roll of her eyes. "I can't believe my home's been… invaded."

"What, invasion of the white trash people?" Chelsea asked with a snort, and the corner of Catherine's mouth lifted in a sardonic smile.

"Something like that. Did you bring the music?"

Chelsea held up the CD she'd burned before she laid it on the table beside her water bottle. "So archaic, but I brought it. We're going to finish up the routine today, right?"

"We only have a couple weeks before school and football season," Catherine replied, ignoring Chelsea's comment about the disc. "Might be a good idea, especially with Phoebe gone. Now… where the hell is our captain?"

"Doesn't it kill you?" Chelsea asked before taking a drink of water.

"What?"

"Not being captain."

Catherine rolled her eyes. "Please. We'll be seniors next year, and besides… Bethany is so easily led, we run this team anyhow." There was no mistaking, though, that when Catherine said 'we', she meant herself. She always had, and probably always would. It was simply the price others in her presence had to deal with—to Catherine, she was always Number One. No matter what.

Rather than argue or point out the obvious, Chelsea merely grinned. "So true, Catherine," she said. "So true."

"So tomorrow," Brody was saying as he and Tyler passed the girls, wiping the sweat from his brow, "we'll work on this some more."

"Um, elsewhere," Catherine snapped.

"I thought we were…" Chelsea stopped as Catherine shot a glare in her direction, so the fact that they were supposed to practice at Bethany's was left unsaid.

But as he had earlier, Brody merely ignored Catherine, acting as if she didn't even exist. Her mouth dropped open for an instant, appalled by his behavior, completely angered that he dared ignore her with her friend by her side. Just as quickly, she remembered the look of pure hatred he'd shot her earlier, and decided her safety was much more important.

"Hello to you, too," Chelsea called out to the boys. Brody didn't respond, and put his hand on his little brother's shoulder, guiding him into the house when he'd looked over his shoulder.

"Why didn't you say anything?" the girls heard Tyler ask.

"Remember what I told you?" Brody replied, his voice light and teasing, a far cry from the tone he seemed to reserve for Catherine alone.

"Ah, if you can't say something nice," Tyler began, and the last the girls heard was Brody's soft laughter before the door closed.

"How rude," Chelsea commented.

"See what I have to deal with?" Catherine asked, gesturing towards the house. "See?"

"Perhaps you should ask your father if you could move in with him," Chelsea suggested, looking at her perfectly manicured nails. Catherine scoffed, crossing her arms in front of her.

"And change schools?" she asked, her eyes narrowed, knowing with her out of the way Chelsea would be Queen Bee. "Not a chance."

Chelsea's smile feigned innocence. "It was just a suggestion."

"Sure." Catherine stood and stretched as a couple more of the girls arrived.

"Your step sister is so adorable," Taylor said dramatically, placing her hand over her heart.

"She's not related to me," Catherine said sharply, her green eyes flashing in anger. "And believe me, if you want to take the brat, you can have her."

"Seriously, could she really be that bad?" Bethany asked, her hips swaying as she joined them outside. Bethany, their leader, whom Catherine knew was far inferior to her. The way she'd been so publicly dumped by Mitch's brother less than a year before was enough evidence that she was too weak. Even with her naturally light blonde hair and pale blue eyes, she was no match for Catherine's classic beauty.

"Let her ruin your jeans and your boots, let her dump all of your lotions in the sink, and then tell me she isn't that bad," Catherine answered as she picked the CD up and opened her portable player. Her nostrils flared as she saw a disc of children's music in there and she angrily tossed it aside, barely missing the other girls. "Stupid little snot," she muttered before placing Chelsea's CD in and carrying the box out towards the lawn. She glanced over her shoulder, looking at the other girls who merely stood there gaping at her. "Are we going to finish this routine or not?"

As the other girls followed Catherine out to the lawn, just as she knew they would, Brody stepped outside. He scowled, walking over to where his baby sister's CD sat on the ground, broken.

Catherine turned around, shooting Brody a challenging look, crossing her arms. A chill passed through her as he nodded ever so slightly in her direction before silently returning to the home to console the sobbing little girl who stood just inside.

She'd thrown down the gauntlet.

He'd accepted the challenge.

May the best person win.

CHAPTER 5

Leverage

Catherine's parents—more specifically her mother—had pushed her from a very young age to excel at everything she did. When she'd told them she wanted to dance, they signed her up for every class they could. When she wanted to ice skate, they rented the rink and hired a private instructor. When she announced on the first day of second grade that she was going to win the gold medal in gymnastics, they took her to the top gym in the state.

And she excelled.

She showed such a true gift for the sport that they built a gym of their own, on their land on top of that hill, so that she could practice whenever she chose to. They loaded said gym with the best equipment money could buy, from the mats, to the bars, to the balance beam. For many years they continued pouring money into that gym and the myriad of instructors that would come and go whenever Catherine wanted them to, all the way until gymnastics interfered with her budding social life. Catherine then traded the grueling schedule for all things social, including cheerleading as all popular girls gravitated towards. This also came with ease, even more ease than usual, securing her rightful place in the eyes of her peers.

On top.

The gym still existed, not far from the house, despite Frank wanting to turn it into a garage. Catherine had complained loudly, promising to bring the wrath of her grandfather down on Frank's head. It was an empty threat, of course, as Catherine's grandfather was more concerned with his own personal life at the moment, but it seemed to pull Theresa from her haze long enough to side with her daughter.

And Catherine was almost grateful.

Her mother was so far removed from her life that she had no way of knowing the time Catherine still spent in that gym honing her skills. It wasn't just about checking her drills or cheers in the mirrored wall; there was so much more that the young girl did in her precious spare time. She would perform old balance beam routines, or practice on the uneven bars. There were times, though, that she would turn on her music and hit the mat—sometimes dancing, sometimes tumbling, sometimes doing both. It was those times that Catherine was closest to being human. This was her space, her time.

And heaven forbid anyone—or anything—interrupt her.

She could sense a difference the moment she entered the building, when in spite of the air conditioning it was still on the warm side. The air was sticky, humid, and she could hear the distinct sounds of Frank's younger children, the same sounds she was trying to escape from.

She walked along the wall, her eyes narrowed as she approached the two small windows that were set up high. They had been strategically placed so that Catherine could see the weather, or if time had passed and the sun had set while she had been busy. She stopped as she heard a distinct crunching beneath her feet, where shards of glass had fallen to the floor below.

"What…the," she muttered. Her eyes darted around the floor before they finally came to rest on the culprit.

A baseball.

If she wasn't mistaken—and she was Catherine, so she was always right—she knew exactly who that baseball belonged to.

"You!"

Catherine called out to Tyler as she stomped across the lawn towards Frank's youngest children. Sam's eyes widened in fear, but Tyler kept his back to her, ignoring her as his older brother did. This only fueled Catherine's anger, and her voice rose as dramatically as her gestures when she stood in front of the young boy, waving the baseball in front of his face.

"I know you can hear me, you little brat! You threw a baseball through my window!"

Tyler glanced up at the back of the house, where the three large windows in Catherine's bedroom sparkled in the afternoon sun—unopened, unbroken. With a shake of his head, he turned from Catherine again.

"In my gym!" she exclaimed as she grabbed his arm and roughly turned him in the direction of the building. He seemed to pale but remained silent.

"Oh no, Ty," Sam whispered, loud enough for Catherine to hear.

"Oh no Ty?" she mocked. "Is that the best the two of you can do? What do you think is going to happen when your father,"

"What's going on?"

Catherine wasn't the least bit surprised to see their older brother, their knight in torn baggy clothing, run to their rescue.

She turned her nose up at the sight of him and scoffed, "Nothing that concerns you, unless you plan to pay for that window."

A glimpse of something—Catherine wasn't quite sure what—shown in Brody's eyes for the briefest moment, even as Sam began to cry.

"I didn't mean to," Tyler stammered.

"Not another word," Brody said to him. "I've got this."

"You've got this?" Catherine's voice was even louder than before. "You... you who can't even afford a decent vehicle... you've got this? Do you have any idea how expensive those windows are?"

That question was a bluff, of course, as Catherine had no idea how much they cost either, but to see the two younger children nearly shaking in fear had her on the edge of gloating.

"You don't need to concern yourself,"

"I what? Are you kidding me?"

The bang of the back door flying open announced Frank's arrival, and Tyler finally began to cry when his father demanded to know what the hell was going on.

"Your son broke a window in my gym." Catherine tossed the baseball in his direction, which he caught with ease.

Frank's eyes were hard and cold as he stared Tyler down. "Come here!"

Before Tyler could move, Brody stepped forward. "I'm sorry, I lost control when I hit the ball, and it broke her window. It won't happen again."

Catherine's eyebrow raised as Frank used a tone she'd never heard before when he said, "Step aside."

"Tyler didn't do this. It was me."

Brody stood still, firm, insistent as his father stared him down while Tyler and Sam cowered behind their brother.

"Are you kidding me?" Catherine nearly shrieked, wanting the child to pay for what he'd so obviously done.

"You and I both know," Frank continued, and Catherine noticed a vein in his temple was visibly pulsing, "that you don't lose control, do you, Mr. Baseball?"

"It's just Brody."

"Hey!" Catherine shrieked as Frank nearly pushed her down while he lunged for his eldest son, grabbing him by the t-shirt. "God! Too much drama already! I don't care who takes responsibility as long as someone pays for it."

She huffed past her mother's boyfriend, who was obviously having a bad day, only to nearly be ran over when Brody told his younger siblings to go inside.

"Your whole family is crazy!" was all she said before she slammed the door, leaving Brody and Frank—who still held onto his son's shirt—outside alone.

"What is going on out there?" her mother asked as she looked up from her latest reading material, her eyes glazed over from her afternoon vodka.

"Drama, Mother," Catherine said as she stepped closer. "Drama, drama, drama! And you brought it here!"

"Ms. Catherine…"

"Ah, Greta." Catherine turned towards their housekeeper. "Would you mind calling a window repair place and having them come fix that broken window on my gym? And make it ASAP, of course."

Would she mind translated into it best be done immediately, which sent Greta scurrying to fulfill Catherine's wishes as she always did.

As everyone always did.

Or… as everyone used to.

"Mother has got to get rid of that whole… psycho, trashy family," she muttered as she stomped down the hall towards her room. She paused as she overheard the two younger children.

"Don't be sad, Tyler."

"But it's my fault."

"He'll be okay. He's always okay."

Catherine stood in the doorway, her arms crossed. "If you're so worried about it, why did you let him take the blame for you?"

"Why are you so mean?" Sam asked, her gray eyes full of tears, which didn't faze Catherine in the least.

"Don't you have a mother to harass?"

Tyler glared in her direction. "Our mother's in the hospital."

"Like that's my problem."

"How do you even have friends?" Tyler continued, his sister too distraught after the mention of their mother.

"Oh… oh, you silly, silly boy." Catherine stepped towards them, shaking her head as a smirk touched her lips. "I don't just have friends; I have people who worship me. And if you grow a backbone of your own, maybe someday you can have friends, too." Her smirk grew wider as she heard Frank reenter the house, barking his orders for Brody to get cleaned up. "Shall we test that? Shall I call him up here?"

Tyler remained silent, but Sam was begging, "No, please… please."

And Catherine suddenly had leverage.

Leverage was something she strived for.

"The both of you will stay the hell out of my way from now on, got it? Or I'll go get the big bad Daddy and sic him on you."

She didn't wait for their response before turning and walking back to her room. Her door bounced back slightly when she attempted to slam it, but she didn't pay it any mind; she was certain the children wouldn't come anywhere near her anymore.

"What to do, what to do?" she muttered. She opened her laptop, checking Twitter and seeing that the normal group of people was heading to the movies. It didn't occur to her that not one of them, including Chelsea, had bothered to invite her; she'd merely show up, looking fabulous, driving her custom painted pearl white convertible, and be the hit of the evening.

Catherine was reapplying her lip gloss when she heard Brody's voice, in the same hushed tones he's used for his sister their first night there. "Hey, it's okay," she heard him say, and instantly rolled her eyes.

"Oh yeah, what a great big brother you are, not teaching them squat about responsibility," Catherine muttered, as if she knew about taking responsibility herself.

"Does it hurt?" That came from Sam, and Catherine groaned as she reached for her keys and her designer bag.

"Nah, I'm good. See? You two just stay out of trouble, stay out of harm's way."

"Stay out of my way is more like it," Catherine said under her breath.

"But what about..."

"Let me handle her, okay?"

And Catherine froze.

Brody—Mr. Psycho Boy—was obviously talking about her.

"Trust me; she'll never be a threat again."

With her heart pounding, Catherine quickly made her way out of her room and down the stairs, not bothering to look back over her shoulder to see if he was following her. She figured once she was safely outside and away from the house, she would call her mother and tell her of Brody's threat, which she was beyond certain was against her life. She was so self-absorbed that she was blind to anyone else's problems or fears.

Just as she had been so self-absorbed that evening that she missed the droplets of blood on the otherwise pristine carpet that had trailed behind Brody all the way to Tyler's room.

CHAPTER 6

Not in Your Nature

Catherine was never one to accept defeat, nor would she back down from an unsettled fight. When it came to convincing her mother that her boyfriend and his children absolutely needed to go, however, it was a never-ending battle.

"You're being unreasonable," Theresa said with a tired sigh.

"It's been three days." Catherine held up her fingers for added measure. "Three. And you have yet to answer me."

"I believe I just did."

"No… huh uh… he's… he's crazy."

"Brody? He barely says a word."

Catherine crossed her arms. "I was talking about Frank."

Theresa's laugh was short and unkind, quite like her daughter's. "Neither Frank nor his children are going anywhere… just yet."

Catherine's eyebrow jumped at Theresa's last words, and she remembered Tyler saying their mother was in the hospital. To her, the answer was now simple and clear; once their mother was available, Catherine would reclaim her territory, and send those brats packing. As for Frank…

"What is he going to do with the brats while the two of you go to the beach this weekend? Or are you taking them with?"

"We won't be going."

Catherine stood silent, staring at her mother as if she were waiting for the punchline to a joke. When none came, she said, "You're kidding, right?"

Theresa peered up from her morning paper, her lips in a thin line. "Hardly."

"See? He's disrupting your life."

"I don't have time for this, Catherine."

"Mother…"

"Frank feels it best that we not go."

"Great." Catherine threw her arms up in frustration. "Super."

"Why are you so concerned about my trip to the beach? You'll be at Chelsea's all weekend."

Catherine didn't bother to correct her mother, as that had been the story she was sticking to. Truth was, that Saturday was the annual end-of-summer party, and while it wasn't going to be held at their house, Catherine had planned to bring Mitch to her home. Either they were going to take things a step further, or merely make others believe they had.

And now…

"That's not the point. Am I not permitted to think of you?"

"You're permitted, of course; it's just not in your nature."

"I wasn't really raised that way, was I?" Catherine countered with her best faux smile, leaving her mother to her morning coffee and paper before she could be bothered to come up with a witty reply. In lieu of stomping, Catherine quickly took the steps to the upper level, moving with grace and ease, and quietly shut her door.

She had to play this cool, without acting the least bit

suspicious. While her mother was easily persuaded, Frank was more of a wild card, perhaps even more like a loose cannon. His younger children cowered from him at times as if he were Satan incarnate, not that Catherine ever would. The man held zero hold over her, even if he was ruining her plans.

"This is just one more reason why he has got to go," she muttered as she pulled out her cell phone, scrolling down through her contacts until she saw her father's number. "Now, for Plan B."

She paused for a moment, tapping her foot as she thought of what excuse she could possibly come up with for not seeing him in…

"How long has it been?" she asked out loud, shifting as she continued thinking back further… and further…

She hadn't seen her father since the end of the school year. Here the entire summer had passed, only a few short days left, and while she'd been to his condo it had been while he was gone.

Purposefully.

She was hoping he would be gone this weekend as well.

"Catherine." No hellos, but Colin Garner's voice sounded much more pleasant than anyone's tone in the house she lived in. "What a surprise."

"It hasn't been that long since we've spoken." She tried her best to play it off and sound just as pleasant as he did.

"It's been about a month, sweetheart."

Sweetheart? She was sure he was on something, or around someone he needed to impress. "I'm sorry… time must have slipped by."

"Of course, of course. What is it that you need?"

Her tapped foot went unseen by her father, which was a good thing since she didn't want him to know what she was up to. Somehow, though, he was the only person who could see through her when she asked, "Do I have to need something to call you?"

"Normally you do."

At least he refrained from adding the 'like your mother' line that he would normally throw in for good measure. Catherine took a deep breath, reminding herself that it was best to at least pretend she really wanted to see him. "I was just wondering if you were going to be home this weekend."

"Why yes, Catherine. Yes I am."

And Catherine's smile fell.

"So sorry to ruin your plans to bring your boyfriend over."

"Oh no, Daddy, it was nothing like that." Catherine herself cringed over her lie and the use of the word 'daddy'. It would be blatantly obvious now that's exactly what she'd wanted.

"So, you're saying you wanted to come see me?" She could tell he believed the lie even less than she did, which sparked her quick temper.

"Yes," she replied, her eyes narrowed even though he couldn't see. "Yes, I do… and I will."

"Well, then…" He left the sentence unfinished, as if he was waiting for her to back out already.

"I am busy Saturday."

"Of course."

"I'll see you Sunday," she added quickly. "For brunch."

"Is that so?"

Although she would need to be an expert in her makeup skills and would more than likely be nursing one hell of a hangover, she replied, "Yes. Yes, Daddy, that is so."

"Okay, then." Her father sounded pleasant once more. "Sunday brunch it is."

Now all Catherine had to do was find a way to break the news to Mitch.

Saturday arrived without much fanfare. The house had been eerily quiet since the last go-around between Frank and his darling eldest son just two short days before, not that Catherine minded in the least. It kept the younger children out of her hair if they were hiding from their father, and Brody… well, if he wasn't in with the two of them, he was hiding out in the basement, curled up with a book with only the light from a small lamp. It wasn't that Catherine spent much time studying this strange teenage boy; she'd simply observed this whenever she'd had to find something of hers that had been stored in the basement, or if she was bringing yet another box down to add to the collection.

"If you have to keep coming down for things," he said to her that afternoon without lifting his eyes from the page, "wouldn't that be a hint that you need to keep them in your own room?"

"This is not your room." She felt the need to remind him for the millionth time that she wasn't about to make him feel welcome in her home.

"Keep it up, and I may think you're just spying on me," he called to her as she made her way up the stairs. This, of course, caused her to pause and bound back down to confront him.

"Let's get a few things straight here." She paused briefly, her chest rising and falling dramatically. "I don't like you."

"That's mutual."

"And I don't care whether you like me or not, but… hey! I'm talking to you, you should be respectful and look up from that stupid book!"

"Respect is earned, Lady Cath-er-ine."

"You… you're a real… jerk, you know that?" He didn't respond, but she could almost swear she saw the beginning of a smirk touch his lips. "See? Right there. That just shows how much of a..."

"Jerk?"

"Yes. Yes, it shows how much of a jerk you are. Don't you even have any friends? No one calls here for you, no one stops by. You don't go anywhere, so you obviously aren't going to see anyone."

Brody turned the page of his book, keeping his eyes on it even as Catherine continued on.

"You are going to fail so miserably at life, you know that? Your own father can't even stand you!"

"And your mother's such a prize, isn't she?"

"Hey..." She stomped forward, her anger causing her to be much braver than normal, and she snatched the book from his hands. "My mother let you and the other brats come stay here."

The way he easily stood, his eyes and hands steady, showed he had much more control than she did at that particular moment, even as he began to speak. "Your mother is a pill popping booze hound who could give a shit less that any of us kids were here as long as she's well medicated, and that, Lady Cath-er-ine, includes you."

Brody's lightning-quick reflexes had him grabbing Catherine's wrist long before her hand could reach his face to strike him. The strength in his grasp caught her by surprise, and she struggled against him.

"Get your hands off of me, you pig!"

"I thought it was 'jerk'."

"Jerk, pig, whatever... just get your hands off of me!"

He grabbed her other wrist, pinning her arms to her sides as he leaned down, his blue eyes piercing straight through her. "Don't ever... *ever* try to hit me again, got it?"

"Is that what you say to your big, bad Daddy?"

His grip tightened. "Ever."

"You're crazy!"

"Got it, Lady Cath-er-ine?"

"I swear to you I am going to get you and those brats kicked out of this house!" she screamed in his face, and he merely smiled.

"Good."

He pushed her backwards, away from him. With her excellent sense of balance, she was able to catch herself before she toppled over. She stood there, though, staring at him while she rubbed her wrists, watching his expression darken and change into something she didn't quite comprehend.

"That really hurt," she said through nearly clenched teeth, and only then did he look away. He picked up his book and sat back in his original seat, only his labored breathing giving away that he'd moved at all. "You're going to pay for this, you know that? I'm going to see to it that you pay."

He didn't call out to her this time, said nothing to keep her from bounding up those stairs in search of her mother, or better yet for Frank. Both of her wrists were an angry shade of red, and she was certain they would be bruised before it was all said and done. If she had to miss practice, or if it was visible the first day of school, she would see to it that his time in this house was done.

"Mother!" Catherine called out as she searched throughout the rooms. "Mother, where are you?"

"She's not here."

Catherine stopped as she heard the small, thin voice of Sam. She glared at the girl as she turned around. "Where is your father, then?"

"They went out." Sam clung to the doll in her arms as if it could protect her from Catherine's ire.

"Out," Catherine repeated, the out spoken with pure venom.

"Uh huh, and… and Brody is s'posed to watch us."

"Great. Super."

"Leave her alone."

Catherine rolled her eyes as Brody rounded the corner, coming to his sister's rescue once more. "Or what, you'll manhandle me again?"

"You're angry with me, not her."

"And your mind tricks won't work on me the way they work on Dear Old Dad."

"It's okay, Brody wouldn't hurt you," Sam said, her eyes wide, glowing with admiration. "Brody wouldn't hurt anybody."

"Really? Because he hurt me." Catherine glared as she looked at Brody, staring him down, silently daring him to deny it. "Don't even bother apologizing, either."

Instead of his usual ignoring of her comments, he acknowledged her with a short nod before taking his sister's hand to lead her around the corner and down the stairs. Catherine stood glaring, as if it would change anything, while she heard the little girl saying, "I know better, Brody. You're not like him."

"They're all nuts," Catherine muttered as she finally turned towards her room. Without her mother or Frank there, she wasn't about to stick around. Instead, she pulled out her bag that she'd been progressively packing throughout the week and left for Chelsea's. She wasn't going to put her life in any more jeopardy with what easily could be a serial killer, especially not when the party of the century was only a few short hours away.

It was time for her to shine and show the entire school that she still reigned supreme.

CHAPTER 7

The Queen of Davis High

The end of summer bash was a long-standing tradition among the students at Davis High. The upper echelon of the upperclassmen would host the party complete with illegally obtained alcohol, loud music, and lack of adult supervision. It was seen as the precursor for things to come—who was 'in', who could only wish to be, and, most important to Catherine, who would be at the very top of the heap.

The moment she and Chelsea stepped through the door into the entryway of Bethany Dillon's home, there was no doubt who the Queen of Davis High was.

"Catherine, you made it!" the first of many admirers exclaimed. In lieu of asking why any of them would be foolish enough to think she wouldn't attend, she simply smiled. There was a grace about her as she treated each compliment as if it were the grandest gesture ever. It was, of course, a charade—one she'd learned from years of watching her mother do the same. Just to add fuel to the fire that kept her star burning brightly, she was sure to include Chelsea in all of her greetings, knowing the Queen was only as strong as her closest ally. By the time the pair had made it to the drinks table, everyone in their path had assured them they looked every bit as gorgeous as they already knew they did.

"Did you see Simone's shoes?" Chelsea asked, one eyebrow raised.

Of course, Catherine had; she's recognized the cheap knock-offs of her designer sandals the moment they'd entered. "Passé much?" Catherine smirked, knowing she'd never be seen wearing said sandals again. They chose their drinks from the vast array of bottles, Catherine opting for rum and juice for the evening. She eyed Chelsea, who pulled a glass bottle of beer from the cooler, with a touch of disdain. "That's what you're drinking?"

"Doesn't require much in the maintenance department." Chelsea smiled coolly as Catherine raised an eyebrow. "Relax, Catherine, I'll still be able to get your car back to my house without a scratch."

Catherine's smile was a bit too syrupy sweet. "Let's hope so."

"Exactly where is Mitch taking you after you leave the party?" Chelsea asked, and Catherine shrugged.

Her silence could be taken many ways, but Catherine was sure to not mention the truth: Mitch hadn't spoken with her about their after-party plans. He'd failed to reply when she'd sent texts about him providing the backup, which had her absolutely fuming with anger. This was a public place, though, where Catherine's beauty and poise were exalted. She'd be sure to wait until she and Mitch were alone before berating him for his thoughtlessness.

"Catherine! Chelsea!" Bethany exclaimed with a broad smile as she approached them. "I was wondering when you would show."

Catherine returned her smile. "We wouldn't want to look

anything less than perfect for your party."

"Oh, how sweet. Whatever will you do next year when it's your turn?"

"Have it at my house so she can arrive fashionably late." Chelsea had said this with a laugh that Catherine wasn't buying.

"That's won't be necessary. I'm positive after seeing this enormous success that you won't mind me taking a few ideas, will you Bethany?"

There was no mistaking what Catherine was saying. Not only was she going to be the hostess of next year's party, but she also felt she could put Bethany's to shame.

"That's so sweet."

Catherine could have gagged had she not been keeping up appearances. Sweet seemed to be one of Bethany's absolute favorite words. Of course, the look in Bethany's eyes conveyed that she'd picked up on Catherine's insult, and was merely keeping up appearances with her frenemy as well.

"Are you so sure you can pull it off?" Chelsea goaded, her own smile in place. "Your mother and Frank may decide to stay home again."

Catherine's eyes momentarily flashed anger in Chelsea's direction, but she quickly recovered. "I can be very persuasive when need be."

"I'm sure." Chelsea held up her beer and barely masked a sigh before taking a drink.

"Speaking of, could you not persuade Brody to come?" Bethany asked, and Catherine openly scoffed.

"You can't be serious."

"Of course I am. He is your… what, step-brother?"

Catherine shuddered. "He is not related to me. And I really don't wish to bring up the unpleasant subject of that… psycho."

Bethany grinned and shrugged. "He seemed rather normal to me. Oh! Looks like the second half of the football team has arrived. Ciao!"

"Ciao?" Chelsea snorted back laughter as Bethany floated away, ever the gracious host.

"Yeah, she apparently missed the memo where that phrase had come and gone," Catherine agreed with a roll of her eyes. "And what is up with her sudden obsession with that bookworm?"

"What bookworm?"

"Brody. He's such a… a stain."

Chelsea eyed Bethany with the same suspicion Catherine did. "Well, I say it's one of two things. Either she wants to soften the blow of one of her cheerleaders being associated with him by making him seem acceptable,"

"I'm not one of *her* cheerleaders."

"She is Captain," Chelsea pointed out. "Or two…" She was silent for a moment as they observed Bethany openly flirt with Catherine's boyfriend, as only the boldest of the bold would do. "She's trying to get to you."

Catherine nearly snorted herself before she polished off her drink. "No one gets to me."

"Are you so sure about that?"

The sly smile on Catherine's face was the only answer she gave before she walked away.

The hour was getting late when Mitch led Catherine to a secluded room in the back of the house, the noise of the party muffled when he shut the door. With her senses dulled from the alcohol, her resistance was futile when he began kissing her deeply, nearly swallowing her whole as he pressed her up against the wall.

"Mitch, what the hell?" She barely squeaked, her words a bit slurred, but his lips were on hers once more, his large hands moving to remove her clothing. For the first time in their relationship, her shirt was discarded, his large hands covering her breasts and squeezing roughly as his kisses moved to her neck. "Mitch, I… I don't know where you got the impression…"

"You told me to make other arrangements."

"It would have been nice for you to tell me, too."

He laughed one short laugh as he pushed her back towards the bed. "You knew I was busy with football."

She felt something at the back of her legs and let out a small gasp. His kiss muffled her protests as he effortlessly laid her back, his body half on hers, pushing her into the mattress. She pushed on his shoulders as she always did when his kiss was too deep, too rough, but he only pulled back when he'd succeeded in unclasping her bra and needed to pull it from her body.

"God, what are you doing?" she asked angrily, trying to cover her bare breasts.

He moved her arms out of his way, his lust filled eyes making her stomach turn as he stared at her. "Worshiping you, of course." His lips curled in a smile that she was far too uncomfortable with.

"This isn't… it isn't… worshiping," she stammered before he was kissing her again. She began pushing at his broad shoulders, her movements more frantic until he finally raised up.

He scowled as he looked down at her. "What?"

"Seriously, Mitch, get off of me."

With a roll of his eyes he stood. "There, your royal highness, are you happy now?"

She also stood, trying to cover herself with one arm while she scrambled to grab her discarded clothing. "What has gotten into you?"

"Isn't this what we had planned?" he asked, and her glare answered his question. "Do you know how many girls down there would be more than happy to be up here?"

"Do you know how much you would suffer if it wasn't me you were with?"

And his mouth instantly closed.

Of course he knew. Being with the hottest girl, the one that every boy wanted, and every girl wished she could be, came with many perks.

"That's what I thought." She adjusted her top, smoothing it with unsteady hands. "Now… where are we going?"

"I'm going to get another drink," he said as he stepped past her.

"No, we're leaving."

He walked out of the room without answering her, as if he knew she wouldn't dare cause a scene in front of all of her royal subjects who worshiped her so. He was right, of course… Catherine had to be the epitome of perfection, her words carefully chosen, her appearance immaculate.

Finding him was a bit more difficult than she'd anticipated, perhaps because her vision wasn't quite as clear as it should be. She walked up to him, her jaw set. "Let's go."

He leaned down, speaking low enough so that others couldn't hear. "I'm not ready to go, Catherine."

Her smile was false, for the show of anyone looking. "I didn't ask if you were ready."

"I'm not leaving," he reiterated, then turned and grabbed another beer leaving his girlfriend staring incredulously in his direction.

"Oh, he's so paying for this." She stomped off in the opposite direction, her eyes searching the crowd for Chelsea. If Mitch just had to stay at this party, he would have to stay without her. And when he was ready to apologize for his behavior, she would make him grovel for forgiveness. Hell, she may draw this out, make him take her some place fancy, some place they would be seen, some place where word would get out that Catherine knew how to keep her man in line.

That's what she would do.

"Chels," Catherine said, her voice and gait not quite steady, "let's go."

Chelsea placed one hand on her hip. "What do you mean?"

"I said… let's go."

"You were supposed to be 'going' with Mitch," Chelsea reminded her, and Catherine waved it off.

"I'm not… I'm not feeling all that well."

"Yeah, well, it's not even eleven o'clock. I'm not going anywhere. Just go sleep it off."

"Give me my keys then."

Chelsea's eyebrow raised as Catherine held out her hand. "Excuse me?"

"It's my car, Chels. Give me my keys."

"Fine, fine." Chelsea placed Catherine's keys in her outstretched hand. "But if you end up splattered all over the road, it's your own fault."

"Right." Catherine stumbled through the crowd and to the doorway. If others thought it best to prevent her from leaving, they never spoke up, and Catherine sped away from the bash in her custom painted convertible, oblivious to most of the world.

Some would say it was a miracle she made it home at all, much less made it there in one piece without a single scratch on her prized possession. With the alcohol dulling her senses, she didn't notice that her park job was less than stellar, nor did she realize she was stumbling as she reached her front door. All she was focused on was that churning in her stomach, the feeling that everything she'd eaten and drank for the past year was about to end up all over her designer shoes.

"Where are my keys?" she muttered in spite of the fact that they were in her hand, and her attempts at being quiet enough to not draw attention to herself weren't succeeding as well as she had planned. She paid it no mind, though; her powers of persuasion were legendary, and besides… Frank adored her. He called her Lady Catherine, after all, and seemed to dote on her more than he did his own children, and…

"What the hell are you doing?"

Catherine squinted up at Brody, who had somehow appeared in front of her and was whispering harshly. "Did you open that?" she asked, pointing at the door.

He moved in quickly, his voice was low, his breath hot against her neck. "Shut up."

Her eyes widened with surprise for one brief moment, but before she could protest, he had his arm around her and was practically dragging her down the stairs.

"Hey, stop manhand…" Her eyes widened again as Brody placed his hand over her mouth, halting her words.

"Listen, just… shut up. You're sick, okay? You're sick."

"I am?" she asked, her voice muffled from behind his hand.

"Make it convincing," he added as he pushed her aside and walked quickly back towards the stairs, where Frank's voice could be heard bellowing.

And that was all she wrote.

Catherine was lucky to find a trash can in time to lose the

contents of her stomach in. The wretches coming from her drowned out whatever Brody was saying to his father, but it was hardly Catherine's concern. All she needed was to finish puking and crawl into the covers of her own bed, which would hopefully not spin nearly as badly as the basement was doing.

"See?" she heard Brody say. "She's sick. She couldn't even make it to the bathroom."

Catherine lifted her head to argue that yes… yes, she most definitely could have made it to the bathroom had he not drug her into this dungeon to probably kill and maim her, but another wave of nausea had her retching once more. She was fairly certain she heard Frank tell Brody to 'take care of it', and she knew she had to get out of there.

"Oh god." She stepped back, wiping her mouth. "No, I'm not staying down here for you to kill me."

"For… what? Fuck, you are just like your mother, aren't you?"

"Did you kill her, too?"

Brody rolled his eyes. "No, shithead, you're drunk," Brody was still keeping his voice down. "And you're an idiot for coming back here."

"This is my home." She stood upright, swaying only slightly. "My home, not yours."

"You can keep it, okay? Just shut the hell up before he comes back."

"I don't need any favors from you." She poked him once in the chest as if it would prove her point. "I don't have to be afraid of your big, bad daddy."

"Just… shut up."

"Or you'll what?" she asked, and gasped when he firmly gripped her upper arms.

"Listen, I'm not doing you any favors, got it?" Brody's voice was hushed, even quieter than it was before. "Does that make you feel any better? You're going to owe me for this. Just shut…"

He barely had her turned in time before she was vomiting again, this time on the carpeting.

"See what you did?" she asked after he muttered a curse.

"Uh huh." He steered her towards the fold out bed he'd obviously recently vacated. "Now you really owe me."

She had every intention of demanding that he take her to her room, just as she had every intention of asking him exactly what he meant. Her body had other ideas, though, and she was fast asleep the moment her head hit Brody's pillow.

CHAPTER 8

As If

Catherine groaned as she rolled over, unsure if it was her aching head or her ringing cell phone that had woke her up. She opened one eye and glanced around the room, searching for wherever she had set her phone down.

And she jumped, startled fully awake.

This was not her room.

This was the basement.

She was on the folded-out couch bed with only a thin blanket to ward off the chill she felt. She could feel her pulse quicken as she looked around, noting the dimmed lighting, and how nothing, aside from her, seemed out of place. She tried to remember… she knew she'd been drinking… she knew she'd been with Mitch… but how did she get here?

"Looking for something?" she heard Brody ask, and she turned her head in the direction of his voice. He was standing several feet away, holding the now-silent phone in his hand. After the initial shock, she regained her composure, her eyes narrowed as she took in his nonchalant expression.

"What the hell am I doing down here?" Her voice sounded a

bit scratchy and unfamiliar to her. As she placed one hand delicately on her throat, he began to answer.

"That would be where you passed out." He made a slight gesture towards her. "And that," he added as he gestured yet again, this time behind him, "would be where you lost the contents of your stomach."

She pulled the thin cover up over herself—after ensuring she was still fully clothed—and again glared at him. "Really?" Her nose wrinkled in disgust. "It certainly doesn't smell that way."

He took one small step towards her. "It doesn't smell that way because I was tasked with cleaning up after you, after I'd told Frank that you were sick."

She paused, biting the inside of her lip as she contemplated her words, yet never let her expression soften. "Why?"

"Why what?"

"Why tell Daddy dearest that I was merely sick? Why not tell him I'd been drinking?"

"And tarnish his view of his precious Lady Cath-er-ine?" There was no mistaking the biting tone in his voice. "I wouldn't dream of it."

"Yes, you would." She nearly recoiled in fear when one side of his mouth lifted in a wry grin.

Just nearly.

Catherine would rather die than show weakness.

"You obviously didn't do this to be chivalrous, so spill."

With one short nod, he pulled up a chair, turned it backwards and straddled it, resting his chin on the back as he stared at her. "You're a real piece of work, you know that?"

"Of course I do."

"It wasn't meant as a compliment," he said quickly, his expression never changing. "But you want me to spill, right?

What's going to keep me quiet?" A muscle in his jaw twitched slightly, and Catherine noted the annoyance in his voice at his next words. "I know Frank is giving you money this Monday, money for clothing…"

"That your bratty sister destroyed."

"…that you don't need, and I'm fairly certain I can add that you don't deserve."

The silence in the room was thick with tension as they sized one another up—Brody in his well-worn clothing and baseball cap turned backwards, and Catherine, still fashionably dressed, her hair still looking as if it were meant to lay that way, expensive makeup still on her face. His eyebrow raised in a challenge, as if he were letting her know that this time, he won.

Her eyes narrowed. "You're such a jerk."

"So you keep telling me."

"So, you're blackmailing me, is that it?" He shrugged slightly, which only annoyed her further. "I'm supposed to give you money to…"

"No, you're going to be buying clothes," he cut her off. "Just not for you."

She gaped at him then, her mouth slightly open as she finally realized what he was demanding of her. A million comments and insults were running through her clouded mind, and yet she seemed unable to form a single sentence to tell him how absurd this was. As if Catherine would spend money on anyone other than herself.

"You're going to take that cash, and you're going to buy some new school clothes for Tyler and Sammi," he said aloud, confirming that she had, indeed, been right.

She finally found her voice. "Excuse you? That's your father's job."

"And you're going to be the one who gives them the clothes," Brody continued, ignoring her obvious comment. "As a peace offering."

She scoffed at his words, nearly asking if he'd been the one drinking the night before, and not her. When he remained silent, one eyebrow again raised to show he was serious, she grew even more angry.

"In what alternate universe?"

His demeanor remained calm, cool. "Because from here on out, you're going to be nice to them. You're going to refrain from your shitty comments…"

"Can't you even speak without cursing?"

"…and your dirty looks. Why yes, I can, Lady Cath-er-ine, but you seem to bring out the worst in me, what can I say?"

"You can apologize to me for… for being such a…"

"Jerk?"

She folded her arms in front of her, her voice holding a hint of warning she wasn't quite sure she could back up. "No one speaks to me this way."

"Maybe if they did, you wouldn't be such a pretentious bitch."

"That's it." She threw her arms up and stood from the bed, ignoring how dizzy it seemed to make her. "Frank's not my father, I don't care what he has to say. You can take your blackmail, and… and… you couldn't even prove it anyway!"

"Really, now?" Brody hadn't even moved. He glanced down at her phone and began to pull up a screen, only moving when Catherine attempted to pry it from his fingers.

"What are you doing?"

"Someone," he said as he held the phone out of her reach, but the screen still visible, "is a bit of a picture whore."

Her eyes widened as he swiped across the screen of her phone, photograph after photograph of Catherine with alcoholic beverages in her hand, and noticeably intoxicated in every one. There were others in the pictures as well, as was the burden of someone so popular—everyone wanted their picture with you.

What was she to do now?

She placed a hand on her hip. "You don't have a cell phone."

"But I have yours."

"And you're going to give it back, or…"

He smirked at her, still holding her phone. "Or you'll what? What I do have is a web-based email account, Catherine… and several of these have been sent to it. Call it insurance," he added as he finally allowed her to take her phone from his hand.

She searched frantically through her phones history and saw that yes, he had indeed sent several pictures to an email address that she could only assume belonged to him, especially with as generic as it sounded. Her heart was racing at an uncomfortable rate as she faced her first true foe in ages.

But this wasn't some meek little school girl.

This was a life-hardened boy who didn't seem to care what anyone thought of him.

Her face flushed with anger. "You're a pervert, you know that? And like I said, Frank isn't my father…"

"That doesn't mean dick."

"Must you be so crude?"

He let out one short laugh. "It's the joys of being a serial killer." His smirk widened at her shocked expression.

"You went all through my phone!"

"Tsk tsk, Lady Cath-er-ine," he chided. "One mustn't wake the sleeping dragon."

The sleeping dragon.

That is what she'd called Frank in one of her private online blogs, his behavior had particularly disturbed her. She'd contemplating deleting the entry, not wanting to sound like someone could possibly unnerve her. Besides, Frank wasn't exactly her problem. She'd actually forgotten about her one brief bout of conscious until just that moment.

But the fact that Brody had read it was unforgivable.

How dare he invade her privacy this way?

Her voice was shaking in anger. "You have no business going through my things. You stay away from me. You and… and those brats stay away. Do you hear me?"

"Now, I can't exactly do that." His shrug was so slight it was almost unnoticeable. "See, I'll be going with you tomorrow, to the mall."

"You think I'd be caught dead anywhere near you?"

His smirk showed his amusement. It figured that he'd be amused; she'd likened him to a serial killer on more than one occasion that he'd obviously spied on.

"You think you have a choice?" he countered as her phone began to ring again. She squinted at the screen and saw her father's name and number just as Brody asked, "Want me to get that?"

"No."

"Just checking." He turned towards the stairs, not looking back at her. "Tomorrow morning, bright and early… it's mall time."

"I'm not doing this willingly," she called after him.

"That's the best part," he replied with a laugh, and she nearly threw her ringing phone at the back of his head.

Just almost.

But she wasn't like him, or his darling father. She was Catherine Garner, she was untouchable.

And he was going to be sorry that he'd messed with her.

Catherine was picking at the food on her plate, wondering how she was going to make it through this meal without throwing up yet again. She had an appearance to keep up, though... one with her father in his condo, just as she'd promised.

"Are you sure you're feeling up to this?" he asked, and Catherine looked over at him, her eyebrows furrowed. He'd never really been one to show concern, at least not in her self-centered memory.

She pasted on her best smile, one that she'd mastered so well that people couldn't quite tell the numerous hateful thoughts running through her mind. "Of course I am."

"Your mother said you were ill."

Catherine averted her eyes from her father's intense gaze. "When did you speak with her?"

"This morning, when you didn't answer your phone." She could hear the clink of his fork as he set it down, every single noise resonating in her head that just wouldn't stop pounding.

"Well, I'm here now, aren't I?" She made a mental note, though, to berate her mother for not informing her of said phone call. Her father nodded once before he took a sip of his orange juice, and Catherine could still feel his eyes on her.

"How are things at home?"

Catherine licked her lips, knowing she could very well tell him what was going on—that her mother had moved her boyfriend in, that his children were heathens at best, that her whole life was being disrupted. In the next thought, she also knew that he would want to speak with her mother, which in turn would lead to a discussion with Frank, which would piss Brody off, which would ensure that certain photographs would surface, which would…

"Are you in there?"

Catherine jumped at her father's gentle touch on her arm, instinctively jerking her arm away before mumbling an apology. "Things are fine," she lied so expertly. "Just fine."

"That's good," he said in return.

And Catherine immediately noticed that he didn't suggest she move in with him.

It was something he'd done nearly every time she saw him. Since she'd made it a point to only venture to the condo when he wasn't there, it made the occasions few and far between. It was still a standing discussion, though; Catherine was more than welcome to come stay with him.

As if she'd give up her status at school.

As if she'd…

"Yeah, we'll be getting more news about layoffs soon." He picked up his perfectly buttered slice of toast, a not-so-perfect smile on his face.

"Oh, Daddy, you have nothing to worry about," Catherine said with a wave of her hand. "You're Colin Garner, financial genius; they'd be foolish to let you go."

He let out a resigned sigh. "I could always go back to teaching. I couldn't stay here, though." He glanced around the luxurious condo with all of its high-end finishes, extravagant furniture, and overpriced art. Catherine bristled slightly as she also looked around, imagining all of her friends there and gushing over every single detail as they did every time.

"Why not?" There was an almost-panicked tone in her voice. She'd already lost her game room, her basement, her privacy… she didn't want to lose this, too.

Her father smiled at her again, a kindness in his eyes that she was unfamiliar with. Who was this man and what had he done with her corporate shark daddy? "Fear not." He patted her arm gently, "I'll still have a home."

She didn't let on that she wasn't concerned about that, per se. "Where?"

"The Valley isn't far from here." Before she could voice her less-than-stellar opinion of all things from that rundown area, he added, "There's nothing wrong with it, Catherine."

Which, to her, wasn't the least bit true. There was everything wrong with the Valley; there was a stigma attached to the small town down there, one that consisted of crime and drugs, and only the worst of the worst would bother going to their schools. She couldn't imagine her father living there, and certainly would never take her friends to his home. What would she say to her friends if he had to take a teaching job there, of all places? No, the Valley was one area that was so far beneath the Garners that the scenario wasn't even worth considering.

She would have to come up with even more clever excuses, if he were as certain of his move there as he seemed to be. Luckily with the Valley being almost 90 minutes from her treasured house on the hill, excuses would be easily found.

Still, she was angry. This was now her only reprieve from Frank and his brats, aside from her time in her private gym. And as she drove home later that afternoon—after seeing all of the concerned posts and tweets from her friends over her well-being, of course—she wondered briefly how her life could possibly get any worse.

Until she arrived, and Frank so proudly placed over $500 in her hand, in front of his children, no less.

The 'look of death', as she so coined it, from Brody reminded her exactly how it was going to get worse.

The very next morning, he was forcing her to be seen in public with him.

And even as Catherine assured the adoring masses in her social media circle that she was, indeed, just fine, she had the distinct feeling this was only the beginning.

CHAPTER 9

Foreign Concept

Catherine made sure her large sunglasses were in her designer purse the next morning. If she was going to be forced to be seen in public with the stain known as Brody, she would at least have the option of trying to disguise herself as best she could. The one thing she wouldn't forgo, however, was her impeccable taste in clothing. She was again dressed in an outfit that had cost a small fortune, her hair styled with products that would make a supermodel envious, and her makeup, while light, was still the best, professional grade, sure to withstand nearly any element thrown her way… including the ghastly beast who casually strolled up the stairs into the living room wearing torn jeans and a faded concert t-shirt.

Catherine wrinkled her nose up in disgust. "Surely you're not going out in public looking like that."

"Of course not." One corner of Brody's mouth lifted in a smirk as he placed a worn, sweat-ringed ball cap on his head, pushing his shaggy dark hair further into his eyes. "There, all set."

"Oh no you don't," she snapped, and she pointed towards the stairs. "I know you have better clothes than that."

Ignoring her demands, he walked towards the front door. "There's nothing wrong with these."

"Excuse… hey! Excuse you!" She quickly followed him out the front door, visibly frustrated that he refused to cave to her.

"I'm fairly certain the proper way of saying that is 'excuse me'." He walked towards his dented, rusted Ford Escort when she finally caught up to him.

"Don't try impressing me with some vast knowledge of the English language. I said exactly what I meant, and…" She shook her head when he opened the dented door. "Oh no, I am so not getting in that car."

He turned to her, one hand resting on the top of the vehicle that had seen its better days. "Yeah, you are."

"No," she said, her arms crossed, "I'm not."

"Okay, Lady Cath-er-ine, how do you propose we get there?"

"You said we had to go together; we're riding in my car."

Brody's expression never wavered as he looked from Catherine, to her car, and back to her. "Not in this lifetime."

"That car is a custom painted Mustang convertible with leather interior, and…"

"It's pink."

"It's not pink."

"Yes, it is."

"It's custom painted pearl white, thank you very much, and in the sun—"

"It turns pink, and I'm not riding in a pink car."

"Yet you have no problem dressing like a bum." Catherine gestured at his clothes, as if he didn't already know what she was referring to. "Frank is your father; I know you own better clothing than this."

Brody was silent for a moment, his expression unreadable. He glanced down at his car, which Catherine was still refusing to get into, and then back at her. "You really are blind, aren't you?"

Unfazed at the change in his tone, she simply glared at him. "What is that supposed to mean?"

"Never mind," he muttered, slamming the door to his Escort, then nudging it a second time when it didn't shut entirely.

"If any one of us is blind," she ranted, even as he reluctantly walked towards her car, "it would be the person who can't seem to put a decent outfit together. Oh, is it suddenly okay to be seen in a pearl white car?"

"It's pink," he corrected her as he opened the passenger door.

"It's... oh, forget it. You're too pig headed to ever admit when you're wrong." She slid into the driver's seat, checking her appearance in the mirror first as she always did. As she buckled her seatbelt, she noticed that Brody was merely staring at her, his blue eyes narrowed. "What?"

"What about you?"

"What about me? I know when clothes match, I know when they're worth being seen in public in. I know how to use a brush, and how to... well, lucky for you, you know how to brush your teeth."

Brody rolled his eyes and shook his head, then turned in his seat to face forward. He was still scowling, even as she smoothly began the drive towards the mall.

"I'm no happier about having to spend time with you than you are with me," she said before she turned her stereo on, the latest pop tune blaring from her speakers.

Brody instantly reached over and turned it off.

"Hey, don't touch my stereo!"

He rubbed his temple, not that she was paying him any mind. "I have a big enough headache as it is."

"You think you have a headache? Look what I'm being forced into! I have to drag you to the mall, actually have to run the risk of being seen with you, to spend my money—"

"Frank's money."

"Whatever, do you think this is pleasant for me? Do you think—"

"You know, on second thought," Brody cut her off, then he reached over and turned her stereo back on. "Much better."

Catherine contemplated turning the stereo off just to give him a piece of her mind, but since she had no idea just how he would react, she thought better of it. Instead, she merely smirked as if she'd won, and continued the drive to the mall, doing her best to ignore Brody's presence the whole way.

"No."

That was the one syllable Catherine snapped in Brody's direction when he tried to lead her into the discount department store in the far corner of the mall.

"What do you mean 'no'? This was the deal."

"No, the deal was I spend this $500 on clothes for your precious siblings. The deal said nothing about being seen in there."

"Look…" He pushed is ball cap back, moving his hair out of his eyes, "I hate this just as much as you do, okay? But… but they need clothes, and you can get more here—"

"Need?" she scoffed. "With Frank?"

Brody growled in frustration, turning away from her momentarily, then he sighed as he faced her once more. "Fine. Give the money to me; I'll do the shopping."

"No. Way," Catherine said, each word punctuated.

"Then you're coming with me." He grabbed her hand and began to drag her along.

"What are you… get your hands off of me!" The words were harsh, but she made a conscious effort to keep her voice down.

"You're the one who doesn't want a scene. Just walk with me willingly."

"I'm not some animal," she said, taken aback by the strength he obviously had in his hands and arms. Catherine was a skilled gymnast; she should have been able to break his hold without working up a sweat.

Brody released her hand roughly. "Animals are far less cruel."

She continued following him, her eyes blazing with anger as she began to fire one insult after another in his direction. Nothing seemed to be off limits, either, from his hair to his clothing, to his lack of proper manners, to his rather plain looks.

"Considering who your father is, you should have been drop dead gorgeous," she snapped, even as he was pulling little girl's clothing off the rack and placing it in the cart. "You're nothing like him."

"Well, what do you know? That's the first compliment you've ever given me," Brody said as he pulled out a pair of pants to go with a top.

"That was not a compliment! And… are you kidding me? Those don't even go together." She yanked the clothing from his hand. "You think you're so smooth, don't you? Trying to win brownie points with your father by showering your siblings with gifts. Here… these match and will go better with her coloring."

"These aren't coming from me," he reminded her. "They're coming from you."

"And what the hell do you care whether or not I'm nice to them?" She sighed again and his choices and replaced another mismatched outfit with something more suitable.

"Because I love them, Catherine."

"So?" She yanked the boy's shirt from his hand. "That color is all wrong for him! Geez, what is wrong with you?"

"There's nothing wrong with green."

"It's an olive green, and it will wash out his skin the way it does with yours. If these clothes are supposed to be from me, they need to look like it."

"Fine, whatever," he said with a roll of his eyes.

"And… and who cares if you love them?"

"I do."

"So? I love Chelsea, and I'm going to be brutally honest with her regardless of whether or not it makes her cry."

Brody shook his head slowly. "Love is obviously a foreign concept to you, Lady Cath-er-ine."

"And would you stop calling me that? It's annoying."

His grin almost reached his eyes. "I know."

She nearly snorted as she took a shirt of a rack they were passing, along with another pair of jeans. They weren't quite the current style, but they would do.

Brody reached for the clothes, but she pushed his hand away. "Those are too big for him."

"These are for you." Her green eyes clouded over as she looked at his current ensemble with even more disdain than she had all day. "And the moment they're paid for, you're changing into them."

"No."

"Um… yes."

"No, that money is for Sammi and Tyler, and—"

"Then I'll pay for this myself, all right? But I'm not going to run the risk of being seen here with you like…" Her words trailed off as she wrinkled her nose in disgust again. "Just… no."

He shook his head as turned from her, his jaw set tightly.

"You're welcome," she said coldly.

"I didn't ask for charity, Lady Cath-er-ine."

"It's not for your benefit; it's for mine."

"All the more reason for me to refuse it."

"You know…" She placed her hand on her hip as she glared at him. "You have a lot of nerve to preach to me about my attitude, bud. You have been nothing short of… of…"

"A jerk?" he asked when words failed her.

"That's the nice version of it, yes. So if you want to continue acting high and mighty…"

"Oh, look who's talking."

"…and berate me about everything, then your own behavior should be above reproach, don't you think?"

A muscle twitched ever so slightly in his jaw, which was set as he returned her glare. "I believe we had this covered, Lady Cath-er-ine. You bring out the worst in me."

Her eyes narrowed. "I don't like you."

"Fine. Dandy. I could give a shit less about you, too, sweetheart."

"Sweetheart?!"

"Let's just get this paid for and get out of here."

"Fine." She placed both hands on the cart as she pushed it towards the checkout lane. He had no problem keeping up with her, even with her brisk pace of walking.

"You need to put those back," he said, keeping his voice lower as other customers were now within earshot.

"What, the clothes you're changing into when we get out of this store? Not on your life."

"I won't wear them."

"Why not? The jeans will actually fit you, and the shirt matches your eyes instead of making you look all… jaundiced, really, you should not wear anything olive green, okay?"

"Catherine, I won't accept them."

"Oooo, without the condescending 'Lady' in front of it. You know, you really should add an extra 'o' to your name. Broody sounds more appropriate than Brody." Her head snapped around as she thought she'd heard him let out a short laugh, but if he had he covered it up well with a cough.

He gestured towards the nearest lane that had the fewest people in it, and she pushed him back when he tried to stand beside her in the line.

"No way, pal," she said sternly. "I'm buying these clothes, and you're changing into them."

The cashier grinned at the two of them. "I wouldn't argue if I were you, honey. Girlfriends tend to win."

"I'm not his girlfriend," Catherine said, in unison with Brody's denial.

The cashier laughed softly as she began to ring up the purchase. "Sure thing, sweetheart. Sure thing."

Brody picked up the shirt Catherine had chosen for him. "We're not buying that."

"Yes, we are, and these jeans as well." Catherine flashed her award-winning smile in the cashier's direction. "But I'll be paying for them separately."

In spite of Brody's protests, Catherine did purchase every item that had been in the cart, the $50 for his outfit going onto a charge card that her mother would be writing a check for at the end of the month. She handed the change from the $500 to Brody, along with the bag with his clothing the moment they stepped out of the store.

"Go change, and then you're getting your hair cut."

"No, and no."

"Yes, and yes," she said, crossing her arms in front of her. Again, he growled in frustration at her insistence.

"How about no and I'll think about it."

"How about yes and yes."

"Yes, and I'll think about it," he countered. "Will that suffice, Lady Cath-er-ine?"

"If you call me that one more time," she said through clenched teeth that she hid from the public with a smile, "you're going to be speaking about three octaves higher."

"So, I stop calling you that, and maybe get my hair cut. Fine. Deal."

She pointed in the direction of the bathrooms. "Go change."

"You are insufferable," he muttered, clutching the bag in his tightly closed fists as he turned as walked towards the bathroom, cursing beneath his breath the entire way.

Catherine found the nearest bench to sit on so she could file her nails as she waited for her less-than-cordial… whatever he was to emerge in clothing that wasn't quite as horrible as the outdated oversized clothing he'd been wearing before. She pulled a nail file from her bag and began to work on a perceived flaw, her jaw set, her eyes narrowed. "It's a good thing we didn't run into anyone," she muttered.

But she should have known.

Because this was the mall… the mall where the who's who of her town, and her class, shopped. And when she heard her name called, she could only cringe.

"Catherine!" Bethany exclaimed as she quickly leaned down and gave the obligatory hug and kiss on the cheek. Catherine looked up to see herself surrounded by no less than three other members of the squad all ooo-ing and aaah-ing over Catherine's bag and shoes.

There was nowhere for her to hide.

Her day had officially gone from bad to worse.

CHAPTER 10

She Buries You

Catherine's smile never faltered as Bethany and the others began firing one question after another in her direction, mostly about her abrupt exit of Bethany's party. The rumors had run rampant, with most of them having Catherine on death's door. She would never miss a social event for any reason less than that, most had concurred.

"I didn't even see you leave," Bethany added, a certain twinkle in her eye.

Catherine didn't acknowledge her obvious attempts at fishing for a story, nor was she about to tell a soul about the spat she'd had with Mitch. She gave a nonchalant shrug instead, suppressing her desire to smack the feigned concerned look off Bethany's face. "I wasn't feeling well."

Bethany's frown was transparent to Catherine. "Oh, you poor thing. I see you're feeling better now."

"Much," Catherine agreed, and she was about to come up with an extremely witty excuse as to why she was at the mall without any members of her entourage when Laura, the newest edition to the squad, spoke up.

"Tell me those bags are not yours."

Those bags, of course, being the bags that held Tyler and Samantha's clothing, so in a way they were. But the young cheerleader, who had yet to learn her place in Catherine's world, was pointing at the shopping bags from the discount department store with her nose wrinkled in disgust, the same way Catherine's had been when Brody had insisted upon going in there.

"Do you honestly think I'd wear anything from that store?" Catherine fired in return, which caused those in the circle who knew her well to laugh.

"Then what, someone just left them sitting here?" Laura asked, and Catherine could feel her blood begin to boil. Laura, Catherine decided, would need to be taught a lesson, and quickly.

Catherine's smile was sickening sweet, albeit false. "Ah, Laura, you have much to learn. Speaking of…"

Catherine had meant to distract them by suggesting more practice, more of anything to change the subject. She certainly didn't want any of them around when Brody returned, but judging by the look on Laura's face…

Laura was no longer sneering. Instead, her eyebrow was raised, and she was biting her lip as she stared into the distance, in the same direction the rest of the girls seemed to be drooling in. Catherine turned her head and inwardly cringed at the sight of Brody walking in their direction, his head down as he messed up his unruly hair even more.

Could he be more embarrassing?

Her mind raced as she tried to think of an excuse while Brody continued his approach, the wrinkled-up bag in his left hand matching the bags that set beside her. There would be no denials that the bags were his, any more than there would be denials that he was with her, and to Catherine it marked a complete social suicide. There was no way she could ever get out of this.

"Hello, sexy," one of the girls murmured, and Catherine shot her an incredulous look. Were they blind?

"There, are you ..." Brody's voice trailed off as he raised his head and realized that he and Catherine were not alone.

"Is she what?" Laura asked with a smirk.

"Oh, Catherine, you've been holding out," another girl added.

"And what is Mitch going to say?"

"Oh, please," Catherine cut them all off as she stood, waving her hand as if all of their questions were no more than a bothersome fly.

"You're Brody, aren't you?" Bethany stepped forward, offering her hand. A murmur went through the rest of the girls, as they all knew that Catherine's house had essentially been invaded.

He eyed her hand warily before he shook it, and his awkwardness caused a wave of giggles through most of the girls. "Yeah," was all he said. Catherine, of course, was not the least bit amused.

"I'm Bethany." She stepped in even closer, and Catherine had to refrain from rolling her eyes at her cheerleading captain's lack of subtlety. "And you look absolutely handsome today."

Catherine's eyebrow shot up as she looked Brody over. Sure, his clothing fit his lean form much better, and perhaps he was more than just skin and bones judging by the way his shoulders and forearms filled out the blue shirt she'd chosen for him. His hair was still shaggy, though, and he was far too small to be anything that she considered remotely masculine or 'handsome' in her eyes. Besides, to her, even though when his eyes were visible the shirt really brought out the color, he was still the plain, annoying jerk who had blackmailed her into coming here.

"Thank you?" The lift at the end made it sound more like a question.

"I take it you're not used to compliments," Bethany added, just as another of the girls informed him this was where he was supposed to tell her how stunning she looked.

"That goes without saying," Brody said, a smirk of his own touching his lips, and it was all Catherine could do to keep from gagging.

"That you're unused to compliments or that I look stunning?" Bethany asked, and Catherine's mouth literally hung open at the girl's audacity. Brody actually winked at her, which was all Catherine could take.

"Are you ready?" she asked him.

"For what?"

"To get your hair cut." She tried her best to keep the exasperation out of her voice, and much to her chagrin the girls surrounding them began to protest.

Laura began to fawn over him as well. "Oh no, your hair's gorgeous!"

If Brody was the least bit uncomfortable, he didn't let it show. He merely shook his head slightly to get his shaggy bangs out of his eyes and turned his smirk in Catherine's direction.

She'd never wanted to smack someone so badly in her life.

"Since that's settled," Bethany spoke up, hooking her arm through Brody's as she did so, "I say we all go to the food court and have lunch. My treat," she added when he opened his mouth, in case it was to tell her no.

Despite feeling her blood pressure rise, Catherine grinned and agreed, only shooting a glare in Brody's direction when she was sure no one was looking. Brody picked the bags up off the bench, which prompted another line of questioning about the store, only this time…

"They have some awesome deals, don't they?" Bethany smiled in Brody's direction, and the girls who had come with her quickly agreed.

"Seriously?" Catherine was unable to keep her mouth shut any longer, her eyebrow raised as she looked at Bethany.

"I get all of Ty and Sammi's clothes from there," Brody said, ignoring Catherine's biting comment.

"You have kids?" Laura asked, and Catherine turned her glare in the young girl's direction. She could easily give the squad a horrid reputation if she were truly that ignorant.

"No," Brody said slowly as Bethany laughed Laura's question off.

"So those adorable kids we saw at Catherine's house are your brother and sister, then?" she asked, as if Catherine hadn't told her this already. They had arrived at the food court by this time, and as the girls all spoke rather loudly and animatedly about how 'precious' Brody's siblings were, Catherine was positively sure she was going to heave all over again. She wasn't quite sure just how much more fake her fellow cheerleaders could possibly get, but she pressed on, her own false smile in place.

The conversation during their lunch was more of the same: Bethany and the others fangirling over all things Brody, acting as if he were the most gorgeous specimen of man on the face of this planet. Catherine made a mental note to have a nice, long chat with her cheerleading captain as soon as she could, but in the meantime, she had an appearance to keep up.

"So, Catherine," Bethany said, actually turning her attention away from Brody for a moment, "why is Chelsea not with you today?"

Catherine could have stated that she didn't need her hand

held, nor did she need an entourage to follow her everywhere. However, she knew it was a rare occurrence when she would come to the mall without her best frenemy. "I was merely offering Brody a ride." She dared him with her eyes to say differently.

She should have known better.

"She was helping me pick out their clothes." His own eyes conveyed that he accepted her challenge, knowing that she would rather be dead than caught in that store. He, of course, wasn't anticipating a couple of the girls to dramatically place their hands over their hearts as if it were the most precious thing on Earth.

"Oh, they'll be immaculately matched, I'm sure," Bethany said, and the other girls quickly agreed, just as Catherine knew they would. "So, they're your pet project then?"

Catherine ignored the twitching muscle in Brody's jaw. "I have no project this year, I have far too much going on. Speaking of…"

"Oh, the lake party!" Laura suddenly spoke up.

"I already know." Catherine held up a hand and had her smile in place. "I'll be there."

"I'm sure you will." Bethany turned to Brody. "But what about you?"

Brody paused with his cup halfway up to his mouth. "What about me?"

"You'll be coming to the lake party, right?"

"I didn't know anything about it."

"Oh, shame on you, Catherine, you should bring him!" Bethany said to Catherine before she turned back in Brody's direction. "The Saturday after the first home game, we hold a party out at Bass Lake. Everybody goes."

"Everybody," Laura added.

"So, you'll come, yes?" another girl asked, and as Brody

shifted uncomfortably in his chair, Catherine sensed his apprehension.

And it was the perfect time to take advantage.

"I'm sure Brody wouldn't want to be away from his brother and sister for too long. Oh, unless your father won't… I'm sure he won't mind, what am I saying?"

Brody's glare was dark as she smiled her sweet, fake smile—the same one the other girls used so often as well. She'd hit the nail right on the head and ensured that he would not be interfering any further in her social life.

"And speaking of…" She briefly glanced down at her cell phone, then back up at him. "It is getting kind of late. Shall we?"

She knew Brody wanted to stay, if for no other reason than to annoy her. She also knew that he never wanted to leave Tyler and Samantha for too long. It wasn't as if they were being left alone; both Greta and Catherine's mother were there, and Frank would often return early in the afternoon.

"Of course." His smile was a bit tight as he stood. "Ladies…" He paused as a couple of them giggled, then Catherine watched him jump slightly as Bethany shoved a small piece of paper into his front pocket.

"My number," she said, as if it hadn't been obvious to begin with. Catherine was sure it was done to spite her, as Bethany not only was the captain but was also a senior. Why would she be interested in a junior, let alone someone so far beneath her?

"We'll be seeing you soon," Laura added.

"Oh, Catherine," Bethany said as she turned to her, "Practice tomorrow."

Catherine nodded. "At your house, I know."

"Oh, I totally forgot… my house is unavailable tomorrow. I'm sure you'd be kind enough to have us all over for practice at the usual time."

Catherine seethed even as she smiled. "Oh, of course." Without another word, she walked away, with Brody right on her heels.

Brody huffed as Catherine began to walk faster. "Wow. You can slow down now; I'm sure they're not following you."

Catherine's teeth were clenched as she spoke to no one in general. "They are so fake."

"And you so have no room to talk," he countered, not the least bit intimidated by the glare she shot him. "What's the matter, Lady Cath-er-ine? Did I steal your thunder? Take you out of the spotlight for a moment?"

"Listen." She stopped abruptly and turned to face him. "I don't want you dating my friends, any of them. Got it?"

He stepped around her and continued walking towards the exit. "I'd hardly consider any of them friends of yours."

"Really? And who are you to talk, Mr. No-Friends-At-All?"

"It seems I made some today."

"Whatever."

"And this…Bethany…"

"Oh, please," Catherine scoffed. "Bethany isn't actually interested in you."

"And what's she after then, my daddy's money?" he asked tauntingly, then he held up the shopping bags. "Last I checked, he gives it all to you."

She came to a stop again, one hand braced on her hip. "Is that what your problem is? You're angry because your father…"

"I have a lot of reasons to be angry, Catherine, and I don't have time for your theatrics. If you don't mind, you're the one who wanted to leave."

"Yeah, well… I have a lot of stuff to do." With a huff, she

resumed walking towards her car. "And why would you want to date Bethany anyway?"

"I didn't say I did. She is cute, though."

"Really? Because Mitch says that compared to me, she's nothing."

"And then you open your mouth, and there is no contest. She buries you."

Catherine scoffed at him. "What is that supposed to mean?"

"It's self-explanatory. You spew so much shit and venom that no matter how fake you claim she is, she's far more genuine than you."

Catherine's face flared red and she grabbed his arm and pulled him to a stop. "You are… well, you're no one that I want to be seen with. You stay away from me, you stay away from my friends, you make yourself scarce when they come over for practice, got it?"

"Sure," he said, drawing the word out. "Are you done with your temper tantrum now?"

Her frustration over his complete reaction to her demands and moods was transparent. "Just… don't speak to me."

"Gladly."

She ignored him, telling herself he only thought he had the last say-so. She was sure, though, that she'd found his Achilles heel in those small children who greeted him so happily the moment he stepped in the front door.

And she was every bit as sure that she would use that knowledge to her advantage in the very near future.

CHAPTER 11

Not Now

Catherine scowled for about the millionth time that awful day, this time as she glared at her phone. Mitch had yet to answer her text, and when she checked the clock, she knew that his break was over and he was back at practice. She was thoroughly disgusted by his less-than-attentive manner but knew that his spot on the football team was what gave him over half of his appeal. Without being such a star, he'd be nothing more than a pretty face, and probably wouldn't be sought after by over half the school's female population.

"As if he would be interested in anyone but me." She typed another text out, hitting send without regard of how mean it sounded. She was Catherine Garner, after all; mean was to be expected.

And with that thought, she glared at her door as if the giggling children in the hallway could see her.

"Before I am done with you, Brody Harris," she said out loud, "you will so be sorry."

Her phone buzzed, signaling a text message which she incorrectly assumed would be from her adoring boyfriend. When she noticed it was Chelsea, she almost ignored it out of annoyance.

Just almost.

Instead, she saw CALL ME typed out with an entire row of exclamation points after it, which meant that her best frenemy had some hot gossip to tell. Catherine's interest was piqued, and when she called Chelsea, she was unable to even get a single 'hello' out of her mouth.

"What is this about Bethany and Brody?"

"What?" Catherine waved her hand, brushing off the thought of it. "Oh, please… there is no Bethany and Brody, trust me."

"Really? Because Laura called Tina, who called Erica, who posted it on Twitter."

Catherine had already begun to fire up her computer before she replied. "I swear there was nothing, other than…"

Drooling. Lots of drooling and stupid girly giggling and giving him her phone number. So transparent it was cringe-worthy, but it meant absolutely nothing.

"She was just trying to get to me."

"That is totally not what it sounded like."

"Then what did it sound like?" Catherine searched for, and found Erica's Twitter account, scanning over the recent posts with a quickness. The only mention was something about a new hot couple, their names, and a question mark.

"Okay, so I did the backup research," Chelsea began, which meant she'd contacted Erica who fed her backwards.

"Why not just call me?"

"I'm getting to that! Shesh! Anyhow, so when I finally call Laura, I asked her what was up, and she would not shut up about the hot piece that Brody apparently is."

Catherine shuddered with revulsion. "So not."

"But she said there was a ton of chemistry, and that you were ten kinds of jealous."

"What?!"

"And that is why I called them first," Chelsea added. "To get the gossip before going straight to the source. So?"

"So, they acted completely irrational the moment they saw him." Catherine rolled her eyes at the memory. "It was embarrassing, actually. And jealous? Hello, did they all forget I have the worshiper known as Mitch?"

"Did she give him her phone number the way Laura said she did?"

"Yeah, desperate much? But nothing is going to happen."

"They're not going to the lake party together?"

Catherine paused, her back stiffening considerably. "What did you say?"

"Laura says he's already called her, and they're going to the lake party."

Catherine silently seethed as Chelsea continued on, talking about how it may actually be a good thing since Brody was tied to her. There would be no reason for him to bring her status down, especially if he was dating the captain of the cheerleading squad. All Catherine was thinking of was how this plain, ordinary, annoying jerk was worming his way into her inner circle, and she would have absolutely none of it.

"Chelsea, I have to go."

"Uh oh, Catherine is on the warpath." Chelsea let out a short laugh. "Tell me how it ends, yes?"

"Of course."

Brody may have blackmailed her into the mall trip, and he may be forcing her to be 'nice' to his brother and sister, but there was no way she would allow him to date one of her friends.

Not if she had anything to say about it.

She shut her door with a bang and stomped down the hallway, taking the stairs down to the basement, her heavy footsteps echoing. As she turned the corner to confront him, she saw Brody standing with his back to her, his posture stiff, his hands at his sides, still wearing the outfit she'd purchased for him. The once pristinely cleaned basement had a few items thrown about and a chair toppled over, which Catherine had to step around before she spoke.

"Hey, I need to talk with you."

"Not now, Lady Catherine."

Those words didn't come from Brody; instead they'd been spoken by Frank, who she only then realized was standing in the shadows in front of his son. Catherine disregarded his command and stood in front of Brody, whose face was expressionless.

"I said I need to talk with you, so…"

"On second thought… I would like to know what you have to say to him," Frank said, and only then did Catherine glance in his direction. "Go on. I'd love to hear how he stole the money from you."

"He… what?" She snapped her head back in Brody's direction, noting the way a muscle twitched in his jaw before he spoke to his father.

"Catherine bought the clothes for them, sir."

"Bullshit."

"Hey… hey!" Catherine snapped in Frank's direction. "Lay off the testosterone, bud. I bought those clothes, okay? Me." The words left her without hesitation, knowing the evidence of her activities lay in Brody's Internet email account. There was no way she was going to test him now and have her plans for the following weekend ruined.

"What did you say to me?"

"I said..."

"She bought the clothes, sir. All of them," Brody added before Catherine could repeat herself, and it was all she could do to keep from visibly rolling her eyes.

"Yeah, and while we're on this subject," Catherine continued in Frank's direction, not noticing Brody's slight tug on the hem of her shirt, "these are your kids, pal. You're Frank Harris; they should look the part, too. They should be in clothes that fit, that match, that scream success. Yes?" Her eyes flashed a hint of a challenge in her mother's boyfriend's direction, one that he seemed to ignore.

"Tell me, Lady Catherine," he said, his tone very calm and even, "what so inclined you to spend that money on children you've wanted out of your space since day one?"

"Call it a peace offering." Catherine mirrored Brody's words, just as he'd told her to. Actually, he had drilled them into her brain, making her swear up and down this is what she would say without questioning him, which she now planned to do once they were alone.

"I wasn't aware that you made peace with anyone."

Of course she didn't. What she also didn't do was tolerate anyone calling her a liar, whether she was or not.

"I tend to prefer a happy home life, Frank." She smiled a bit too sweetly. "One that is harmonious, where everyone gets along. Is that too much to ask?"

"What does he have on you?" Franks eyes narrowed in Brody's direction. Catherine turned her head towards Brody, noting that his own expression had never changed, and that his eyes were fixated on some spot on the far wall.

"Him?" Catherine asked incredulously, then she turned back

towards Frank. "Nothing. As if anyone could have anything on me, Frank. And for the record, it's rather insulting of you to insinuate otherwise."

Frank stepped in closer, his eyes never leaving Brody. "You best not be lying to me."

"Excuse…"

"We're not, sir," Brody interrupted Catherine, who only then saw two small heads peering around the corner and into the basement. They quickly disappeared back up the stairs before their father noticed, and Catherine again had to refrain from rolling her eyes. Her mother was so going to pay for bringing so much drama into her life.

"Where is my mother? If you're going to interrogate me, someone who actually has the right to do so should be present."

"Theresa is indisposed."

Indisposed, meaning she'd probably had too much to drink yet again.

"Then this is going to have to wait," Catherine said with a wave of her hand, and then she turned back to Brody. "I need to… hey!"

No sooner had Frank's hand grabbed her shoulder when Brody roughly shoved her to the side. He stood nearly eye to eye with his father, and the silent communication between them crept beneath Catherine's skin.

"I will not be manhandled, got it?" Her eyes drifted back and forth between the two of them, neither of whom acknowledged her. Instead of sticking around to prove her point, as she normally would, she instead stepped past them and quickly went up the stairs, taking them two at a time. The tones coming from the basement were low, the words indecipherable, but she would still have none of it.

"Catherine?"

She almost cringed as she realized that Sam was standing before her at the top of the stairs. "What?" she asked almost dismissively, forgetting momentarily of her 'deal' with Brody.

"Did you really buy the clothes for us?" she asked, her gray eyes wide. "And made them match and everything? I knew Brody couldn't do that, 'cause his never match."

"No kidding," Catherine muttered, and much to her chagrin the small child actually giggled. If she'd been unprepared for that, she certainly didn't expect Sam to throw her arms around her waist and squeeze her tightly before running away. She stared incredulously at the children who were chattering happily about what they would wear on their first day of school, never remembering being that excited about either school or new clothing a single day in her life. It wasn't something she could comprehend, nor was she in the mood to try and decipher it. With a shake of her head, she walked back to her room, the bang of her shutting door muffling a thud coming from directly below.

CHAPTER 12

Blue and Gold

Catherine enjoyed the reprieve that the first two days of school had brought to her. At Davis High School, where she reigned supreme, she had been doted on, fawned over, and worshiped in a way that was second to none. When she walked the hallways either alone, with her boyfriend, or with a member of her entourage, she was greeted with more adoration than she'd been getting at home, thanks to Frank and his children. At school, there were no such distractions.

Until the first Friday, when their enrollment was complete.

"Heads up," Chelsea was saying the moment Catherine answered her phone. "It's Brody's first day."

"You think I don't know this?" Catherine cringed as she heard the giggles of his young siblings. "I'm stuck living with them, remember?"

"Then you know that Bethany will be driving him."

Catherine paused mid-stride, her nostrils flaring as she inhaled sharply. "Over my dead body."

"Well, it beats the alternative, you know." Catherine heard the pop of the gum Chelsea was obviously chewing "You could be stuck driving him the way dear old Frank wanted you to."

After Brody's extreme protests of ever being seen in her car again, it would almost be worth the torture. Instead, Catherine shook her head as she pulled the summer cheerleading uniform out of its protective packaging. "I just need to find a way to get them out of here," she muttered, more to herself than to Chelsea.

"Tsk tsk, Catherine, what would your mother say?"

Catherine stopped short of telling Chelsea that lately Theresa was lucky to form a coherent sentence, as that would be sure to spread like wildfire throughout the school. A wry grin touched her lips instead. "I'm working on it, fear not."

"Oh, and Bethany said…"

"Summer uniforms for during school," Catherine finished for her. "And, actually, I was the one who suggested it to Coach."

The coach who, to Catherine, was merely a formality, same as Bethany being named Captain. It was Catherine who essentially ran the show, Catherine who created the routines, Catherine who coordinated most practices without a coach even being present.

"Ah," was all Chelsea would say to that. "So, is Mitch picking you up?"

"No, I'm driving myself." Catherine certainly hadn't insisted upon this custom painted convertible to have it sit idle while she rode with her boyfriend, no matter how amazing his car was as well.

"Just as well, since the day is so busy." Chelsea's smile could almost be heard. "First home game and all."

Which also meant the lake party was the following day, and nothing in this world would keep Catherine away from it.

Even if it meant biting her tongue all through breakfast.

"So, your colors are blue and yellow," Tyler was saying. Catherine glared sharply at the young boy, who was none the wiser as he ate his bowl of cereal that Greta had fixed for him.

"No, they are blue and gold," Catherine replied before she returned her attention to her orange juice.

"Then why is your dress blue and yellow?" Sam added.

"It's a uniform, and it's blue and gold," Catherine corrected her.

"Looks yellow to me," Tyler commented, and Sam quickly agreed.

"It's gold," Catherine reiterated, this time through clenched teeth.

"Are you so sure about that?"

It took everything in her to keep from visibly cringing at Brody's light, teasing tone as he entered the kitchen. His playful attitude, she surmised, was more for Tyler and Sam's benefit than for hers, as he instantly had them giggling.

"Yes," she said with an air of superiority, "I am quite sure. The colors of our school are blue and gold. I suggest that be one of the things you study on your first day."

"Yes, because it's so important." The tone in his voice was flat, although he was still grinning. Catherine noted with a slightly turned up nose that he'd chosen to wear his old, tattered clothing in lieu of what she had bought for him, or what Frank had insisted that he owned. If he noticed her look, he ignored it and continued his playful banter with his brother and sister, ensuring they were both ready for school.

Catherine stood and faced him, trying to keep her expression neutral. "When you're done here, I need a word with you."

"Yeah, well…" He scratched at the light scruff that he hadn't bothered to shave. "I'm not going to be done for a while, so..." He shrugged and sat next to his little sister, who looked up at him with blind adoration. To Catherine, if this was their role model, these children were doomed.

And, of course, she wasn't going to let it slide.

"I don't want you riding with Bethany. I've already told you that my friends are off limits."

Brody looked far too pleased that this bothered her. "Well, she's my friend, and she offered."

"Bethany is not your friend," she said, a faux smile painted on when he shot her a warning look.

"Sure thing, Lady Cath-er-ine," he said, his own fake smile in place. "But until I get a parking permit, she's been generous enough to offer me a ride."

"You're not driving that thing out there, either."

"Well, it beats riding in a pink car." One corner of his mouth lifted as her nostrils flared. "Wow. Anger does not suit you at all."

"Neither does…"

"Change."

Frank's barked order, which had obviously been aimed at Brody, brought all banter in the kitchen to a screeching halt. After mumbling his apologies, Brody quickly left the room, brushing up against Catherine as he did so.

"Ugh, watch it," she called after him, knowing that he wouldn't dare reply. Suddenly losing her appetite at the sight of her mother's grimacing boyfriend, she dumped the remainder of her breakfast in the trash.

"You'll be driving him to school, yes?"

She turned towards Frank then, one hand on her hip and her eyebrow firmly raised. "I hope for your sake you're not attempting to give me an order, Frank."

"Oh, Lady Catherine." His trademark grin was in place, the words flowing so smoothly off his tongue. "It was merely a suggestion."

Catherine rolled her eyes at his term of endearment that his son had long since tarnished. "Well, the answer is a firm 'no'." And without waiting to see if he was going to reply, she turned on her heel, her ponytail swaying as she left the room.

She was light and graceful that morning, choosing to avoid any injury that stomping around might cause. She'd brushed her teeth and gathered her things together quickly, wanting to make her grand appearance at her usual time, annoyances be damned. After she glared in the direction of her mother's closed door, she was bounding down the stairs once more, hoping to stop Brody from riding to school with…

"Good morning, Catherine."

"Bethany," she greeted the cheer captain with a smile she didn't feel. "I honestly don't know why you felt the need to offer Brody a ride."

"It's my pleasure to."

Catherine nearly turned up her nose at the blush that was touching the other girl's cheeks. "Really?" Catherine asked the question before she could stop herself, but before Bethany could answer, Catherine heard Brody climbing the stairs from the basement. He emerged not in the outfit that Catherine had bought for him, but the clothes were suitable just the same. The fit was nearly perfect, and the black and gray shirt went rather well with his coloring.

And yet he looked uncomfortable in them.

"Hey, are you ready?"

And what was up with this soft voice he suddenly developed?

"Um, hello…"

"I know, I'm blocking you," Bethany said to Catherine, her arms up in defeat. "Sorry about that. But we're leaving now, yes?"

"One sec," Brody said, actually grinning at her before he

quickly walked up the stairs, where Tyler and Sam had gone to their rooms.

As Catherine heard him saying goodbye to them, she turned to Bethany once more. "Seriously, you didn't have to go through this trouble."

"Oh, it's no trouble." Bethany's eyes were still on the stairs that Brody has just ascended. "Besides, Mitch may have had a problem with you driving him."

Catherine shifted her weight uncomfortably to her opposite foot, clearly irritated by the statement. "Mitch has no say in what I do."

"True, and he could hardly say anything if you did drive Brody to school, could he?" Bethany asked, this time smiling at Brody, who was walking down the stairs to the entryway. Before Catherine could demand to know what her off-handed remark was in reference to, the two of them had left, so wrapped up in speaking to one another that they ignored her open-mouthed glare.

"Oh, this is so not happening," Catherine muttered as she walked out to her precious car, more determined than ever to remove all things Brody from her life.

CHAPTER 13

Both Ways

Davis High was abuzz with a newfound energy that Friday. Not only was the first home game happening, along with the lake party the following day, it seemed there was a new couple for everyone to gossip about. Senior cheerleading captain Bethany was not only dating a junior, but he was somehow tied in with Catherine.

And Catherine couldn't have been more displeased.

"He is not related to me," she said for the umpteenth time, each one with more venom behind it than the last.

"Then what exactly is he?"

Several choice words entered her mind any time someone asked her that, none of which were appropriate for a person in her position to say. Again, she found herself repeating that Brody Harris was her mother's boyfriend's kid, and that her home had essentially been invaded. Instead of the expected sympathy, she found herself staring in disbelief at the girls who would begin firing question after question about her 'intriguing' houseguest.

"He's no more intriguing than I am common," she said during lunch, where she and most of the other cheerleaders congregated together beneath the large oak tree.

"And you are definitely not common," Taylor spoke up, sating a little of Catherine's wounded ego.

"Amen to that," Chelsea added, raising her diet soda in Catherine's direction, and Catherine acknowledged her with a nod of her head.

"But you have to admit," Laura chimed in, shifting so she could see where Bethany was saying her goodbyes to Brody before they parted ways, "it certainly does fair better for you. You know, so the rest of the school won't be so fixated on his bargain clothing."

Catherine looked over her shoulder, her eyes narrowing as she took in Brody's appearance yet again. Oh, those definitely weren't bargain clothes that he was wearing. Perhaps they weren't bought this season, but this was more in line with something that Frank would buy, even if it wasn't a suit. In lieu of correcting Laura, in case it would seem she was defending the stain that so bothered her, she remained silent. She'd said her peace where Brody Harris was concerned, now all that was left was chastising Bethany for lowering herself in such a manner.

"Ah, young love," Chelsea teased as Bethany took a seat with the rest of cheerleaders.

"I wouldn't go that far," Bethany said in return, clearly enjoying the positive attention.

"Then how far would you go?" Catherine asked, and the group silenced at her sharp tone. "I mean, after all... you are a senior, are you not?"

"And Captain of the squad," Bethany added.

"Shouldn't you be interested in someone more, say, in our league?" Catherine asked.

"Like a football player?" Bethany asked rather quickly, then shook her head as she let out a short laugh. "Been there, and no thank you."

Bethany's 'been there' had been Mitch's older brother, who had graduated just a few months before and nearly destroyed Bethany's social status. Catherine had been more than happy to not have to play 'sisterly' with Bethany when she'd been unceremoniously dumped at Travis's graduation party. It had stung enough to have to 'answer' to her as Captain. But now, if Catherine was reading Bethany's body language correctly—and it was something she prided herself on—Bethany definitely had intentions of being much more than friends with Brody.

"So, why a junior?" Catherine asked, her eyes narrowed as she waited for Bethany's reaction.

"He's not just a junior, Catherine," Bethany said, her own eyes on Brody as he entered the school building. "He's fresh meat. And besides..." She turned her brilliant smile in Catherine's direction. "It certainly helps you, doesn't it?"

Laura beamed at Bethany's statement. "I was so just telling her that."

As the rest of the girls continued fawning over Bethany's new infatuation, Catherine had to repress the urge to outwardly roll her eyes. It wasn't so long ago that these same girls were in Catherine's own back yard practicing the routine that she had come up with, and there they'd all agreed that Brody and his siblings were the equivalent of the spawn of Satan. Now here they all were, wearing near replicas of outfits that she herself had worn over the summer, their hair styled similar to the way she'd originally worn hers after her last cut. And now what... all of a sudden, the same Captain who most had chastised and made fun of, who most had gossiped about her lack of leadership, was suddenly their hero because she decided to pursue Brody?

And she claimed it was, in part, to help Catherine.

But Catherine was far too perceptive to fall for it.

"I want to talk to you."

This was how Catherine 'greeted' Brody when she stomped down into the basement. Brody was putting a box back in place and hadn't even bothered to turn around.

"Hey! Did you hear me?"

"I think the entire neighborhood hears you, Lady Catherine," he muttered, still not turning around as he searched through the boxes.

"I don't..."

"...want me hanging around Bethany, yeah, I know." He turned then, one small box in hand. "And I don't give a shit."

She placed one hand on her hip and glared ominously at him. "You should."

"It's not like you can do a damn thing about it, and quite honestly this whole 'stay out of my life' thing is getting a bit redundant." The way his voice had raised an octave or two when he'd said 'stay out of my life' only fueled Catherine's ire.

"You think I can't make your life a living hell?"

"If it's any consolation, it already is."

She ignored his comment as she stepped forward, her eyes narrowed as she read the writing on the box. "Brian? Who the hell is Brian?"

Brody paused for a brief moment before he resumed removing the clothing from said box, albeit a bit reluctantly. "No one you need to concern yourself with."

"Is another one of you coming?" she nearly shrieked, only to fall silent when Brody's hardened glare turned in her direction.

"No," was all he said.

It took a moment for Catherine to regain her composure, but her bravado hadn't faded in the least. "I know she's taking you to the lake party tomorrow."

"And?"

"And… just… don't speak to me then, got it? Tomorrow you don't exist to me."

"If only," he said with a wry grin, then rolled his eyes at her glare. "Whatever, Catherine. Just remember that goes both ways."

"Fine."

"Fine," he said, and he turned his back on her to continue with his task.

Catherine was far from satisfied with their 'talk', and more than a little angry that both he and Bethany ignored the fact that she didn't want them together at all. At least she knew that Brody wasn't going to the football game that night, but still… things just weren't going the way she wanted them to.

Yet.

"You know what?"

Mitch didn't pause when Catherine spoke, and continued leaving wet kisses along her neck. The windows of his car were again steamed up, but the night was so dark no one could have seen as he reached across her and leaned her seat back.

"Brody thinks he's so damn smooth, and he… ow! Did you just bite me?"

"A little," Mitch said with a chuckle before he resumed his quest, his hand now trailing up her thigh.

"But he thinks that he can just… Mitch, what are you doing?"

"Celebrating the first win of the season." He lightly nipped at her earlobe as his hand continued moving up her thigh, beneath the short skirt of her uniform. "Celebrate it with me, Catherine."

He silenced whatever protest she may have had with a kiss, the same kind of kiss that left her unable to breathe at times. With the celebratory shots of liquor that she had snuck from his flask, her senses were slightly dulled, but when his hand cupped between her legs, she managed to push him back. "Mitch, c'mon."

"You've had a shit day," he said, and he returned his hand to where it had been, only this time it was beneath her underwear. "I'm going to make you forget all about it."

Her entire body jolted with shock when he touched her intimately, the foreign sensations his touch caused completely unexpected. His fingers were rough, seeking, and as she struggled to catch her breath, he urged her legs further apart.

"I don't think this is such a good idea," she said, her hand on his wrist even as he probed further.

"I think you think too much."

"Mitch…"

"Just trust me."

"I'm not having sex in a car," she said, her voice not quite as strong as it had been before. The grin he shot, while nowhere near sinister, was far less from friendly.

"I didn't say we were going to," he replied before he kissed her again. Her mind was going in several directions—telling her this was wrong, telling her everyone else was doing it, telling her that Travis had humiliated Bethany because she wouldn't do things like this with him.

Catherine wasn't about to be humiliated, especially not now. Not when the whole school practically worshiped her, not when she was nearly certain Bethany was trying to take that away from her, or at least put herself a notch above.

So when Mitch again mumbled the words 'trust me', she went against that nagging voice in her head and did as he asked.

It was past midnight before Mitch dropped her off in front of her home. She had a piece of cinnamon gum in her hand, ready to pop it into her mouth to drown out the smell of alcohol in case Frank decided he was going to attempt to assert whatever authority he mistakenly thought he had over her. When she noticed that her mother's car was missing from its usual spot, she stuffed the wrapped piece of gum back into her bag.

"Looks like I don't have to worry about them tonight," she muttered as she opened the door. She scowled as she made her way up to her room, noting the discomfort between her legs. Just as Mitch had promised, they hadn't had sex. It hadn't stopped him from being rough, though, and she would be sure to give him an earful when he picked her up for the lake party the following day.

"How long are you going to be gone?"

Catherine paused outside her door as she heard Tyler's voice. She refrained from demanding to know why the brats were still awake; they were hardly her problem.

She had other problems of her own.

"I won't be there long. Greta's going to watch you and Sammi while I go to the lake party."

"With Bethany."

"Yeah, with Bethany."

Catherine rolled her eyes as she unlocked her bedroom door. Brody was the last person who belonged at that party. She thought of him having to ask the housekeeper to babysit for him, scoffing quietly so that they wouldn't hear her. The last thing she wanted was to see or deal with any of them.

"Why can't we go?" Again, Tyler was firing more questions in his brother's direction.

"It's not a place for little kids."

"Or losers," Catherine added under her breath. She finally managed to get her door unlocked, and she quickly retreated to her room, where she could block all things Harris related from her mind.

She kicked her shoes off and grabbed her night clothes, preparing for the shower she felt she so desperately needed. She was still wincing as she removed her clothing, but she paid it no mind. Her livelihood, her reputation, her place as Queen of the school was being threatened, she could feel it. No amount of discomfort would dissuade her from preserving the title that was rightfully hers.

CHAPTER 14

Trouble in Paradise

That Saturday afternoon couldn't have been more perfect for the lake party. There was a slight breeze, but it was still warm enough to go without coats. This worked out perfectly for Catherine, who had no intentions of hiding the outfit she'd so carefully planned out. She smiled her obligatory smile at every person who commented, and more often complimented her as she stepped out of her car.

She had driven herself to the party, in spite of her earlier insistence that Mitch come pick her up. Between her nagging headache, which she blamed on the alcohol from the night before, and this uneasy feeling that remained with her, she had decided it was best to drive her own car, which sparkled in the sun.

"And it's not pink." She clicked the button, locking up her prized possession, and made her way towards friends who had already arrived.

Not once did her smile falter. Not once did she let on that she'd felt even more uneasy from the moment she'd arrived, when Mitch had swooped her up into his arms and practically shoved his tongue down her throat. When she'd smiled up at him and asked if he hadn't done that enough the night before, he took it upon himself to make a crude remark to his friends, one that suggested they'd gone much further than they actually had. If said comment would hurt her reputation, she would have given Mitch an earful regardless of who was standing by. Apparently, though, being the 'it' couple had its perks as well as its responsibilities.

"Seems that love is in the air this fine day, doesn't it?"

Catherine glanced in Laura's direction after she'd asked her question to no one in particular. "I suppose," she replied, far more subdued than normal.

"Your step brother is certainly enjoying himself."

Catherine rolled her eyes. "He's not my step brother."

Laura shrugged as she picked up her red cup, which was filled to the brim with beer that no one at said party was old enough to have. "He may as well be. Too bad, though… for you, anyway."

"What is that supposed to mean?"

"Look at him." Laura gestured over towards the lake, where Brody was crouched down looking out at the water. He wasn't exactly dressed to the nines, or however the phrase went—it seemed to be escaping Catherine's mind at the moment. At least he wasn't in his ratty clothing, though. The breeze was catching the edges of his hair, and Laura actually sighed, causing Catherine to look at her in disbelief.

"There's nothing special there, trust me."

"I wonder what he's thinking about," Laura said, an almost dream-like trance in her features. "I bet it's about Bethany."

Catherine opened her mouth to tell her she was clueless, to tell her he was probably thinking about that morning when he'd promised his brother and sister that he'd be back long before Frank ever got home.

But she didn't.

Instead, she frowned in her nemesis's direction, turned, and walked away.

If he knew that Frank hadn't wanted him to leave, hadn't wanted him to entrust those brats to Greta's care, he never should have agreed to come here with Bethany. And for that matter, perhaps he should have driven his own beat up car that was such an eye sore, especially when it sat in front of that sprawling house on the hill. He wouldn't have to worry about the time, or about Bethany not wanting to leave just yet.

Not that Catherine was paying attention.

Not that Catherine cared.

She spotted Chelsea, who had decided to finally make an appearance. Her best frenemy was frowning, apparently as irritated with the day as Catherine was. Or perhaps Taylor was bothering her with whatever she was animatedly speaking about.

"Ohmygosh, Catherine, is it true?" Taylor asked her as she walked up, interrupting their conversation.

"Is what true?"

"Did you and Mitch, you know… do it in his car last night?"

"Do it?" Catherine asked mockingly. "Do it? How old are we here?"

"I think she's asking if you had sex," Chelsea chimed in, her eyebrow raised as she and Catherine shared silent communication agreeing how Taylor's words were sure to be mocked from that day forward.

"Hmm, let me think." Catherine tapped her fingernail on her chin a couple of times, squinting up at the sun. "I'm going to say… none of your business."

"Seriously?"

Both Chelsea and Taylor said the word, with much different

tones. Taylor's was full of excitement, Chelsea's disbelief.

"Seriously." Catherine's smile was obligatory, in spite of the fact that she didn't feel it.

Taylor leaned in closer to the girls, her eyes sparkling with a mixture of laughter and alcohol. "Well, you may just want to tell your boyfriend it's no one's business then." With a wink, she turned and hurried away towards Laura, probably to share the forbidden news, no matter that there was no proof and without verification from Catherine herself.

"Seriously, Catherine?" Chelsea's smile was nowhere near as genuine as she attempted to portray, prompting Catherine to roll her eyes.

"As if I'm going to say something in front of her." Catherine shook her head and dismissed Taylor with a wave of her hand. "Anyhow..."

"Did you?"

"What is this sudden need-to-know about my sex life?" Catherine crossed her arms in front of her as she waited for Chelsea's answer.

"Since when have you had one?" Chelsea retorted. "Last you'd said to me, he was going to have to grovel for it. And," she added before Catherine could speak up, "you also said it was far too beneath you to screw him in his car."

Catherine's eyes narrowed as she contemplated Chelsea's words, that nagging uneasy feeling settling over her again.

"I did say that, didn't I?" was all she added to the conversation. She smiled then, one that was every bit as fake as the one Chelsea had given her, and then she stepped around her and began to walk in her boyfriend's direction.

Under normal circumstances, she would be fuming that Mitch had been making statements or spreading stories about their relationship and how far they'd gone. That day in particular, though, she was almost glad that he had.

But for Catherine, almost was never good enough.

When she reached Mitch, she ran her fingernails lightly down his arm, her smile beguiling as she motioned for him to follow her. Those who watched them walk away let out catcalls, their comments every bit as lewd as she would expect them to be. Once they were finally out of earshot of the others, she turned her chin up slightly as she looked up at him.

"I'm hearing rumors today, Mitch."

And his smile fell. "What kind of rumors? You know how these people are. They're always..."

"Rumors apparently started by you," she cut him off, one of her eyebrows raised. "I had no idea we actually had sex last night."

He chuckled softly before taking the last swallow of beer out of his red cup. "You know how it is, Catherine." He leaned in closer, his dark eyes raking up and down her body the same way they had the night before. "We could always make them true."

'Not likely,' she thought to herself, but only smiled up at him. "In front of everyone?"

She wasn't prepared when his hands closed around her arms, or when he pushed her up against the tree they stood beside. He was kissing her deeply, the same way he'd kissed her the night before. Today, though, in the sun, with others watching, without the aid of alcohol, Catherine's reaction was far different. It wasn't indifference, nor was it curiosity. Instead she couldn't begin to describe the rush of anxiety washing over her.

"Mitch, stop," she said sharply as he began to kiss down her neck. His hands tightened slightly on her arms before he pushed himself back, his grin less friendly.

"For now," he replied, his smile only intensifying her irrational fear.

He planned on a repeat of the night before, she could tell just by the look in his eyes as he again raked them over her. No… he planned on taking it further, he planned on his stories becoming true.

This was Mitch, though. They had known one another since elementary school, they had risen to the top of the popularity ladder together. He knew above everyone else that whatever she wanted to happen, whatever she desired, whatever she chose was the law.

But as he took her hand in his that day and led her back towards the crowd, who had been cheering the spectacle that Mitch had created, she knew she had to plan her escape before this fear, this uneasiness, this overwhelming sense of something being wrong consumed her.

"Bethany, I have to get back."

In spite of their avoiding one another, occasionally throughout the day Catherine had come close enough to Brody to hear his voice, which grated on her raw nerves. Catherine cringed as another twinge of pain throbbed in her temple.

"But I'm not ready to leave just yet."

One glance at her phone let Catherine know this was the fourth time in the past two hours that Brody had told Bethany that he needed to leave. Each time Bethany had sounded more and more impaired, and less than eager to leave.

"Aw, is there trouble in paradise already?" Chelsea quipped in Catherine's ear.

"What are you… oh, them?" Catherine shook her head. "Who

cares?"

"Not feeling well?" Chelsea asked, and Catherine shook her head. "Well, that will put a bit of a crimp in your boyfriend's plans, wont it?"

"Why do you care so much about that?" Catherine asked suddenly. "Are you hitting a dry spell since you and Jeff broke up?"

"Hardly. I'm just giving you a hard time, Catherine. Shesh, sensitive much?"

Catherine shook her head slightly and rolled her eyes as Chelsea stomped away. "Whatever," she muttered. She really wasn't feeling up to being in a big crowd, but Mitch had insisted that they stay just a little while longer until…

Well, until they disappeared to do things she really didn't want to do.

Mitch had already made a snide comment about how she'd left Bethany's party, so she couldn't leave this in the same manner. No, she knew exactly what she had to do.

That didn't make it any easier for her to do it.

"Bethany, c'mon…"

"Oh, for crying out loud, would you stop your whining?" Catherine said it loudly enough for Brody to hear. "All of this 'boo hoo, I need to get home' is just… ugh. Just ugh."

Brody's head snapped in her direction, and for a brief moment she almost thought she'd seen a glimpse of…

No, Brody was merely being a jerk. There was nothing for him to possibly be afraid of.

"Shut it, Lady Catherine."

"Well, I tell you what… what will it take for you to shut it? Will it take you having to stoop low enough to get into a pearl white convertible and…"

"It's..."

"Pearl white."

He huffed out a sigh, obviously giving up the argument over the color of her car. "Did you drive?"

"Aw, you act like that actually hurt for you to ask," Catherine said mockingly.

"Fuck, forget it." Brody's hands were in his hair as he turned and began to walk away. Catherine spoke quickly before her ingenious plan to leave the party walked away.

"Geez, fine, I'll drive you home. No need to have a conniption."

Brody kept his back to her as she dug her keys out of her bag, and Catherine tried to ignore Bethany's drunken pleas for him to stay.

"Mitch," she said with a huff of feigned annoyance, "I have to drive Brody back to the house. He's about to have a major meltdown or something here."

"But you'll be back."

She swallowed as she tried desperately to come up with a reply that would suffice for now. "Unless he creates some major home front drama. I'll text you."

Mitch's attention was elsewhere, though, until Catherine turned his face in her direction. "Hmm? Oh, yeah, right. We can always pick this up later. Say... homecoming."

Homecoming, the night that he would be following her out to her father's condo after the dance.

She smiled tightly and nodded. "Of course." She forced herself to not stiffen when he kissed her goodbye, then she quickly made her way towards her car. She caught herself just before she wiped her mouth a bit too forcefully, removing the wetness that Mitch had left there. "Are you coming?" she snapped at Brody, who was already beside her.

Neither of them spoke as they began their drive towards the house on the hill. Catherine didn't comment on her relief to leave a party she should have been more than pleased to be at; Brody didn't thank her for his ride back to the house. She didn't speak of her uneasiness, of her unnecessary fear, and he didn't speak of what could possibly be waiting for him when he returned.

She chanced a glance, merely out of curiosity, as they were stopped at a red light. Brody's eyes were fixated on something straight ahead, his hands balled into fists on his lap.

And her uneasiness increased tenfold.

It wasn't in her nature to care about anything or anyone other than herself, unless if affected her. Perhaps that was the problem; perhaps she was angry that whatever consequences he faced if Frank had already returned would somehow impact her.

That had to be it.

And that just wouldn't do.

"You shouldn't have gone, you know," she said, and scowled at herself.

Her words had been spoken much more softly than she'd intended.

Her scowl deepened when he nodded, agreeing with her without saying a word.

The light changed to green, and that uneasiness in Catherine's chest was now bordering on anxiety, even more so than it had earlier. For reasons she didn't quite understand, she hit that accelerator just a little harder, drove her car just a little faster up the hill.

What did she care if Frank was already home? It wasn't any of her concern. He wasn't her father, and those brats weren't her responsibility. They were Frank's, and… and she supposed that they were Brody's too, which definitely meant that it had nothing to do with her.

Absolutely nothing.

But that didn't stop her heart from sinking, or the gasp from leaving her lips as she pulled into the driveway and saw her mother's car already there.

She didn't speak as Brody threw his door open and ran towards the front door before she'd even parked properly. She only sat there, her mouth slightly agape as she stared at the door to her home, the one he'd left wide open when he'd sprinted through, the same way he hadn't bothered with the passenger side door of her car. She reached over and pulled her car door shut, frowning as she noted the slight shake in her own hand as she did so.

"What the… ugh, I just need to…"

She didn't finish her sentence, nor did she bother with going through the front door that someone had slammed shut. Instead, after giving herself a few minutes to calm down, she walked around the side of the house and took the path towards her gym. Maybe that was what she needed—time to decompress, time to go over everything that had happened the past 24 hours, time to gather her thoughts, her feelings, time to get some perspective.

She didn't care what was happening in that house. She didn't care that something was just wrong, that something had been wrong ever since…

Ever since they'd moved in.

"They just have to go," she muttered under her breath as she reached her gym. "They can go, and my life can just… return…to…"

She pushed the door slightly, and it eased open, a sliver of light spilling across the lawn. Someone was in there, someone who had turned on just the minimal amount of light.

Someone who was speaking in a low, angry tone.

She took a tentative step forward, no longer talking to herself, holding her breath as she listened to a thud, a crack, a grunt that made her stomach turn.

"Who the fuck do you think you are?"

Catherine could see the floor to ceiling mirror, the one that helped her with her routines.

The one that showed Frank holding Brody up with one hand wrapped around his throat.

And she couldn't move.

She was frozen in place, her hand over her mouth as she felt a scream building from deep inside her blackened soul.

This wasn't happening.

It couldn't be.

"I leave for one afternoon, one damn afternoon, and what do you do?"

She watched in horror, in disbelief as Brody's hands grasped desperately at the fingers clasped around his throat. She tried to speak, tried to scream, but could only shake uncontrollably as Brody's head slammed against the mirror that splintered, red dots spraying in a pattern as Frank released him and watched him fall limply to the floor.

CHAPTER 15

Deafening

The silence was deafening to Catherine, who only on instinct moved to the shadows just before Frank stalked past her, slamming the door shut on his way out. He couldn't have seen her; she was sure he would have said something.

But Brody…

Tentatively she stepped forward, one foot in front of the other, her body trembling as she made her way towards the open floor of the gym. Brody was still on the mats in front of the mirror where he'd fallen forward, a trickle of blood making a trail down his pale face. His eyes were closed, but as Catherine inched nearer, she could see the slight rise and fall of his back, indicating he was still breathing.

"Okay," she said to herself in a whisper, "he's not dead."

But he was obviously hurt, obviously in need of help. Feeling the panic rising within her, she glanced between his unmoving body and the door, wondering if she should make a run for the house and call an ambulance, and then…

What?

And then what?

"Brody." Her voice was still a whisper, so she spoke a little more loudly as she finally reached him. "Brody, it's… it's me, it's Catherine. Are you awake?"

Her voice was shaky, and for a brief moment she was angered that it had the nerve to betray her, to sound as if she cared, to sound as if she were crying.

Until she realized she was.

"Oh, god," she whispered harshly, wiping the tears from her face as if they were full of disease. She inhaled sharply, instincts kicking in as she knelt beside him. "Brody, are you awake?" Her voice was stronger now, louder. She saw the twitching of his fingers and hesitantly she reached out and touched his shoulder, not wanting to move him too much. "Brody?"

With a slight groan he began to stir, and she nodded to herself, as if his moving meant that everything would be okay.

"Listen, you… you've been hurt." She winced involuntarily at the most obvious statement in the world before she continued. "I… I'm going to call an ambulance, okay? And…" She let out a slight screech as his hand shot out and grabbed her wrist.

"No… no, I'm okay." His speech was slightly slurred, his movements not nearly as fluid as they should be.

"You're hurt, you're… you're bleeding, and it's… it's getting everywhere."

"I'll clean it up, okay? No… no ambulance."

"You… you're crazy, you know that?"

"So you keep telling me." Brody forced himself to a sitting position, but leaned forward almost immediately.

"Oh God, are you going to be sick? Because if you're going to be sick, then you…"

"Where is he?"

"He? He who, Frank?"

"No, the boogieman. Yes, Frank."

"Don't snap at me!" Catherine scowled and closed her eyes tightly as she tried to gain control over her emotions, tried to make sense of the nightmare unfolding right before her eyes. When she finally opened her eyes, Brody was looking at her, his own expression guarded.

"What did you see?"

"Enough to… enough to get him arrested, okay? So let's just do that, and…"

"No."

"Yes! Yes, and then…"

"I have to go," Brody said, and Catherine watched in disbelief as he tried, but failed to stand.

"Where are you going? Just… stay here and…"

"Ty and Sammi."

"What? They're not here, they're back…" Catherine's voice trailed off and her eyes widened in horror as she looked towards the door. "What did he do to them?"

"I don't… I don't know, I have to…"

"No, you stay put, okay?" She stood and brushed her trembling hands down the front of her shirt. "You stay here, and… and I'll…"

"Please don't call anyone."

"Fine!" She inhaled deeply again, as if it would clear everything away. "Fine, if you insist that I don't call anyone, then… then you still need cleaned up, and… and I'll… I'll just…

"I don't need your help."

"Really? Because you're bleeding all over my mats, your head left one big impression in my mirror, and—"

"Don't sweat it, Lady Catherine." Again, Brody tried unsuccessfully to stand, his legs trembling as he slid to the floor.

"It isn't like you would help. So sorry your precious mats and…

"Oh, just… shut up," she muttered as she walked towards the door. "And stay here, and… and I'll be back."

"No police, no ambulance, no…."

"And when I get back, you…" She pointed at him for effect. "You are going to start talking."

"Why would I talk to someone who won't listen?"

His words were barely audible, his eyes closed as he sat with his back against the mirror. She wanted to argue with him, to tell him he was wrong, but instead she turned and walked as quickly, as inconspicuously as she could, towards the house.

If Frank was still there, she had to act as if she hadn't seen anything. She would simply slip past him quietly, act as if he didn't exist while she found a first aid kit. And she'd check on Tyler and Sam, just to shut Brody up. She'd make sure her cell phone was charged, she would talk that stubborn boy into letting her call the police, and she'd make sure that monster her mother had brought into her home would go to jail.

And her problems would be solved.

She could go on about her business, go on about her life, and…

"Ms. Catherine?"

She jumped at the sound of Greta's voice, her hand instinctively covering her mouth to stifle a scream that had yet to truly surface. She had barely made it through the back door, and she had so much to do that…

"Ms. Catherine, are you all right?"

Greta's words spoken in broken English would, on any other day, set the girl off on a tangent. That evening, though, Catherine merely stood, looking at the housekeeper, a million questions going through her mind.

What did she know? What had she seen? Where…

"What are you doing?" Catherine asked as her eyes rested on a couple of plates of food.

"Oh, oh, I… I was just… putting the leftovers away, and…"

"And it's late." Catherine walked slowly over towards the plates, not quite recognizing her own voice. "That's… that's so much food."

"I… I apologize, and…"

Memories, broken and ignored, began to invade Catherine's mind, scream at her conscience.

"Did they eat?" Catherine asked suddenly, her eyes never leaving the plates. "Did they eat at all?"

Greta was silent for a moment, her hands wringing in front of her as she looked between the plates and Catherine, whose own demeanor was far from normal. Her shoulders slumped slightly and she shook her head. "No, Ms. Catherine. They didn't get to eat."

Catherine was frozen in place, her eyes still fixated on the plates as she recalled so many nights of putting her headphones on just so she wouldn't have to hear the children complain about being… about being hungry…

"This… this happens all the time." Catherine heard herself say the words, felt the anxiety building again, felt her eyes grow hot and begin to burn. "And… and I'm so blind, so blind, and… and Mother is…"

"Ms. Catherine, do you need some help?"

Catherine sniffled slightly, shaking her head, trying to get this nightmare to stop. "No, I…" She paused then, a sudden calm settling over her. "Greta, I'm going to take these upstairs."

"Ms. Catherine, I…"

"And I'm going to have Tyler and Sam in my room for a little bit, okay? I… I'm going to shut and lock that door, but… I need you to find the extra key to it."

"Extra key, yes."

"Yes, and… and I also need the first aid kit." Catherine turned to Greta, her eyes clearly focused now. "Is he still here?"

"No, Ms. Catherine," Greta replied, without needing clarification. She knew exactly who Catherine was asking about.

"Okay, good, I… I'll be back downstairs in just a few minutes, but just in case… if he comes back, I need you to leave, okay? And… and I need you to put the first aid kit…" She glanced around, then her eyes rested on the cabinet by the sink. "Put it and the key in there."

"Mr. Brody…"

"He's…" Catherine paused, then shook her head. Instincts told her to stay quiet about this part, at least for now. "I'm going to take care of him."

"You?"

Catherine nodded as she picked the plates up. "Yes, I… I can do this."

"They're good kids, Ms. Catherine, just like…"

Greta didn't finish her sentence, didn't say that Catherine was good, too.

And in that moment of clarity, Catherine understood why.

She didn't say another word to the housekeeper, nor did she stomp her way up the steps as she sometimes did. She paused as she looked down the hallway at the closed master bedroom door, wondering if she flung it opened and demand her mother do something about this mess if she actually would.

But she knew better.

Just as she'd known Brody was right when he'd said her mother was more concerned about money, about status, about that drink in her hand than she was about her own daughter.

"Catherine?"

This time it was Sam's small voice that got her attention, and Catherine looked down at the frail child, her eyes seeing the truth for the first time. This little girl shouldn't have hair that looked like it hadn't been brushed, she shouldn't have dark circles under her eyes, she shouldn't be so small, so thin, so frightened of her own shadow.

"Hey," Catherine said in a soft whisper, in a friendly tone that was so foreign she had no idea where it came from, "I need you to go get Tyler, okay? And..." She held out the plates of food, the ones that made Sam's eyes widen. "And both of you come to my room, okay?"

"Is it okay?" Sam asked, and Catherine nodded.

"Hurry, though, and be as quiet as you can."

Sam nodded before she ran towards Tyler's room, giving Catherine time to unlock her door and carry the plates of food inside. Both children followed shortly after, and Catherine placed her finger to her lips as she closed and locked the door. She motioned to the plates, which the children began to eat from, as she turned her television on, bringing the volume to one that could muffle soft sounds of whispers. She then turned towards the children and motioned that they could sit on her bed.

"But..."

"No buts," she said, interrupting Tyler. "I don't know how long I'm going to be, so go ahead and sit up there. Eat," she added, pushing the plates of food toward them. Sam was more than happy to oblige, but Tyler looked at her warily.

"Where's Brody?"

"In my gym," Catherine said, keeping her voice down. "I'm going to go out there with him for a little while."

"Where's..." Tyler paused, as if he was unsure of what he should call his own father, and it caused an unfamiliar, uncomfortable tightening in Catherine's chest.

"Listen," Catherine knelt beside the bed, keeping her voice low. "Frank isn't here right now." When both of the children nodded, she continued. "Okay, so I don't know when he's going to be back, but... Brody wants you both to stay put, in here," she said, thinking quickly, saying whatever she could to make them agree.

"He does?" Tyler asked skeptically.

"See?" Catherine held up the small key, and when both children had looked, she closed her fist around it. "When I go back out to the gym, I'm going to lock that door. But I have a key, and no one else will. When we come back, we'll unlock the door. If anyone knocks, don't say anything, don't answer, don't open that door for anyone, got it?"

"Why are you being nice?" Tyler asked, still eying her suspiciously.

"Brody said she would be," Sam spoke up between bites of food.

Catherine placed one hand on his small arm—the first contact she'd ever had with him—and she wasn't surprised when he pulled back. "I need you to do this. Brody needs you to do this. There's a bathroom right there, I have water bottles stashed... somewhere in..."

"Under your bed," Sam said, and Catherine's eyebrow shot up as she recalled the great lotion debacle.

"Yes, under the bed. There's plenty to drink, a place to go to the bathroom, you have food... and we'll be back."

"Soon?" Tyler asked as Catherine reached under the bed and retrieved three water bottles.

"As soon as we can," she replied, her voice full of conviction. She handed a water bottle to him, and he reluctantly took it from her and crawled up on the bed beside his sister. She handed another water bottle to Sam, who held it out for her brother to open for her. "And remember…"

"Don't open the door, and be quiet," Sam said in a whisper, and Catherine nodded as she gave the children a reassuring smile that she just didn't feel.

She quietly closed the door and locked it with the key in her hand, jiggling the knob before she left to ensure it wouldn't just open. After closing the doors to the rooms the children had left, she quietly made her way to the kitchen, retrieved the supplies she needed, and walked toward the gym.

Her heart was pounding uncomfortably in her chest as she went over the myriad of questions swimming around her brain. It wasn't just what was happening though, it was the logical side of her wanting to know why…

Why would someone be so cruel to another human being, especially their own child?

But Catherine wasn't a stranger to cruelty, not by a long shot. She'd spent much of her life being cruel, being indifferent, being so self-absorbed that others' thoughts and feelings were of little to no consequence to her.

She wanted to go back to that… to that place, to that time, where the entire universe centered around her. Because that was so much easier than the unfamiliar, unwanted thoughts, feelings, emotions that she was drowning in.

This… this was supposed to be her time. She was supposed to be at the lake party still, with her boyfriend, being exalted.

But when she walked through the door of her gym, her heart slowing from relief as Brody's eyes opened to see her standing there with supplies to help, she knew that there was little chance of ever going back.

CHAPTER 16

Consider it Payback

"Ow! Damn, be careful."

Catherine sighed and rolled her eyes at Brody's crankiness. The boy who hadn't so much as let out a whimper with his father wasn't pleased with Catherine's care. She had expected him to be moody, given this was Brody she was dealing with, but it was as if he'd taken it to the next level.

"Stop moving," she said for what she was sure was the millionth time in the past half hour. "I've got the glass out, I have it cleaned, now I'm just trying to get this closed up."

"By what, yanking all my hair out of my head?"

She sighed and rolled her head from side to side to alleviate some of the strain on her neck. "I told you, either go for stitches, or thank me many times over for doing this for you."

"Doing what exactly?"

Catherine nibbled on the inside of her lip as she prepared to answer him for the third time. "I am tying strands of your hair together to hold this closed." She paused her task and looked up at his reflection in the mirror. He was still pale, still had a bit of dried blood on his face, and his eyes were downcast. "Brody?"

"I'm not feeling so good," he finally admitted, and Catherine had just enough time to grab a wastebasket and hand it to him before he was throwing up. She turned away to give him as much privacy as she could, and when his retching subsided, she handed him the water bottle she'd brought along.

"I think you have a concussion."

"Don't."

"I know, I know, you won't go to the hospital." She nudged his shoulder to get him to sit up a little straighter before she continued with her task. "I still think you should."

"Stop it."

"Stop what?"

He sighed, his eyes narrowed as he met her gaze in the mirror. "Stop acting like you give a damn. We both know that you don't."

Catherine remained silent, not voicing her offense at his statement. She shouldn't have been offended, though. A few short hours before, she would have agreed with him wholeheartedly. Now, here she was caught up in the middle of this drama, and… did she care? Or was she just angry? Or…

"You don't know me well enough to make that assumption."

"Yes, I do. Ow!" He winced as she pulled a bit too hard on his hair. "And I think you're enjoying this too much."

"What, being subjected to you heaving all over the place?" she countered, trying to keep him engaged in conversation, keep his mind focused.

"Consider it payback."

"Payback for what? Oh." She instantly remembered what he was referring to, and again began chewing on the inside of her lip. "Brody, why did you lie to Frank that night?"

"Don't worry about it. Where are,"

"Tyler and Samantha are in my room," she repeated before he

could ask the question again. "Look, I want answers, and you better start talking."

"What do you want to hear, Lady Catherine?"

His sardonic tone was more like the Brody she'd become accustomed to, which eased a bit of her anxiety. "I want to hear how long this has been going on." The only response she received was a slight shrug. "That's not an answer."

"It doesn't matter. There, that's your answer."

Catherine's frown deepened, partly from his reply and partly from the unwarranted, unfamiliar feelings it stirred within her. "It does matter," she said slowly as she tried to get a handle on her emotions. "Has it always been this way?"

This time only one of his shoulders lifted.

"Is… is this why your mother is in the hospital?" she asked, trying to keep her tone nonchalant when that couldn't be further from the truth.

"What do you know about her?" His question was sharp, the anger in his eyes piercing as he met her gaze in the mirror once more.

"I know that she's in the hospital, and that's all." She tied another knot and carefully picked up a few more strands of hair. "Is this why?"

"How did you know that?"

"Because Tyler told me, now would you stop being so difficult?" She watched as one corner of his mouth twitched upwards, and her eyebrow shot up. "What was that for?"

His smirk was intact when he answered, "Payback."

Her eyes widened a fraction, her snarky retort ready to roll of her tongue, but she didn't.

She couldn't.

"Touché," she said instead. "This also means it's my turn to blackmail you."

"Don't."

"Just... answer my questions, okay?" She sounded far calmer than she felt, and had no idea where this strength was coming from. Perhaps it was a natural instinct, perhaps she was in shock. Either of those would be far more acceptable to her than to find that she honestly cared.

"Before Sammi was born."

This time her eyes were wide from shock, which she tried her best to cover while she continued tending to him. "How old were you then?"

"I don't know... ten? Ish?"

"Why?" Her voice was barely above a whisper, but in the silence that enveloped them he could hear her.

"I pissed him off."

Again, it was silent as Catherine contemplated his words, as she tried to think back to when she was ten. What had her home life been like? Her parents had still been together, she was in gymnastics, she had been just as cantankerous as any normal child, at least to her. But not once could she think of anything she possibly could have done to anger her parents to the point of them striking her, let alone do something like this.

"What did you do?" she finally asked, without adding that there was no way it could have been bad enough.

"It's hard to say. It could have been forgetting to take out the garbage, or waking him up when he was taking a nap."

"But you were just..." Her voice trailed off as she scowled and sighed.

"A kid," he finished for her. "Yeah, I know."

"But *why*?"

"Because he could." Brody winced as he shifted. "He couldn't fulfill his promises of riches and glory, he couldn't hold a job, he couldn't be this all-powerful being he'd had us believing he was… but he could control *us*."

"But…"

"He gets off on it, okay? Isn't that obvious?"

She licked her lips, which were suddenly dry, and forced her hands to remain steady as she finally finished closing his wound. She stepped back and crossed her arms to hide her now-trembling hands. "So… What about now?"

He moved then, slowly standing from the chair he'd been sitting in. Catherine watched as he steadied himself, forced himself to look her in the eye. "Name it."

As much as she didn't want to hear it, didn't want it confirmed, she couldn't stop herself. "The window."

"Yep."

Her cringe was visible as guilt assuaged her. "But that wasn't even you! That wasn't you, and… and I didn't… I didn't know that he…"

"Really?" he asked, his head tilted slightly to the side. "You didn't know?"

"No! No, he was always so… so charming, and so… I don't know,"

"Manipulative?"

"I… wouldn't… no, okay, I would. Because he can't be that… charming. And… there's no way my mother knows." Brody let out something that sounded like a bit of a snort as he turned from her and she grabbed his arm. "And what was that supposed to mean?"

He glanced over at her briefly then looked away as he bent down to help pick up the broken glass. "It means I find it hard to believe." He paused for a moment, then looked over his shoulder.

"But she is just as self-absorbed as you are; maybe she doesn't."

"Hey!"

"What?" he asked as he rubbed his temple.

She put her hands on her hips as she glared at him. "That's rather rude of you, considering."

"You think this makes us BFFs?" he asked mockingly.

Her anger was rising, but she decided against arguing with him. She told herself it was to save anymore headache from forming, but she knew deep within her that he was right. They weren't friends, just as they hadn't been before she'd witnessed all of this, which she couldn't even put a name to.

"Let's just get back to the house," she said with a sigh. "This can get cleaned up tomorrow." She walked towards the door, only realizing when she was almost there that he hadn't followed. "Aren't you coming?"

"Not yet." Before she could protest, he added, "He can't see us leaving here together, Catherine. He can't know that you know."

She tilted her head slightly to the side as she contemplated his words. "Why?"

"Isn't it obvious?"

The silence stretched between them as they stared at one another, neither one finishing the thought for him. It was obvious why; with her supposed oblivion, Catherine was safe for the time being. He wouldn't turn his anger on her, not yet, not when he was so convinced he had her fooled.

And for Catherine, that also meant as long as she acted aloof in front of Frank, she could intervene whenever necessary.

"You're just lucky I'm too tired to argue with you right now," she said to Brody, and he merely nodded, one short nod, in her direction as if he were telling her to go. "Fine, but I'll be watching for you. And I'll be waking you up every hour or two."

"You can't be..."

"You have a concussion, Brody, I'm almost certain of it. Now if you want my cooperation, you're going to have to accept my..."

"Your what?" he asked when her voice trailed off. "Your charity?"

She didn't acknowledge the sad tone in his voice, nor the way his eyes held no anger when he asked the question. "My help."

And she left the gym without waiting for his response.

Frank had already come home and gone to the bedroom he shared with Catherine's mother before she ever made it back to the house. She was as quiet as she could be as she unlocked and opened the door to her bedroom to check on the children, pocketing the key as she stepped inside and shut the door behind her. Sam was fast asleep, curled up on top of the blankets, but Tyler was wide awake and eying her warily as she stepped into the room.

"Where's Brody?" he asked, his voice barely above a whisper.

"He'll be back in a minute," Catherine replied, without adding that if he wasn't, she was going back out to the gym to drag him back into the house herself. "Coast is clear, so long as you stay quiet. You can go back to your room now, and I'll get your sister back in hers."

Tyler sat there for a moment, staring at her, unblinking.

"What?" Catherine asked as she moved a few items out of the way before attempting to lift Sam.

"You called them our rooms."

Catherine faltered for a moment before regaining composure. "I guess I'm just tired or something," she said in an almost teasing tone, ignoring the voice in her head that asked her what in the world she was being nice to him for.

"I want to see Brody."

Catherine lifted Sam up with much more ease than she thought she would have had, then glanced over at Tyler, whose expression was full of more worry than a child his age should ever have. "I'll be sure he comes up, okay?"

"Will he listen to you?"

"Well, no, but he'll want to come see you anyway, so…" She shrugged slightly and shifted Sam in her arms before she took the sleeping child to her room. She wasn't surprised when Tyler followed behind, ensuring that his sister was, indeed, placed in her bed.

"She's going to want her bear," Tyler was whispering while Catherine pulled the covers up.

"I don't think it will matter."

"No, it will… because she'll wake up and won't have it, and she'll be scared."

Catherine sighed as she glanced around the darkened room. "Where is it?"

"I don't know, she had it…"

"Here."

Catherine turned abruptly when she heard Brody's whisper from behind her, her hand covering her racing heart. He was holding a stuffed bear in one hand as he hugged Tyler, who had immediately thrown his arms around his big brother. She silently began to back out of the room, feeling like a voyeur, as if she shouldn't be watching Brody with these children, but she couldn't turn her eyes away. She watched him reassure Tyler that he was fine, a dull ache forming in her chest as he tucked Sam's bear into bed with her, kissed the child's forehead, and smoothed her hair back out of her face. This was such a contrast to the anger he always threw her way.

And yet now she understood.

Had she been in his shoes, had this been happening to her when she was convinced that people were refusing to help, she would be angry, too.

Before he turned to see her watching them, she retreated to her room, where she gathered the plates and empty water bottles to return them to the kitchen. She didn't follow Brody when he went to his own bed in the basement, choosing to only interact with him as little as possible. Things had to appear normal in this house, or so he'd said to her in the gym. Besides, she had so much to process in her head, she wasn't sure if speaking with Brody at that moment would help her or not.

When she went to set her alarm on her phone to wake him up was when she finally saw several texts from her boyfriend, each one angrier than the last, demanding to know where she was. "Well… crap," she muttered. She sat down on her rumpled comforter and typed a quick apology, leaving out any details at all, without expecting any sort of a reply. When one came less than a minute later with him telling her not to worry about it, she wondered for a brief moment if she should.

She simply couldn't at the time.

Every hour—as she was far too uncomfortable waiting for two to pass—she went down to check on Brody, waking him enough to have him grumble something angrily at her before she would shuffle up the stairs, each time more difficult than the last. She'd lost count of how many times she gone, how many times she'd sat on the edge of his bed, how many times she'd beg him to just say one word so she could finally get some sleep.

Until morning came.

She reached for her phone, its hourly alarm sounding, only to have a larger, warm hand cover her own and take the phone from her. "I'm fine, Catherine. Go back to sleep."

And when she woke again, much later in the day, she was curled up in Brody's bed, alone.

CHAPTER 17

The Truth

Catherine busied herself with her normal primping routine, regardless of the late hour she'd woken up. Once freshly showered and dressed with her makeup just so, she pulled her hair up in a messy bun and took one last look in the mirror.

Nothing had changed.

Everything had changed.

She looked the same, and yet now when she looked in the mirror something was just… different, and she wasn't at all comfortable with it.

Her cellphone began to ring, snapping her out of her slight daze, and she frowned as she saw Mitch's name and smiling face looking back at her. He would never understand what had happened the night before, even if she could tell him. And waking up in Brody's bed… that was simply a coincidence, or an accident. She'd definitely never tell Mitch that, because she knew without a doubt he'd get the wrong impression. She was still tired from her interrupted sleep and had yet to really face what the big house on the hill had in store for them today.

But ignoring Mitch any longer would surely be social suicide.

Not that he would dare break up with her so close to homecoming, but Catherine certainly didn't want to risk it. She could afford to say she'd wasted close to $500 on a dress, she could cancel her hair and nail appointments, she could come up with some excuse to not go stag, or better yet she could find someone else to go with who may or may not be able to procure a matching tux combo. What would never recover, though, was her status.

And at that moment it was all she could depend on.

"Hey, sorry… I just woke up a little bit ago."

"Sleeping your life away?"

She breathed a sigh as his tone was friendly, almost teasing. Perhaps he wasn't as angry with her as she'd originally thought. "Oh, you know me… needing my beauty sleep."

"With as hot as you are, you must sleep your life away."

She suppressed a groan at his words, or lack thereof. He did tend to repeat himself like that quite often. Mitch was far from a smooth talker, or an expert kisser. Even when his hands were on her, they were rough, sometimes a little too much so. But he was worshiped, just as she was. This was her normal, this was her life, this is what she looked forward to day in and day out—wasn't it?

"Some of the guys are getting together this afternoon."

"Yeah? What's up?" she asked as she sat on her bed, smoothing out an uncharacteristic wrinkle before realizing she hadn't even made her bed that morning. As Mitch spoke again, telling her it was just some guy thing, some football thing, she moved to the chair in front of her mirror.

"I was hoping you wouldn't be mad that I said yes."

"Why would I be mad?" she asked, averting her eyes from the stranger staring back at her in the mirror and focusing on her nails instead.

"Ah, you forgot."

"No," she lied, then shook her head as she remembered her demanding he take her out to a nice restaurant that evening. "I just… get it."

"You get it," he said, his voice a little flat. In her quest to sound normal, she'd apparently forgotten that Catherine never 'got' why anyone would put her second in their lives. She did her best to quickly recover.

"Yeah, it's… football season, you do your guy thing. I'll probably just call Chels or something."

"I don't think she's feeling so hot."

"Why's that?" Catherine asked, frowning as she almost sounded like she cared.

"She had a rough day yesterday," Mitch replied with a laugh.

Ah, the lake party. Chelsea was known for getting rather drunk at parties, and for making a spectacle of herself from time to time. Perhaps it was a good thing that Catherine hadn't stuck around. "I'll just call her later, see how she's doing," Catherine said.

"Sure you will. Uh, well… Chad's coming to pick me up, so I gotta go."

"Not even taking your car?"

"Nah, not today. I'll see you at school tomorrow."

She frowned slightly. "Yeah… sure."

"And we can talk all about our after-homecoming plans."

Her shoulders relaxed at his words, even though they shouldn't. "Of course," she purred, sounding more like herself. It wasn't that she wanted to discuss the night she'd promised would be the night, but knowing the plans were still in place eased her still-troubled mind at least a little.

She and Mitch were still together, still the 'it' couple. Her life wasn't nearly as upside down as that uneasy feeling in the pit of her stomach was telling her it was.

What was it that Brody had said? He'd said many things, actually, but he'd told her she was forever lying to herself.

"Not today," she muttered to no one, knowing it wasn't the lying she was avoiding.

It was the truth.

"Catherine, dear."

Catherine stared almost blankly at her mother, who sat on the back porch with her special Sunday drink on the table beside her.

"I was a bit concerned with how late you slept in."

"You noticed?" Catherine snapped, and instead of wincing she smiled inwardly. She sounded just like herself in that moment.

"Of course." Theresa's tone was undeniably flat when she replied. She must not have had enough of her special drink this morning, or perhaps she'd had too much already. "I figured you'd be gone the moment the sun rose. Where are you off to?"

Catherine's eyes narrowed at her mother's question. "We're in the back yard, Mother. I'm obviously not off to anywhere."

"Well, if you're wanting to go to the gym, Frank has informed me that it was broken into."

A chill passed through Catherine, one that she tried her best to shake off. "Oh, really?" she asked, not informing her mother she was well aware it was a lie. "And what did this intruder take?"

"Oh, I doubt they took anything," Theresa replied, the ice cubes in her glass clinking as she picked her drink up. "But they made quite a mess. He's being a dear and cleaning it up."

Catherine felt a surge of anger course through her. "I don't want him in there. Ever."

Theresa scoffed and set her drink back down. "Don't be so dramatic, Catherine. It isn't like Frank's the one who trashed the place."

"Seriously?" Catherine snapped before she could stop herself, then she shook her head. She had to be normal, she had to continue pretending she didn't know what was going on.

"He's right, you know," Theresa called out when Catherine turned on her heel to stomp her way towards her gym. "You are ungrateful. You do need to learn some manners."

"Finish your drink, Mother," Catherine called over her shoulder. Perhaps it was foolish of her to be so bold as to confront Frank, but she knew she wouldn't be demanding answers for the night before. No, she would simply be ordering him away from her gym, the same way she'd ordered everyone else out of it. Then she would have Greta call the locksmith and ensure that Catherine was the only one with a key. That way Frank couldn't use her space to… to…

She rubbed her temple, which was beginning to pound, as she pushed the door open and continued stomping her way inside. "Hey, excuse you! I don't want you in my…"

She faltered as she saw the scene in front of her. Frank stood, his back against the far wall, his arms crossed as he watched Brody clean up the broken glass.

"Is there a problem, Lady Catherine?" Frank asked, his voice far too calm for her. Today she saw past the charming smile, heard the true tone behind his words. Today she saw Brody pause when her name was mentioned, and the memory of his face as he struggled to breathe overcame her.

"Yes," she said, wishing she could go into every problem she had with this entire situation. Instead, keeping true to her promise to Brody, she crossed her arms and glared at her mother's boyfriend. "You know I don't want anyone in my gym, Frank."

"Not even a 'thank you' that I'm overseeing the cleanup from the break in last night?"

She didn't flinch as the lie passed his lips so easily. She knew exactly what talent it took to lie so well; she was an expert in it.

"That's what clean-up crews are for, that's what the contractors that will be replacing my mirror are for, that's what the locksmith replacing the lock on my door are for."

"Your lock doesn't need changed, Lady Catherine."

"It does if I say it does," she countered. Perhaps she should have felt some fear when Frank pushed off the wall to walk closer to her, but she followed Brody's lead and ignored Frank's actions.

"I think you need to learn your place."

"I think you need to remember who lives here on a permanent basis." Her eyes narrowed as she followed a hunch, as she reached for a reason that Frank would act so differently towards her than he did his own children. "Isn't my grandfather coming out here today, Frank?"

And he stopped.

As much as she'd wanted to avoid the truth, it wasn't going to happen that day. Catherine knew every accusation that Brody had thrown out there was accurate, far more accurate than someone who knew so little about her and her life should be.

Her grandfather essentially bankrolled her mother. Her grandfather was the reason they had this home, the reason that Theresa had a never-ending supply of cash, of pills, of her special drinks. Her grandfather's fortune had been the sole income, and a rather substantial one at that, since her parents had split.

And, like so many others, her grandfather worshiped her.

So far one of the only people who hadn't worshiped her, at one time or another, was still picking up broken glass—broken glass that had caused the injury that Catherine herself had to clean. "Stop it," she snapped at him, but like the dutiful son, or perhaps just like the son who didn't want to be hit again, he continued on. She glared at the person responsible, the person she felt an absolute rage towards. "Frank, tell him to stop."

"Brody, go check on your brother and sister. Make sure they're not causing any trouble."

With a mumbled "Yes, sir," Brody emptied his dustpan into the trash one last time, stealing a sideways glance at Catherine, one full of warning, as he left the gym.

The dread and fear that Catherine should be feeling was absent. Instead, she stared her mother's boyfriend down with the same disdain she saved for all those she deemed beneath her. He took one step towards her, then another, and still she didn't back down.

"You are a feisty one."

"I always have been," she reminded him. "And I meant it when I said I don't want anyone else in my gym, Frank. I'm certain I've made myself clear."

"You're not the parent."

"You're not my father."

"But in his absence,"

"You're still not my father," Catherine interrupted him yet again, ignoring the angry glare Frank shot her way. "Your relationship with my mother doesn't change that, got it? Now get out of my gym."

Her chin tilted up further and further as she kept eye contact with Frank as he stepped closer and closer to her. Not so long ago, she'd seen her mother's boyfriend as charming. He was always so polite, so attentive, so agreeable. He had certainly been a master manipulator, and apparently thought he was still winning this game.

But Catherine was the master.

"Easy on the testosterone, Frank," she said, her voice never wavering. "You're still only my mother's boyfriend, still only a guest."

"Oh, did your mother not break the news?" he asked, one corner of his mouth lifting in a slight smirk that anyone else would mistake for a grin. "She's agreed to marry me."

Catherine didn't miss a beat. "And what does your wife have to say about that?"

She inhaled sharply as he patted her head in a true condescending fashion. "Be sure you're here for dinner, Lady Catherine. Your grandfather would frown upon you missing it."

If looks could kill, Frank would have dropped on the spot. Instead he casually walked out of the gym, leaving the door opened for her to follow. She stood there fuming, her mind going into overdrive as she thought of something, anything, that would get that monster out of her life. With a huff, she turned to pick up a few items off the floor, as she tried to come up with some brilliant plan.

"Have you lost your fucking mind?"

She screeched and turned quickly in the direction of Brody's voice, her heart hammering in her chest. "Would you stop doing that?"

"Do you have any idea what he would do, Catherine? Do you?"

She stood up a bit straighter and narrowed her eyes. "I can handle myself, thank you very much. Oh, and you're welcome."

Brody growled in frustration, his eyes closing as he ran his hands through his hair and turned from her. He winced almost immediately, his hands falling to his sides as his head dropped forward. "This isn't about you, Catherine."

"Are you being serious?" Her footsteps were heavy as she walked towards him, her cheeks flushed with anger. "This is my home, my gym, my… my mother that…" She stopped as each of her words somehow sounded empty, shallow.

Hollow.

"What did he say to you today?" she asked quietly, and he only shook his head. "Brody…"

"Nothing, Catherine. He said nothing. He never fucking does."

"Could you try not cursing, please?"

She nearly gasped at the coldness in Brody's eyes when he finally looked over his shoulder at her. "Why, does it offend you? Does it tarnish your perfect fucking world?" She didn't answer, couldn't answer, and with one short, bitter laugh, he turned and left the gym as well.

And it was Catherine's turn to growl in frustration.

Catherine's turn to grab her hair, the pain distracting her from the anxiety building, threatening to swallow her whole.

It was Catherine's turn to close her eyes tightly, to wince at the way her eyes stung, to suppress the scream she wanted to let out, one that was sure to be heard for miles around.

She could come up with a million reasons why, each one more disturbing than the last. None of them could be true, none of them could be further from.

She didn't care about them, it wasn't her concern if Frank hit Brody, it wasn't her business if he decided the younger children needed punishment by having them go to bed without dinner. It wasn't her place to feed them, to hide them, to help them. It wasn't her nature.

In the end, as she gathered her thoughts, as she calmed herself down, she convinced herself she knew exactly what her problem was, and it had everything to do with her and her alone.

Because her perfect world wasn't perfect anymore.

CHAPTER 18

Short of Perfect

Monday morning couldn't come soon enough.

Catherine had never dreamed those words would form in her head, but during the visit with her grandfather, she found herself wondering how she could have possibly come to feel so uncomfortable in her own skin. Her family had doted on her, pampered her, coddled her in so many different ways that she'd long been the envy of more than one of her peers. There was something she noticed that Sunday evening though, something that had been severely lacking.

"This girl here," her grandfather was boasting once more as he pointed in her direction, "could have easily been an Olympic gymnast."

"That's hardly true," she murmured with a smile that she wasn't close to feeling.

"Ah, nonsense," he said with his large, booming voice, but she'd known it was. Sure, she'd been good, but she didn't have the discipline to be an Olympic gymnast, not to mention that at 5'3" she was considered a giant in the gymnastics world. She'd also grown a healthy, albeit somewhat on the small side, chest, which would have hindered her perfect balance.

But it was far from her grandfather to think of her as anything short of perfect.

"Can you flip backwards?" Sam asked, wide eyed, before being chastised for interrupting the adults. Her gray eyes were downcast once the criticism started, and Catherine watched as Brody reached over and took her hand in his to give it a squeeze.

And it felt as if that grip was around her chest.

"Yes," Catherine answered her, and her grandfather fell silent as he looked in her direction. "I was answering her question," she explained, and he nodded and continued on and on and on... about her.

Catherine watched as a muscle in Brody's jaw twitched, watched as he continued helping his brother and sister, watched as there was always a gentle touch that passed between them.

"What is this I hear about you not going for the Homecoming court?" her grandfather asked, and Catherine kept her smile sweet and demure.

"With a school so large, you can go for the court for Homecoming or Prom. I chose to hold out for Prom."

"Ah, going for the big guns, that's my grandbaby."

He said it with a wink. Not with a pat on the head, or a hug, or holding her hand.

She watched Frank and her mother interacting as well, watched how they would exchange glances, but never a touch.

Catherine looked down at the meal that Greta had prepared, the one she'd been called in on her day off to cook and serve, and thought back as far as she could remember. Where other children were often held, hugged, consoled in a physical manner, had she ever been? Had her mother, or her father, ever tucked her into bed, ever brushed her hair back out of her face, ever left a kiss on her forehead to tell her goodnight? Had they done it when she was small and simply stopped? Was that one of the many things her mother referred to as a weakness?

The rest of the meal was relatively uneventful, with Catherine smiling at the appropriate times, answering questions as she should, staying silent when it was necessary. If only her mind would remain silent. If only she didn't know the meaning behind Frank's warning glare in Brody's direction, if only she was oblivious to the reason Brody would occasionally rub his temple, the way his eyes glazed over a time or two before he'd been chastised as well. But once the formalities were done, once the children were dismissed from the adult's presence, Catherine was also able to slip away unnoticed, to tend to her own aching head.

"This just won't do," she mumbled to herself as she sat in her chair, her back to the mirror, her arms wrapped around herself. "This… I can't…"

Her phone began to ring, pulling her from her own head that was still trying to wrap itself around the madness. With a glance, she saw Bethany's name, and almost ignored the call, but thought better of it. Bethany wasn't one to call for idle chitchat anyhow. If she called, she had a reason.

"What's up?" Catherine asked, almost hating the sound of her own voice.

"I was wondering the same thing," Bethany replied, and Catherine's frown deepened.

"What do you mean?"

"Brody was supposed to call me today."

Ah, Brody. Why else would Bethany be calling her? With a sigh, Catherine stood and walked out of her bedroom as Bethany continued on and on about how she was certain that Brody was angry with her, how she hadn't meant anything by wanting to stay at the party, how she was wanting to talk to him about Homecoming. All the while Catherine remained silent, not knowing what Bethany knew, not wanting to divulge any secret Brody wasn't willing to share.

And she stopped.

Since when did Catherine give a damn about keeping anyone else's secrets?

"Do you think he's angry with me?" Bethany finally asked.

Catherine shook her head in disbelief. "How am I supposed to know that?" She continued down the last set of steps, ignoring questions from her grandfather as she made her way to the basement.

"I was wondering if he'd said something to you."

"Why not ask him yourself?" she said as she stood in front of Brody, then held her phone out, even though Bethany was still talking. "Here. It's for you."

Brody looked curiously from Catherine to her precious phone that she'd threatened him beyond reproach if he ever touched it again. She shook it once for emphasis, and he took it from her, pink case and all, and held it up to his ear.

The last thing Catherine wanted to hear was his side of the conversation with Bethany, so she turned and began walking up the steps, out of Brody's designated bedroom area. Her grandfather stood in the entryway, eying her curiously as she rounded the corner. "Something going on between you and that boy?"

She blinked several times as his question sank in. "No, no," she finally said.

"You're not yourself, Catherine."

She swallowed over the lump in her throat, the one that wanted to scream obscenities that only the boy downstairs would dare to. Of course she wasn't herself, not after what she'd witnessed, not after what she'd been drug into. But her grandfather… he was so like her mother. Not with the drinking or the 'happy pills', but with his complete disregard for anyone else's feelings, his complete lack of compassion.

The same traits that Catherine had latched onto so readily, had prided herself on.

"I've just been running myself ragged," she said, lying as easily as ever. "Between cheerleading practice, and the start of school, and…"

"What about that boy you've been seeing? That… Mitch?"

She nodded once. "Him, too."

"Now that's the kind of man you need to associate with. That one downstairs doesn't seem to have learned a thing from his father."

"It doesn't look that way, does it?" Catherine didn't add how it was a blessing, how no one on this earth should be like Frank Harris.

Her grandfather stepped in closer, and for a moment she thought he was going to give her a hug. Instead, his eyes were dark, full of warning. "Princess, if that boy ever lays a hand on you, they'll be out of this house so fast it would make your head spin. I've told your mother as much also."

Catherine nodded once more, feeling as empty as ever when he stepped back and continued on his way to the living room. Frank was in his normal spot, and this evening even Theresa had decided against retiring early, although the hint of anxiousness in her eyes showed she was longing for her escape.

"Go on to your room, now," her grandfather ordered, just as he ordered everyone in his life around. "I'll make sure that boy brings your phone back to you."

"That isn't necessary, Grandfather, he will." As soon as the words left her, Catherine stiffened as she waited for him to berate her for speaking back. Instead, she was met with his booming laugh.

"See? Cut from the same cloth, that's my Princess."

She continued on to her room, ignoring the voices of the children as they got ready for bed at what Catherine considered was an insanely early hour. She pushed her door shut behind her and made her way towards her bed, the bed that was supposed to be some kind of a reprieve but somehow didn't seem to be this evening. She sat on the edge with her arms wrapped around herself, and she waited.

When Brody knocked gently on her door before pushing it open, she didn't even glance up at him. Her eyes remained on her shoes, even as he stepped in her room and she heard her door click shut. "What the hell is wrong with you?" he demanded in a harsh whisper. This broke her from her daze, and her eyes burned with anger as she turned them on him.

"What's that supposed to mean?" She stood up, still having to look up as she continued. "I brought you my phone when your… whatever she is called it looking for you."

"And you sic your grandfather on me, making it sound like I'm taking advantage of you?"

Her eyes widened, then narrowed once more. "I did no such thing. How dare you accuse me after…"

"After what? After you stepped into a situation that I told you to stay out of?"

"What other choice did I have?" It was an effort to keep from yelling at this point as she stepped even closer to him. "Was I supposed to just leave you there? Was I supposed to let them go hungry?"

"It never stopped you before."

"I didn't…" She paused and inhaled sharply, hating how her next words cut straight through her. "I didn't notice before."

The silence in the room stretched past the point of being uncomfortable, still neither of them moved. She watched as his expression changed, as her words sunk in no matter the unwanted guilt they brought. He held his hand out, and she almost cringed until she saw her phone there. With one slight nod she took it from his hand, careful to not actually make contact with him. His now empty hand went to the back of his neck, where he scratched lightly as his own eyes drifted to the ground.

"I still don't like you," she finally said, her tone much less harsh than the one she normally reserved for him.

He let out one short laugh as he tilted his head and brought his eyes to hers. "I'm not your biggest fan either, Lady Cath-er-ine." Just like hers, his voice was softer, more reserved. Still he didn't move, as if he were struggling with the right words to say to her, and the silence once again had stretched on for just a beat too long.

But she knew.

And for once, she understood.

"You're welcome," she said to him, one eyebrow raised. For a brief moment she almost thought she saw the corner of his mouth lift up in the beginning of a smile. She didn't expect him to say anything, to correct her by telling her he hadn't thanked her for anything. Instead, he turned and left the room, left her standing there staring at her closed door feeling just a little less empty than she had been.

CHAPTER 19

Of Course it Was

"What is with you this week?"

Friday was already upon them, and Chelsea was once again complaining to Catherine about her behavior. Even in the alcove at lunch, Catherine just couldn't seem to shake the feeling that something was about to happen. "I told you I'm just moody." She picked at a non-existent loose thread on her cheerleading uniform before she smoothed her hair back into its perfect ponytail. She wasn't about to elaborate to Chelsea, or to anyone else, exactly why.

"Well, I'm not buying it. Moody is normal for you. This is all… emo or something."

Catherine narrowed her eyes as she stared Chelsea down. "You know me so well, don't you? Well enough to know that I don't do emo."

"Of course not. Your life is perfect." The words were biting, even for Chelsea's less than cordial side.

"Hardly," Catherine muttered, not realizing it had been out loud until Chelsea asked her to repeat what she'd just said. "Look, my life is… my life. Don't worry about it."

Her life had also consisted of listening extra closely for sounds that were out of the ordinary, making sure that Brody was fine even though he insisted that if she checked on him one more time, he was going to question her motives. It was acting as normal as possible so that Frank would be unsuspecting, yet always on edge that something would set him off again.

It also consisted of conflicting emotions, ones that reminded her how she wanted the children out of her hair, and ones that ached for their loss of innocence and all they had to endure.

"Plans for this weekend?"

Catherine frowned as she pulled at her skirt. "Same as yours, I presume."

"Beyond the game," Chelsea huffed as Catherine eased herself down to the concrete, laid back, and propped her feet on the wall in front of her, legs fully extended. "Aside from giving the whole school a show. Geez, Catherine, what is with you?"

Catherine's head fell to the side as she watched other students out on the lawn enjoying the warm afternoon sun. The football players were all huddled together, passing the ball back and forth, making snide remarks to and about others not in their precious circle. Right in the middle of that group was Mitch—Catherine's Mitch, the same Mitch who had groped and probed her with his prying hands, had nearly devoured her more than once this week with his lips and tongue. With a sigh she remembered her promise to him.

Homecoming.

At her father's condo.

She was finally going to give in, finally going to have sex with him, even though she could hardly see what the fuss was all about.

She should know it, though. She was Catherine Garner, Queen

of the school. And Mitch, he was her King. No one could touch them, no one could take them down off the pedestal the entire student population had put them on.

"You comfortable?"

The words were barely audible as Brody passed, hardly acknowledging Catherine aside from his comment as he walked towards Bethany, who was waiting for him. Somehow, though, she'd heard the words much clearer than she heard any of Chelsea's rants, or Laura's sighs as Brody leaned forward and placed one gentle kiss on Bethany's forehead.

Catherine swallowed over the lump in her throat, forcing her eyes back to Mitch, reminders of the night before fresh in her mind.

"Damn it, I don't want to wait," he panted in her ear as his fingers moved between her legs, beneath her panties.

"I'm not… Mitch, I'm not having sex in a… car." How many times had she told him that already?

He mistook her whimper of discomfort as one of pleasure when he roughly pushed two fingers inside of her. "You just wait, Catherine," he breathed in her ear, "you just wait until that's me inside of you."

Those words should have made her hot, made her want him with the same abandon he seemed to want her with. Instead, they made her blood run ice cold, even with his deepened kisses, the kind she was beginning to despise.

She caught a glimpse out of the corner of her eye, a couple moving into the shadows. Unable to draw her eyes away, she watched as Brody gently caressed Bethany's face, as he left soft kisses on her lips, kisses where she could still breathe, kisses that didn't leave that disgusting wet ring around her mouth.

Kisses that left Catherine wondering what the hell was wrong with her that Mitch couldn't kiss her in that way.

Her frown firmly in place, her eyes darted out to the football players once more. She squinted slightly, taking in Mitch's massive form. He was taller, broader, with larger muscles than everyone else at this school. That was what she found attractive about him… that, and his chiseled good looks. He wasn't some slender, almost too lean random guy with ordinary features who treated her…

How did Mitch treat her?

"Giving a preview?" he asked with a wink when he finally walked over. Catherine quickly regained her composure, regained her senses about her, and smiled up at him devilishly.

"Took you long enough to notice." Making him, and everyone else, believe that she was simply wanting attention was so much easier than admitting that at times now she wanted to disappear.

He held his hand out to her. "I don't need everyone here seeing my girl's goods. Those are for my eyes." As she placed her hand in his and easily stood from her position, moving with a grace that only she had, he added, "And hands, and mouth, and…"

His voice trailed off as she elbowed him, the fake smile on her face letting everyone else think she was playing. He was laughing as well as he trailed along behind her, making remarks about her 'fine ass' loud enough for everyone to hear. She held her head high as he proclaimed his love, even as he added 'of her body', and how he would 'worship' her every night of the week.

Because that was what she wanted, wasn't it?

The hottest guy in the school drooling every time she walked by, unable to keep his hands to himself because she drove him wild.

And that would mean so much more than sweet, stolen kisses

in the shadows, with longing gazes as they parted ways. Wasn't the way Mitch adulated her so much better than the way Brody shyly glanced over his shoulder as he walked away from Bethany?

Of course it was.

Of course it was.

The house on the hill held an eerie calm when Catherine returned from the football game late that evening, feigning illness to get away the first moment she could. Most of the lights were out, and her mother's vehicle was gone from its normal spot. Once not an issue of any sort, it now had her panicking.

Had Frank done something to Brody and just taken off again?

She moved quickly to the front door, fumbling with her keys as her hands were shaking uncontrollably. After two failed attempts, she successfully opened the front door and wrestled to get her keys out of the door. Once she had, and had the door shut and locked, she stood for a moment, her heart hammering wildly.

Where should she look first?

Being the closest alternative, Catherine took the stairs down to the basement at her quickest pace, not calling out for Brody, but instead taking in her surroundings as she searched for him. A small lamp was on beside the couch, which hadn't even been pulled out to make his bed, but Brody wasn't down there.

"Oh no… oh no, no…" She turned and ran back up the stairs, not going down the hallway to the living room and instead taking the second flight to the bedrooms above. Her own door was closed and locked, just as she'd left it. And she hadn't been there that night, in case anything happened. No one could get into her room to hide for safety, if they'd needed to.

Her eyes wide, she ran a few more steps down the hall and threw open the door to Tyler's room, and he jumped slightly, roused from his sleep. "Brody?"

"No, it's Catherine," she said softly, not wanting to alarm him. "Sorry, go back to sleep." When Tyler mumbled something incoherently, she closed his door with a soft click and quickly walked towards Sam's room. Her door hadn't been shut all the way, and Catherine eased it open. When she saw the empty bed, her heart sank.

"Oh god," she whispered in a rush before she turned and ran towards the stairs, taking them so quickly she barely registered that she wasn't alone.

"Hey!" Brody's harsh whisper broke into her thoughts, and she finally paused for a moment, barely able to catch her breath. He was there in front of her, looking at her as if she'd lost her mind. "Where's the fire?"

"Where have you…" She blinked a couple times as he motioned her to be quiet, and only then did she notice the sleeping child in his arms. She moved to the side as he passed, her eyes trained on her shoes as she sunk down onto the steps, succumbing to the trembling in her limbs. She placed her arms on her thighs and lowered her head there as she took slow, calming breaths.

Everything was fine. She had panicked over nothing.

"What the hell, Catherine?"

Brody's voice was still low as he neared her again, this time making his way down the stairs. She raised her head, her eyes narrowed as she looked up at him. "What do you mean, 'what the hell'?" she demanded.

His jaw was clenched as he motioned for her to follow him, obviously not wanting to be overheard. So, follow him she did—

back down the first flight of stairs, towards the entryway, and then down the second set of stairs into the basement. When she finally entered the basement, as her legs were carrying her much more slowly, she found him pacing, his hands in his hair.

"Damn it, Catherine, what the hell part of act normal do you not understand?" he asked without once looking at her.

"What part of you took all the normal out of my life do you not understand?" she snapped back. "I don't know from one day to the next if he's going to just… kill you or something, and… then what, huh? Then what? And… and your mother, she's in the hospital, right? Did he put her there?"

"Don't ask about…"

"No, I'm going to ask!" Catherine shouted, then when he threw a warning glance in her direction, she lowered her voice. "If you want me to act 'normal'," she added air quotes for emphasis, "then I want my questions answered! What hospital is she in?"

Brody was looking down at his worn Converse, which he was shuffling slightly in the carpet. "I don't know."

"Well, what… did she have surgery? Did he… did he beat her so badly that,"

"It's a fucking mental ward, okay? Are you satisfied, Lady Cath-er-ine?"

Momentarily stunned silent, she stared at Brody as he continued to pace, as he continued to run his fingers through his already tousled dark hair.

"She ended up there, and we ended up here, and I don't know how the fuck we're going to get out of here," he kept on. "But we will, all right? We will. And…"

"What… is it… permanent?"

"I'm not fucking staying here forever, Catherine."

"No, your… mother."

It was his turn to be silent, his eyes still averted. "I don't need your pity."

She was about to ask what the hell he was referring to now, but then she realized the change in her tone, the one that…

The one that sounded as if she cared.

Ignoring his comment, she asked again, "Is it permanent?" When he shook his head, she added, "Will she come back for you?" He shrugged slightly. "Frank should be fine with that, right? I mean, if she came back for you, then he wouldn't…"

Her voice trailed off as Brody shook his head slowly.

"I don't get it, Brody."

"What's there to get?" He looked over at her then, his eyes showing how tired he really was. "Is that all for now?"

"Did you take care of them before?"

"Before what?"

"Before he brought you here."

He licked his lips and swallowed, and she already knew the answer before he said a soft, "Yes."

"And what…" She gestured back towards the boxes, the ones she'd asked about before. "What about Brian?"

"Tell me, Lady Cath-er-ine, what's it like?"

She blinked a couple of times, startled when the edge had returned to his voice. "What is what like?"

"What's it like to be so fucking perfect, huh?" He took a step forward, gesturing towards her cheerleading uniform. "What's it like to be idolized? What's it like to have everyone exalt everything you say and do?"

"I… well, being… popular has its good points, but…"

"How does it make you feel, huh? To be so high up on that pedestal that nothing can touch you?"

"That's not necessarily true," she said, choosing her words

slowly and carefully.

"Do you believe the hype, then?" he asked, each word more biting than the next. "Do you honestly believe all the bullshit they feed you? Do you feel perfect?"

Her chin rose in defiance, her eyes narrowing as he stepped even closer. "What the hell would you know about how I feel, or… or who I am, or…"

"Or does it eat you up inside?" he interrupted her, his jaw clenched tightly. "Does it make you want to scream at the top of your lungs, huh Catherine? Does it make you want to put a fucking bullet in your head to show them how imperfect you are?"

Her eyes grew wide as he finished. "No! No, what makes you…" She glanced again at the boxes, then at Brody, who had turned away from her and was pulling the cushions from the couch to fix his hide-a-bed. "Brody, I…"

"Leave."

Shaken to the core, she turned and slowly began to climb the stairs. Midway, though, she stopped and turned, watching as he continued to fix his bed. "You really like her, don't you?"

"What?" he asked incredulously, glancing over his shoulder to stare at her.

"Bethany… you really like her."

"What does that have to do with anything?"

"Nothing… and… and everything," Catherine stammered, not even making sense to herself. Brody merely shook his head at her.

"You are strange."

"Oh, you're one to talk," she said quickly. "Do you?"

He sighed then, a deep thoughtful sigh as he features began to relax. "Yeah… yeah, I do."

"Okay, then," she said, then she turned, ignoring Brody as he called after her.

"Okay then? What the hell is that supposed to mean? You giving your bless… you think I need your blessing?"

She had already rounded a corner then, so responding wasn't necessary.

Nor was it necessary for her to stop the corners of her mouth from lifting in the beginnings of a smile.

CHAPTER 20

Feeling's Mutual

Homecoming week around Davis High was full of energy, the students all chattering about the Court, the dance, the party that was sure to follow. Catherine's demeanor had begun to shift back to the norm, at least around her peers, and whispers of her 'breakdown' had subsided. Little did the rest of the students know, it was because of said whispers that Catherine made it a point to be extra sharp, more on her game.

Helping her in her matters was the fact that Frank had decided to take some sort of sabbatical from being a monster. Perhaps it was the pending nuptials, although they couldn't take place until his divorce was final. Perhaps her grandfather had made it clear that no harm better come to Catherine, and Frank had taken it to heart. No matter the reason, though, Frank had left the children to their own devices, leaving Catherine to focus on herself.

"They must be getting it on quite a bit now," Chelsea remarked that Thursday afternoon, after Frank and Theresa had made a hasty exit when the rest of the cheerleaders had showed up. Catherine squinted over at Chelsea, who was doing her usual warm up routine on the plush lawn, the same lawn they'd practiced at nearly all summer as well.

"Um, ew," was Catherine's reply, her nose firmly in the air. "Let's just not go there."

"Rumor has it you're 'going there' this weekend," Taylor added, waggling her eyebrows.

"Why else would you and Mitch not be attending the party?" Laura asked between stretches before Catherine could even answer.

Catherine wasn't about to outright answer the question. "Are we about ready? Where's Bethany?"

Chelsea rolled her eyes, which were already showing her agitation. "Need you ask?"

With a huff, Catherine stood and stomped her way back inside towards the stairs to the basement. She could hear Tyler and Sammi upstairs, so she knew that Brody and Bethany would be alone. Ever since the two of them had started dating, Bethany had deemed Catherine's house the place to hold practice—saying, of course, that it was in preparation for the younger girls for the following year. It was no secret, though, that Bethany's main drive was so she could steal moments like this, alone.

"I'm so glad you get to go Saturday," Catherine heard Bethany say, and she paused on the steps, just out of sight. It wasn't what Bethany had said, since Catherine knew that somehow Frank had agreed to let Brody go to the dance. Instead it was the manner in which she'd said it—breathless, quiet. If Catherine wasn't mistaken, she could almost swear she actually heard the girl whimper.

"Seriously?" Catherine whispered with a shudder. This was hardly what Catherine wanted to be witness to, and the fact that Brody was so bold as to do any of this in that basement—her basement—was making her anger soar.

"Okay, okay… we need to stop."

And those words came from him. Catherine's eyes grew wide and her mouth hung open, but still she stood there as if she were frozen in place.

"Your father's gone."

"But Tyler and Sammi aren't, and… aren't you… supposed to be… practi…"

"Ssssssh."

Well, for the prude that Bethany had been pegged for, crucified for, she certainly wasn't acting like one now. And as Captain, she certainly didn't need to be doing this during practice time. As for how she could go about not getting caught eavesdropping…

"Catherine's going to come down here looking for you." Brody's voice was firmer now, clearer, almost as if he'd seen her or her shadow. Catherine took a couple steps backward, then stood still once more when Bethany responded.

"What, will she be jealous?"

Catherine's eyes narrowed, not only at Bethany's words, but at the way Brody chuckled after she said them. Oh, did they both ever have nerve! What in this world would make Brody think that…

"You know better, Bethany."

"You better believe that, jerk," Catherine muttered, then decided she better not stick around to hear any more. She was certain to become too angered, speak her mind, be accused of… well, be accused of eavesdropping, which is exactly what she was doing, but not for reasons that they would think.

Once securely back on the landing, Catherine called down, "Hey, Brody? If Bethany's down there, would you please remind her she's the one who called for practice today?"

And without waiting to hear anyone's response, she turned on her heel and stomped her way through the house and out the back door, which slammed behind her.

Catherine's mood had only continued to sour throughout the evening, and during dinner she barely spoke a word. She was a bit too preoccupied with shooting her glare of death in Brody's direction, which he, in true Brody fashion, ignored. She was so wrapped up in her own anger that she didn't notice that the entire table was silent, the tension nearly palpable.

Until Frank spoke.

"What went on this afternoon?"

"Nothing, sir," Brody answered, keeping his eyes averted.

"Catherine?"

Catherine huffed in annoyance. "Practice. You knew that already."

"Young lady,"

"Oh, don't start," Catherine cut him off. She had nothing to worry about; Frank wouldn't treat her the way he treated the others. Honestly, she'd had enough of that day and wasn't about to have an argument with Frank or anyone else. Without another word, she grabbed her plate and stomped into the kitchen, where she discarded the leftovers and left the plate in the sink.

She avoided the dining room and chose to head upstairs, put on some music, perhaps post something on Facebook or Twitter and wait for the dozens of responses that were sure to come. That had always worked before, so why change the norm?

Only she had nothing to say.

Absolutely nothing.

"What am I supposed to write?" she mumbled out loud. "My

mother's boyfriend's son is a… jerk who likes to make out with my friends? No, that doesn't sound stalkerish. Um… the cheerleading captain is a big skanky ho? Hell, if that was the truth…"

If that had been the truth, then Mitch's brother wouldn't have humiliated her. She wouldn't be trying so hard to redeem herself, make herself seem worthy of her social status, worthy of being someone's girlfriend. Of course she'd had to stoop to dating a newbie Junior, but still…

What would Catherine have done?

"That is something I just don't have to worry about," she stated, again out loud, again for her own benefit. She clicked on Bethany's profile, where a sickening cute picture of the couple served as her avatar. Her profile also clearly stated 'in a relationship', although it didn't say with whom. Brody didn't use Facebook, or Twitter for that matter. As far as Catherine knew, he didn't even have a cell phone, which was something she just couldn't comprehend.

Her curiosity had her clicking through Bethany's photos one by one. She smiled whenever she saw one of herself, making a mental note that she never seemed to take a bad picture. There were a few from Bethany's party, too. There was when Catherine and Chelsea had arrived, looking absolutely gorgeous as per always. There was one of Catherine and Mitch, several random crowd shots, and one of Mitch with…

"Chelsea?"

Catherine's eyes narrowed as she looked at the picture, which seemed innocent enough to the normal bystander. But to Catherine, who knew her best frenemy all too well, it looked like a girl hell bent on stealing someone else's man. Her man, to be precise.

She clicked on another album, this one from the lake party. Oh, there were many pictures in this one—such as when Mitch had nearly devoured Catherine, on more than one occasion, that day. And there were the obligatory pictures of Brody with Bethany, because they were so cute it would make a puppy nauseous. Someone had a snapshot of Brody and Catherine leaving together, which Catherine stared at for quite some time. It wasn't that they looked like a couple, or that they even looked cordial with one another. It was because, not so long after this, everything had changed.

"Oh god…"

Catherine set her laptop to the side, a nervous worry settling over her. She'd been so rude at dinner, even though it was justifiable. But Frank… he was in a mood as well. What if she'd done something to set him off?

"I can't… I can't worry about that. It's not my problem. It's…"

She cringed as she heard the slamming of a door—her mother's door, or the door she shared with Frank. This wasn't good. This… this could never be good.

After taking a couple steadying breaths, she opened her door as inconspicuously as possible. One glance to her right let her know that the master bedroom door was still closed, so she silently made her way to the stairs. She took the first flight down and paused, wondering where she should check first. She was turned towards the direction of the living room when Brody's voice behind her made her stop.

"Relax, you missed the fireworks."

She glanced over her shoulder, one eyebrow raised. "What makes you think that…"

"Right, my apologies, Lady Cath-er-ine," he interrupted her, and she could feel the heat creeping up in her cheeks knowing that he'd been right in the first place; she was on her way to check up on him.

"So, he gets pissed off at me, and takes it out on you?" she asked in lieu of coming clean.

"Wow, you really..." Brody paused, leaving his thought unfinished.

"I really what?"

"Well, unless you left this in the couch cushions, then no... it wasn't about you."

Catherine looked down at his hand, where he held a tube of Bethany's lip gloss. "Huh, well..."

"Hell, if it had been yours, I'd be looking for a new place to live, I'm sure," he added with a half-laugh as he passed her and walked towards the kitchen.

"Oh, as if I'd... hey! I'm talking to you!" She kept her tones hushed as she followed him into the kitchen, where he threw the lip gloss in the trash. "You could have given that back to her, you know." Brody only shook his head as he grabbed a bottle of water, wincing slightly as he bent. "And what was that comment about, huh? If it had been mine."

"I was making a joke." He sounded tired, almost defeated, and he let out a sigh. "It doesn't matter, though."

"What doesn't... what did he do?"

"Her dad is still one of his clients, so I still get to take her to Homecoming, yay me."

"I thought you wanted to go with her."

"It's just a stupid dance, Catherine."

Catherine's eyes widened a bit at his words. "Yeah, and your girlfriend is a Senior, and likely to be voted Homecoming Queen, so... it's more than a stupid dance."

But Brody wasn't paying attention to her; instead, he was

staring out the window into the darkened back yard, as if it held all the answers to his future.

But what sort of future could he possibly have?

"I really don't have time for this tonight, Catherine," he said, as if he could tell she was about to quiz him about his life before he'd moved there.

As if she'd listen.

"Did you have friends, back where you lived before?"

He sighed again, still looking out the back window. "Yeah."

"A lot? Or a few?"

"Real friends, Catherine. You should check into that sometime."

She ignored his comment, instead asking, "And a girlfriend?"

He took another drink of water, and his eyes narrowed slightly before he answered. "I did, but…"

"You broke up before you moved."

"Yeah, she didn't do long distance."

"Well, it didn't take you long to get over her."

"Why are you so curious about all of this?" Brody asked, finally turning to meet her gaze.

"I just… you don't have a Facebook, you don't have a cell phone, you don't do Twitter… I was just curious."

"If I was some loner psycho serial killer?" he asked, one corner of his mouth twitching upwards.

And hers began to do the same.

"Have you made friends here?" she asked him, and he shrugged.

"Time will tell, I guess. Why? You wanna be my friend?" he asked, almost teasingly, and her eyes widened.

"No! No, not… well, I'm friends with everybody, but,"

"But you don't like me, remember?"

She crossed her arms in front of her, almost angry at herself that her bad mood was forgotten. Still, she said, "You're right. I don't. And the feeling's mutual, isn't it?"

"Damn straight it is." He was grinning when he said it, and it was accented when he finished his bottle of water and threw it in the trash. "If you weren't coming down here to check on me, then what the hell were you doing?"

"Oh, you're... insufferable." She turned on her heels and walked out of the room, hiding her own grin from her face that was so foreign, and she honestly had no idea where it had come from.

"I'm fine; thanks for asking."

"I didn't," she called over her shoulder. "And if you'd quit making out with your girlfriend, then she wouldn't lose..."

"You were spying on me."

He was directly behind her now, and that had been enough to startle her, make her lose her balance. She was quick to recover as she turned around and looked up at him. "I was doing no such thing."

He was close enough now that she could see the rim of dark blue around the lighter blue of his eyes, close enough to see how dark and thick his eyelashes were. Her heart rate increased slightly as he took yet another step closer, and her eyes caught the hint of a dimple in his left cheek when he smirked down at her.

"Liar."

"You should have given your girlfriend's lip gloss back to her," she said as she stood just slightly taller, her chin lifted in defiance as she waged this inner war with herself. He crinkled his nose up slightly, and Catherine felt an unfamiliar dip in her stomach.

What. The. Hell.

"It was in the cushions. I probably sat on it. That would be gross."

And she almost laughed.

Just almost.

Except her pulse was racing, her palms were sweaty, and her cheeks were flushed in a way that was reserved only for her boyfriend.

Her boyfriend who failed to evoke such responses from her.

Her boyfriend who was probably clueless over her best friend's obvious infatuation with him.

"Personal space, Brody," she said as she placed her hands on his chest and shoved. As she did, his face paled and he grabbed his side before he could stop himself. "Wh… Brody, what's…"

"Nothing," he said with a shake of his head, but Catherine was moving his shirt up to see where a bruise was already forming along his ribcage, after averting her eyes from the definition is his abs. "It's… Catherine, quit, I've got this." He was back to being short, angry, withdrawn.

And as the ache in her chest grew, she realized she understood why.

"I can get the…"

"Greta left it under the counter," he said as he gestured back towards the kitchen. "It's probably just a couple cracked ribs. I'll just tape them up."

"Brody,"

"And I can do this myself."

"I just want…" She gasped as he grabbed her wrist and moved her hand away. His grip was firm, but nothing like the way it had been the day he'd hurt her. And that night, it sent her pulse racing at an uncomfortable rate, had her breath catching in her throat, had her looking up at him with a different kind of fear.

A fear of herself.

"Go upstairs, Catherine," he said, seemingly unaware of his effect on her. Instead of arguing, she merely nodded and turned away from him, absentmindedly touching her wrist where his own touch seemed to have burned her. "Hey…"

"I'm fine," she said with a shake of her head, not turning around and she made her way to the safety of her room.

CHAPTER 21

So Tired

Anything Catherine set her mind to, she not only could do but would be the master of. She'd had her fair share of people in her lifetime that she'd chosen to ignore, those who she deemed unworthy of her time or her presence. Just as with everything else, she was the queen of acting as if someone didn't even exist.

Until that next morning, where no matter what she did Brody seemed to be everywhere.

He was exiting the washroom, freshly showered, as she left the safety of her room to get her breakfast.

He was in the kitchen, helping the children, shortly after.

He was just outside the door as she left to get into her convertible and head to school.

And he was kissing Bethany softly, in a way that made Catherine beyond uncomfortable.

"Would you mind moving your car?" she snapped as she bounded towards her own, which was sparkling in the sun. She scowled as she heard Bethany's giggle behind her, one that made Catherine want to gouge the other girl's vocal cords straight out of her throat.

She could easily decipher her bad mood that morning. It had nothing to do with Brody, of course—no, anything he may think had happened between the two of them was strictly in his own imagination. She, on the other hand, was furious over what she saw as a betrayal.

And the two people she wanted to speak with were standing next to Mitch's car in the school parking lot when Catherine pulled in beside it.

Mitch's smile, to Catherine, seemed to be lacking that morning. When her eyebrow rose at his greeting, both he and Chelsea took it as their cue.

Catherine was in a mood.

"I'll see you in class," Chelsea said, her tone a bit flat.

Catherine didn't move her eyes from her boyfriend when she snapped her reply. "Was that for him or for me?"

She wasn't surprised when Chelsea didn't answer, choosing to walk towards the school instead. Mitch was eying his girlfriend almost suspiciously as she stared him down.

"I don't know what you heard,"

"Save it," Catherine said as she stepped in closer, her voice quiet but full of anger. "I know exactly what's going on."

"Care to enlighten me then?"

"Enlighten." Catherine repeated the word, almost surprised it was in Mitch's vocabulary. She'd never given much thought to how smart he could possibly be, only knowing his intelligence never matched hers. "I've seen the pictures; I know that Chelsea is rather fixated on you."

"Yeah, well..." Mitch left it at that, never finishing the sentence even though Catherine was glaring at him.

"Yeah well what?" she demanded, then shook her head. "You know what? Doesn't matter. I'm putting a stop to it right now."

A smirk touched his lips. "Is that so?"

"Yeah, that's so, Mitch. The homecoming game is tomorrow. Tomorrow. The dance is the day after. Do you know what else happens then?"

He leaned down, not bothering to mask the way he peered down the front of her shirt. "Yeah, I know what happens, Catherine." He stepped in closer, his hand possessively sitting at her waist. "We go to your daddy's condo, the one that he's not going to be at. Then I strip that dress off of you and we do what we should have been doing this whole time."

Her eyes narrowed, partly from anger, and partly because anger seemed to be the only emotion, the only thing fueling her in her own boyfriend's presence. "Or would you prefer to take Chelsea?" she asked, her eyes issuing the challenge that he damn best not ignore.

Mitch's size would have been intimidating to nearly everyone, but even though he towered over her, even though his arms were so large his shirts cut into them, she never backed down from him. She'd never once wavered even if he was in a mood of his own. So, when his look of anger failed to make her retract, make her apologize, make her beg him to not ditch her at the last minute, humiliate her in front of the entire student body, his glare subsided. His grip on her waist tightened, though, as he leaned close enough to speak directly in her ear.

"If I wanted to go with Chelsea, don't you think I would?"

He stood back with that same smirk, but just as Catherine was about to accept his challenge, call his bluff, and tell him that no, there was no possible way he would hurt his own reputation in that manner, she heard Bethany's voice behind her.

"Is everything all right?"

Without turning to see her standing there with Brody,

Catherine instead tangled her hands in Mitch's short dark hair and kissed him brazenly. She didn't bother with soft and sweet, the way that Brody seemed to always be kissing his girlfriend—again, he just couldn't stay out of her way. Instead, she kissed Mitch the way he always kissed her. It didn't matter that it wasn't what she wanted; it was what was expected of her.

Of them.

The golden couple, the It Girl and Boy.

And when the kiss was done, as she discreetly wiped her mouth with the back of her hand. "You'd miss out on that if you did."

Without another word, she turned on her heel and walked towards the high school. She didn't need to look back to see if Mitch was following her; there was no question that he was.

Mitch was devoted to her.

All she had to do now was convince herself that was enough.

Catherine was quiet, contemplative, but not bothering to hide her annoyance with Chelsea as they sat in the classroom, equally ignoring the lecture. Chelsea, on the other hand, wasn't in the mood for quiet. "What is your damage lately?"

Catherine didn't even glance in Chelsea's direction. "Retract the claws you have embedded in my boyfriend."

"You think I have-"

"You think he would dump me for you?" Catherine asked the question as quietly as she could without losing its intended tone. "Leave prime real estate for second rate goods?"

"Second… rate." Chelsea let out a short laugh. "You are more full of yourself than the rest of the student body combined, Catherine."

"Start a war with me and find out who's on top." Catherine's smile didn't come close to reaching her green eyes. "And does your current homecoming date know you're pining away for someone who will never be yours?"

"Look, I don't know who's been talking,"

"Who needs to talk when there are pictures all over the internet of you drooling all over my boyfriend?"

Chelsea was quiet for a moment before she said, "So that's it? You saw a few pictures and decide I'm screwing your boyfriend?"

Catherine turned her gaze to Chelsea then. "If you were slut enough to screw my boyfriend, you know you could kiss away any dreams and aspirations of being seen as anything better than second best. And," she smirked slightly, "we both know how much that would kill you, don't we?"

Chelsea's eyes narrowed, and she leaned in a little closer. "Open your eyes, Catherine. Stop being so absorbed in your own existence, notice the world around you, and maybe you won't have to be so paranoid over pictures you see on the internet. You'd actually be there to know what's going on. Or are you too preoccupied with your current housemate?"

"What does Brody have to…" The girls both straightened as the teacher cleared his throat, letting them know they needed to be paying attention. Once the attention was no longer on them, Catherine whispered harshly, "What does Brody have to do with any of this?"

"Everything," Chelsea countered in a whisper of her own. "In case you didn't catch the memo, Ms. Perfect, your boyfriend thinks you have a thing for him. I'm the one who's been trying to talk some sense into him. You're welcome, by the way."

"Mitch knows better."

"Why, because you dote on him? Please."

"Brody is with Bethany,"

"Whose own words don't mean squat to him, considering it was his brother who almost ruined her. God, Catherine, seriously! Get it together, or you're the one who'll be visiting the whole second-class-citizen tier."

The quiz being handed out to the room wasn't the only reason that Catherine was silent now, although it gave her a perfect excuse without feeling the least bit guilty. She had nothing to feel guilty over; she was merely caught up in all the drama that Brody Harris and the whole lot of his family had brought into her once-perfect world. She would show Mitch, show Chelsea, show Brody how insignificant her 'housemate' was to her.

There was no way she was going to throw away everything she'd worked so hard for over him.

After dinner, Catherine holed herself up in her room, blocking out any potential drama from the people she was doing her best to ignore. Mitch was under strict orders from his coach to rest up, as were all of the cheerleaders. This particular year, their playoff hopes were riding on the outcome of this game, so the players were all taking their coach's advice. The cheerleaders had already prepared the gifts for the senior players, so Catherine was also taking it easy.

And checking social media outlets, ensuring there were no Chelsea and Mitch sightings that she wasn't aware of.

A chime on her phone signaled a text from Mitch, one that made her smile a wicked smile.

This weekend. Epic.

Ah, there he was… her football player of few words. She shot a text back to him, telling him she was locked in her room, alone.

As she'd expected, when she'd insisted to him that she wasn't the least bit interested in Brody, he'd scoffed at the thought that she potentially had been. Chelsea was insistent, though, that he hadn't wanted to worry Catherine since she'd done such a good job convincing him that nothing was going on.

"I'm so not an idiot," she said as she awaited his reply.

Same here, babe.

And he was even calling her babe. Even though she hated the endearment, it was back after an absence. Things were well on their way to being all right.

Before she'd even had a chance to reply, though, he shot another text to her.

Just don't listen to what people are saying.

So of course, she needed to know what he was referring to. She wasn't about to post any questions, to bring attention to any potential problems the It Girl and Boy may be having. She also wasn't about to ask Chelsea, or any other the other cheerleaders, what he could possibly mean by it.

But there was one person who may know, though... one person whose secrets she kept, who wouldn't go running to his girlfriend over any questions Catherine may ask for fear of her spilling his secrets as well.

"Okay, Brody," she muttered, "time to pay up."

Catherine quietly made her way from her bedroom down the first flight of stairs, pausing to see if Frank was paying attention, or had heard her. With a grace only years of gymnastics could have given her, she was so quiet taking the second set of stairs that even Brody hadn't heard her coming, and was startled when she spoke.

"I have a few questions that I need answers to."

"Jeeeezus, Catherine, what are you... you shouldn't be down

here," he said as he stood, keeping his voice down low.

"This is my house, I can be wherever I want. And besides, those things?" She pointed to a few boxes in the far corner. "Those are mine. He won't think anything of it."

"Look, I'm… fuck, I'm not going to argue with you, okay?"

"Could you not be so crude?"

"Would it make you go back upstairs?" he asked, then turned as if he was trying to stop himself from saying anything else.

"What are people saying, Brody?"

He sighed, his shoulders drooping in defeat. "About what, Catherine?"

"You, me. You living here."

"Nothing to me," he said, his back still to her as he shuffled over to his stack of books, thumbing through them as she stepped in closer.

"Then why would Mitch tell me to not listen to what people are saying?"

Brody shook his head slightly. "Can't help you with that."

She was standing beside him now, her hands on her hips. "I don't believe you."

He glanced over at her, and she took in his appearance—the dark circles under his eyes, the pale pallor of his skin. The distant look in his eyes was even more pronounced, before he looked back at his books once more. "Believe what you want, then."

A rush of anger overtook her, and she opened her mouth, inhaling deeply as if she were going to yell, call out for Frank, bring him to her non-needed rescue, and that was enough. Brody turned towards her, his voice full of an emotion she just didn't comprehend.

"Please, Catherine, I'm tired… I'm just… so tired."

Her voice was soft, a complete contradiction to the glare she was shooting at him. "Of what?"

"Everything."

That one strained word, spoken barely above a whisper, coupled with the raw emotion finally showing in Brody's eyes affected Catherine more than any other experience ever had. It held her heart in a vice grip, had her eyes stinging, her stomach dropping.

"Brody,"

"If it means that much to you, I'll find out, just please… please go."

While his words stunned her, making her nod in agreement, that wasn't what had rendered her speechless.

In that one moment, without a single touch, without anything remotely intimate happening between them, she knew.

Whatever the rumors were, there was at least some truth behind them.

CHAPTER 22

What's Expected

The cool night air was settling in after Davis High's win that Friday, prompting several of the students and other patrons of the game to hurry towards their vehicles rather than linger behind. Catherine was close to the locker rooms, her mind wandering as she proceeded to stretch out her muscles. Strong arms wrapped around her just moments before her lips were covered in a heated kiss, one that was deep and passionate, both startling and slightly angering her.

Not that she could let on.

"Okay, okay," she said in a breathless rush when Mitch's lips kissed a wet trail to her neck, in spite of the crowd surrounding them. "Don't you want to save this for tomorrow?"

"I just want a taste of what's to come." His words were hot in her ear, and he chuckled at his own double entendre. "Come with me, Catherine."

Amidst the shouts of 'Get a room!', Catherine stared up at her boyfriend, the one she'd claimed as hers well over a year ago based on his social status alone. Her heart hammered in a traitorous fashion, one that reminded her she didn't want that preview, but with all eyes on her—especially the eyes of her own boyfriend, and the rest of the cheerleading squad that had them in full view—she simply smiled up at him.

"You," she said, with one finger on his chest, "need to go shower."

He was chuckling as he stepped away. "Wait for me."

She swallowed over the lump in her throat, the one that reminded her of everything that could be happening in her home. She pushed it down, not wanting the burden. "Of course." She continued smiling for his benefit, for the benefit of all eyes that were upon her, as she walked towards her car.

"Seems you two have certainly kissed and made up." Chelsea had fallen into step beside her as she walked to her own car, which was parked two spots over from Catherine's.

Catherine chanced a side glance and took in Chelsea's blank expression. "There was no making up to do." She stopped suddenly and turned to face her closest frenemy. "What was that whole line about what people were saying about Brody and me? Because, funny enough, neither of us has heard it."

"Like people are going to say it directly to you." Chelsea stood with one hand on her hip, her blank expression now closer to bored. "You know how it goes, Catherine."

Of course she did, which is why she'd dug a bit deeper. "And Bethany hasn't heard it, either."

"You spoke to Bethany about it?" Chelsea asked, and when Catherine's eyebrow merely shot up, a smirk touched her lips. "Of course not. You asked Brody. You see why people think the way they do?"

"Are they thinking it, Chels? Really?" Catherine resumed walking towards her car and called back over her shoulder. "Or is that merely your guilty conscience trying to worm your way out of something?"

She didn't wait for Chelsea to answer, and had her car headed towards where Mitch had parked in a matter of seconds. No need for him to come looking for her, any more than there was need to give Chelsea time to go looking for him.

Catherine had a reputation to uphold, after all.

That reputation had her kissing Mitch back once they were alone, parked on a darkened deserted street, despite the warning bells going off in her own mind.

It had her agreeing, easily saying yes when he eased her seat back.

It had her closing her eyes tightly, biting her bottom lip to keep from protesting as Mitch's hands roughly pulled her underwear down her thighs, had her muffling her whimpers of pain as his fingers probed. When she'd finally whispered, "Mitch, please..." she didn't correct him when he thought she'd asked for more.

What humiliation would that have cost her?

And would it have even closely mirrored the mortification she endured as his mouth replaced his hand?

With Mitch's tongue now stroking where his fingers had been, Catherine sucked in a shuddering breath, one mistaken for passion instead of the horror and dread she felt. Her stiff limbs also went ignored, and as she covered her face to hide her shame, to hide that this was not something she wanted to do, she repeated over and over in her head.

This is what they're all doing. This is what's expected of me.

And instead of first love's joy, all she looked forward to was when she could go home.

For once, Catherine was nervous about the lateness of her arrival back at her house. She reminded herself repeatedly that it wasn't Frank's business where she went, who she was with, when she got home. He wasn't her father, he couldn't punish her if he felt she'd done something wrong. She'd never stand for it.

But he'd already shown he wasn't above punishing someone else.

Her mother's car wasn't in the drive, but Catherine wasn't sure if it had been parked elsewhere, or perhaps had been taken back to the garage for more mysterious repairs. Unwilling to take any chances, she decided to go straight to the basement to see if anything had happened. It was better than making a trip up to her room and then having to come all the way back down, after all. She would check on him before her much needed shower, the one she convinced herself would wash this feeling away. This urge, this one to make sure that Brody was all right, far outweighed any other emotion she was feeling, any fear that Frank would find her, think something else entirely.

Besides, she was still in uniform. She could use the excuse, if caught, that she was letting Brody know that they'd won. Or perhaps she could be conveying a message from Bethany, and Frank's treasured client would want his daughter's wishes fulfilled.

As quietly as she could, she crept down the stairs, checking for any signs of him. The lights were off, but she could see the outline of the mattress—the pulled-out bed was already in place. Still wanting that extra reassurance, she whispered loudly into the darkness. "Brody? Brody, are you all right?"

"I'm fine."

Those whispered words came from behind her, frightening her, setting off her already frazzled nerves. As she stumbled, arms that she at one time hadn't considered strong reached for her, and one hand muffled her startled cry.

"Ssh, please." His whispered words sent a chill through her that had been absent all evening long, and the feel of his breath hitting her neck and ear had her heart hammering against her ribcage. She nodded once, briefly, her breaths coming out in tiny gasps when he removed his hand from her mouth. She could see just the outline of his face as he pulled back, see where his dark hair was sticking up in disarray, and her eyes dropped to his lips.

Only then did she realize she'd completely missed what he was saying.

"What?" she asked with a shake of her head.

"What are you doing down here?"

His hands were still holding her steady, the heat from his touch making her warm in places that should have been on fire earlier in the evening.

When she was with her own boyfriend.

"I was… making sure you were okay," she finally managed to whisper. He was silent for a moment, and she wondered if she'd said or done something wrong.

And just as quickly dismissed the idea.

She was Catherine Garner, after all.

"I suppose you're going to tell me it's none of my concern," she added when he remained silent.

"I'm fine," he repeated, still close enough that she could feel his breath on her, smell the mint of his toothpaste. She shifted slightly where he stood, yet one of his hands remained at her waist, holding her steady with a firm but gentle grip.

"Are you?" she asked without thinking, her own hand instinctively touching his side, just barely a brush of her fingertips over where the tape was placed on his ribcage. When he sucked in his breath sharply, she pulled her hand back, thankful for the darkness that hid the blush she could feel in her cheeks. "I'm sorry if I..."

"I'm fine." His hand slowly released her waist, as if he were unaware he'd still been touching her to begin with. "I promise."

"Fine enough for the dance tomorrow." Her words were more of a statement than a question.

"Yeah." He inched slightly farther away, but made no move to pass her.

"Frank's..."

"Yeah, he's here, in... upstairs." He gestured enough for Catherine to see, and she stifled a laugh.

"In the bedroom. With my mother."

"Thanks for the visual," he muttered, and this time she allowed herself to laugh, albeit quietly. She watched in the shadows as his lips twitched slightly before giving way to a smile.

And it took her breath away.

"I should be going," she whispered as she backed up a couple of stairs, afraid and confused over her reaction to this plain, ordinary boy. "I... need..."

She needed to shower, get the feel of her boyfriend's hands off her.

She needed to clear her head.

She could see him nod, so she turned to go back up the stairs, go to the privacy, the sanctuary of her own room. Just as she reached the top, she heard him call her name. Ignoring the dip in her stomach, the tingling in her waist and across her lips where his hands had been, she glanced over her shoulder at him.

"Are you all right?"

The sincerity behind his question—one that seemed to be lacking whenever anyone else had asked—had her lower lip trembling, but only for a moment. She held her head slightly higher as she replied with, "Of course."

"Are you sure?"

She wasn't sure.

She'd allowed her boyfriend to do things that she hadn't wanted him to do. She had convinced herself that is was fine, it was what was supposed to happen. Mitch, after all, adored her. And besides, she had to dispel the rumors that she was in any way interested in the boy in front of her.

The only one who seemed to notice that something just wasn't right.

"Of course," she finally said, thankful that she was talking in a whisper, sure that her voice would have faltered. She took in a deep breath as Brody climbed the stairs after her, standing just one step below, his face now visible in the dim lighting.

And she took in everything.

His hair was slightly shorter—had he had it trimmed?—and, as she'd suspected, looked as if he'd been lying down. His thick, dark eyelashes rimmed his blue eyes, the ones that were narrowed slightly as he looked over her face, her hair, her clothes, and his expression darkened.

"What happened?"

She opened her mouth to protest his question, to tell him there was no need for him to even ask such a thing.

Then she realized that for the first time that she could remember, she hadn't checked her appearance before entering the house. It hadn't seemed all that important to her, when she considered what may have happened inside.

Her hand went up to her hair, which was falling from the standard ponytail that Bethany had ordered they all wear that evening. She was sure her makeup was smudged, perhaps even a trail or two of mascara from the tears that had dropped, the ones that she'd sworn she'd never shed again.

"It… I'm fine," she said with a shake of her head, throwing his own words back at him. She didn't have the conviction behind them that he'd had, though, and he gently placed one hand on her arm.

She'd never known a simple touch could burn.

"Did he hurt you?"

The words Brody whispered weren't demanding of an answer. Instead he'd said them in a manner that was open, inviting her to confide in him. To Catherine, there was nothing to confide. Mitch hadn't hurt her; he hadn't done anything to her that she hadn't allowed him to do. So, Mitch wasn't the problem.

She was.

She shook her head slightly, the remnants of her ponytail swishing across her back.

"Cat, it's okay. I'm not… always a jerk."

Her eyes widened at his shortened form of her name. On one hand, no one had ever dared try to give her a nickname. She wouldn't have stood for it. She was Catherine, and that was that.

But right at that moment…

"Sorry," he mumbled, dropping his hand, leaving a void in her she never felt when free of Mitch's touch. "Just… are you sure you're fine?"

He had come up with his own pet name for her, the same way he had with his brother and sister. And now, he was looking out for her, the same as he did for them.

That was what she convinced herself of before she nodded once and turned, this time taking the stairs at a much quicker pace.

Just as she convinced herself that the racing of her heart, the warmth spread in places that had felt so cold and violated earlier was simply a delayed reaction to her own boyfriend.

The football god who was going to be taking her to the dance the following evening, taking her to her father's condo after.

And taking her virginity not long after that.

And before she closed her eyes that evening, she had almost convinced herself that she was ready.

CHAPTER 23

As Ready as I'll Ever Be

Catherine's hair appointment in the early afternoon went off without a hitch. Her hairstylist had asked repeatedly if she was sure she wanted her curls to cascade down her back, a clip holding the front and leaving a few stray tendrils around her face. After all, the other girls who had come in for their Homecoming hairstyle had their hair pinned completely up; it was apparently all the rage.

Which was all the more reason for Catherine to decline.

She did so with a smile, of course. There was no reason to anger the person in charge of making her hair absolute perfection. Her strapless pale green gown accented her eyes and showed off the remnants of her summer tan. So after carefully applying her makeup, and even more carefully slipping the silky dress over her matching lace undergarments, she stood before the full-length mirror in her room observing the final outcome.

Even without the shoes, even without much jewelry, she knew she looked beautiful, looked far more mature than her teenage years. There was a glow to her skin, and her eyes sparkled in a way that could be interpreted in so many different ways.

But she knew. She understood, no matter how wrong the reason was.

Only a few moments before, she'd been in the hallway, after checking to see if she'd left her bag with her shoes in her car. She'd heard a rustling behind her, heard Sam's gasp, heard the young child exclaim, "You look like a princess!"

She'd paused and looked over her shoulder, wondering if the comment had been directed at her. Sam stood there in her doorway, her grey eyes wide as she stared up at Catherine.

She looked down at her dress, almost commenting that she wasn't done getting ready, but instead had decided a smile and a 'thank you' was more appropriate.

"Doesn't she look like a princess?" Sam had asked, and without turning Catherine knew who she'd been talking to before he even spoke.

"She sure does."

And here Catherine stood before her mirror, arguing back and forth in her mind—why had Brody said those words? Had he meant them, or was he simply trying to appease his sister?

She hadn't asked him, of course, when she'd turned to see him standing there in all black, aside from the blue tie and cummerbund for his tux. His hair had been trimmed, yet was long enough to still hang slightly into his eyes. She resisted the urge to push his bangs back to see those crisp blue eyes more clearly.

So she'd merely stood there, a soft smile touching her lips.

And he'd done the same.

"Damn it," she muttered as she stood alone in her room staring at her reflection, "I didn't get my shoes." Then she shuddered at her rude language. "Too much Brody."

Those words were about more than just her language.

Had the seed merely been planted in her mind by Chelsea, or

had the recent events propelled her thoughts into that boy's direction? He shouldn't have even been a blip on her radar screen; she certainly wouldn't have taken notice of him had he simply shown up at her school.

But he hadn't simply shown up at her school. He and his family had invaded her home, taken over her mind, consumed her in more ways than she was comfortable with.

Perhaps this weekend was just what she needed. The dance with her boyfriend, the… planned evening with her boyfriend at her father's condo, then much needed time alone.

"I won't be thinking of you when I'm there," she whispered with closed eyes, willing the statement to be true. She knew without any doubt in her mind that one little slip would send her entire world crumbling down around her.

More than it already was.

When Mitch texted Catherine—right on time, of course—to let her know he'd arrived, she grabbed her overnight bag, her clutch, and the keys to her car. She'd told her mother that she would be spending the night with Chelsea, which was about as far from the truth as she could get. She wasn't even sure who Chelsea was going to Homecoming with, let alone what Chelsea's plans for the evening were. Catherine was sure, though, that she didn't want to run the risk of her father knowing she planned to use his condo this evening.

'Not that it would matter,' she thought to herself. She knew that her father was on a business trip, one that would have him gone until late Sunday evening. She also knew that her mother rarely spoke with her father, unless it was to argue some point or other over who was responsible for what financial… whatever after their divorce. Besides, neither parent seemed overly concerned with Catherine's plans, her social schedule, her life.

A slight scowl was on her lips as she descended the stairs in her bare feet, her shoes still missing in action.

"A little underdressed, aren't we?"

Of course Mitch would notice, and of course he would think that he was being hilarious by pointing out the obvious. "I thought they were in my car," she said with a sigh as she sat her overnight bag down. "I'll just have to go look again."

"You're honestly not ready?"

One of her eyebrows shot up at the amusement still in his tone and expression. "I suppose there's a first time for everything."

"Here."

She was startled as she felt the keys being taken from her hand, and she turned abruptly to see Brody by her side. "What are you doing?"

"You don't need to ruin your dress," he said, pointing down to the ground.

"I could hold it…"

"Ah, let him get it," Mitch insisted as he pulled her to him. His mouth a fraction of an inch from hers, he smirked and asked, "Shall I risk ruining the makeup?"

"Before pictures?" she countered.

"Oh, pictures… yes, yes." Only then did Catherine realize that her mother was standing there, and she resisted the urge to roll her eyes as she stepped out of her boyfriend's rather rough embrace. If she'd expected her mother to fawn all over her, she would have been sadly mistaken. Instead, she heard Theresa call for Greta to get the camera, to take pictures of them all before they left.

"All?"

"Yes, of course Catherine," Theresa said with a dismissive wave of her hand, one that Catherine used quite often herself. Tonight, the gesture made Catherine wonder if it grated on others' nerves the way it did with hers. "Bethany should be here any moment as well."

"Well, we need to get this done. Quickly," Catherine added. "We have reservations at the club, don't we?"

Mitch nodded once, continuing his appraisal of her dress with his eyes. Or was he simply imagining her out of it? She shook her head slightly and glanced over her shoulder at the door as Frank entered the living room, commandeering Mitch's attention.

"Great," she muttered under her breath. "Super." She lifted the hem of her dress as she walked towards the front door just as Brody walked through, her shoes in his hand. She blinked a couple of times in surprise before reaching for them. "Where were they?"

"Behind the passenger seat." His voice was low, soft, a complete contrast to the boisterous laughter coming from the living room. The silence between them stretched a bit too long as they held one another's gaze, their expressions soft, full of wonder.

What was happening? It seemed to be the unspoken question, even as her cheeks turned a slight shade of pink.

She watched as he swallowed, as he inhaled sharply, as he licked his lips—the realization hitting her that she wanted to know if those lips were as soft as they looked.

"Be sure you're home by midnight."

Frank's gruff voice broke the spell, and Brody's eyes dropped to the floor as he stiffened. "Yes, sir."

Frank seemed a bit distracted as he pulled out his own set of keys, as Theresa walked out the door in front of him. "We'll be going out."

"Yes, sir," Brody repeated.

"Don't disappoint me again, Brian."

Catherine didn't miss the way Brody flinched as he was called the wrong name, but before Catherine could correct Frank, he had shut the door. Her eyes drifted from that closed door to the boy who stood before her, his eyes closed, his breathing forcibly slow, as if he was trying to keep his emotions in check. She took a tentative step toward him, her voice barely above a whisper. "Brody?"

He shook his head. "Don't."

"But… what was…"

"Don't."

"Brody, who is…"

"Don't, Cat. Please."

His whispered plea had her heart racing, had her reaching for his hand, had her stepping in even closer. "You can talk—"

They both jumped as the doorbell rang, and Catherine stepped back abruptly, her hand still burning from the feel of his. Her fingers trembling, she opened the door to Bethany, who stepped right into Brody's waiting arms. Her hair was all pinned up, just as Catherine's hairstylist had suggested to her, and her royal blue gown matched his tie and cummerbund every bit as perfectly as Mitch's matched hers.

Because that's who they were with.

That's the way things were supposed to be.

She quietly slipped her shoes on as Mitch's booming voice called for everyone to come to the living room, where Greta would have them all stand in front of the picture window, would snap picture after picture in various poses, as she had over the years.

Always Greta, never Theresa.

Catherine pasted on her best smile, the one she reserved for the spotlight that she was so accustomed to, the same spotlight that she basked in under normal circumstances.

There was nothing normal about this evening, though.

And the photos would be sure to show the glances she kept throwing in Brody's direction.

Perhaps… perhaps they'd also show him looking over at her, the way she thought he had a time or two.

"Okay, so we're ready then." This was Catherine's way of announcing she was done having her photo taken. "We don't want to be late."

"We'll be right behind you," Bethany said, and Catherine turned to her with a puzzled expression. "You're not the only ones who can get reservations at the club."

Of course not. Bethany's father was incredibly loaded, ran in the same social circles that Catherine's mother—and now Brody's father—belonged to. The same social circle Catherine's father shunned after he'd left that house on the hill.

And for the first time, Catherine wondered why.

The moment was brief, though, as she searched the entryway for her overnight bag, which she was sure she'd left there. She pressed her fingertips to her temples and took a deep cleansing breath, one that should have had her calming down.

"Brody, did you see my… whoa."

Catherine opened her eyes to see Tyler near the bottom of the steps, his eyes wide as he stared at her. "What?" she asked, and her inward wince wasn't at any harshness in her voice but more from the lack of it.

"You look pretty, Catherine."

"Eyes in your head, kid." Mitch was fishing his keys out of the pocket of his tux, and Catherine shot him a glare.

"Be nice, Mitch," she said in hushed tones. Mitch's eyebrows raised at her words, but he said nothing even as Sam came bounding in from the kitchen.

"She… looks like… a princess." The young girl was winded from running, her eyes shining even as she held up her small hands. "I didn't bring my drink."

Catherine swallowed over the lump in her throat as guilt assuaged her, the great Kool-Aid incident almost forgotten until that moment. Brody was chuckling as he came up behind her and he mussed the top of her hair, causing the little girl to giggle.

"Be good tonight," he was telling both Tyler and Sam as Mitch opened the front door. Mitch held his arm out to Catherine, and she slipped her hand around it, the bulk of his muscles almost feeling foreign to her.

But they shouldn't.

The sun was still shining, catching the flake of the cherry red paint on Mitch's Dodge Charger, the same car that she'd counted as such a perk to dating him. Now it was nothing more than just a car, just a means to an end… sometimes a much different end than what she truly wanted.

"I've been assured we'll have the best table," Mitch murmured in her ear. Of course he would see to such a thing; it was one of the stipulations she'd put on this evening when they'd planned it long before.

Somehow the detail didn't hold the importance it had before.

"And I'll make sure they're nowhere near us," Mitch continued, "so no reports can make it back to Mommy Dearest."

"Why would you call her that?" Catherine snapped, then shook her head at his amused expression. "No, never mind."

She didn't want to know if he could see the same indifference in her mother's eyes, the way she had.

"So, Catherine," he said as he opened the passenger door for her, "your chariot awaits."

Which was exactly what he'd said to her the night of the Kool-Aid incident.

The day her entire world had begun to change.

"Thank you." She smiled demurely at him, consciously avoiding looking in Bethany and Brody's direction as they stepped outside. She folded into the seat, the same seat where she'd been so uncomfortable the night before, her heart rate picking up pace before Mitch had even walked around to the driver's side.

This was Mitch, though. She'd known him for years. They were the 'It' couple, the two who could do no wrong, the ones whose relationship was envied by all, including those in the Senior class.

There was no reason for her to feel nervous as he slid into the driver's seat and flashed his infamous grin in her direction. "You ready for tonight?"

Catherine painted on her best smile, one even more radiant than the smile she'd shown for the camera mere moments before no matter that it felt forced. "As ready as I'll ever be."

CHAPTER 24

Pet Names

The number of phones out at the dance, each one snapping photo after photo, was incredible. Catherine wondered as she glanced around the room if anyone was bothering to just enjoy themselves rather than trying their best to have photographic evidence that they were. The irony wasn't lost on her as she pulled her own phone out to snap self-portraits with friends and frienemies alike who would idle up to her with their own phones out to do the same.

"Here… Brody, take my phone," Bethany commanded to the boy at her side, who merely chuckled.

"Again?"

"This time, one of all the girls." Bethany was pulling Catherine's hand, who gave a mock-exasperated look in Brody's direction.

"Do you want me to take one on your phone, too?" Brody asked her, but apparently every member of the cheerleading squad had thought he was speaking to them, and several different phones were stuffed in various pockets of his jacket. "Shesh, fine," he said in a teasing tone, then he gestured to all of the girls to gather together in front of one of the many backdrop decorations the committee had in various locations throughout the gym.

Catherine was sandwiched between Bethany and Chelsea, with Taylor and Laura rounding them out until Bethany instructed that Taylor go to the other side, in front of Laura. Catherine didn't comment on how the original arrangement would have had her dead center, instead she merely smiled for picture after picture with them aligned in 'pecking order'.

No matter that, technically, Catherine's popularity outshone Bethany's by a mile.

"You know," Bethany said in between photos, "we were all supposed to have our hair done the same." There was no doubt who she was speaking with.

"This isn't an official cheerleading function," Catherine replied softly, not the least bit miffed that she seemed to be one of the only girls at this dance with their hair down.

"We held a meeting on it."

"Really? When?"

"You were probably busy," Chelsea said from her opposite side. Catherine refrained from a biting remark, and simply smiled.

"You're probably right." That was all she said, refusing to elaborate. "And I certainly didn't get a memo for… this." She gestured slightly with her head before Brody announced it was time for another photo. It wasn't lost on Catherine how some of the other people in their circle had come closer, also taking their phones out for pictures of the group. Such was the way with her crowd, with the girls she was huddled together with for the barrage of pictures taken.

It always seemed as if they were on display.

Perhaps they always were.

The rest of the girls may have been content to stand there and pose, their smiles painted on their faces, but Catherine was definitely through. "Okay, girls… I don't know about you, but I didn't come here to just stand around." With her head held high, she walked towards Brody, her hand outstretched for her phone. She wasn't immune to the whispers, or the incredulous looks the rest of the cheerleaders were shooting her way, but she wasn't going to be sucked into the drama that evening. "Let me guess, daggers aimed right at my back?" she half joked, low enough for only Brody to hear.

"You have no idea," he murmured his reply. She turned her head to him, about to ask exactly what it is that he was privy to, but Mitch was now there by her side, his arm holding her securely to him.

Her questions for Brody would have to wait.

Mitch and Catherine seemed to have all eyes on them wherever they went that evening. On the dance floor, he would crush her body to his during every slow dance. At the refreshment table, he would act as if he was spiking her drink, although he knew if he did, she wouldn't be able to drive her car to her father's condo. When the obligatory pictures of the cheerleaders with their dates were taken, Mitch was the one whispering his dirty thoughts into her ear, making suggestive remarks, placing his hands where he shouldn't.

All of these things should have been bothersome to Catherine. She couldn't even seem bothered when Chelsea would shoot dirty looks in their direction; she'd already accepted that Chelsea was jealous, just as Chelsea needed to accept that Mitch would never exchange the notoriety that their relationship carried.

No, what bothered Catherine that evening was the gentle caresses exchanged between Brody and Bethany, the soft kisses that she'd convinced herself were all for show. Certainly, two people who barely knew one another, or hadn't known one another for long, couldn't possibly be in love.

No… Catherine surmised that it wasn't love. It was infatuation. What she shared with Mitch, that was…

It was…

Well, it was certainly more than any other couple in that entire gymnasium had. And that night, she would live up to their reputation, she would follow through with her promise.

And then, she was bound to feel the normalcy return to her life.

"Oh, no." She rummaged through her small clutch purse, trying to find the keys to her car before she and Mitch left the dance. The plan was simple; he'd drive her back to her car, which she would have the keys ready for, and she would just leave without stepping in to say goodbye to anyone. Trouble was, she didn't have her keys. She couldn't even remember where she'd set her overnight bag, only then realizing she'd never tried to find it before they'd left.

"Ready, babe?"

"Just a minute." She shuffled through her clutch once more, knowing her keys weren't in there. "Hey, give me just a moment. I need to find Brody."

"Why?"

"Because he had my keys."

"Why did he have your keys?"

Catherine sighed. "Because he went to get my shoes, that's why. Have you seen him?"

"He was playing tonsil hockey with Bethany, in all her crowned glory."

Ah, yes. Bethany had won Homecoming Queen, just as predicted. And after her official dance and obligatory basking in the glow, she had attached herself to her date's side. And his front. And his face.

It was enough to make Catherine nauseated.

"Wonderful," she muttered. "Which direction?"

Mitch pointed to the opposite side of the gym, and Catherine began walking, not asking Mitch to follow, and not waiting for him to. She smiled at those saying hello, asked a couple of the upper echelon of the senior class where their Queen and date had gone, and soon found herself in a darkened hallway, with lockers lining both sides.

"Oh, this just has horror movie written all over it." Her voice was low, though, as to not call any undue attention to herself in a part of the school that was strictly forbidden for the evening.

Except, apparently, to the Homecoming Queen, and the person who held her in his arms.

Catherine inhaled sharply before she cleared her throat to let them know she was there. Brody instantly stopped, peering over Bethany's shoulder as she continued kissing his neck. "Hey," he said, not only letting Catherine know he saw her, but letting Bethany know they most definitely had company. Bethany murmured something in Brody's ear as Catherine stepped in closer, making him squirm uncomfortably before he stepped out of her arms. "What's up?"

"I was wondering where you'd put my keys," she said, her eyes taking in his disheveled appearance. Surely they hadn't, not here of all places.

"Oh… shit, they're in my jacket." He began walking towards Catherine as Bethany called out that she was going to fix her hair. "Yeah, okay," he said over his shoulder when she'd asked him to meet her at 'their spot'.

It was enough to make Catherine want to gag.

"Seriously?" she snapped.

"Seriously what?"

Catherine huffed as she followed him back into the overly decorated gym. "Forget it."

Brody shrugged, apparently deciding that 'forgetting it' was the smartest thing he could do at that point. He greeted a few of the school's varsity baseball players near the bleachers, people that Catherine was familiar with but hadn't been aware that Brody was. He picked up one of the discarded tux jackets, fished around in the pockets, then dropped that jacket and reached for another.

"What are you doing?"

"Trying to see which one's… ah, got it." He held the jacket in his hands, his back to her, while Catherine waited impatiently.

"Come on, Brody, I have to,"

"You don't need to go through with this." His back was still turned, his words barely audible above the music.

She stepped in closer and crossed her arms in front of her. "Excuse you?"

Brody turned then, his head still lowered as he looked at the jacket in his arms. "You don't need to go through with this," he repeated.

Her heart beat an unsteady rhythm, one that she chose to ignore as she held out her hand. "Give me my keys."

Slowly, almost reluctantly, Brody pulled the keys out of his pocket, the lights from the dance reflecting off of her key chain. "You just… after last night,"

"You don't know anything about last night."

Brody stepped in closer, his arm brushing up against hers,

sending a current through her body. "Look, you've made no secret about what your plans are. And he certainly hasn't, either."

"At least we're not going to do it at the school," she said through clenched teeth. "Have a bit of class, please."

"Do it?"

He leaned down even closer, so close she could turn her head just so and feel just how soft his lips were…

"It's called sex, Catherine. Are you even ready for this?"

Her eyes widened, and a wave of anger mixed with nausea came over her. "You actually…"

"No! No, we… stop turning this around, okay?"

"So, you didn't?"

His hand touched her—deliberately this time—and her pulse took off at a dizzying pace, the way it should have with Mitch. Brody's eyes skimmed over her face, and for one brief moment she was sure he looked at her lips. Her eyes widened a fraction again as he leaned in even closer. She was so sure this was it, he was going to kiss her…

But she was mistaken.

"Why?" he asked, his fist still clenched around her keys.

"Why what?"

"Why are you so curious about Beth and me?"

"Does she know you call her 'Beth'?" Catherine asked, one eyebrow raised as she did, his close proximity affecting her still. "The last guy who tried that ended up limping. Badly."

With a sigh, he pushed one hand through his hair, causing it to stick up in various places, and Catherine resisted the urge to run her fingers through it, to fix it.

Or mess it up more.

"This isn't about me, Cat. You just shouldn't go."

Her eyes narrowed, her anger evident as she took a step away from him. "Pet names must be your thing," she said, and it was Brody's turn for his eyes to widen. Had he realized his mistake, or been that surprised over her reaction? Neither would matter to Catherine, though, as she roughly grabbed the keys from his hand. "I don't get played, Brody."

"I wish that was the truth."

She shifted her weight slightly as she glared up at him. "What's that supposed to mean?"

"Catherine,"

"No, don't… don't Catherine me, don't… and don't ever call me Cat again, got it?"

He nodded once, his eyes almost sad as he looked at her.

"And… and that look? I'm not the one who needs pity, Brody. That would be you. Does your girlfriend even know what your life is really like?"

Brody glanced around, perhaps seeing if they had an audience—something that Catherine had nearly forgotten about.

Was it the possibility of an audience that had her chest feeling heavy, or that look… that pleading look in Brody's eyes.

Of course he didn't want anyone to know. And Catherine… she shouldn't want them to know, either. Wouldn't that hurt her reputation as well?

Her eyes closed briefly as she realized it wasn't her reputation that mattered… not about this…

And that just wouldn't do.

"I have to go."

"Catherine,"

"I still need to grab my bag," she said as she looked down at the keys in her hand. "And I just… I just need to go. You can enjoy your reprieve from all things me this weekend, I'm sure it will be welcome, and…"

"It's in the trunk."

"Excuse me?"

She stopped her ramble, focusing on Brody again, no matter how uncomfortable it made her feel. "Your bag," he said, and he reached to scratch the back of his neck. He was obviously uncomfortable, too.

That knowledge shouldn't have given her butterflies.

"I put your bag in the trunk for you."

She stood a little taller, refusing to show anything other than the anger she was so desperate to hold onto. She was prepared to tell him to mind his own business, to take care of his own bags, or Brian's bags, whoever that was. Those were Catherine's intentions, pure and simple.

Until someone walked past roughly bumped into her, sending her stumbling forward.

Until Brody caught her, his arms securely around her waist.

Until she felt the hammering of his heart beneath her hands, which had instinctively gone out to break her fall.

She watched the rise and fall of his chest as she slowly backed away, not even acknowledging the apology of the person who'd expected the wrath of Catherine to rain down upon him.

She didn't dare lift her eyes, didn't dare glance up at the face of her rescuer, the face of the person who had been the bane of her existence—who still should be. Instead, she murmured her thanks as she stepped away, her head held high once she'd turned, and she walked towards the exit.

Her footsteps slowed when she realized he hadn't followed her. Catherine didn't know if she was disappointed or relieved, before she decided upon indifferent. Brody wasn't supposed to mean anything to her anyhow; Mitch would be waiting for her, to take her to her car and start their journey.

Their night together.

Brody's haunting words, the words that almost had her doubting, all but disappeared when she rounded the corner of the building towards the parking lot. Standing with Mitch beside his Charger was none other than Chelsea.

This time, Catherine's anger overpowered her nerves, and her footsteps increased in pace and intensity as she neared them. She knew when she'd been spotted; Chelsea's demeanor changed dramatically. If Catherine had expected her to act busted, then perhaps the smirk of satisfaction on her frenemy's face would have come as a surprise.

But Chelsea was too much like Catherine. She'd wanted to get caught, wanted Catherine to be suspicious.

"Gee, Chels," Catherine said with feigned kindness, "thanks for keeping him company. As you can see, I'm here now, and he certainly doesn't need anything you can give him."

"Sure thing." Chelsea drew out the words as she walked past, her hips swaying with every step.

"Aw, there's not going to be a catfight on my behalf, is there?" Mitch's words were murmured in Catherine's ear, and he misinterpreted her shudder for one of pleasure.

But she wasn't going to let it get to her. She was going to carry on with her evening, have Mitch take her to her car, go to her father's condo just as they had planned.

Nothing was going to get to her.

Not Chelsea, not that uneasy feeling, not Brody's words, not the note he'd left in her car.

Don't go.

That was all it had said, and Catherine nearly wadded the piece of paper up and sent it flying into the backseat.

Instead, she brushed it aside—the way she was brushing

everything aside—and drove off into the night, checking her rear-view mirror only once to ensure that Mitch was following her.

Of course he was. She was Catherine Garner, after all. And he worshiped her.

All she had to do now was convince herself that was enough.

CHAPTER 25

Maybe Later

The first rays of morning sun were beginning to peek through the blinds, casting a soft glow on the tan carpeting, making the shadows dance in the corners. In one of those corners, the one furthest from the door, Catherine sat on the ground, her legs drawn up, her arms wrapped around them. Her eyes stared forward, her expression blank. An occasional tremor would pass through her, though not one of cold, as the night's events played out in her mind.

The alcohol, and the abundance of it.

The hard kisses, the ones she'd asked him to please ease up on. He'd merely laughed at her, telling her he'd kissed her the same way the whole time they were together.

Her clothing being discarded, piece by piece—not that there was much to it to begin with. She'd already changed out of her dress and into a tank top and shorts for comfort, those comfort clothes now wadded in a ball.

The blanket spread beneath her, with nothing covering her. He had wanted it that way.

The tearing of the condom packet, echoing through her mind

even though she knew that wasn't possible.

And the pain.

The searing, blinding pain that followed the first push of his hips.

And the second.

And the third.

The grunting and panting in her ear as he finished what she'd started, what she'd put in motion by agreeing to all of this.

And all the while, she remained silent. She said nothing. She didn't ask him to stop, she didn't tell him no, she didn't even cry.

Until he had left.

Left her feeling broken, used, and discarded—but he couldn't have known that, could he? No, because he'd also left her of promises of more of 'this' to come.

And she'd gone straight to the shower, scrubbing underneath the hot water until her skin was as raw as her nerves. She'd thrown the bottles away, thrown the condom wrapper away, thrown away the soiled blanket, with the damning spots of blood.

But she left her clothes there, wadded in a ball... a ball she stared at from her seat on the floor in a corner across the room of this luxurious condo her father called home.

She hadn't checked the time when Mitch had left, she had no idea what time it was now, she wasn't sure how long she'd been sitting there before her phone began to ring from across the room. She jumped at the suddenness of sound filling the space, snapping her out of her daze, and she slowly unfolded herself from her sitting position. Her muscles were stiff and sore, for more reasons than she wanted to admit to herself as she reasoned that maybe, just maybe, if she acted like last night didn't happen, maybe he would, too.

Her hand was shaking as she reached for her phone, that

phone that had since stopped ringing. She hit a few buttons, pulling up the missed call list, and began shaking again as she saw the name.

Bethany rarely phoned at an early hour, especially not the morning after such a significant event. She'd been crowned Homecoming Queen, she'd had her evening with Brody…

And Catherine realized, with a sickening lurch in her stomach, that she'd simply left Brody there, at the dance, reliant on Bethany to get him home on time.

Apparently in lieu of leaving a voicemail, Bethany chose to text Catherine instead, with a simple *Have you heard from Brody?*

"Heard from him?" Catherine squeaked out, her eyes wide with a new kind of fear. She typed back her reply that no, she hadn't heard from Brody since she'd left him at the dance with her. While waiting for Bethany's reply, Catherine began gathering her things together quickly. She stuffed her discarded dress back in her bag with little regard to its condition, dressed enough to make herself presentable without worrying about perfection, and quickly glanced over the condo to ensure everything was in place.

And she froze when she saw her discarded clothing, still wadded in a ball.

The chime from her phone alerted her to another text, and this one had her equal parts angered and panicked.

They'd gone to the party, the one that Mitch's best friend was throwing.

The same party that Mitch had announced he was making an appearance at when he'd left Catherine there, alone.

And Brody had to leave, had to be home before his curfew.

So he had walked.

"Oh no… no… damn it." She didn't think twice about cursing at that moment, not as she grabbed her phone, her keys, her bag and rushed out the door.

It was a forty-minute drive from that condo to her house. It was forty minutes of discomfort, of anxiety, of a different kind of fear. And as thoughts of the previous night, her own personal hell, tried to creep in and take over, Catherine pushed them aside, as far away as she could.

Sunday mornings were always fairly quiet around the house on the hill, so the lack of activity didn't come as a surprise to Catherine. She remained quiet herself as she took her bag up to her room, setting it just inside her unlocked door, which caused her to pause for a moment. Had she left the door unlocked? It was highly likely, considering she hadn't even remembered her keys or to take her bag to her car to begin with. She hadn't noticed any noise coming from the main level of the house, so she assumed that Frank and Theresa were still in the bedroom they shared at the end of the hallway. As quietly as she could, Catherine checked on Tyler and Sam, who were both sleeping soundly, before making her way down both flights of stairs.

Using her phone screen for light, she checked around the basement for any signs of Brody. The bed wasn't pulled out, nor was Brody sleeping on top of the cushions, as she'd inadvertently seen him doing when she'd come down to retrieve some of her possessions. A quick glance around the room confirmed that Brody wasn't down there, causing Catherine's heart rate to spike.

She took the stairs to the main level of the house, searching the living room and the kitchen before her eyes finally caught a glimpse of a tattered baseball cap sitting on the table outside on the deck. As she stepped outside, wrapping her arms around herself in the morning chill, she spotted the lone figure, holding a baseball in one hand and a bat in the other. Catherine had seen him do this before, only he'd been hitting pop fly balls for Tyler to catch.

That morning, he was out there alone.

When he tossed the ball into the air, he swung his bat with so much force it sent the ball flying.

Then he picked up another and did it again.

And again.

Each crack of the bat echoed in the stillness of the morning, the birds scattering away as he hit the next one.

And the next.

He never faltered, never missed, never seemed to put enough strength into each swing, and each crack, each snap, each thud of the ball only caused the tension to grow.

And when he'd run out of baseballs, he stood there, breathing so heavily she could see his shoulders move. Just as Catherine was about to call out to him, she watched as he swung the bat up above his head and slam it to the ground over and over, each thud causing her to jerk, until the stinging behind her eyes became unbearable.

"Brody?"

He didn't seem to even hear her as he continued over and over, and when it seemed too much—or not enough—he threw the bat as hard as he could, away from the house, away from the gym, and he dropped to his knees, his hands fisted in his hair.

He was still there, rocking back and forth, pulling at his hair when Catherine finally reached him. She was a bit winded from her quick sprint, but she ignored her discomfort as she dropped to the ground beside him. She didn't speak, unable to even ask what had happened as she knelt beside him. The tenseness in his body, the strangled sounds he was making made it seem as if he was trying to keep from screaming. She still couldn't tell if he knew she was even there, and as much as it frightened her, she still reached over to him, and gently placed her hand on his arm.

And he stilled.

Slowly, his hands relaxed, letting go of his hair, but the rest of his body remained just as tense, though no longer moving.

Catherine took in a shaky breath and caressed his arm with her thumb. "It's me."

"I know."

His words were barely above a whisper, his hand unsteady as he placed it over hers.

Her eyes dropped to their hands—hers on his arm, his covering hers, and she watched as his fingers curled around, fitting between hers, as if he was holding her there.

As if he were craving just a little bit of kindness, of gentleness, that he'd long been denied.

Neither one of them knew how much time passed as they knelt there silently together, each one seeming to draw strength from the other. They didn't speak of their night, or what had led them both here in such a fragile state of mind.

But they didn't need to.

When they were finally interrupted by two rambunctious, ravenously hungry children, Catherine chanced her first glance into Brody's eyes, the haunting pain there nearly taking her breath away. She watched his own eyes widen ever so slightly, and felt his fingers curl a little tighter and give a light squeeze.

He must have known her night had been hell, too.

Almost reluctantly he stood, then gave her hand a gentle tug to help her to her feet as well. Even with Sam dancing around them asking for cereal, and Tyler running to retrieve the bat and baseballs, it was almost as if they were the only two people around.

Just almost.

Catherine licked her lips, not missing how it drew Brody's gaze to her mouth. "Are you all right?"

"Are you?"

She felt his thumb caress the back of her hand, the gentleness squeezing her already bruised heart all the more. "You're deflecting, Brody," she said in lieu of answering.

His eyes lowered, his dark lashes fanning across his cheeks before he raised his gaze to her once more. "I'll live. You?"

One corner of her mouth lifted in a sad smile, but she didn't answer.

She couldn't answer.

She hadn't yet wrapped her head around what had transpired any more than she could possibly fathom what the big deal was, and why everyone she knew was in such a hurry to 'do it', or to continue to.

Brody's gaze darkened, his grip on her hand tightening. "Catherine,"

"I'm… fine," she lied.

She was an expert at lying; no one could lie better than she could.

So she kept telling herself.

But Brody—he wasn't fine, and he couldn't lie to her about it. And for reasons that eluded her, she wanted to fix it, make it better. "Maybe… maybe we could go up to the batting cages later, and…" She paused when he shook his head, his eyes looking down at the ground. "Oh, um… well, the gym. My gym." She squeezed his hand, which she was still holding. "All of us could just… hide out there, or something." She said it with a soft laugh, one that she hoped didn't sound as forced as it felt. "We could just pull out the rackets, hit tennis balls off the wall."

"And break another window." One corner of his mouth was lifted in a grin, though, and she took it as a good sign.

"Nah, they're too high up. Unless you really suck at it, or if they do. Or, hey… we could all do gymnastics."

"No." This time he was genuinely chuckling. "No, that… would be disastrous at best."

"But fun to watch."

Their smiles were small, tentative.

Healing.

"We could get pizza, too," she added.

"Oh, pizza… now you're talking."

They were still holding hands as they began their walk towards the house, Sam chattering excitedly about her cereal, about the pizza they would have later, about how Tyler could hit tennis balls with Brody while Catherine taught her how to tumble.

"Oh…" Catherine paused as she felt her phone vibrate in her pocket. "Bethany, she wants you to call her."

Catherine watched as a muscle twitched in Brody's jaw, and he shook his head slightly. "Maybe later." He glanced over briefly before looking forward. "What about you?"

"Hmm? Oh, I don't need to talk to her. Oh!" She faltered a bit as she realized Brody had actually been referring to Mitch.

Mitch, who was the last person she wanted to speak to at that moment.

"Maybe later," she said, using Brody's own words.

Maybe later she could talk to Mitch, maybe later she could explain to him that she just didn't want to do *that* again any time soon.

And maybe he would agree, maybe he wouldn't humiliate her the way his own brother had done with Bethany.

And maybe... just maybe it would matter to her again.
But that Sunday morning, all that mattered was forgetting.
Even if it was only for a little while.

CHAPTER 26

It Shouldn't Be

The small private gym was bustling with more activity than it had seen in years. Even back when Catherine was telling everyone she could that she was going to be on the Olympic team, she rarely had others join her. It was normally her, her coach of the moment, and occasionally an assistant. That Sunday, though, the echo of a tennis ball being hit off the wall was almost as loud as the chatter, the excited squeals from young children, the occasional bursts of laughter.

And yet all the noise would fade away when Catherine's eyes would find Brody's, when their smiles would be soft, bordering on shy.

"Did I do that right?" Sam asked excitedly, capturing Catherine's attention.

"Hmm? Oh… yeah, yeah, not bad." The words didn't taste bitter at all as she watched the young girl take to gymnastics as if it were second nature to her, the same way Catherine had as a child. "Be careful when you do your cartwheel, though. Don't bend your arms, keep them perfectly straight. Like… this." She exerted little effort showing Sam the proper form, and somehow the young girl's smile and enthusiasm topped every award she'd been given.

"Like this?" Sam mimicked Catherine's moves perfectly, and Catherine's smile broadened.

"Exactly! Exactly like that. You're really getting the hang of this. Would you like…" She screeched and ducked as a tennis ball flew past her head, which had Sam giggling. Catherine was also smiling and shaking her head as Tyler jogged past.

"Oops."

"Oops?" Catherine mimicked, but there was no biting sarcasm in her tone. Tyler's reciprocating grin only lightened her heart more.

"When are we ordering pizza?" Sam had executed another couple of cartwheels and was once again asking for food. Catherine shook her head at the young girl's never-ending appetite, not that her size was any indication.

"Soon." She sat down on the mat, quietly observing Sam practice the few things that she'd taught her, her fingers absentmindedly twisting a piece of her hair that had fallen free from her ponytail as she did. So many things were still weighing on her mind—what would happen when she finally answered her phone, when she went to school and faced everyone the next day?

And did it even matter?

She shook her head at that. Yes, it mattered; her entire universe was centered around her social status, around what others thought of her more than what she thought of herself.

One glance over her shoulder, at the boy she'd once thought of as so plain, sent her thoughts in a tailspin again.

"Whatcha doing?" Sam had sat on the mat beside her, her head tilted to the side as she studied Catherine's face.

One corner of Catherine's mouth lifted in a half-grin and her hand dropped from her hair. "I'm resting. I don't have your kind of energy today."

"My mommy rested a lot, too. In her bed, though. We didn't have a gym."

"But you had a nice house." Catherine made the statement lightly, her curiosity piqued. She watched as Sam contemplated her question, her small mouth twisted ever so slightly.

"I liked it." Sam nodded once, as if confirming to herself she was telling the truth. "It wasn't this big, though. That's good, 'cause Brody couldn't have kept it clean. We didn't have a Greta."

Catherine didn't bother to correct her, to tell her the proper term for Greta was a housekeeper, not only because Greta was proving to be so much more. Still, Sam's reply bothered her. "Brody cleaned?" Catherine was picking at a string on the hem of her shirt, trying to casually ease information from the young child, ignoring the side of her that said she should ask Brody instead.

"Mommy was too tired."

It made sense that she'd been tired, especially if she was so sick that she'd been hospitalized. "So, she's been sick a long time, then." Again, it was more of a statement, and Catherine pushed the guilt down deeper, still driven to get as many answers as she could.

Sam was silent for a moment, and Catherine watched as a frown settled over the young girl's features. "Just since Brian went to heaven."

Catherine licked her suddenly dry lips and her heart was pounding uncomfortably in her chest. *Brian*. The Brian, the one whose name she'd seen on boxes, the one whose name had slipped from Frank's lips when he was speaking to Brody. She was certain knew the answer to the question before she asked, "Who's Brian?"

"Our other Brody."

Catherine's eyes narrowed for a moment in confusion, and when she finally understood what Sam was saying they stung uncomfortably. Their other Brody. Her older brother. "His twin."

Sam's nod confirmed her suspicions. "Uh huh. Catherine, my mommy tells me not to pull on strings on my clothes. She says I can put holes in them. Didn't your mommy tell you that?"

The abrupt change of subject made Catherine blink a couple of times before Sam's question truly registered in her brain. She smiled sadly as she looked down at her hand, where she was still pulling at that string making it longer and longer. No, her mother hadn't bothered telling her that. She'd simply told her to stop fidgeting, it made her look nervous. True winners were never nervous, she'd said, and Catherine had never once thought to disagree with her.

"Brody pulls on his strings, too." Sam's quiet statement caused Catherine's chest to ache even more. Of course he would have nervous habits. He'd lost his other half, his mother was sick, the children had been left to him to care for when their father...

Well, Frank was simply someone Catherine added to the list of people she didn't want to think about at the moment.

"What..." Catherine cleared her throat, which felt constricted to her. "Why did Brian go to heaven?" She didn't want to bluntly ask how he'd died, partially from fear of who or what had caused it.

But she wasn't prepared when Sam simply stated, "Because he wanted to."

Catherine inhaled sharply as she closed her eyes, knowing that if she didn't, she would have been looking over her shoulder again, over at the boy who was taking over her thoughts, making her feel things foreign to her. She was powerless to stop the one tear that escaped, but quickly brushed it aside. She didn't want to ask why, didn't want to pry any further, but Sam wasn't quite finished with her story.

"Daddy wasn't mean to Brian like he is to Brody."

'Like he is to all of you,' Catherine thought, but she remained silent.

"Daddy just wanted Brody to be like him, that's what he said."

Frank had played one twin off the other. Somehow this didn't surprise Catherine, although the outcome must not have been near what Frank had anticipated. What was it that Frank had said to Brody? Something about disappointment?

"And my mommy, she would tell Brian it wasn't his fault."

Even as Sam sat now silent, watching her brothers play, Catherine could tell she'd already told why Brian had taken his own life. He'd felt responsible, he'd felt the guilt of what his other half had to endure.

"How long ago was that?" Catherine asked, and she watched Sam shrug slightly.

"Dunno. But my mommy wanted to go see him."

Catherine couldn't suppress the gasp that left her, instinctively—where had the instinct come from?—reaching out to hold the little girl's hand. She squeezed it, albeit gently, as she tried to send a little comfort.

Perhaps their mother wasn't ill, not in the traditional sense.

It seemed, through the words of a small child, their mother had been heartbroken, and like the son she'd lost she'd been unable to cope.

"But Brody takes care of us."

'But it shouldn't be Brody,' Catherine wanted to say.

It shouldn't be a young boy taking care of them. It should be their father, the same poor excuse of a man who used that young boy as his own personal punching bag. That boy… he should be free to live, free to have friends, free to cut up at parties, free of the responsibility of raising, of protecting two young children from the one man who should love them all the most.

"Brody says when Mommy's well again, we'll go be with her."

There was so much trust, so much conviction in those words. What else did the children have to look forward to? Besides, hadn't her own mother promised her this was only temporary?

"Can we have pizza now?"

"Hmm? Oh… yeah, yeah. I'll order it." Catherine patted the young girl's hand before she stood to get her phone. Her eyes drifted to Brody, to the easy smile on his face as he played with his brother, and paused for one brief moment. She didn't turn when his eyes found hers, when his smile fell as he looked at her unguarded expression.

As if he knew his secrets were no longer buried.

She could have asked him a million questions, but the only words that left her were, "What do you want on your pizza?"

The rapid-fire answers from Tyler and Sam had her smiling, even if it didn't quite dispel the sadness in her eyes. With her attention diverted, she was only mildly aware of Brody stepping closer and closer, until he was there beside her, close enough for her to feel his shallow breaths on her neck as he leaned in.

"Are you all right?"

Chills spread across her skin at his words, and she took a step away from him, alarmed. "I'm fine," she said, without adding she knew that he wasn't… and she truly understood how far from fine he was. Before he could reply, her phone began to ring, with Bethany's name and face showing on the display. Catherine held the phone out to Brody. "I'm supposing this is for you."

He looked down at the phone in her hand, a troubled scowl on his face. "Not necessarily."

"Did you have an argument?" The question was innocent enough, though his eyes showed his suspicion for one brief moment before he shook his head. By then, the phone had stopped ringing, sending the caller to voicemail. Brody turned to walk away, only stopping when Catherine put her hand on his arm. "I'm sorry I didn't bring you back with me."

He lifted one shoulder briefly. "I didn't ask you to." Which was true, but didn't assuage her feelings of guilt.

"But the lake party,"

"Please don't."

She couldn't tell from his expression which was more important—her not knowing what had happened, or her not discussing it in front of Tyler and Sam. She merely nodded her agreement, slowly withdrawing her hand from his arm. "Another text," she said softly, "asking to have you call."

Catherine barely heard his murmur that he'd see Bethany tomorrow as she scrolled up through her unread texts. There were several mentions of her on social media sites, inquiring about her absence from the party the night before. Mitch had sent her one brief message, letting her know he was busy, not that she would have wanted to contact him that day anyhow. Nothing from Chelsea, aside from mentions of her being at the party as well. Each piece, each name drop, each snippet of information floating to her seemed disconnected, unimportant. Even the group text reminding her and the rest of the squad of the following week's practice schedule, the last for the season, seemed meant for someone else.

"When is... when is it going to get here?" Sam asked breathlessly as she bounded up to Catherine, who only then remembered she hadn't ordered the pizza yet.

"Give me just a moment," she said softly as she clicked on a link someone had sent her, a link to a picture on Facebook at that party.

Of Mitch.

With Chelsea.

Just 24 hours before, she would have been screaming, livid, even though it was nothing more than a photograph of two people laughing, either at something they shared or a story someone else had told. But in that moment, in that room, even with the dull ache in her chest that matched the ache in muscles and places on her body, it was merely another picture for her to look at.

Nothing more.

"He just left you."

She didn't jump at the sound of Brody's voice, nor ask for clarification of what he'd meant by his question. She only nodded as she closed the browser, the picture still engrained in her mind.

"He shouldn't have."

"Please don't." She repeated his own words, not wanting to discuss this further, whether Tyler and Sam were there or not.

This time when her phone rang, it was Mitch's name and picture on the display. Without hesitation, she hit the ignore button, sending his call to voicemail as well.

That action alone stunned her, and she stared at her phone as she tried to contemplate why… why would she do such a thing?

Her fingers tingled as Brody took the phone from her. "I can call for the pizza, if you'd like."

She only nodded, not trusting her own voice, her own mind, her own words to not betray her. As she watched him turn, smiling at his little brother while he began to dial the number to the local pizza place, she knew there were things out there far more important than her own current drama. He winced slightly as he moved, showing the soreness from whatever had transpired the night before, and if her mind hadn't already been made up it would have been then.

She'd sworn to Chelsea this boy wouldn't be her project, and he wasn't... he really wasn't. She wasn't going to go out of her way to change his image, she certainly hadn't gone to any lengths to bring him into her circle of friends.

No, he needed more than that.

He needed his freedom, the freedom that could only come if he wasn't forced to live here, in this house on the hill.

She wasn't sure how, or when... all she knew was she would do whatever it took to help him.

And for once, the reasons had nothing to do with her.

CHAPTER 27

From the Inside Out

When the pizza arrived, they all gathered just off of the mats, each one of them still smiling. Paper plates and napkins were passed around the small circle, and when the stack reached Catherine, she looked at it curiously. "We have these?"

Brody grinned, just slightly where his dimple wasn't quite showing. "Napkins? Pretty sure we have them at every meal there, Lady Catherine."

Catherine's eyebrow was raised, even though she felt a grin coming on as well. "Ha. Ha."

As Brody opened up the pizza box, he stole a glance over at her. "Greta picked them up."

Catherine nodded, understanding immediately. "For when you have to hide food?" Her question was asked softly, so the younger children wouldn't hear her over their own conversation.

She watched as Brody's eyes were drawn to her lips, but he averted them quickly. "Um ... yeah. Yeah, it's... they can just be thrown away, you know? Don't have to get them washed and put away." He was grinning once more, as if he was wanting to dispel the tension. "Unless of course you really want to."

This time, Catherine couldn't stop her grin from forming, and it only faltered when she reached for a slice of pizza and her fingers accidentally brushed against his. "Sorry," she murmured as she pulled back, the same time he did.

Brody gestured towards the box with his head, his dark hair falling into his eyes as he did so. "Go ahead."

"Thank you."

She was fairly certain the expression on his face was one of surprise. It made sense; just a few short weeks ago, Catherine wouldn't have muttered a single apology to anyone. No, a few short weeks ago, Catherine would have insisted everyone wait for her, wait on her. She'd been convinced these were things she was entitled to.

That day, though, her eyes wandered over to Tyler and Sam who sat smiling, waiting patiently.

And she smiled in return.

"You two go first," she said, and she sat back as they happily took their pizza, their excited chatter again filling the gym. When she glanced back at Brody, his smile was gone, his expression contemplative. It caused her own smile to fall, and she silently took her slice of pizza before she sat back to give him room.

Catherine kept her eyes on her own food, carefully picking the mushrooms off and setting them to the side. Once she was sure she'd removed them all, she took her first bite, savoring the food considered so unhealthy for her. A soft satisfied sigh left her, and she heard Brody chuckle. Her cheeks heated slightly as she asked, "What?"

He held his hands up in defense. "Nothing, nothing at all." His eyes dropped to her plate, then locked with hers. "Don't like mushrooms?"

She wrinkled her nose. "Ugh, no. They're gross."

"But you didn't say anything."

It sounded more like a statement, but because she'd taken another bite, she could only shake her head in response. Once she swallowed, she said, "Everyone else wanted them. I can pick them off. See?" She held up her plate for his inspection, but his eyes never left hers. He stared at her with the same contemplative expression, the one that had unnerved her earlier.

Now it warmed her from the inside out.

"Would you like them?" she asked, still holding her plate up.

One corner of Brody's mouth lifted in a half-grin, this one showing the dimple that she'd noticed, the dimple that she could now admit was kind of… adorable? No, it wasn't adorable, she argued with herself. It simply wasn't… ordinary. "Sure," was all he said, and he carefully moved the mushrooms from her plate to his.

They were silent as they ate and passed around the bottle of soda—something Catherine would have scoffed at not so long ago, but since they'd forgotten cups it seemed the best short-term solution. In between bites, she watched Brody's eyes as he took in everything around him, from the repaired mirror to his brother and sister, who seemed more carefree than Catherine could ever remember them being. In spite of Brody's smile, his eyes reflected a sadness that Catherine had only begun to understand.

"Do you miss him?" she asked as she picked up another slice of pizza, promising herself she'd work out twice as hard tomorrow.

Brody's eyebrows drew together slightly. "Miss who?"

"Brian."

If she hadn't been watching for his reaction, perhaps she would have missed the subtle change in his expression, or the way his hand faltered for a fraction of a second before he set his slice of pizza down. One shoulder lifted slightly, and he kept his eyes on his plate. "I guess."

She felt a bit relieved that he hadn't played the denial game and continued on her in quest. "You… guess?" She tilted her head to the side and watched him as he scooted a little closer, this time turned directly towards her.

"I really don't think this is the right audience for this conversation." She'd seen this look in his eyes before—the hardened, shut down, off-limits look. It was the same look that had convinced her he was bad news, perhaps with a serial killer streak to him.

"Sam didn't mind,"

"And don't… don't bring them into this, okay? If you want to interrogate someone, then it needs to be me."

She leaned forward, her own tenacity showing through. "Then you need to start talking."

He shook his head slightly and returned to his pizza, taking another bite of it. He didn't move away from her, and his close proximity had her heart beating wildly in her chest.

"Is this why you did this today?" he finally asked, and her eyes grew wide.

"No! No, I just… I thought that… well, I thought it might do some good."

"It won't, you know. It's not going to change anything. Frank's still going to be an asshole, they're still going to be minus both parents, and I'm still…" He shrugged again, as if he didn't want to put it into words.

Catherine sat up a little straighter as she wiped her hands on her napkin, contemplating her next question carefully. "Does Bethany know?"

"No." The word was quick and forceful, letting her know he

had no intentions of Bethany ever finding out.

"Do you talk to anyone?"

"I'm talking to you, aren't I?" Again, one corner of his mouth was lifted in a half-grin, but this time she wouldn't let it slide.

"Yes, and no." She watched his eyes dart over in her direction before they returned to his plate, where he busied himself pulling his piece of pizza apart in tiny pieces. "Do you miss him?" she asked again.

This time his lower lip trembled.

He quickly recovered, and with a sniffle that perhaps he thought she missed he said, "Yeah. I'd be an asshole if I said I didn't."

"Like your dad."

"He's not my dad."

Catherine blinked several times as the shock and surprise washed over her. "But… but you're…"

"My dad's… well, he's just gone. Mom married Frank when I was her age," he said as he gestured towards Sam. "Yep, I was six. Well, we were… Brian and me. And because things have to be just so, he made sure we had his last name."

"So, there's a few years between Sam and Tyler then."

Brody shook his head. "Not really. She's almost seven; he's eight."

Catherine blinked a couple of times. "He's… tall."

She refrained from adding 'like Frank.'

Frank, whose height only added to the intimidation.

Brody merely nodded, remaining silent.

Catherine leaned in a little closer, her voice extra soft as she said, "Sam told me a lot today."

"I kind of figured that out, Cat. Sorry… Catherine."

"Brody, I…"

"He picked his favorite, you know… out of me and Brian." Brody continued picking at the crust of his pizza, the pieces getting smaller and smaller. "It was an easy choice." He inhaled sharply as Catherine placed her hand on his arm, but he didn't shrug away. "And you know he's dead, and I'm guessing you figured out how he died."

"Not the details, no."

"Well, you don't need them." He shook his head, his eyes shut, his expression pained. "And you know why we're here and not with Mom."

"But when she gets out?"

He glanced over at her then, his eyes shining. "Don't lose any sleep, Catherine. I already told you, as soon as we can, we're gone."

She did her best to hide the hurt his words had caused, just as she questioned her own sanity over them. "That's… well, I'm still going to say that's good, just not for the reasons you think I am." She looked down at her own plate, unsure if she had an appetite left or not. "It is good… right?"

She heard his sigh and glanced over as he shoved one hand through his hair. His blue eyes conveyed the depth of his pain—the one no physical scar would ever show. "It has to be."

Without realizing what she was doing, Catherine reached out and took his hand in hers, their fingers interlacing perfectly. Only when he gave her hand a small squeeze, one that sent a shock straight through her system, did she acknowledge, at least in her own mind, the depth of what she felt for this boy. So many new, conflicting, confusing emotions were fighting for control in her mind… caring, compassion, awareness… infatuation?

As he looked down at their joined hands, she found her voice again. "You can talk to me, you know. Any time you need to."

His thumb slowly moved back and forth, tracing a small pattern on the back of her hand, branding her with his touch, sending chills spreading across her skin. His eyes followed the chills up her arm, to where they disappeared beneath her shirt, up the curve of her neck, and finally to her face. She felt her cheeks warm under his close inspection, especially when his eyes focused on her lips, the same time she watched him swallow slowly.

And she knew she wanted to kiss him.

That realization alone caused her pulse to take off again, the rush similar to the adrenaline kick she would get when she would get ready to perform. It was unfamiliar, and she tried to argue with herself that it was unwelcome. This was Brody, a plain, ordinary boy who had invaded her home, invaded her life. He was rude, manipulative, he'd blackmailed her, taunted her, forced her outside of the bubble where she was the center of the universe. She should hate this boy, with every fiber of her being.

Instead, she felt drawn to him, consequences be damned.

The buzzing of her phone between them interrupted her thoughts, and she quickly dropped Brody's hand to see who was texting her. Seeing Bethany's name brought another sliver of reality back to the day. Catherine read the message, a blaring reminder that Brody wasn't hers to kiss, or to have any of these feelings for.

Just as she wasn't his.

"Bethany will be here at the normal time to pick you up," she said softly. "I suppose you're going to be riding with her."

He shrugged nonchalantly. "Well, you know... her car's not pink. Hey!" He dodged a mushroom that Catherine threw at him. "I'm not cleaning that up, you know."

Those words, which would have angered her before, only made her let out a short laugh, one that had Brody's face lighting up with a smile. "Oh," she said as she inhaled sharply, without realizing she'd done so.

"What?"

She was blushing under his scrutiny, but never one to back away, she answered him with absolute honesty. "You should smile more often."

If she wasn't mistaken, he was the one blushing now. He was looking down at his plate, picking at his pizza crust again, his words so soft she nearly missed them.

"So should you."

Unsure of what to say, she shyly looked down at her hands, where her phone vibrated once more. This name took the smile from her face, let the outside world creep back in.

Mitch.

He was telling her that he'd meet her in the parking lot the following morning, just like they always did, as if nothing had changed.

"Hey… hey Brody, watch this!" Sam was standing on the mats, grinning at her big brother before she showed him the perfect cartwheel. Even as Brody cheered, Catherine called out to her, letting her know she would want to wait for her food to settle. Sam and Tyler were already back at play, though, leaving Brody and Catherine sitting with their unfinished plates of food.

"You on the team?" Brody asked, gesturing out to the vast amounts of equipment in the room, and Catherine shook her head. "Why not?"

"I decided to stick with cheerleading. Less time consuming, more… you know."

"Social status crap," Brody finished for her, his grin showing he was still trying to be lighthearted. Catherine felt anything but, though.

"Pretty much," she admitted. "I wanted it all. I wanted to be the best, to be on top, to have everyone's attention, to be adored."

"Did you get it?"

She was quiet for a moment as she watched Sam go over a few of the moves she'd shown her earlier. "What do you think?"

"Was it worth it?"

It wasn't lost on Catherine how he honestly hadn't answered her. She knew his opinion where her friends were concerned, and on days like today—when she was contemplative and being honest with herself—she could almost see where he was coming from. But was it worth it? She would have said yes not so long ago. She would have berated him for having the nerve to ask such a question. But in that moment, with everything she'd given up, with everything she'd endured, with being unable to know who in her life she could trust, she couldn't.

"I don't know," was all she said in return.

And long after their day had ended, when she laid in bed staring at the ceiling, her mind continued to taunt her. She had it all: the social status, the boyfriend that many envied her for, the legions of friends who followed and worshiped her every move…

The ordinary boy just two floors below, who had proved himself to be anything but.

But he wasn't hers, nor was she his.

Instead, in a few short hours his girlfriend would be picking him up, driving him to school. And Catherine's boyfriend, the one so unconcerned with how the night before had affected her, would be waiting for her, expecting his perfect girlfriend with her perfect smile and her perfect life.

Again.

As if nothing had changed.

But Catherine knew, deep within, that everything had.

CHAPTER 28

The 'It'

That Monday morning was buzzing with a different kind of energy, one that Catherine wished she couldn't comprehend. The day before had seemed like such a good idea, and in many ways it had been. But in the morning light that followed, she couldn't decide if it had been wise or not.

Brody's smile had been heartwarming, genuine. The way he'd interacted not only with Tyler and Sam, but with her as well, showed his razor-sharp sense of humor, a caring disposition, wit beyond any of Catherine's peers, and an intellect that was mirrored only by a few select students at Davis High—Catherine included in that small circle. She'd walked away with a greater appreciation for his likes and dislikes, and was under the impression that he felt the same.

The biggest problem, for her, was now she could see 'it'… the 'it' that Bethany saw, the 'it' that the other girls would sigh over.

The 'it' that had Catherine checking her appearance a million times over in anticipation of his reaction.

She, of course, knew it was wrong, and kept trying to convince herself that it simply wasn't true, wasn't the case. No one boy was worth turning her entire world upside down over. But then… wasn't her life already upside down?

As Catherine continued getting ready for school, making sure her hair, makeup, and clothes were just so, she wondered what the day would bring for her own social status. It certainly hadn't concerned her the day before, when she'd ignored Mitch the same way that Brody had ignored Bethany. In the Monday morning light, though, with the bustling of activity throughout the house, she was second guessing herself.

And second guessing herself was not something that came naturally.

"This… this is all wrong," she muttered as she looked in the mirror, disgusted with herself. These were the clothes of someone trying too hard to impress. With very little time to spare, she changed into something more comfortable, something that didn't scream 'look at me' when she wasn't quite sure who, if anyone, she would want to… or should want to.

Some things about that morning remained unchanged. Frank and Theresa were absent, Frank having left for work for the day already and Theresa returning to the sanctuary of her room rather than listen to the children chatter as they got ready for school. Greta was tidying the house after Brody had declined her help making breakfast for Tyler and Sam, as he did any morning he wasn't running behind. It seemed like nothing had changed from last Friday morning, even though nothing could be further from the truth.

"Juice and fruit?" Sam asked Catherine as she entered the kitchen, and Catherine could only nod. She didn't trust her voice that morning, nor did she truly trust putting anything in her stomach. She couldn't even glance at Brody, who seemed far more content and happier with the morning than she did.

"You all right?" His repeated question, the one she'd asked him several times as well, resonated deep within her.

But it was easy for her to lie to him, her eyes averted as she told him she was fine. She'd been so sure of her plan to help him, to help them, but as she stared at her orange juice, her stomach churning, she didn't have any idea how she possibly could. What good would it do to hide them away when Frank would be waiting for them eventually? And what if their mother returned… would Frank allow the children to go? Theresa had been adamant that the situation was only temporary, and in some ways, it was comforting. But what if it was no better than the way they were living now? At least here, in this home, she could help them, try to buffer for them, try to…

Catherine jumped as she was nudged slightly, causing a tiny bit of juice to slop out of the cup and onto her shirt. As Brody apologized, perhaps a bit too forcefully, she cut him off with a shake of her head. "I'll just go change," she said, her voice soft. She placed her juice and banana on the counter and left the room as quietly as she'd entered.

The text waiting on her phone from Mitch filled her with even more dread. His simple *Meet me in the parking lot, usual spot* lacked the exhaulation that she'd grown accustomed to. Instead, it seemed like an order, one that he obviously expected her to obey.

What other choice did she have?

It wasn't really any different from the text he'd sent the day before, but somehow it seemed to be. Perhaps it was her overactive imagination, or her lack of sleep.

Or her memories of that Saturday night, the ones that made her anxious, sick to her stomach.

She waited in her room as long as she could before grabbing her bag and throwing it over her shoulder. Her keys jingled slightly as she made her way down the stairs, coming to a halt at a familiar, yet unexpected, visitor in the entryway.

"Hello, Catherine," was Bethany's greeting, one that seemed sincere enough and yet Catherine's instincts were screaming at her that it was anything but. "Is it okay to have practice here this afternoon?"

Catherine scowled slightly before she remembered. "Yeah, sure."

"I'm giving Brody a ride," Bethany added, "just in case you were waiting on him."

There seemed little reason for her to remind Bethany that she'd sent a text to her phone the day before telling her that she would be there. "I wasn't," was all Catherine said. She didn't take time to contemplate Bethany's words before she stepped around her and out into the crisp morning air. The sun's rays bounced off her pearl white convertible, and she once again was reminded how Brody had claimed it was pink. With a shake of her head, which let loose a few strands of her hair, she climbed into her car and drove away without so much as a backward glance.

As she always did, Catherine checked her appearance before stepping out into the parking lot at school. To the outside world, she was certain she looked the same. To herself, the one person she seemed unable to lie to anymore, she was anything but. She held her head high, though, as she walked towards where Mitch stood, propped up against his Dodge Charger, the same car Catherine used to love seeing. Now she was filled with trepidation as she walked towards it, towards the boy she'd thought she knew, who seemed so focused on himself he had little to no regard for others.

That had been his appeal though, hadn't it? He'd been so similar to her in that way, except for the fact that he'd at one time worshiped her the same way the rest of the student population did.

She wasn't certain what kind of greeting she would receive from him that morning, but she steeled herself for the fight, the accusations he was sure to throw her way. Instead, she was stunned as he took a handful of her jacket and pulled her close, nearly smothering her with his familiar kiss. His grip was firm as he held her against him, causing her heart to beat an unsteady, unwelcome, uncomfortable rhythm against her ribcage. In her mind she felt the fear, the pain, the shame, all of it washing over her in waves, causing her to put her hands against his chest and push, a bit more forcefully than she thought she could. His smirk when he observed her taking panting breaths, saw the small sheen of sweat across her forehead, seemed out of place to her, until he spoke.

"Ah, you did miss me."

Again, some things that Monday morning hadn't changed at all. Mitch was as clueless as ever, so self-absorbed he misinterpreted her response. Catherine, however, wasn't as self-absorbed, nor as unobservant as her boyfriend. Once she'd regained control of her breathing, her eyes focused on a small purplish mark on his neck.

"What's that?" she asked, gesturing with her hand, and his smirk widened.

"How quickly you forget," he said as he threw his arm around her shoulders and steered them towards the high school. Other students moved out of their way, the same as they always had, but always extending a greeting as they passed by.

"What are you talking about?" Catherine asked, stiffening

under his touch.

"Just one of the marks you left on me," he replied, not bothering to lower his voice. She felt the heat invade her cheeks as she tried in vain to recall doing anything that would have left any kind of mark on him. "And you blush over that." His fingertips on her cheek, not nearly as gentle as she felt they should be, snapped her back to the present.

Before she could say another word, ask him what had actually happened, he had backed her into her locker and kissed her hard, possessively. "Last game this Friday."

"Aside from playoffs," she added, his close proximity unnerving her and making her hands shake.

"We're going to your dad's condo after," he said, ignoring her comment, and his smirk again appeared. "And we're going to continue what we did on Saturday." Without waiting for her to protest, he pushed himself off the locker and walked down the hall, a strut in his step that at one time had appealed to her.

"Looks like you two had one heck of a weekend."

Catherine cringed inwardly when Laura stopped beside her locker. Unwilling to harm her reputation, she merely replied with, "Of course."

"Did you hear about the big blowout?" she asked. "Oh, of course you did. You live with Brody, after all."

Catherine looked down at the small girl, knowing she was fishing for information. She could play into it, of course, to see what she could learn, but had long since learned the way to play the game. "It seems everyone is forgetting that Brody and I rarely fraternize."

After the previous day, though, that was hardly true.

"Oh of course, of course." Those words seemed to be Laura's favorite that morning, and Catherine hardly had the patience for the young upstart, in spite of the fact that once her time came, she'd be destined to be the Queen at this school.

"Is there something you needed?" Catherine retrieved her books for the morning and was annoyed to see Laura still standing there when she shut her locker door. Laura wasn't paying attention to her, however; her eyes were fixated a little further down the hall, where Brody now stood with Bethany at his side. Instead of staying to watch whatever spectacle there would or wouldn't be, Catherine made her way towards her class, ignoring the lump in her throat that surfaced when she watched Bethany kiss him, when she saw his soft response.

When, for the first time, she could admit that maybe… just maybe… she wished that it was her.

"We have the routine down pat. Why are we even here?" Chelsea stood with her hands on her hips, sweat dampening the ends of her hair. The girls were in Catherine's sprawling back yard, the same back yard that Brody had beaten with his bat just the day before.

"This is it, the last regular game of the season," Bethany replied.

"Oh, bull, that's not why we're here and you know it." Chelsea stood a little taller, eyeing her cheer captain with the same death glare that she'd been reserving for Catherine since their most recent argument. "You set up this entire week after lover boy in he broke up with you at the party."

"He did not break up with me, obviously."

"Could we not do this? Please?" Catherine's words were much nicer than her tone, in spite of her curiosity piquing over Chelsea's statement. She'd already had a long enough day as it was and was eager to retreat to the privacy of her room, without being under watchful and scrutinizing eyes.

"Well, obviously you had broken up, just as obviously as he and Mitch got into it over our girl Catherine, here." Chelsea's smile was about as far from friendly as it could get as she turned in Catherine's direction, daring her to say something in her defense.

"What are you talking about?" Catherine's hands were now on her hips as well.

"Oh, is this something else Mitch is keeping you in the dark about? Maybe you're just turning a blind eye to it the same way you have everything else. And what about the way you and Brody are trying to snow everyone?"

"Chelsea, enough," Bethany snapped, but Chelsea threw up her hands as she shook her head.

"Huh uh. No. When there is something relevant for us to do, or some wardrobe thing I need to know, then you can involve me. But this? You?" She pointed at Catherine for effect. "Everyone is going to see through you soon enough, the way I have."

Catherine's eyebrow shot up. "And exactly what is that supposed to mean?"

But Catherine didn't need to ask, any more than she expected Chelsea to answer. Instead, she watched in silence as her closest friend and fiercest enemy walked up to the door of the house, away from cheerleading practice without saying another word.

Catherine didn't feel the need to refute Chelsea's accusations, didn't feel the need to claim she wasn't a fraud by any means.

She knew better.

She could barely stand the majority of those she called friends, and barely knew anyone else outside of that circle.

She was with her boyfriend for status purposes only, and just the thought of his hands on her now made her cringe.

She was unsure of herself, her home, her future.

And there was this boy… this boy who, along with his family, had disrupted her entire life. This boy who she wanted to help. This boy whose past—and present—were so full of pain that it made her heart hurt. This boy who was dating the girl standing in front of her, this boy who had said all Catherine had to do was open her mouth and this girl buried her.

This boy who just yesterday had made her heart skip a beat with just a smile.

Practice had ended shortly after, with all the girls making it a point to talk Chelsea into returning the next day. Catherine had begrudgingly agreed as well, if for no other reason than to stop the rumors that were sure to be floating freely the next day. Her mind stayed elsewhere, though, even long after everyone had gone. She didn't want to speak with anyone, including her father who had left a message inquiring about the clothes she'd left behind and letting her know he needed to speak with her.

She was wandering about the house after nightfall, her feet seeming to have a mind of their own, and she paused as she realized where they'd taken her.

"Spying on me, Lady Catherine?" Brody hadn't even bothered to look up from his book when she'd come downstairs.

Catherine let out a heavy sigh. "No. And stop calling me that." She flopped on the opposite end of the couch and pulled her legs into her chest, her heels setting on the cushion. "You didn't tell me you guys broke up." She glanced over at him, not surprised when he still didn't lift his eyes from his book. "I'm guessing you're back together then."

"It's high school. Couples break up all the time." He turned the page, still not looking over at her. "Is that it? You came down here to pry about my girlfriend?"

Her face flamed at his choice of words—girlfriend. They must have gotten back together. "I was merely curious."

"You know what they say about curiosity."

She scrunched up her nose. "Yeah, I'm fairly certain it involves dead cats."

He laughed softly, but still didn't look up from his book. "Is that all?"

"What was the fight about?"

"Now you're being nosy."

"With Mitch, Brody… what was the fight with Mitch about?"

He slowly set his book down before he turned his eyes in her direction. "It wasn't right. That's all."

"What wasn't right?"

"Him, being there. Without you."

"He goes places without me all the time, as do I without him." Her words were perhaps a bit defensive, if for nothing more than to hide her stunned reaction to his response.

"That's not what I meant, and you know it."

She shifted uncomfortably, but stayed seated, in spite of her urge to run. "Well, obviously I'm fine."

"Are you?"

Her eyes widened at his question. "That's an incredibly rude thing to say."

He shrugged, his head tilting to the side as he examined her expression closely. "I'm a jerk, so I've been told. Rude kind of come with the territory."

"You can't charm me," she shot back, and one corner of his mouth lifted.

"Yes, I can."

"No, you… Brody, why did… never mind." She stood and

quickly ran her fingers through her hair. "It's been a long day, and I'm tired, and I'm never going to get a straight answer from you, so…"

"That was a straight answer, Catherine."

She turned to look at him, his face slightly hidden in the shadows as he held her gaze.

"He never should have…" He licked his lips, and for a moment almost looked nervous before he spoke again. "It's supposed to be special, to mean something."

"I don't know what you're talking about," she lied, calling upon her own strength, her own resilience to keep tears from forming in her eyes.

"So, he was lying then?"

She bit the inside of her lip to keep it from trembling. Of course, Mitch would tell people, of course he would brag. Wasn't that the point? For everyone to know? Wouldn't that stake her claim, and not destroy her the way Bethany had nearly been destroyed the summer before?

Brody stood, and Catherine took an involuntary step backward. "I'm not going to hurt you," he said, his voice soft and soothing, which only served to spark her anger.

"I'm not a child, and I don't need coddled."

"But you need a friend?" He asked the question just as softly, staying where he was when she took yet another step away from him.

"I'm fine," she snapped, even though she felt anything but. "You need to just… stay out of my business."

"Like you are with me and Beth."

The fact that he had a slight grin on his face only fueled her already fragile temper. "Just… leave me alone."

"Sure, sure." He held his hands up as she stomped her way

across the room, back towards the stairs. "Hey, Cat?"

She huffed as she turned around, one hand on her hip. "What?"

"I'll be here when you're ready." He scratched the back of his neck, his expression unreadable in the shadow. "I kinda owe you that, you know."

"No, you…" She stopped herself from snapping at him again, and sighed heavily.

He was right. Which, of course made her angrier, but…

He was right.

She needed a friend, even more than she needed to understand why her heart always beat so uncomfortably around him.

And she wanted to go to him, throw her arms around his neck, and just let it all go.

Just cry.

But she wasn't ready.

"Thank you," she said instead, then she turned and walked in silence to her room.

CHAPTER 29

She Wished

In spite of everything appearing to be normal, Catherine couldn't shake the uneasy feeling that followed her everywhere she went. She had been convinced that people were whispering about her behind her back, making a point to stop talking when she would turn her attention their way. Chelsea had continued to avoid practice, Mitch had continued to remind her to check that the condo was free and clear, and Brody…

Well, Brody had continued being Brody, riding to school with Bethany every day and not speaking to Catherine just as he had before. She wondered why he had decided that, even after the day they'd spent in her gym, he'd decided to act as if she had the plague. Was it because of rumors about her, about them? Or was it because she'd told him not to speak to her in a public setting?

And home… Frank's mood had been sour, and he hadn't been going out in the evenings as much. Perhaps it was because Theresa had a function she had to be particularly sober for, or perhaps it was to keep his suspicious eye on Brody. Whatever the reasoning, Frank's presence meant Brody's disappearance. Wasn't this what Catherine had wanted? For Brody to disappear?

Her curiosity had been piqued, though, and there was only one way to assuage it.

So, Catherine began to do homework, of sorts. She pulled out her laptop, opening up the page to Google any and everything she could that would answer the questions that she'd left unasked. Not that Brody had lied to her; he'd merely told her that the details were unimportant. That, of course, was the wrong thing to tell this girl, although she had respected his wishes and not discussed the matter further with him.

She typed in his brother's name—Brian Harris—and her finger hovered about the enter button. Did she really want to know? What good would it do anyhow?

"It would tell me his mother's name," she reasoned aloud. "I get her name, I find her, and… poof! Troubles be gone."

She chewed absentmindedly on her bottom lip as the webpage pulled up a myriad of articles and pictures all related to that one name. Of course his name would be popular, making the narrowing of her search all the more difficult. Now if she knew what city he'd come from, then perhaps…

"Wait a minute," she muttered, refining her search, this time entering in the name of the boy two flights of stairs below. She was rewarded instantaneously with pictures and newspaper articles about the star of Valley High's baseball team—their pitcher, Brody Harris.

She inhaled sharply at the first image she saw, one of his intense glare while in his baseball uniform. Upon closer examination, she could see the faintest bruise above his eye as well as what looked like stitches along his brow.

"His scar," she murmured to herself, wondering if it had been a baseball injury or at the hands of Frank.

Momentarily forgetting her search for his brother, she began to consume all of the information she could about Brody himself. He was a few months older than she was, meaning she'd missed his birthday while she'd been busy doing her best to ignore his existence. It seemed he'd been well-liked by his old classmates, some of whom had rather open profiles on Facebook and Twitter. Only when she clicked on a public picture and read the caption with it did she remember her original intent.

Miss you brotha—RIP Brian Harris

His date of birth, and date of death, were typed in beside it, causing the fine hairs on the back of her neck to stand on end.

"Christmas?" She whispered the word, recalling then how the children had gotten quiet when she'd offhandedly asked them what they'd wanted this year, while they'd been playing in the gym. Brody had quickly changed the subject, as he so often did, and Catherine had thought nothing of it. She'd simply assumed that with Frank being Frank, Christmas had less than fond memories for them.

This… this was so much worse.

Her hands were trembling as she retyped Brian's name into Google, adding in the high school name since Valley High serviced several cities. This time, the search was far more narrowed, boasting of an academically gifted young man, one whose life had ended far too soon.

One who had been found by his twin brother, dead of a self-inflicted gunshot wound.

Article after article quoted Brian's many friends, all of whom couldn't believe that someone as happy and seemingly carefree as this boy was would take his own life. Catherine understood far too well, though—not only what he was going through, but to what lengths a person would go to keep up a façade. She'd proven to herself just the past few days what a master she'd become at doing just that.

She jumped as her phone began to ring, her father's name flashing on the display. Knowing she needed to take the call, as he'd been trying to contact her, she sniffled and quickly wiped the wetness off her face, tears she hadn't noticed before. One more sniffle and she put her best fake smile on, knowing it could be heard through the phone line as she answered.

"Hey there, Princess."

Yet another title, another nickname she felt the burden of this day. "What's up?" she asked as nonchalantly as she could.

"Listen," he began with a sigh, "I don't have the best news to tell."

Her fake smile faded instantly, and her heart began hammering in her chest. "What's wrong?"

"No, nothing… well, something, but nothing life threatening," he said with a short laugh, and Catherine was surprised at the feeling of relief that washed over her. No… of course she should be relieved. This was her father, and in spite of their distance, she did care for him and believed he cared for her as well.

"That's good then, right?"

"Right, but… well, the shoe has dropped. Today was my last day on the job."

"Oh, Daddy, I'm so sor…"

"I know that you enjoy coming out to the condo," he continued on quickly, cutting off her apology, "but unfortunately that won't be able to happen. I am putting it on the market, hoping to at least break even on it. The realtor will be showing it this weekend."

Catherine's shoulders slumped, this relief one that she could understand. She wouldn't have a place to take Mitch, she wouldn't have to face another night like the previous Saturday.

"I'm sorry to hear that, Daddy," she said, her words honest as she felt a true concern for her father. "Do you have somewhere to go? And do you need help?"

"Well, I… I'll be fine, Catherine. Thank you." His tone showed an element of surprise, one that made Catherine feel guilty. He was silent for a moment before adding, "You've changed, you know that?"

"What's that supposed to mean?" she asked, frowning as she looked down at the chipped polish on her fingernails. A manicure was definitely in order, but would have to wait; she'd just have to do with removing the polish this evening.

"For the better," he said, and she almost smiled. There was so much her own father didn't know about her, her life, or her friends. "Listen, I found some clothes you left here," he began, and her body instantly tensed, her heart rate spiking once more.

"Throw them away."

"Ah," her father said with a short laugh. "Wear them one too many times?"

She cringed at his joke, but knew he had no clue… and she wouldn't tell him.

She couldn't.

"Something like that," she said instead, her eyes watering as they lifted to the screen of her laptop.

She blamed the sound of her voice on allergies when her father asked, and she blamed her tears on the information about a boy gone too soon, and for those he left behind. The only time she allowed Mitch's name to enter her conscious was when she sent him a text, letting him know the condo was permanently off limits, through no fault of her own. Without waiting for his response, she turned off all of her electronics and curled up beneath her covers, wondering what she could do to help… just help.

Maybe helping could ease her mind.

In spite of the community's high hopes, Davis High lost their last regular season game that Friday evening, ending their bid for a spot in the playoffs. Catherine hadn't been any more surprised at the outcome than she had at Brody's absence at the game as well as the after party that Mitch had insisted they go to. At least Mitch had agreed when she'd said she wanted to drive herself, just as he seemed to believe her excuse for her distance was due to the drama in her father's life.

The real cause, though, was her own boyfriend—the boy whose size had once been something she prided herself on, but now was intimidated by. He was unfazed by her attitude, as he always had been. What he didn't seem to notice, though, was the lack of spunk from the normally headstrong and outspoken girl. Instead, she retreated within herself at that party, sipping on her drink instead of downing several, making excuses to wander away from the crowds to get some peace and quiet.

The night air was cool against her bare legs, making her wish she'd worn a pair of jeans rather than the mini skirt that Mitch had insisted upon. She'd felt so guilty, though, for pushing him away, when she'd convinced herself it was her own mind playing tricks on her. She pulled her jacket closed, hugging her arms around herself as she walked through the back yard towards the small patch of trees on the property. She wasn't quite sure which one of the football players lived here—if she thought enough about it, she was sure to remember—but all that mattered to her at that moment was a bit of solitude to clear her head.

There was a rustle in the trees to the right of her, and she stepped back as a couple of her classmates emerged from the wooded area, laughing amongst themselves. Catherine recognized them almost instantly, and the way the boy tugged at the girl's hand to stop and kiss her made her feel uncomfortable at best. She stepped further into the shadows as the couple disappeared, going towards the house as they chattered about the 'perfect' evening.

"Seems we had the same idea."

Catherine screeched and turned at the sound of Mitch's voice. "Don't do that, you scared me!" she exclaimed, blaming her pounding heart on the fact she hadn't known he was there. She took another step back as he came closer, only stopping as she leaned against the tree behind her.

"Where you going?" Mitch's words were slightly slurred as he stood before her, his hand reaching out and tugging on her clothing. When she didn't step closer to him, he closed the distance between them, pressing his body up against hers. He ignored, or perhaps didn't notice, her cringe when he began to suck on the side of her neck. She heard the bottle of beer he'd been holding hit the ground, the leaves rustling beneath it as it rolled away.

This could not be good.

Catherine placed her hands on his shoulders, applying enough pressure to get his attention. "I don't think this is…" She gasped as his fingers, still cool and wet from the bottle he'd been holding, pushed her panties aside and began probing her roughly.

"That's more like it," he said, the smell of alcohol on his breath nearly overpowering, and Catherine's heart took off at a crippling speed.

"Mitch, wait," she said, grasping his wrist, trying to pull his hand from her.

"Such a damn good thing you aren't like Bethany, isn't it?" he asked, his thumb rubbing against her as his fingers continued to move, and she jolted in his arms. "That's it. See? Damn good thing you're not a prick tease."

Catherine hesitated as she thought of Bethany, of the humiliation she'd suffered at the hands of Mitch's older brother. She remembered the sneers, the laughter, the way so many others—including herself—had scoffed at the girl, remembered how she thought that kind of embarrassment just wasn't worth it. Why hadn't Bethany just had sex with him? He was her boyfriend, after all.

Those words haunted her as she followed Mitch's lead, further back into the woods, where a blanket was spread out in a small clearing. Without thinking how odd it was, without wondering how many others had used this blanket on this night alone, she laid back on it, closing her eyes tightly as her boyfriend moved first her clothing aside, and then his.

Because this… this is what girlfriends did for their boyfriends, wasn't it?

He moved on top of her, inside of her, stretching her uncomfortably as he panted in her ear. She could only cling to him, her eyes clamped tightly shut as he continued on and on. He pushed her legs further apart, and when he pulled one up, holding it up with his arm as he thrust in deeper, she cried out at the sharp pain.

It was a cry he, once again, misinterpreted.

"Finally into it, huh?" he grunted into her ear, pushing harder still.

She opened her mouth to ask him, beg him to stop, but cried out again as he pulled her other leg up.

"That's it, let them all hear you. Don't let them know you've been a dead lay."

Catherine's eyes flew open at his words just as he began shuddering above her, his jerky, frantic movements increasing in intensity as his face contorted, his grunts and groans louder still. She felt a burst of liquid heat within her as he thrust forward one final time, and she whimpered at the pain that lingered behind, even as he put her legs down.

"At least that one was worth it," he muttered, as he pulled out of her, a light gush of liquid following and trickling between her thighs.

"What was that supposed to… oh… oh God…" She stared at the damp spot on the blanket, shuddered as she felt more leak out. "Didn't you use protection?"

"Huh? Oh." He was still breathing heavily as he adjusted himself in his pants. "Nah. Didn't want to. I wanted to feel you."

"This… Mitch, what the hell? What were you thinking?" she asked as she stood, shuddering again as she felt the dampness between her legs.

"I just told you, Catherine," he said as he stood, towering over her. "If you're going to be such a diva about it, go home. Shower. It's no big."

"No… ugh!" She leaned down and wiped her sticky hands on the blanket, only afterward wondering who else had done exactly the same thing that very evening. "Mitch, this is…"

"Well, at least you were into it this time. Who needs your daddy's condo, right?"

She stood staring at him, her eyes wide, her shame and panic warring each other to take over. "What are you…"

"Look, Catherine, if you're going to be a little girl about it, stop wasting my time." He ran his fingers through his hair, then raked his gaze over the girl who'd been so sure he worshiped her.

"There are too many other girls who know what they're doing, and actually like it. Make up your mind. Do you want to be on top, or not?" He started to turn, then glanced back at her with a less than friendly grin. "You can take that however you wish."

However, she wished.

She wished she hadn't agreed to do this to begin with.

She wished she hadn't come out to the woods.

She wished she hadn't come to the party.

She wished she wasn't so conflicted, so confused.

She wished she hadn't questioned whether or not her friends were genuine, whether or not her feelings for her boyfriend were real.

She wished she hadn't spent that time with the boy who'd invaded her home, her thoughts.

She wished she had something to say to Mitch before he walked away from her, taking everything she'd once thought was important to her with him.

She wished she didn't have an overwhelming urge to cry… to just… cry.

But she waited until he was gone, until she was alone in the cold, dark shadows of the woods, before she let the first—and only—tear fall.

CHAPTER 30

Who Are You

The house was eerily silent when Catherine returned home, but she paid it no mind. The silence was a welcome reprieve from the loud voices, the clinking of bottles, the booming music that all had meshed together at that party.

That damn party.

She should never have gone.

With sheer determination, she made her way up to the top floor, down the hallway to her bedroom. Her hands were less than steady when she retrieved her keys and opened her door. She left the light off until she was inside with the door closed, so she didn't disturb anyone. Once her light was on, its muted tones casting a warm glow across her sanctuary, she let her bag and jacket drop to the floor. On the side wall, several pictures adorned her desk. Some were in frames, others shoved in along the edges of the mirror's frame. Her legs felt weak as she walked over to it, the bile in her throat as she took in the many images before her.

Mitch.

Mitch with her at the Homecoming dance.

The cheerleading squad all together, blowing kisses at the

camera.

Pictures of her and Chelsea, who wouldn't even speak with her now.

Pictures of the same people who hadn't even seemed to notice when she'd grabbed her things at the party and disappeared.

Pictures of her and Phoebe, who had left the school when no one believed her. She'd said Mitch was… what was the word? Predatory. She'd said Mitch was predatory. No one had listened.

There were no texts, no missed calls, no one wondering where she'd gone, or why.

She reached out to a picture that had been taken at the end of the previous school year, when everything had seemed so simple, so carefree. Even then, as much as she'd smiled, it just hadn't seemed genuine. It had been in her attempts to one-up Chelsea, or whomever else was near her. It had been a show for Mitch, who'd eaten it all up.

Or so she'd thought.

As her fingertips traced around the group of people smiling up at her, she whispered, "Who are you?"

The question was as much for herself as it was for all of them.

Who was she?

She shuddered at the damp feeling between her legs and began roughly stripping her clothing off her body, piece by soiled piece. Barely able to contain her disgust, her revulsion, only needing everything off of her, needing to be clean, she ripped the scraps of fabric from her and tossed them. It didn't matter to her where they landed, only that they were off, that they would never touch her again. Once naked, she stared down at her dirty, scratched, slightly bruised body.

And she bit back a sob.

She covered her mouth with her hand, trying to hold

everything back before she rushed into her private bathroom. Dropping to her knees in front of her toilet, the contents of her stomach emptied quickly, in wave after wave. She reached up and flushed, watching it all wash away.

"Oh… god."

She was trembling still as she stood to rinse her mouth out. Her towels were all in the cabinet, so there was no reason to step out before taking her shower.

Before washing all the remnants of this horrible evening from her.

The steam had already filled the room before she stepped in and beneath it, gasping as the hot water pelted her tender skin.

But it was needed.

So needed.

She wasn't sure how long she stayed in there, scrubbing until her skin was red and raw, until she was certain not a single drop of him was left behind. Only when the water began to cool did she turn it off, open the curtain, step out onto the plush towel she'd set on the floor beforehand. She wrapped another around her body without patting the droplets away and grabbed another towel to absorb the water from her hair. She opened the bathroom door, the rush of cool air from her bedroom hitting her damp skin and spreading chills across her.

Still she felt numb.

Her head was down, her hair in her face as she continued patting it, closing the towels around the ends, so when she heard a throat clearing, she jumped with a slight squeak. She dropped the towel that she'd been drying her hair with and stared, wide-eyed, at Brody.

In her room.

His head was turned, his eyes closed, and he was holding her robe in his hand. "I'm sorry, I was just checking on you."

Just checking on her.

"Why?"

"I just heard, you know." He gestured with the hand that held her robe, his face still turned, his eyes still closed.

She roughly grabbed the robe from his hand and pulled it on, securing it around her before shimmying out of the towel she'd wrapped around her body. "Heard what?"

"You getting sick. Too much to drink?"

Of course he would ask that. She hadn't given him a reason to think anything but. "No. And I hardly think you could hear me from the basement." She didn't even have it in her to sound angry or accusatory. Even she recognized her flat tone and could only shake her head.

"No, I was with Sammi, and,"

"I have the robe on."

He opened his eyes then, taking in her appearance with a knowing gaze. "Are you all right?"

She tightened the robe around her, her arms crossed as she returned his stare. "I'm fine."

"What's..." He gestured around the room at her discarded clothing, some of it torn. "What happened, Catherine?"

She only shook her head. "I'm fine, Brody."

"Catherine,"

"I don't think Frank would buy that you're up in my bedroom to check on my welfare," she said tiredly as she shuffled over to her bed and turned down the covers. "Nor would my mother, or my grandfather."

"Yeah, well, I'm not Mitch."

She hesitated for only the briefest of moments before continuing on her task, never acknowledging his statement. And

Brody never said another word before he left her alone in her room—alone with her thoughts, her questions, her shame.

Only as she pulled the covers around her, trying to erase her memory of the evening, did it finally occur to her.

Brody was the only person in the past twenty-four hours who had even asked about her welfare.

The sun was peeking through the crack in her curtains, letting Catherine know the day was well underway. Still she lay beneath the covers, staring at her dresser and the pictures that adorned it. On the side closest to her set her phone, which was buzzing for the first time since the night before.

But she didn't want to answer it.

She didn't want to move, to think, to deal with anything outside the sanctuary of her bedroom. Life had other plans for her, though, as Sam opened her door slightly and poked her head inside. "Your mom says your grampa is coming today, and we all have to behave, and we can't be hooligans. What's a hooligan?"

She sighed as she mentally cursed her forgetfulness. Why hadn't she locked the door the night before? She chose to not correct the young girl's pronunciation of 'grandpa,' opting instead to keep conversation to a minimum. "Ask your brother."

"Tyler doesn't know."

Catherine pulled the covers closer around her. "Ask Brody."

"Daddy's talking to him."

It wasn't just the words that Sam had said, but the sad tone she'd used when she'd said them that had Catherine's full attention. She sat up, realizing then that she had slept in just her robe. She pulled it further closed and shook her head slightly. "Where are they?"

"Basement."

Basement. Of course. Because it was out of the way, and because Frank no longer had access to her gym without breaking in.

"Give me a minute and I'll be up."

Sam merely stood there, still staring at her. "Okay."

Catherine pointed in the direction of Tyler's room. "That means go bother Tyler until I'm up and dressed."

Sam shrugged. "Okay," she said, then pulled the door shut as she left.

"Shit… shit, shit, shit." Catherine threw her covers back and tugged her robe open as she pulled out a fresh pair of underwear and a bra from her dresser. She closed the drawers with such force that a couple of the pictures toppled over, but didn't bother to right them. Instead she grabbed a pair of yoga pants and a fitted t-shirt, quickly dressing before she ran a brush through her tangled hair. "Fu… forget it." She stopped herself from cursing this time, and she pulled her hair back into a messy bun, foregoing makeup before she rushed out of her room and down the two flights of stairs. She paused in the stairwell before reaching the basement, listening for any signs of Frank. When instead she heard his voice coming from the floor above, she continued her descent into Brody's domain, her eyes searching the darkened room for him.

Furniture was in disarray, and paperback books were strewn about as if Brody's entire collection had been tossed. A lamp, which hadn't worked to begin with, laid in several pieces on the floor by a broken chair.

And then she saw Brody.

Brody, whose shirt was torn, whose head was bowed as he gathered the broken pieces one by one and placed them in a garbage bag, once again hiding what that monster continued to do to him.

Catherine's chest ached, and she rubbed it absentmindedly with the palm of her hand as if that would make it stop. "Brody?"

Even though her voice was barely above a whisper, Brody's head snapped up. His eyes were wide, fearful as he saw her standing there.

"Are you… can I help?" she continued.

Brody moved with a quickness and grace that took her by surprise, pulling her into the shadows in the far back corner of the basement. His fingers were over her lips, motioning for her silence, but his actions alone had rendered her speechless.

"What are you doing down here?" he whispered harshly, his hand still gripping her arm.

Catherine brushed his fingers aside and exhaled in a huff. "Checking on you."

"Don't."

He was close to her—so close that she could feel the heat radiating off his skin, feel his breath on her face, see the slight tremor in his hands that he was trying to hide. Her fingers tingled as the overwhelming urge to reach out and just touch him hit her full force. She shook her head once, slightly, then noticed his nervous glancing toward the stairwell. "What's going on, Brody?"

He motioned her to be quiet again, until he was sure no one was coming. She watched his shoulders relax slightly, but the urgency in his voice, in his eyes was still present when he turned his gaze to her. "You can't come down here, Catherine. Not anymore."

Her eyes narrowed. "Why not?"

"Listen…" He stopped just shy of placing his hands on her shoulders, dropping them to his sides instead. "I'm sorry that I came into your room last night. You know, when I heard you getting sick. I'm sorry."

"You already—" She stopped abruptly, her eyes widening with realization. Alarm, mixed with anger, coursed through her veins. "Frank was in my room?"

Brody didn't answer her, his eyes dropping to the floor as his breathing picked up. As her eyes fixated on his chest moving up and down, her mind took off at a breathtaking pace.

She'd slept in nothing but her robe.

Her clothing had been thrown everywhere.

Frank knew that Brody had been in there with her.

She gasped, grabbing Brody's hand as she did. "Frank thinks that we..."

She couldn't finish the sentence. She didn't need to; the look in Brody's troubled eyes as he looked down at her said it for her. His fingers twitched slightly, neither pulling away nor intertwining with hers as her grip on his hand tightened.

"But we didn't."

Brody swallowed and licked his lips. "I know."

She stood slightly taller, her chin raised. "I can make this right."

Brody only shook his head. "You can't, Catherine." He looked again at the staircase, then back down at her, his eyes pleading. "If he says anything to your mother, or to your grandfather—"

"There's nothing to say!"

He took a step closer, and they were nearly touching head to toe. "I don't know where my mom is, Cat." If she didn't know better, she could almost swear that was said with a sob. "If it was just me, I'd be fine leaving. I would have been gone a long damn time ago. I wouldn't look back; I wouldn't give a damn. But I can't leave them behind."

Tyler and Sam.

He was forever protecting them.

She licked her lips, trying to come up with a plan. "I can get you a key, to my room."

"Don't."

"I can put it in the first aid kit," she continued, ignoring his protests, "like I do the key to the gym."

"Don't." He leaned down just a little further, their foreheads touching just enough to cause her heart to race. "Please, Catherine, don't."

Her lower lip trembled as her emotions threatened to consume her. "I just want to help."

In the shadows, she could still see the slightest bit of a sad smile on Brody's lips. "I know."

Her fingers tightened around his, her eyes fixated on his lips briefly when they heard the front door open, followed by voices in the hallway. Catherine's heart began to race as she heard footsteps on the basement stairs, and Brody squeezed her hand once before he stepped away. She nodded, her assurance that she would remain silent, and she could almost swear he mouthed the words 'thank you' in her direction.

"Brody?"

Bethany's voice filled the otherwise silent basement, and Catherine thought she saw Brody cringe. Before she could wonder why, she remembered his state—disheveled, torn shirt, evidence of Frank's anger strewn about. "Yeah, give me a minute," he called out.

"I tried calling Catherine's phone."

Catherine's eyes narrowed and she shook her head, knowing that was a lie. No one had attempted to contact her.

"Just… I'm not dressed. Please wait upstairs."

"Goodness, what happened down here?"

Brody quickly took his torn shirt off and threw it aside just before Bethany rounded the corner, and it was all Catherine could do to not roll her eyes at Bethany's blatant gasp.

"Please go upstairs," he said as he stepped closer to Bethany, steering her away from the far darkened corner, where Catherine stood taking in the spectacle before her. She crossed her arms angrily as Bethany's fingertips trailed down his bare chest before hooking in the belt loops of his jeans.

"Are you sure you want me to?" she asked suggestively, even as Brody moved her towards the couch. With one swift motion, he pulled her to him, and Catherine's eyes widened in shock and disgust as he kissed her thoroughly, his fingers tangled in her hair.

"Seriously?" she whispered angrily, not sure exactly why her chest was hurting now.

And then she saw his free hand gesturing towards the staircase, before it rested on Bethany's hip, holding her to him.

Catherine slipped by them, unnoticed, but not without glaring over her shoulder.

A glare that met Brody's eyes, which fixated on her as Bethany's kisses moved to his neck.

A glare that faded when he mouthed the words 'go, please.'

She nodded once before she turned, and just as silently as she'd descended, she made her way back up the two flights of stairs, and down the hallway to her room.

She closed her door, turning the lock after she heard the distinctive click of the latch, and looked around the mess in her room. "I can't," she whispered, her arms wrapping around herself as she tried to block out everything from the night before.

There was nothing she could do about that now.

But there was something she could do about the nightmare

playing out before her eyes under her own roof.

She pulled out her laptop and logged into her Facebook account, ignoring all of her notifications and going straight to a profile she had bookmarked.

Sandra Harris

Their mother.

With a deep breath, she began to type the most important message she'd ever sent in her life, knowing she was doing the right thing, and praying that it would be seen.

CHAPTER 31

Whatever

The week following the party was an odd one, at least in Catherine's book. Everything about it just felt off.

"What is with you?" Mitch had asked her on more than one occasion. Every time he'd placed his arm around her, she would stiffen. Every time he would kiss her, she would flinch, make up excuses, tell him she wasn't feeling well.

That was actually the truth. She was tired, lethargic, anxious. She had daily headaches, which seemed to drain all of her energy. All she wanted to do was sleep, curled up beneath her covers, shutting out the rest of the world.

With whispers running rampant, people stopping their conversations when Catherine would pass by, she occasionally would wonder what it was they found so fascinating.

But she should have known.

Even Brody, Tyler, and Sam seemed nearly non-existent to her that week. Brody was going out of his way to not speak to her at school, which was no different than other days. She, after all, had been the one who insisted that he act as if she didn't exist there. He was acting the same at the house as well, which also left his antics with Bethany up to her own imagination to come up with.

She simply didn't want to.

She didn't want much of anything anymore.

When Friday finally rolled around, even as she readied herself for another day, putting on another show for the masses at school, she knew that it was different.

With her favorite jeans, her perfect designer top, and her $200 boots on, she at least looked the part. Her honey blonde hair was styled to perfection, her expensive makeup absolutely flawless, her designer bag that matched her shoes and her coat was on her arm. Her look was complete, screamed 'Queen of the School' just as it did every other day.

But Catherine could sense it.

This was the day everything was going to change.

If only she'd known how much.

The break up was inevitable; Catherine could have seen it coming from a mile away.

Had she been paying attention.

Had it mattered as much as she once thought it did.

She saw Mitch leaning against his Charger, his arms crossed in front of him, the scowl on his face as he watched her approach letting her know the day had come. Her steps never faltered, her expression never changed as she walked up to him, her head held high. She paused just out of arm's reach, holding her books in front of her almost like a barrier between her and this boy.

This boy who she had seen as another piece of the perfection puzzle, another subject to fall down at her feet.

This boy who she now associated with pain, anxiety, and shame.

His size was more intimidating than ever, but she kept her gaze steady, locked with his as he sneered when she refused to come any closer. "Jeez, Catherine, look at you."

Her eyebrow raised, challenging him to continue. It didn't surprise her in the least when he stood taller, when he shook his head slowly, when he raised his voice to grab the attention of everyone walking by.

"Just look at you, standing there trembling in your shoes, hiding every chance you get. You're busted, bitch, and you know it."

If he'd hoped to anger her, to escalate to a screaming match he was going to be disappointed. Catherine had long come to the conclusion that on her best day, she was the biggest bitch of all. And this display Mitch was putting on was child's play compared to what she could dish out.

"You're not happy unless there's a drink in your hand, just like dear old Mommy."

The most that the rest of the school had seen of her that year had been at parties, where she'd had more than her fair share of alcohol.

Just as they all had.

But that didn't stop the snickers or the dirty looks from everyone surrounding them now.

"That bitch doesn't even bother to hide it in her coffee anymore," Mitch continued on, and in Catherine's peripheral vision she saw Laura and Taylor smirking in triumph. The cheerleading squad had spent quite a bit of time at Catherine's house, and Theresa had been in various states of inebriation nearly every time. Again, though, Catherine refused to react, refused to say a word, even though she could.

Even though she could point out that Taylor's father was in

jail on drug charges, even though Mitch's own father was under investigation for embezzlement, even though half of the kids watching in glee had parents who were less than desirable as human beings.

"So, is that it, Catherine?" Mitch walked in a circle around her, eying her up and down. The look of disgust on his face was far less disturbing than the way he'd once looked at her like a piece of meat; she would be more than happy to replace that memory. "Is that why you've been walking around like a zombie? Because you've been dipping in Mommy's happy pills?"

She could have screamed in his face, told him that her problem was the nightmares she was having. She could have shouted that the nightmares were of his hands, his mouth, his body. She could have spit in his face, finally say she should have told him no.

Instead, she remained silent, expressionless, each word coming from him etching into her brain.

"You're so stuck on yourself."

This coming from the king of narcissism.

"You're so concerned about appearances, about who you're seen with, about who you are associated with."

She had been. He had been. Isn't that why they'd dated each other? To be the King and Queen of Davis High, in their junior year no less?

"Now look at you. You've gone downhill in a matter of weeks."

He said those words with such contempt, even though she stood there with flawless makeup and hair. He sneered at her designer clothes, her bag which cost more than most other high school students' outfits. She looked the part; she always looked the part.

She just didn't feel it anymore.

"Ever since that Brody kid—"

"I told you to leave him out of this."

Bethany *was* there. It was only fitting; Catherine had been on the sidelines, smiling triumphantly just a few months earlier when Mitch's brother had publicly decimated her. As Catherine's eyes finally looked over the faces of those gathered around, she saw a good half of the student body standing there—Mitch's buddies, the rest of the upper echelon, most of the middle rung on the social ladder, the entire cheerleading squad, including Chelsea.

And she looked the happiest of all.

Mitch stood in front of her now, looking down his nose, shaking his head. "You're done, Catherine. Finished."

Done.

No more ruling the school. No more planning the next year's party, which would have to be held in her home—the same home that was its own set of nightmares now. No more lunches under the tree with her subjects all around her, trying to pry into her business.

No more Mitch. No more 'It Couple'.

No more avoiding him, fighting him off, letting him do things to her that made her stomach turn.

She took a deep breath as that hit her, taking a weight off her small shoulders, which she shrugged. When she finally spoke, it was one simple word.

"Whatever."

And with that, she walked past him, through the crowd which still parted to let her through, although it could have merely been from habit.

Or perhaps it was revulsion, just as it had been with Bethany not so long ago.

"She really has lost it," she heard someone say.

She could have scoffed at that one statement, at all of it.

They honestly had no clue.

The gossip had spread like wildfire all through the school, the whispers of the other students making their way to Catherine's ears on more than one occasion. They'd also made it to the front office, where her guidance counselor had called her in and began quizzing her about her non-existent drug problem. She'd only replied with a simple "Really?" before she'd stood up and walked out, calling over her shoulder that she was late for her lunch.

Her lunch where she sat alone on a bench, staring at her carrot sticks and banana, not wanting a bit of it. Others who passed assumed her state of mind was because of the breakup, or because she must have gotten into her mother's pills. Those whispers barely registered with her, but the other rumors had her shaking her head.

Rumors of her and Brody, and how Catherine had been cheating on Mitch all this time.

Brody hadn't even made an appearance at lunch, not that Catherine expected him to. He still avoided her at school, just like she'd asked him to do. At this point, he might have even been avoiding her to steer clear of being a part of the rumor mill. No one could think Brody and Catherine had anything between them, in case it would somehow get back to Frank.

Frank, who would hurt him, or make him leave.

Catherine stood and tossed her small lunch in the nearest garbage can. She didn't need food that day. She didn't need anything; she didn't need anyone.

She was so convincing in her performance that she almost believed herself.

Even when she was home, where she'd spent the afternoon and evening in her gym working out vigorously in spite of her fatigue, she believed she wasn't the least bit disappointed when she wasn't joined by Brody, Tyler, or Sam.

At dinner, where she barely ate, she told herself it didn't matter that Brody avoided eye contact with her. Even the younger children were silent, their eyes on their plates as Frank stared them all down.

It didn't matter. None of it mattered.

Neither did the nasty messages on her Facebook wall, the ones boasting about how the mighty had fallen. One by one she deleted them, blocking those who had left them, noting how her friends' list had already depleted considerably. It was fine with her; if they'd truly been friends they would be there now. Just like…

She paused as she looked over those left on her list, many of which had been there smiling in triumph as Mitch had publicly dumped her. 'Like trash', one of the posts had read. Should she just delete them all? No, she would simply disable the option of letting others post on her page. As she fixed her page, noting how her status now read 'single', she remembered why she'd wanted to check it in the first place.

Her messages.

She could see there were several waiting for her, but as she'd expected most of them were nasty, hateful. They were reminiscent of ones she'd sent herself to others who had been in the same predicament she'd found herself in that very day. With a heavy sigh, she deleted them one by one, not even bothering to open them. Twenty-two, that's how many there'd been. Perhaps she didn't rate as high as she'd once thought, since the number was so low.

Then there was the message she'd sent to Brody's mother.

Unread.

She closed out of Facebook, her finger hovering in her bookmarks over the Twitter icon. Perhaps she shouldn't have clicked on it, but her curiosity won out in the end.

Again, her followers list had depleted, by nearly half. In another browser, she pulled up her unfollower page and did the automatic deletions, not needing any of them in her life either. The posts with her username were just as high as ever, only this time they were full of rumors, innuendos. Some were even talking about seeing Catherine in the woods with Mitch the night of the party.

Talking about how she'd thrown herself at him, screwed him there right in the woods.

As if no one else had done the same thing that very night.

She cringed as she thought of that night, though. The images, the memories, the creeping sensation that made its way up her spine as she could almost feel his hands holding her too tight as he moved between her legs brought a fresh wave of nausea over her. Pushing her laptop aside, she barely made it to the bathroom in time to empty her stomach into the toilet, heaving over and over until there was nothing left.

Absolutely nothing left.

With a nearly blinding headache, she climbed into bed, pulling the covers up to her chin, where she slept most of the entire weekend away.

CHAPTER 32

She Had Been

When the alarm sounded Monday morning, Catherine peered out from under her comforter. She glared at the clock, as if she could somehow change the time, no matter that she knew it was impossible. The last thing she wanted to deal with that morning—or any morning, for that matter—was the stares, the whispers, the cruel actions she was sure to be subjected to at school. It didn't help that she was still exhausted, in spite of the fact that she'd slept for most of the weekend.

It wasn't as if she'd missed much of anything.

There were no missed calls on her phone, no unread texts. No, if people were going to go after her, she knew exactly where it would be—online. It would be there on Twitter, on her Facebook wall, for all the world to see.

Just the way she, on more than one occasion, had.

And she didn't miss much around the house, either. She could guess that Frank and Theresa had been gone most of the weekend, with the sounds of Sam and Tyler's laughter that she'd heard. They made themselves more than scarce when their father was around. If she wasn't mistaken, she'd heard Brody telling Sam to not knock on her door, to let her be, let her sleep.

Everyone had let her be, actually.

But today was Monday, where Catherine was expected to make her appearance, whether she felt up to it or not. With a heavy sigh, she threw her comforter back and swung her legs over the edge of the bed, regretting it almost immediately. A wave of dizziness and nausea held her in place, saying a silent prayer that it would go away so she could at least make it to the bathroom. She hadn't showered in days, or done much of anything else for that matter. The thought of that alone would normally cause her to shudder in revulsion, but not that morning. No, that morning she could let it all slide as she shuffled her way in to her private bathroom, groaning when she turned on the light that caused her head to pound.

"Forget it," she mumbled. She would take care of herself that day, take her shower—or perhaps a bath, so she could just soak—but she was not going to school feeling less than human. They were already waiting to tear her apart; she knew this from past experience, along with the sporadic checks she'd made to Facebook and Twitter during her brief moments of consciousness over the weekend. All the comments seemed to be the same, too.

She was no longer the Queen of the school.

She wasn't part of the It-Couple.

She didn't have her cheerleading to fall back on, as she'd been on the Varsity Football squad, and their season was over.

How was she going to act at the awards banquet? Would she even have the guts to show up, knowing how she'd "hurt" both Mitch and Bethany by being such a whore?

It was so repetitive; Catherine almost wondered why she bothered to even look. Twitter, she could do without, so she bypassed checking it that morning. But Facebook... well, in her messages, she was still searching for a sign that her message to Sandra Harris had been read. Once again, she found that it hadn't been. After deleting several sure-to-be-hateful messages without even reading them, she wondered if Sandra had done the same to hers. She shook her head, not even wanting to deal with it at the time, and closed her laptop instead.

Catherine stayed sitting on her bed, her knees drawn up to her chest, staring at her closed computer while life outside her room bustled with activity. She could hear footsteps up and down the hallway, some small and shuffling, some loud and heavy. She could pinpoint when Frank had left for the office, because the small footsteps were now joined with small voices, full of joy when their big brother came down the hallway to check on them. Catherine closed her eyes tightly as she heard Brody speak to them, his voice full of patience and compassion, full of...

She jumped when she heard a soft knock on her door, her eyes flying open.

"Catherine? You okay?"

Her lower lip trembled when the voice she heard belonged to Brody, not her own mother. Taking in a shuddering breath, she sat up straighter. "I'm sick," she said, blinking a couple of times at the softness, the scratchy sound of her voice.

"What was that?"

She attempted to clear her throat, then decided against it when another wave of nausea hit. Instead, she shuffled over to her door and opened it a fraction, barely peeking out. She kept her eyes focused on his tattered Converse when she spoke again. "I'm sick," she said, still barely audible.

"Hey,"

"Have you informed Greta?" Theresa's clipped words interrupted whatever Brody was going to say to her, and

Catherine's head shot up automatically. When her gaze locked with Brody's, the concern in his blue eyes caused an ache in her chest, and she dropped her head again.

"No," she said as her mother passed by.

"Ah, well, I suppose I will call the attendance line then. Close the door, Catherine, no need to get everyone else ill."

As Catherine pulled back bringing the door with her, Brody reached out and grabbed the edge. "Are you okay?" he asked again, his voice softer still. Swallowing over the lump in her throat, she could only nod and motion for him to remove his hand. After a moment, one that seemed to last for much longer, he finally withdrew, leaving Catherine alone once more.

She waited until all commotion had ceased, until she was certain the kids had left for school and Theresa was—well, Theresa was doing whatever she had going on, since she'd sounded fairly close to sober that morning—before she ventured outside of her room. The house was eerily silent as she shuffled down the hallway, holding her robe closed tightly around her. Her head was held low, her eyes on the carpeting, counting rust colored dots marring the otherwise pristine high-end carpet. She paused, kneeling as she stared at the dots before she ran her hand over them.

This carpeting had been cleaned, yet the dots remained.

And she had no doubt exactly what the dots were, or who they belonged to.

"Catherine?"

Catherine looked up at the sound of Greta's broken English, her hand still in the carpeting.

"Miss Catherine, I tried to—"

"I know." Catherine stood, ignoring her nausea.

"You need some toast." It wasn't even worded as a question,

and it brought a ghost of a smile to Catherine's lips.

"I can get it, Greta." She began to walk away, but paused, glancing over her shoulder. "Is that new?" she asked, gesturing to the carpeting, and Greta shook her head. Catherine fought against the ache in her chest, the stinging behind her eyes. "How did I miss it before?" she asked as she turned, not waiting for an answer.

She already knew the answer, anyhow.

She'd missed it because she'd been so wrapped up in herself, in her own world, in what she thought were colossal problems whenever she couldn't find just the right outfit, or if her hair was out of place, or if someone had posted a less than flattering picture of her. She'd missed it because she'd been coming up with excuse after excuse to not go to the condo to see her father. She'd missed it because she'd been so busy being the person that everyone expected of her because… well, because it was the person she'd let them all believe she was.

No, she *had* been that person.

She had been.

Forgoing her usual breakfast of fruit for two dry pieces of toast and a cup of tea, she shuffled her way back up to her bedroom, where she locked herself in and proceeded to sleep the rest of the day away.

It was late afternoon when Catherine finally woke with a stretch and a yawn. The first thing she noted was that it was almost 5 pm; the second thing she noticed was her stomach growling in protest.

"Oh, finally."

Feeling almost human, she decided to shower, dress, and

apply light makeup. There was no reason for her to miss dinner, the way she had all weekend long. She was hungry enough to not even care that Frank was so obviously home, which she could tell by the lack of chatter from the children. Knowing that dinner would be at 6 pm sharp, she ensured she was ready in time; no need to make Frank or Theresa angry, or angrier, or…

"Whatever," she said with a shrug before she unlocked her door and stepped out into the hallway.

"Catherine."

She stopped at her mother's sharp tone and glanced over her shoulder where her mother was emerging from her own bedroom, her hair and dress immaculate. "What?"

"If you're still ill, you should be in bed."

"I'm fine. And hungry."

"Well, then, I suggest you change." Theresa paused and looked over her daughter with a frown on her face. "Your grandfather is expected at any moment."

Catherine blinked a few times. "Grandfather?"

"Yes, I know I spoke clearly. And stand up straight," Theresa added as she passed Catherine, who was now frowning as well.

"I think I prefer you drunk," she muttered, but did as she'd been instructed to do. A designer dress, the pearls her grandfather had given her, and a several-hundred-dollar pair of heels replaced her comfortable clothing, and she smoothed her hair into a low ponytail in lieu of the messy bun she'd had it in. Confident that her grandfather would approve, she left the confines of her room to join everyone for dinner for the first time in days.

When she finally made her way to the dining room, ten minutes past six, everyone was already seated and being served by Greta. The tension in the air was thick, even with Frank chuckling at something her grandfather had said before she'd entered. Theresa sat in her normal spot, back completely straight, her mouth in a thin line as she assessed the way Greta was serving the food, which probably wasn't up to her standards. Sam and Tyler sat subdued, their expressions sad, their hands on their laps. When she finally dared to look at Brody, she swallowed over the lump in her throat. He didn't look sad or forlorn the way the younger children did; instead, his blue eyes seemed full of anger even if they were fixated on his plate before him. His jaw was set, his breathing deep and even, and when she looked at his hands, they were balled into fists on his lap. Whatever Frank and Catherine's grandfather had been speaking of had affected Brody, and seeing Brody this way…

Catherine shook her head slightly to clear it, her smile tight as she moved her gaze to her grandfather. "Hello," she said politely, demurely. "I apologize for,"

"Are you feeling well, Catherine?" her grandfather asked, cutting off her words. She paused for a moment, then proceeded to sit, still forcing herself to smile.

"I'm fine."

"I would hope so," Theresa spoke up. "I have the ball and auction coming up, Catherine."

As Catherine let her mother's words sink in, it occurred to her that this was typical of Theresa. No words of comfort, no concern over her welfare. It wasn't about whether or not Catherine was feeling well, it was whether or not she would inconvenience Theresa, or interfere in her plans. Had her father been the same way? She racked her brain trying to recall as she stared down at the food she'd been so sure she wanted but now looked less than appealing.

"As I was saying," her grandfather continued, "Colin was so insistent that she get that damn car, but I made it clear he wouldn't be using a dime of my money for it."

Catherine stiffened at the sound of her father's name but continued cutting her baked chicken.

"Now while I don't mind spoiling my granddaughter to no end, the car is simply tacky."

"My car?" Catherine spoke up and was immediately met with a chastising glare from Theresa.

"You know better than to interrupt, Catherine," her grandfather said dismissively without even looking at her. "So, he goes out and finances the damn thing. I would have been perfectly content paying cash for a BMW or a Mercedes, but he was insistent. And now he's insistently stuck paying for it without living on my money."

Catherine sat staring at her grandfather, her cut piece of chicken still on her fork.

"Here he thought if he bought her that car, she'd go with him when I forced him out of here."

The boisterous laugh that the older gentleman was sharing with Frank turned Catherine's stomach more than her own illness had. Was what he was saying true? Had her father tried to buy her affection? And had her grandfather…

"I knew he'd be out of his job before long, just as I knew he'd never been suitable for my daughter. Theresa here, she was bright enough to agree with me."

Catherine set her fork down, her eyes now on her own plate instead of fixated on the adults in the room—the ones who were supposed to be caring for them, setting the example on how to live, how to treat others.

"Who would give up all of this?" her grandfather was saying.

All of this.

The house on the hill, with all of its amenities.

The never-depleting bank accounts.

The country clubs, the resort vacations, the best of everything that money could buy.

"Now you understand, Frank, that you and your children will have to abide by my rules, my standards as well."

Her father had been forced out because he'd wanted to do something for her? Because his job wasn't good enough? Because he refused to do as her grandfather told him?

"And when Catherine is of age, she will be with someone suitable as well," he continued on, plotting her life for her. "Like that Mitch, he comes from a good family."

"Excuse me," Catherine said as she stood, unable to listen anymore.

"I told you not to leave your room unless you weren't ill," Theresa snapped under her breath.

"Yes, yes, please." Her grandfather dismissed her with a wave of his hand. "No need to get everyone else sick as well. I'll keep you apprised."

Keep her apprised.

She almost vomited on the spot.

"Thank you, Grandfather," she said instead, leaving the room as quickly as she could.

She'd barely made it to her own bathroom before she was on her knees, emptying what little contents she had in her stomach into her toilet, tears which she swore were from the exertion dampening her cheeks.

Brody had been right, so very right.

It was all about the mighty dollar, to hell with everything else.

Was this what her life was destined to be? Would this be her a few years down the road—no career of her own, her days filled with booze and pills except when appearances called for otherwise? A loveless marriage to someone her grandfather deemed worthy, just to keep her current lifestyle?

Was any of it what she wanted?

If she did… was it worth the price?

She reached into the cabinet beneath her sink to pull out the mouthwash, so tired of what little of this day she'd participated in, when she accidentally knocked her box of tampons to the floor. "Ugh, what else is going to… go…"

Her voice trailed off as she looked at the scattered contents, her eyes wide, her pulse racing as she thought back… and back…

She pulled out her phone, opening the calendar on it, searching for the dot on the day where she'd mark, just as she did every month.

But none was there.

She counted back, flipping the page to the previous month where she saw the word Homecoming typed in, over three weeks prior.

"No." Her eyes were wide as she whispered that one word over and over.

But she already knew.

Even before she ditched school the following day, easily claiming illness when she was throwing up, she knew.

Before she drove the car her father had gotten for her to a drugstore in the next town, she knew.

Before she took the bag back with her, up to her bedroom in the house her grandfather ruled without even living there, she knew.

And it was back in that private bathroom, sitting on the pristine high-end flooring, that Catherine Garner—former Queen of Davis High—found out she was going to be a mother.

CHAPTER 33

Talk To Me

Catherine was on the window seat in her room, looking out into the sprawling back yard. It was crisp and getting colder outside, but the skies were clear. Brody was out there with Tyler hitting the baseball out for his little brother to catch. Her lower lip trembled for a moment when she remembered the day she'd stomped out there, throwing a fit to make them leave before cheerleading practice.

Oh, how times had changed.

She was unfamiliar with this sense of dread that had overcome her that afternoon. She knew what was coming, knew it had to be done. That didn't make it any easier to watch the clock, or to pick up her phone when the time had come.

The one person she wanted to speak to least answered after the fourth ring.

"What do you want, Catherine?" Mitch sounded bored, which clued her in that he probably had an audience. "And before you beg, you couldn't pay me to take you back."

On a mission, she refused to be goaded into an argument. "We need to talk." Catherine paused when she heard Chelsea laughing in the background. “And it may be in your best interest to not have this conversation in front of others.”

“What, are you calling to tell me your trailer trash boy gave you a disease? Are you telling me I need to get tested? I used protection with you, Catherine.” He said her name with such venom, but instead of angering her it only caused her to roll her eyes.

“Whatever story you’re trying to spin will have to wait, and just a reminder, Mitch? We didn’t use protection every time. You can talk to me, or I can talk to everyone else.”

She was bluffing; there was no way in hell she would go on Facebook or Twitter to announce what she’d found out. She was close enough to throwing up just thinking about it, and as much as she didn’t want anything to do with Mitch, she knew telling him was doing the right thing.

Luckily, he didn’t call her bluff. Catherine could hear the sounds of the others being muffled and the closing of a door before Mitch spoke again. “I won’t be seen in public with you. There is no way.”

Of course not; it would hurt his precious reputation now. “I refuse to be anywhere alone with you.” After the way he’d manhandled her in the woods, the way he’d spoke to her afterwards, she knew how little regard he had for her.

“Just spill it, Catherine.”

Just spill it.

That sounded easy enough.

“I’m pregnant.”

And she was met with silence.

The silence stretched out, and she could almost imagine the oaf counting on his fingers. Just as she suspected would happen, his next words were spoken with absolute venom. “No way are you pinning this shit on me."

"There's no pinning going—"

"I had a condom on after Homecoming," he cut her off. "The only time I didn't wrap it with you wasn't that long ago, and it's way too fucking soon after that for you to try to pull this."

She sighed, going over the list of things she knew she would have to point out to get him to realize that this baby was, indeed, his. "Condoms aren't 100 percent."

"It didn't break."

"That doesn't mean that—"

"Look, you need to be having this chat with Brody, since I know for a fact that you were fucking him the whole time."

Her eyes were wide, her mouth slack at Mitch's 'declaration'. "What?!"

"Chelsea filled me in on everything."

Chelsea. Of course. "How would Chelsea know anything? Does she live here?"

As expected, Mitch didn't answer her question. "And Bethany has admitted that every time she said anything about you to him, he was biting her head off. Hell, any time any of us had shit to say about you, trailer trash boy got pissed. And that's been going on for a long damn time."

She could feel the blood draining from her face as Mitch continued on.

How long had everyone been talking about her?

And Brody had known?

No, of course he had; he'd tried to tell her that the whole lot of them were fake. Not his precious Bethany, but the rest of them? He couldn't find a single kind thing to say about them.

If Catherine had thought that Mitch was done, she was mistaken.

He'd only been getting started.

"So you just go down to your basement where you're spreading your legs every time your drunk ass mother turns a blind eye, and tell him about your kid. Go on and have the thing, pawn it off on your housekeeper to raise the way your mother did with you. Then you can have your booze, your pills, and you can whore it up just like your mother without a care in the world. Maybe you can even do more than just lie there, like the dead lay you are. Just one damn thing you better remember, Catherine… don't ever try to tie me to it again. I have a future. I have scholarships lined up, a reputable family name to protect. Never again, Catherine. Got it? Never again."

After the line went dead, the phone slipped from her fingers, falling with a soft thud to the carpet below. All she'd meant to do was the right thing, to let Mitch know that she was pregnant. She wasn't asking him for anything—not money, not for him to be there, nothing.

But she hadn't even gotten that far.

Instead she'd just sat there, listening to another of his scathing attacks on her, one that was hitting so close to her fears it had rendered her speechless.

Her eyes blurred as she stared at her bedroom door, knowing just down the hallway Theresa had retreated after her meetings for the day, with a cocktail in one hand and a bottle of pills in the other.

Over an hour away, her father was busy with his new job, settling into his new home, getting on with his new life.

How soon before Mitch let the rest of the class know that she had fallen even farther, becoming another statistic?

And, just as he'd so thoughtfully pointed out, she was all alone.

She sunk down onto her bed and laid down on the pile of pillows, her arms circling around her abdomen.

How had it come to this?

What would she do now?

Alone, frightened, confused, and hurt, she curled up on her side, her back to the door, and finally let her tears fall.

The light filtering through the blinds had shifted as early evening descended, casting a shadow across her room. Still she laid there on her side, her back to the door.

Still she cried.

She cried for the loss of innocence, had she ever truly had it. She cried for her lack of hope. She cried over her loneliness, something she hadn't quite experienced before. She cried for lost friendships, which she wasn't sure had been honest or real. She cried the tears she'd denied herself both times she'd had sex with Mitch, admitting deep within her soul that it was something she just hadn't wanted, not with him.

And she cried for her child.

She cried for the baby growing within her that didn't ask to be brought into this mess that was her life. She cried over her fears that she would be like her own mother, the same mother she couldn't remember ever showing an ounce of honest affection toward her. She cried over wondering how she could tell everyone, where she would go, how she would care for a child when she was dependent upon others to care for her. She cried over the possibility that her grandfather would force her into any form of a relationship with Mitch, or worse would force her into any other decision she just wasn't sure of.

"I'm sorry," she whispered, holding her arms tighter around

her abdomen. "I'm so, so sorry."

Even the opening of her bedroom door didn't stop her tears. Instead the realization that she couldn't even remember a simple task such as locking her door had the tears flowing harder, her shoulders shaking with sobs she couldn't hold back.

"Catherine, will you play with me?" Sam's soft-spoken words made her heart ache even more. "Can we go to the gym and get on the mats again? Brody and Tyler are doing baseball stuff, and I don't like baseball."

With every word, Catherine could tell that Sam was walking closer, around to the wall that she was facing. Catherine kept her eyes closed, but there was no disguising the tears that streamed down her face or the sobs escaping her.

"Catherine?"

Catherine could only shake her head, pull the covers up to her chin, silently pleading for the little girl to go away, go back outside, go make her brother play with her.

Just let her cry until she found the courage to get off this bed and face the world.

The sounds of Sam's feet scurrying away, out of her room and down the stairs, still couldn't get Catherine to open her eyes. She stayed there, lying still, her shaking shoulders whenever her sobs would hit the only movement she made. Perhaps if she could just sleep, she would wake much later to find this was nothing more than a bad dream. There was no baby growing inside of her, no school full of people waiting to tear her apart.

Would she want to go back to how it was?

Would she want to be surrounded by people who hated her? Would she want to be associated with Mitch, much less date him? Would she be better off if Brody had never entered her life, bringing chaos and confusion with him?

"But he's not here." That was Tyler's voice that Catherine heard now, along with several sets of footsteps coming closer to her room. "What if he hurt her and left?"

"Like he hurts you?" she heard Sam add.

There was no question who they were talking to.

Catherine tried to suppress the fresh wave of tears threatening to consume her as she heard Brody's soft, gentle tone as he told the younger children to go to the kitchen and ask Greta to help them get something to eat. She listened as he reassured them that he would take care of this, but couldn't find her strength, her voice to tell him he was wrong, so very wrong.

There was no way he could fix this.

After the sound of Tyler and Sam leaving her room, she heard the sounds muffle even further, followed by the click as her door closed. She could sense Brody's presence in the room, hear his light footsteps as he approached her bed.

"Catherine?"

Even with the fear she heard in his voice, she couldn't answer him. She could only close her eyes tighter, curl up even further, try to cry as quietly as she could.

"Catherine, talk to me."

She stiffened as she felt his hand hesitantly touch her back through the blankets, and he quickly withdrew. Still she didn't relax, especially as she heard him walk around her bed, felt his closeness as he knelt beside it. The heat from his hand as he gently pushed her hair back—the kindest gesture anyone had made towards her in quite some time—was almost as overwhelming as the surge of emotions coursing through her veins.

"Catherine?" he asked again. "Please tell me you're okay."

She shrunk slightly away, trying to bury her face in her pillows, but he tangled his fingers in her hair, his thumb caressing her cheek.

"Cat?"

She couldn't stop the sob that one simple word brought forth, any more than she could stop herself from being drawn into his warmth as he gently gathered her in his arms.

"Oh god, Cat," he breathed against her neck as he held her, his hands now caressing her back softly, soothingly.

Slowly, almost unsure of herself, she wrapped her arms around him, turning her face into his chest. Her tears damped his shirt there, where she could hear his heart beating wildly, probably far too fast. She couldn't remember the last time she'd turned to someone for comfort; she couldn't remember the last time she'd needed comfort. Yet there she was, in Brody's arms, clinging to him as she cried. The pounding of his heart echoed with her own as he tried to soothe her, sending an unwanted chill through her body. As she pulled away from him, she felt his hands cup her cheeks, his thumbs brushing away her still-falling tears.

"Tell me what's wrong, Cat." He sounded so close to tears himself, but she could only shake her head. "Did… did Frank—"

Her eyes opened wide and she shook her head. "No! No… not Frank." Her voice sounded so odd to her, but her words caused just the slightest bit of relief in Brody's eyes.

"So, it's Mitch."

It wasn't even voiced as a question; there was no question about it. Her lower lip began to tremble as her tears—the tears she just now noticed had ceased—threatened to consume her again. Brody leaned forward, resting his forehead on hers for just a moment before he sat back, his hands now seeking hers to hold them, give her comfort.

"I know the breakup was brutal, Cat. I didn't have to be there to know; I heard all about it. I… fuck, I should have said something, but he just doesn't deserve you, you know? And people, they're… well, they're assholes."

With each word he said, she began to shake her head slightly harder. "No… no, Brody it's worse." She took in a shuddering breath and squeezed his hands back when she began to shake. "It's so much worse."

Brody was quiet for a moment, his eyes steady even as she felt just a slight tremor in his hands, which still held hers. When he finally spoke, his words were spoken with what she believed to be controlled anger. "Did he rape you?"

An almost immediate reaction, she dropped her chin as she shook her head.

"Listen to me, okay?" She could tell he was trying to see her face as he spoke, but she remained as she was. "I know… I know he has upset you, and I saw you when you came back from that party. Did he force you to—"

"I never said no," she admitted with a sob. "I never told him no, I never told him to stop, but I should have… god, I should have."

Brody's arms were once again around her, his voice soft in her ear. "Don't cry, Cat, please. He should have known, should have asked if it was okay, if you were okay."

She was trembling as she clung to his shirtfront, her tears dripping down his shirt front. "It's nothing I don't deserve."

"Hey, hey!" He pulled back abruptly, his hands cupping her cheeks again. "Look at me, Cat. Look at me." When she finally looked into his blue eyes, the intensity there nearly took her breath away. "Don't say that, do you hear me? Don't ever say that."

"But I'm a horrible person. It's okay," she said, holding a hand up to stop him from interrupting her. "I know I am."

He caressed the side of her face, pushing her hair back as he did. "Look at everything you've done for me, for Tyler and Sammi."

She was shaking her head before he was even finished. "You were right about me before. They're right about me."

"Don't listen to them."

"But they were right." She swallowed over the persistent lump in her throat, continuing on before Brody could interrupt her again. "And- and what happened Friday? That's nothing compared to how I have treated all of them, at least once. And that includes you."

Brody's brows furrowed together as he continued wiping her tears away. "This is you, Cat." He leaned in closer, and she felt her breath catch in her throat. "This girl right here, this is you."

She let out a short laugh. "Who, this? This mess? I wasn't smart enough to tell my boyfriend to get the hell off of me; I wasn't smart enough to break up with him when I couldn't stand him touching me to begin with. I have no friends—you were right on that one. Congratulations."

"You have me."

His words should have warmed her, but she could only shake her head. "No, I don't, because I screwed that up, too."

"You haven't, Cat. I promise."

"Fine, but I would." She sat up a bit straighter, pulling away from his hands. "And I'll end up just like that zombified alcoholic that poses as my mother when it suits her, and my baby deserves better than that, even if it's a part of him."

She hadn't meant to blurt it out, hadn't even realized that she had until Brody's eyes widened with shock. She covered her mouth, wishing she could just take it back, take it all back as her tears began again.

"I don't know what to do." Her breath was shaky as she inhaled, her hands covering her face to hide from him, hide her shame. "I'm so alone, and I've never been—"

"You're not alone." She felt his arms go around her again and she welcomed it, welcomed him, welcomed his comfort. "You're not alone, I promise."

A soft sensation in her hair sent a shiver through her, and Brody held her just a little tighter, his presence calming her.

Soothing her.

And the slightest ghost of a smile touched her lips.

He was right, once again.

She wasn't alone after all.

CHAPTER 34

Anything But

Catherine was sitting on her bed with her arms wrapped around her legs that she held close to her chest when Brody walked back in. She sniffled a bit, still feeling the residual effects of her cry, but didn't bother to hide her face from him. Instead, she gestured with a nod towards his arm that he had bent behind him. "What are you doing?"

He pulled his arm around and presented a plate with several pieces of pizza on it. "Thought you might be hungry." He sat on the bed beside her and placed the plate between them before taking a piece for himself. "We're sharing, of course."

She picked up the smallest piece on the plate, picking the mushrooms off and setting them to the side. "Where are Frank and Theresa?"

Brody paused, perhaps picking up that she'd called her mother by her first name. Instead of addressing it, though, he merely shrugged. "Some kind of fund-raising thing? Or a dinner, or both. Maybe it has to do with the big whatever they have this weekend."

"Frank's going, too?"

After Brody swallowed his bite of pizza, he nodded. “Yeah, yeah he's going.”

“That will be good for you.” Her voice was soft, still sounding odd to her and probably to Brody as well, but again she just didn't care. “Except I can't see how constantly having to be a parent to them...”

But she couldn't finish the sentence.

The silence stretched out as Brody finished his piece of pizza while Catherine picked at hers, taking tiny nibbles every once in a while. When he finally spoke, it took her by surprise and she jumped slightly at the sound of his voice.

“It's not so bad. Taking care of them, I mean. And I'm not just saying that, just in case that's what you're thinking.” He picked up another piece and held it, staring at it as if he was contemplating what to say next. “Kids need the basics, of course, but they also need love. They need guidance, patience, understanding.”

“All of the things I suck at,” she mumbled, and he nudged her knee.

“No, you don't. Your capacity to care, to empathize, goes much further than you think it does.”

She shook her head just a little but couldn't bring herself to roll her eyes. “Someone has been reading too many books.”

He mock-gasped and placed his empty hand over his chest. “Why Lady Cath-er-ine, there is no such thing.”

“Please don't call me that.” Her words were soft, almost whispered, her eyes fixated on her lap. She only looked over at him when she felt his gentle touch on her arm.

“I was just... hey, I promise I won't call you that anymore if you promise not to pick on my reading.”

“That's a little difficult to do, you know.” One corner of her mouth twitched as she felt the beginnings of a smile try to take over. "I mean, for all I know you could be a—"

"Future serial killer!" He smacked his forehead. "How could I forget that one? That was brilliant, Cat. Just brilliant."

This time there was no hiding her smile. "Hey, you creeped me out."

"Is that even a real word? Creeped?"

She pulled another small bit of pizza off of her slice. "Probably not."

The silence fell over them again, without any degree of awkwardness. When she glanced over at him, he would grin at her, warming her all over. The feeling wasn't exactly new; no matter how many times she'd ignored or at least refused to acknowledge it, Brody had had this effect on her for some time now. Where her own boyfriend had caused her stomach to turn, this boy—this simple, plain, boy who was anything but—had conjured a flurry of butterflies, a rapid pulse, quickened breaths.

But there was nothing she could do about it, not in the situation she was in.

"Hey, um…"

Catherine glanced over at Brody after his words trailed off. "Hey what?"

"They're going to be home soon."

She nodded, understanding what he was telling her. "Then you should go, shouldn't you?"

His eyes were piercing, intense as he met and held her gaze. "Are you going to be okay?"

She wanted to answer with a firm yes, wanted to sit up straight with her chin tilted as she had so many times before. Instead, she could only shrug. "I suppose so."

He nudged her knee with his own before he stood. "Of course

you will. If you need anything, I'm not that far away."

She tilted her head to the side as she looked up at him. "But I thought you didn't want me to come down there anymore."

"I didn't..."

And she knew what he was trying to tell her. He wasn't the one who'd ordered that Catherine stay away. She nodded, letting him know it wasn't necessary for him to come up with the words he seemed to be at a loss for. One corner of her mouth lifted in a half smile before she spoke. "I can always sneak down there if I need to. I can be rather stealthy."

She was met with a genuine smile from him, one that reminded her that in spite of her first impression, this was no ordinary boy standing before her.

And without another word, Brody turned and left the room.

"Seriously?" That was about all Catherine could manage after she threw up the breakfast that she'd attempted to eat that morning. She hadn't even managed to close her bedroom door on her mad dash up the stairs, barely making it to her toilet before the morning's pukefest had begun. With a growl, she moved from her kneeling position to sit beside the toilet, unwilling to leave the confines of her bathroom until she was certain she was finished.

"Catherine."

She stiffened, frozen in place as she heard Theresa's voice. "I'm in the—"

"I know where you're at." Theresa was now standing in the doorway to Catherine's bathroom, looking down at her daughter. "You need to go see the doctor. This has gone on long enough."

It took every ounce of willpower that Catherine had to keep her expression neutral. On top of the exhaustion, her emotions were now all over the place. Her once steely demeanor was notably absent, but she couldn't let Theresa see the state of sheer panic her statement caused. "Greta will take me," she said, inwardly cringing that she hadn't asked, but reminding herself that the Catherine of old never would; she would simply make demands.

Theresa's eyebrow raised slightly. "Yes, I suppose that would be best. Only a few days until the fundraiser. Oh, and Catherine?"

Catherine raised her chin, still fighting to keep her expression neutral. For once Theresa's disinterest in her well-being was going to work in her favor, and she didn't want to jeopardize that. "Yes?"

"Until this is over with, be sure to stay in your room. Greta can bring your meals to you."

She nodded, staying put until Theresa turned on her heel and walked out of the room. Only then, did she move to flush the toilet and freshen up. After she brushed her teeth for the third time, convinced the taste was stuck in her mouth somehow, she stomped her way out to her bedroom. Now was not the time for a temper tantrum, not that having one would do any good.

"I heard Theresa tell Greta to take you to the doctor's office."

Catherine screeched, covering her heart with her hand as she spun around. Brody stood in her doorway, grinning at her reaction. Each word was punctuated when she said, "Not funny."

"Guess you're not the only stealthy one."

She sighed, her anger quickly dissipating. "I guess." With a sigh she sat on her unmade bed and picked up a pillow, hugging it to her.

Brody looked down the hallway before he slipped into her room, closing the door behind him. "Hey, listen." He was kneeling in front of her, his eyes a brilliant shade of blue as he looked up at her. "Greta knows, okay? She'd suspected but didn't want to say anything."

"Why didn't she…" Catherine didn't finish the question, her eyes dropping to the pillow she held. "I suppose I haven't been the nicest to her, have I?"

"Actually, lately? You've been fairly awesome to everyone."

Catherine lifted one shoulder in a half-shrug. "I'm trying to not be." Brody's soft laughter pulled her out of her contemplation, and she could only stare at him. "What? I'm just trying to say I don't want them to be suspicious. Theresa and Frank, I mean."

"No, no, I get it." He held up his hands, still smiling at her. "And I think Greta knows that, too. You should go to the doctor anyway, you know."

She sighed heavily and hugged her pillow just a little tighter. "Yeah, I know."

"Do you know what you're going to do?"

Her lower lip trembled, tears threatening once more as she shook her head. "Huh uh."

"Hey." He placed his hands over hers, giving her more comfort than she wanted to admit. "Whatever you decide, I'll be there."

She couldn't answer him, tell him how difficult that was to believe. Instead, she nodded, conjuring up a small grin for him. "You better get going. Bethany should be here to pick you up soon."

There was just the slightest change in Brody's demeanor, one that only a few weeks ago Catherine wouldn't have picked up on. He didn't elaborate, though, and only smiled at her before he stood and walked out of the room.

"Okay," she said out loud in the empty room, "that was weird. Even for him." She turned to her desk, where her laptop sat, ready for her to pry.

But prying meant dealing with the probable nasty messages. At least she'd had the sense to disable posts from others on her wall, but that had only started the barrage of private messages—ones that weren't so private, since they'd been sent to several people in addition to herself.

A brisk knock at her door informed her that Theresa was back. Without waiting for an invitation, she opened the door, but didn't cross the threshold. "They are squeezing you in first thing this morning. Greta will be driving you."

She stated that fact as if it had been her idea all along. Catherine nodded instead of rolling her eyes, and waited dutifully for her mother to continue.

"Brody has been informed that he is to bring your school work back for you. No need for your grades to suffer." When Catherine failed to snap back at her, Theresa's eyes narrowed. "Is there something you're not telling me?"

There was plenty she wasn't telling her, plenty she never bothered to tell her.

"You've never been concerned before, Mother," Catherine replied coolly. "Why start now?"

Seemingly satisfied with Catherine's reply, Theresa stepped back, closing the door as she did so. Catherine huffed out another sigh.

"What is with people?" she muttered as she stood, tossing her pillow aside. She grabbed her phone and her bag, knowing that 'first thing' meant that she and Greta would need to leave as soon as Tyler and Sam were on their way to school. There was no way Theresa herself would stoop so low as to get them on the bus; she certainly never had when Catherine was that young. It hadn't seemed peculiar to her at the time, but now… now it irritated her at best.

She placed her hand on her lower abdomen, frowning as she did so. What kind of mother would she be? Wasn't she destined to follow in her mother's footsteps? Her grandfather certainly wasn't one for outward affection; it was more about what he could buy for her. As far as Theresa, the apple hadn't fallen far from the tree… although at times Catherine's grandfather seemed at least a little more concerned for her than her own mother.

And what of her father?

She glanced down at her cellphone, biting the inside of her lip as she did so. Had he been affectionate towards her? No… no, as far as her recollection went, he hadn't been. Then again, his entire demeanor had been stiff and tense any time her mother was around. And her mother… well, she'd always been the one to reiterate everything Catherine should do—sit up straight, mind her manners, dress to impress, never settle for less than first place.

She opened her contacts, her finger hovering over her father's name. She remembered at the last moment that he was probably at work, at his new job that he seemed to be rather proud of.

As a teacher, at Valley High.

It was a far cry from the prestige that the firm he'd once worked for had given him, at least as far as her mother and grandfather were concerned. He certainly wouldn't be able to afford his Armani suits any more than he'd been able to afford his condo.

Catherine glanced down at her own designer clothing with a frown. Having the money, the car, the clothes certainly hadn't shielded her from life's harshest realities any more than it had given her happiness or fulfillment. It didn't bring any real friends into her life, either. No, the only person she counted at that moment as a friend cared in spite of who she was and what she had.

That realization was still weighing on her mind as she listened to the doctor, who was explaining what options would be available to her. She was early enough along that she could have an abortion, but due to the state law her parents would have to be notified. She could choose adoption, either open or closed, if she would be able to hand over her child.

Or she could raise this child, on her own, with little to no parenting skills, before she even graduated from high school.

"Miss Catherine?"

Greta was standing beside the bed that she was sitting on, and only then did Catherine realize how hard she was squeezing her hand. "Sorry," she replied with a shaky breath as she loosened her grip.

"No, no." Greta's free hand was gentle as it wiped away the tears that Catherine hadn't realized were falling. "No sorry, okay? No sorry."

"If you have any questions before your next appointment," the doctor was saying as he made his way towards the door, "please give us a call."

Catherine nodded, keeping her questions to herself as she pondered what she could do. There was no way around her parents, unless she could somehow find someone to pose as her mother. She was certain Greta couldn't, as her English alone was broken at best, not to mention that Catherine looked absolutely nothing like her. She couldn't do that to her housekeeper anyway, not with the kindness the woman had shown her on this day alone.

She remained silent all the way back to the big house on the hill, barely acknowledging Greta when she'd promised to bring her something to eat. She simply walked up the stairs to her bedroom and crawled onto her bed, pulling the covers around her, wishing that somehow she could rewind the clock, turn back the time to Homecoming night.

Wish that she had listened to Brody and not gone to her father's condo.

But all the wishes in the world wouldn't change what her life had now become.

CHAPTER 35

Not Even Close

Catherine sat on her bed early Thursday afternoon, her books and homework assignments mocking her from their spot on her desk. She supposed she should at least work on them a little, especially since there was sure to be more when Brody returned from school in a few short hours. Instead, she sat on her bed, picking at her ham sandwich watching Star Wars for at least the millionth time. She could nearly quote the movie by heart, not that she'd told any of her so-called friends that bit of information. It was almost like a comfort to her, this tried and true movie that had never failed to let her escape her worries whenever she'd let it happen.

A soft knock on the door only brought a sigh from her. Greta had already brought something for her to eat, so she wasn't quite sure what her housekeeper could possibly want. "Yeah?"

When the door opened slightly, Catherine was surprised to see Brody peek his head in there. "Coast clear then?"

She blinked a couple of times as she sat up a little straighter. "Who else would be in here?" That was all she could manage to say as he came into her room, closing and locking the door behind him.

"Just in case."

She nodded, a smile tugging at the corners of her mouth as he walked towards her carrying a bowl of freshly popped popcorn. She moved over slightly, giving him room to sit, and he placed the bowl on his lap. "You're not going to share?"

He shrugged as he grinned over at her. "You can have all you want."

She glanced down at her ham sandwich, then back over at the bowl of popcorn. With another sigh, she reached into the bowl on Brody's lap and grabbed a handful of popcorn, placing the kernels on her plate. "Now it's movie time."

"Indeed."

She was acutely aware of his presence beside her, distracting her from the movie that she knew by heart. Her cheeks warmed as she acknowledged the fact, at least to herself, that she was happy he was there, that she wasn't sitting in solitude for another day. Not that there were many people she wanted to be around, but Brody was…

"Do you know what you're going to do?"

His question was spoken so softly she almost didn't hear it. She glanced over at him, admiring his profile for a brief moment before she returned her gaze to the television. "I don't know," she admitted. All of the information that the doctor had handed to her had only added to her confusion.

Out of the corner of her eye, she saw Brody lick his lips before he spoke again. "What about Mitch?"

She scoffed as she picked up a few kernels of popcorn, studying them as if they were the most interesting things in the world. "He thinks it's yours."

Brody only nodded, as if he had been expecting that answer from her.

"I'm sorry, you know?" she added. "I didn't mean to cause you so many problems."

He lifted one eyebrow as he looked over at her. "With?"

"Everyone." She swallowed over the lump in her throat. "Frank."

Catherine noticed a slight dimple in Brody's cheek as he grinned. "Eh, he was trouble to begin with."

"And Bethany." Catherine gestured with her head towards her laptop, which also set on her desk. "I know she broke up with you." It had been all over Facebook, along with several scathing remarks in Catherine's inbox, which also held the message that she'd sent to Brody's mother.

The message that was still unread.

Brody's laugh was genuine as he reached into the bowl for more popcorn. "Hardly, Cat. Hardly. Don't believe everything you read."

Her chest ached a little, the pressure unwelcome. She certainly knew that all too well. "So, you didn't… you're still together?"

"Hmm? Oh." He shook his head. "No, we're not."

The pressure in her chest eased a little, which brought a scowl to her face. She shouldn't be relieved that Brody and Bethany had broken up; it shouldn't affect her in the least. "What… well, I'm sorry."

He nudged her shoulder with his as he continued grinning at her. "Don't be." His head tilted slightly to the side. "They don't know, you know. He hasn't said anything; you don't have to hide away in here, alone."

When had he reached out to touch her arm?

And why did it feel like it burned?

She swallowed again, this time to suppress the unwanted butterflies that had taken flight. She found it increasingly difficult to breathe, but she continued to slowly, purposefully.

He had returned his attention back to the movie, perhaps unaware that her reaction to him had changed considerably. "I always knew you were a fan." He grinned over at her. "You know, since I was accused of trying to Jedi mind trick you."

She felt her cheeks heat at the memory, but she grinned at him anyway. "Go ahead, call me a nerd. I've been called much worse this week alone."

The way he wiggled his eyebrows had her grin widening. "It's kinda hot."

The laugh that left her was sudden, spontaneous.

And the first time she'd laughed all week.

That realization had her touching her cheek absentmindedly as she looked back at the screen, trying once again—in vain—to pay attention to the movie. She heard Brody inhale deeply but refrained from looking over at him, even though she could tell his eyes were still on her.

"Look, about Bethany—"

With a mock roll of her eyes she finally turned to him, mirroring his words from months before. "I know, I know. I open my mouth and she buries me, bla, bla, bla."

The smile faded from his face as he held her gaze, his blue eyes burning with an intensity that nearly took her breath away. "Not even close."

If she'd been experiencing butterflies before, she must have graduated to full grown pterodactyls at those words. The silence stretched on a few moments longer, both of their expressions softening to one of understanding, of mutual admiration.

She must have been mistaken when she thought his eyes had flickered to her lips before he turned back towards the television, a playful grin on his face. "Now if you looked like that." He pointed at the television before he licked his lips and smacked them as if he'd tasted the most incredible thing on the earth. "Now that is hot. The whole white sheet for a dress thing? Mmm mmm. And honey buns on either side of your head? I'd never be able to keep my hands to my…" He couldn't finish the sentence as she'd elbowed him, causing him to laugh.

"You only think you're funny."

"I'm hilarious."

"Whatever." She settled back into her pillows, still grinning as she continued to pretend to watch the movie. "Whatever." She was about to make another comment, one that was sure to be funny or witty or both, when it finally dawned on her.

He shouldn't be there.

At all.

"Why are you here?"

"Watching a movie, duh."

"Don't duh me. Seriously." She turned fully towards him and placed her plate to the side. "You should be at school."

"So should you." He grinned but also sat up a little straighter before he shrugged. "I got sent home early."

Her eyes narrowed. "No kidding. Why?"

"Had an accident."

"What?" she asked, alarmed. "What kind of accident? You drove? How are you alive if you were in that rust bucket? What—"

He held his hands up. "Not that kind." He picked up a couple kernels of popcorn, tossing them in the air before he ate them. "Frank is smoothing this over with Mr. Witherspoon as we speak."

Catherine's eyes widened in alarm. "Witherspoon? As in Mitch? As in you wrecked into his Charger?"

Brody's grin couldn't be more suspicious to her. "Nope."

She huffed in irritation. "Then what kind of accident?"

"Oh, you know... my arm slipped." He held up his hand, wiggling his fingers. "While holding a baseball."

Her eyes widened. She knew exactly how much Mitch's precious car meant to him. How was Brody sitting here in one piece? "You broke his windows?"

His grin was now more of a smirk. "I'm sure he's wishing I had."

She growled in frustration and shoved Brody, who only laughed at her. "What did you do?"

He shrugged—something she'd noticed he did quite often. "I could be wrong, but I think good ol' Mitch is minus a testicle now."

Catherine gasped, her hand covering her mouth as she stared at Brody with wide eyes.

"He really should watch what he says about you."

She could only imagine what had left her ex-boyfriend's lips, but for someone—not just someone, but Brody—to have defended her?

"No one else heard, of course. And we both know he won't press charges because then—" Brody's eyes dropped to Catherine's abdomen for the briefest of moments. "Well, he'd have to fess up. And let's face it, he's not man enough to."

Catherine was still stunned silent, although her hand had dropped to her lap. Her lack of response to Brody's confession seemed to worry the boy, though, because he sat up even straighter and took her hand in his.

"Look, the guy's an asshole, okay? He treated you like shit. He should have known to stop because it's not supposed to be that way. And to refuse to stand up now? That's bullshit. Absolute bullshit."

She could feel the telltale sting of unshed tears in her eyes, and she did her best to suppress them, unaware she was squeezing Brody's hand. "What's it supposed to be like?"

His breathing seemed to pick up pace, but his expression never changed as his eyes held hers captive. "It's supposed to be… god, as bad as it sounds, but… like… like poetry. Like your favorite song, and not the one where you want to rip someone's head off. The one where… where your heart is so full, where all that matters is making the other person happy, showing them…" His voice trailed as he glanced down at their joined hands. "Showing them how much they mean to you. No doubts, no questions, because… because if they're there, if you're not sure if you're ready, if it's what you want, then it isn't. And you shouldn't." He looked back up into her eyes, a small smile touching his lips as he did. "You should be treated like you're the most important… the only person in the world." He swallowed, and she felt his thumb caress her hand. "You should feel loved."

She almost asked what that felt like.

But she wasn't sure if he knew, either.

"Was it like that with Bethany?" she asked, and again he shrugged.

"We never did."

She could try to call her reaction to this bit of news surprise, but she knew better. She knew it was relief, it was a tiny bit of jealousy that she could tuck back away. It hardly seemed fair to her, or to him, for her to feel anything towards Brody other than gratitude.

Friendship.

But their hands remained joined as the silence fell between them, stayed that way as they turned towards the television and resumed watching the movie. There was no awkwardness, only an innocent shyness that had them stealing sideways glances when they thought the other wouldn't notice. When she yawned, the familiar grips of exhaustion threatening to consume her, he only shifted closer, where her head would rest comfortably against his shoulder. Her eyes were growing heavier with every breath they took, nearly in unison now, until the slamming of the door downstairs caused them both to jump, break apart.

Frank was home.

Brody stood quickly, making his way to the bedroom door. Catherine watched him, her heart hammering with fear as he pulled it opened just a fraction. They could hear him speaking just a floor below them, giving Brody time to slip from her room unnoticed.

"Brody, you shouldn't have—"

"It was worth it," he cut her off, his voice barely above a whisper, as if he were afraid Frank could hear him.

Catherine's eyes filled with unshed tears, and she blinked several times to keep them at bay. "You know," she remarked, "for someone who insisted you stay away from me, he's certainly leaving us alone quite a bit."

"I could, you know." Brody looked over his shoulder at her as he began to leave. "Stay away. If you want me to."

She knew, in spite of everything, that was the last thing she wanted.

Without waiting for her answer, he began to walk out into the hallway, heading towards Tyler's room, pulling the door with him as he went. Before it shut fully, Catherine finally found her voice.

"I don't mind the company."

She almost kicked herself at the lameness of her words.

Until he smiled.

And without saying another word to her as he left, she knew he would be back.

CHAPTER 36

The Latest Rumor

Days seemed to blend together for Catherine, who by mid-Sunday afternoon had developed a strong case of cabin fever. Unwilling to show her face in public, she instead ventured out to her own haven also known as her gym. In some ways, this was exactly what she would have done before her life had imploded before her own eyes. In others…

"Do you… do you think the boys will… be noisy?" Sam's excited voice was up an octave or so as she hurried to keep up.

Catherine smiled down at the young girl, who was more than eager to practice the moves that she'd been taught. "They're boys. What do you think?"

"I think—" Sam jumped a couple of times, her arms stretched out like a ballerina. "—that we need our music really loud to drown them out."

"How about no?" That was Tyler's response as he ran past them towards the gym door, which he couldn't enter without Catherine unlocking. "Beat you!"

Sam stuck her tongue out. "We weren't racing, dummy."

"We always race."

"But I am a big girl today." Sam peered up with an adoration that Catherine felt she hadn't earned in the least.

"You're a big girl every day," Brody corrected her as he finally caught up. His breathing was a bit labored, and he held his right side—the side that Catherine knew was black and blue beneath his loose-fitting t-shirt. Instead of complaining, he'd simply smiled and promised her that Mitch's 'junk' probably looked worse.

Tyler didn't seem to notice his brother's pain, or perhaps was used to seeing him not quite at 100 percent. "Are we gonna order pizza again?"

Catherine cringed as she opened the gym door, stepping aside as the younger children raced past her. "Again? Can't we get something else?"

"I could get us sandwiches." Brody motioned for Catherine to enter first, and then he stepped in behind her, closing and locking the door. "I do have a car, you know."

Catherine was smiling as she walked towards Sam, who was doing her best to warm up on her own. "If that's what you want to call it."

"Hey, at least it's not—"

"My car is not pink, Brody."

She turned to remind him that her car was, in fact, custom painted pearl white, stopping suddenly as she nearly ran into him. His close proximity was more unnerving to her than the children running on the mats behind her, their screeches of delight as they chased one another nothing more than background noise.

Brody's eyes skimmed over her face as his hand rested on her arm. "How are you feeling?"

Their eyes were locked, their breathing in unison as she replied. "Shouldn't I be asking you?"

"Yeah well..." He raised one shoulder slightly, a half shrug that he so often did. "This is nothing new for me."

Without thinking, she reached out and brushed her fingertips along his right side. "It isn't right."

None of it was.

Not the way Frank treated him, not her predicament, not the way she felt when this plain, ordinary boy was near.

He stepped back first, breaking the spell she swore he had her under. Or maybe it was her hormones; she'd been reading up on that, in lieu of checking social media, where she was still being torn apart. Yes... yes, she could blame her imbalanced hormones, say that was the cause of her checking out Brody's form when he bent over to pick up the ball that he and Tyler would be hitting off the wall. Her eyebrows had probably disappeared behind her bangs, she had them raised so high when she got a peak of his toned midsection, and...

"Were you staring at his butt?"

Sam's whisper was a bit loud, snapping Catherine out of her daze. She shook her head and turned away from the boys, focusing on the little girl instead. "No, no. I... am just... hey, how about let's see your cartwheel?"

Catherine watched as Sam showed her what she remembered, with a perfect form and grace that only the truly gifted gymnasts possessed. While it kept her occupied a great deal of the day, it didn't stop her from stealing glimpses in Brody's direction, or sharing shy smiles with him whenever their gazes would meet. She wasn't sure exactly what was happening—or she was and simply chose denial. Either way, there was no denying the shift, the change between them. The only thing that was certain was the timing, and circumstances, couldn't be much worse.

"Don't even think about it."

Catherine paused as Brody spoke the words that Monday morning, her eyes still focused on her bedroom door. She hadn't been to school since the day of the breakup, since she'd found out she was pregnant with her ex-boyfriend's child.

She wasn't so sure she wanted to now.

She looked over her shoulder at Brody. "One more day."

"Nope." He took her arm, gently guiding her towards the staircase. "Nope, it is Monday, we have school, and you are not going to let them do this to you anymore."

She scoffed at his words. "Do what to me? I just want to sleep, that's all."

"You've been sleeping for a week. Well…" He grinned over at her as they descended the stairs. "Almost. Aren't you feeling better?"

"Well, yes, but—"

"And aren't you Catherine Garner?"

"Well, that's a stupid question."

"And letting them get the best of you is a stupid answer."

They were in the entryway now, and she turned towards him, one eyebrow raised. "What makes you think I was letting anyone get the best of me?"

"You were hiding in your room, Cat."

Her eyes widened for a fraction of a second before narrowing as she glared at him. "I was not hiding in my room." Which was a lie, of course, but one she chose to stick with anyway.

"Wonderful." He opened the front door, letting the cold air in. "Then let's go."

"I swear," she mumbled as she walked around him, shaking her head as she made her way towards her car, "you are the most insufferable human being I have ever met."

"Thanks."

She glanced up at him before she shook her head and turned her attention back to her car. "You always think you're right about everything, and… what are you doing?"

He had the passenger door open, his expression almost pained. "Degrading myself by riding to school with you."

She paused, a brief moment of weakness as she let his words hit her where it hurt most.

"I swear we'd be better off in my Escort, but, you know… it won't start." His grin gave his playfulness away, only then reminding her that he detested the car she drove.

"One would think," she said as she slid into the driver's seat, "that you'd be thrilled to be driven around in a Mustang."

"Well one would be wrong." He was still grinning as she started the car. "Lucky for you, I don't mind the company."

She blamed the heat she felt creeping into her cheeks on her imbalanced hormones—weren't they the cause of all problems?—and she drove the rest of the way to school in silence. Brody had picked the music, so instead of her usual pop station she was listening to some alternative rock, her thumbs tapping along to the rhythm without her even realizing it. When she finally pulled into her parking space, Brody spoke up, startling her.

"Liked it?"

"Liked what?" She grabbed her book bag and opened the door as he did the same, his grin making her pulse race.

"The music."

She shrugged. "It was okay, I guess."

"Wow, look at you." He walked along side of her, both of them ignoring the stares and whispers as they made their way to the school entrance. "Even your taste in music is growing up.

There's hope for you yet."

She was grinning as she shook her head at him. "Shut up, Brody."

"Aw, am I being too much of a jerk?" He laughed as she nudged him, but kept in stride with her. "See? Look. We made it to school and you didn't spontaneously combust or anything."

"Let's just steer clear of churches for a while though."

His laughter caused her smile to widen, and almost... just almost... made up for the uneasy feeling that still was hovering over her. They turned together down the hallway towards their lockers, Catherine's eyes immediately falling on Mitch.

And Chelsea.

And their rather public display of affection towards one another.

Brody leaned close to her, his voice low enough so only she could hear. "Is it just me, or does it look like they're putting on a show?"

An answer wasn't necessary, so she merely smiled at him as they paused at her locker so she could put a few of her unneeded books away. As she contemplated the spectacle still taking place, it suddenly occurred to her that she wasn't the least bit surprised. As far back as the night that Brody had moved in, Mitch had slipped and called her by Chelsea's name, only to back-peddle his way out of it.

And she'd fallen for it, being naïve enough to think that this would never happen to her.

Brody was still beside her, talking low enough so that passers-by couldn't hear. "Does it bother you?"

She thought for a moment before she shook her head. "No." And that part was the honest truth; she couldn't care less who either one of them was with. "I suppose I knew it all along. It was easier to pretend, though." She looked over at Brody, who was studying her intently. "Does it bother you?"

His eyebrows rose. "Mitch and Chelsea?"

Catherine laughed as she shook her head. "No, no." She closed her locker and tilted her head slightly to see his expression better. "That they think you're with me, the school pariah."

Brody rolled his eyes. "You hardly are."

"Yeah, but—"

Brody leaned in closer, his eyes locked with hers. "I didn't say anything to anyone, I swear. And your boy, your ex- boy hardly will either. Got it?"

She nodded slightly, her soft grin one of relief and gratitude.

"Okay, well... I have to get to class." He stood up straighter, giving her one last smile before he walked down the hallway, ignoring everyone around him.

"Well, look who's decided to show the school what incest is all about."

Catherine stared incredulously at Chelsea, who was now standing beside her. With Taylor on one side and Laura on the other, she certainly seemed to be filling the recently vacated Queen Bee spot that Catherine had once held.

"Aw, can't speak without lover boy standing beside you?"

Catherine raised an eyebrow before she took a step towards Chelsea, one that the other girl hadn't expected her to take. "Wow," she said as she looked her former friend up and down, "you really suck at biology, don't you? Or is it just the English language you haven't quite mastered? Perhaps it's both."

Chelsea's eyes widened, but before she could snap back with her own reply, Catherine continued.

"It's called a dictionary, genius. Before you throw around big words that you obviously don't know the definition to, perhaps you might try looking it up first."

And with a toss of her hair, Catherine turned on her heels and made her way to her first class.

"Did you hear about Homecoming? About how Mitch caught them in a hallway?"

That was the latest whispered rumor as Catherine gathered her fruit and milk for lunch, preparing to eat it alone while the others stared at her. It would be no different than her classes that whole morning, or what she was sure to endure that afternoon. Even with the brisk temperatures outside, she preferred to sit on a bench in the courtyard rather than in the lunchroom where even more pairs of eyes would be on her.

"This seat taken?"

She jumped slightly and glanced over her shoulder at Brody, who was grinning down at her. Without waiting for an invitation or an answer to his question, he sat beside her.

"Is that all you're eating?" He gestured to her fruit and milk, his eyebrows raised.

"It's the usual." She sighed as she stared down at it. "Not that I don't wish it would manifest itself into a big greasy cheeseburger, but I'm going to get fat enough as it is."

He laughed then, and she felt her tension melting away. "Hey, heard the latest rumor?"

"I think I've heard them all this morning." She turned her apple over in her hand a couple of times. "He's doing everything he can before people actually find out, isn't he?"

"Yeah, well, he's an asshole, so…" Brody's voice trailed off as he opened up his bag of chips and set it down between them. "Grease and salt, m'lady."

She laughed softly. "You're such a..."

"A jerk?" he teased. "C'mon, say it. It's been so long, and you know it makes me hot."

"I thought white sheet dresses and honey bun hair did that."

Several passersby looked over as Brody threw his head back in laughter. "Oh, right, right... that, too."

She took a chip from the bag, her mouth watering before she even took a bite. The second chip tasted even better than the first, and after the third she was sure she'd died and gone to heaven.

Which, again, she would definitely blame on the imbalanced hormones.

"Hey," she said, and he looked over at her with his eyebrows raised, "what about... you know." She gestured towards the tree, where Bethany was being consoled in an overly dramatic way.

"What about her?"

"Her father? Frank? Client? Did you forget that part?"

Brody shrugged as he took the apple from her outstretched hand. His eyes held hers, spreading warmth throughout her entire body. "To hell with him."

"Brody—"

"Huh uh." He shook his head, stopping her from continuing. "To hell with him. To hell with all of them. Got it?"

One corner of her mouth twitched up in a half-smile. "Got it."

"Now..." He stretched out, grinning over at her as he did so, her body's reaction reminding her of the girls at the mall nearly swooning when he'd walked out of the restroom there.

In the same clothes he was wearing today.

"...about this whole fruit and milk only thing, you've got going... not good, Cat. Not good. If I have to sic Greta on you and make her pack you a healthy lunch, I will."

She rolled her eyes as she ate another chip. "Whatever."

"Whatever? Did you just whatever me?" He grinned over at her as he tossed the apple into the air, catching it without even looking. "Don't be such a jerk."

"Jerk?" She scoffed mockingly and rolled her eyes at him. "Is that the best you can do?" When she nudged him, perhaps she did so a little too roughly, forgetting until he winced that his side had been injured.

Because of her.

"Brody, I'm sorry," she said quickly as she turned towards him, her eyes wide as she reached out, her fingertips again brushing his side. She pulled away as someone sneered at them, telling them to get a room.

As if something this innocent would possibly warrant that kind of reaction.

Catherine's face reddened as she began to gather her things, murmuring her apologies to Brody as she did. She only stopped when he placed his hand on her arm, his thumb discreetly caressing her through her sweater.

"What did I just say to you, Cat?" He was so close to her that she could see the dark ring of blue around the lighter blue of his eyes, so close that his dark, thick eyelashes mesmerized her.

"Huh?"

His smile was soft, inviting as his touch alone seemed to calm her. "What did I say to you, Cat? About them?"

Her eyes wide as she fought the urge to lean into him in front of everyone there. "To hell with them," she finally said.

"Exactly." He sat back slightly, his lopsided grin showing off his dimple she wanted to trace with her fingertips. "Now repeat it one last time."

She laughed and rolled her eyes, not quite sure if she wanted to thank him or throttle him. But this time, when she said the words, they held a conviction to them that carried her throughout the rest of her day.

"To hell with them."

CHAPTER 37

Happy Birthday, Princess

Catherine stared down at the screen on her phone, where she noticed she'd missed a call from her father. It had been almost two weeks since she'd returned to school, and those two weeks were equal parts hell and...well, not quite so much hell. School had been horrid in its own way, with the sneers of the upper echelon of students along with the almost giddiness of those who she had once deemed beneath her. Everyone seemed to go out of their way to be cruel to her, and never once—aside from her confrontation with Chelsea—did she ever fight back.

What was the point?

But with every passing day, no matter that she was nearly feeling back to her old self physically, she knew that time was running out for certain options. Was she avoiding them simply because it was something she just couldn't do? Or was it because she was so afraid of the consequences, of the reaction from her parents?

Would they even notice the change in her?

No, she knew better. She knew her father would comment at least on her absence from his life, even though he was rather busy creating an entirely different world for himself. But Theresa… she was far too narcissistic to notice on her own, at least until Catherine was visibly showing signs of pregnancy. Then she was certain to be sent away, far away so that no one would know that Theresa's daughter had gotten knocked up.

With a heavy sigh, she almost put her phone away, until a ping alerted her to a text message.

Happy birthday, Princess.

Her lower lip trembled as she traced the words from her father with her fingertips. She almost huffed out a laugh that he'd finally resigned himself to text after resisting it for so long, but the grim reminder that he was probably the only person she'd hear that from today settled heavily upon her shoulders. Her grandfather had shown up the night before with a hefty sum of cash for her, one that she stashed away for things she was sure to need in the coming months should she choose to keep her baby.

Or maybe she could use it towards the unthinkable.

She shuddered before she typed back a quick reply, thanking her father for his birthday wishes. She wasn't quite sure what she would say to him when they finally did talk, but didn't have the time to think about it that morning.

She grabbed her bag and coat, noting it was time to go to her own private hell known as school. She had driven Brody every day since she'd been back, every day letting him choose the music and the subject content of any conversation they may have. She wished just once she could tell him that she'd found his mother, but after the latest barrage of unsolicited rude and hateful comments, she decided to deactivate her Facebook account. She didn't know if his mother would ever see her message, didn't know if she would ever rescue her children from the monster that enjoyed his power over them far too much.

And Catherine didn't know if she had it in her to leave them here to fend for themselves without her help.

"No breakfast?"

That was how Brody greeted her that morning as he met her by the front door. She pulled the door open without answering, not even able to conjure up a smile for the one person who could make her smile so easily.

As she walked towards her car, she paused and glanced around. The long, winding driveway looked a bit... empty. Frank's car was gone, her mother's had been sent to the repair shop, and Brody's...

She looked over at Brody, who was digging something out of his backpack. "Where's your car?"

"Hmm?" He glanced up, his eyebrows disappearing beneath his bangs. His expression was so endearing she almost did smile.

Just almost.

"Your car?" She gestured towards the empty spot, which had evidence of an oil leak from the vehicle that used to sit there. "Where is it?"

"Oh, uh..." Brody shrugged as he opened the passenger door of Catherine's Mustang. "Gone."

Her eyebrow was raised as she slid into the driver's seat and set her bag in the back. "Just like that? Gone?" She started the engine, Brody's favorite radio station filling the otherwise silent air between them. She didn't change the station, but turned the volume down as she waited for his response.

"Yeah, well, I couldn't get it to run." He pulled something from his bag before he placed it in the back alongside hers. "So I sold it to someone who could."

She scoffed slightly. "Someone actually bought that thing?"

"Yep, for five hundred bucks. Here."

They were stopped at the end of the winding driveway, and Catherine glanced over to see him holding out a wrapped snack cake. She stared at it for a moment as her eyes began to sting.

"It isn't much, because I can't cook, but…" He shook it slightly, letting her know that it was hers to take. "Happy birthday."

The cellophane crinkled beneath her fingertips as she took it from him, her voice soft as she thanked him before she placed it on top of her bag in the back. She swallowed over the lump in her throat, unable to form words, and continued driving them towards the school.

"Ty and Sammi have a card for you," he continued on. "But it's supposed to be a secret, so act surprised."

She nodded, the muscles in her hands aching from how tightly she was gripping the wheel. "So, um…" She cleared her throat and licked her suddenly dry lips. "What do you plan on doing with the money?"

"Not sure." She heard him sigh but didn't look over at him. "It's a lot less than what I paid for it, obviously. I can't exactly get a job to get more money."

She almost asked him why not, but stopped herself in time. She knew why he didn't get a job; he didn't want to leave Tyler and Sam with Frank, without him. "So, you had a job before?" she asked instead.

"Huh uh. I sold my camera."

"Wow." She blinked a couple of times. "That must have been some camera."

"It was." She could almost hear his smile, but still didn't look over at him. "You should have seen the pictures I took with it, Cat, the way I could filter the light, the way… the way I could see the world."

"How do you see the world?"

"Through my eyes, it's not a pretty place." In her peripheral vision, she could see him picking at a string on his pants. "But… but when I can capture… like Sammi, if I could get a picture of her face at just that moment, when she's hit one of the moves you've shown her… or Tyler, when he catches a ball he never thought he could…"

He was quiet for a moment, and when she pulled up to a stop sign, she finally gave in and looked in his direction. He was staring out the window at the nearly barren trees, their branches swaying with the wind. "The world through other people's eyes can be just as dark as yours is." The words came from her, but she was unsure why she said them. When he nodded once, acknowledging her answer, she returned her eyes to the road and continued forward.

"Sometimes, though…" She wasn't expecting him to speak, so she jumped slightly, tensing when his hand rested on her arm, as if to calm her. "Sometimes you can see the hope, the peace." He removed his hand, and she immediately missed its presence. "The light."

"So, it wasn't always baseball then?" She turned into the school's parking lot, almost wishing that the conversation wasn't close to coming to an end.

"Of course it was. It's just… well, photography is… well, it was…"

She pulled into a spot and turned the car off before she looked over at him. "Your escape?"

He scratched the back of his head absentmindedly as his eyes narrowed, his focus on nothing in particular. "Kind of?"

"A passion?"

One corner of his lips turned up in a grin at her question.

"Photography is… my gymnastics."

"So, it's here." Without thinking, she reached forward, placing her hand on his chest, over his beating heart.

And just like his, hers began to pound even faster.

He covered her hand with his, his eyes scanning her face as he did. "Exactly." One corner of his mouth lifted in another grin as he laced their fingers together, pulling her hand from his chest and resting it between them. "Now about that cupcake,"

"That's hardly a cupcake."

He reached back with his free hand, the cellophane package crinkling in protest as he grabbed his present for her. "All of this chocolatey goodness and you're saying it's not a cupcake?" He shook it slightly, his smile even showing in his eyes, causing her to smile as well. "You can't tell me you're rejecting my birthday present to you."

And her smile fell.

"I never got you anything for yours."

His smile wavered for a moment before he recovered and squeezed her hand. "Of course you did." When her eyes narrowed as she thought of a reply, he continued. "You stopped me from needing stitches."

"I…" She had started to ask what he was talking about, but then…

Then she remembered.

She remembered seeing his head slamming against the mirror, which splintered.

She remembered the blood splattering.

She remembered him dropping to the floor.

"Hey…" He let go of her hand and placed his fingers beneath her chin, lifting it until she met his gaze.

"That was… *oh,* that *was* your birthday."

It was his turn to look confused, reminding her that she only knew his birthday due to her snooping into his past. Before he could inquire, she sat up a bit straighter, taking the cupcake from his hand.

"Split this with me?" she asked quickly. "Since I didn't get you anything for your birthday."

"I already told you—"

"Hey, you're the one that insisted it was 'chocolatey goodness'," she said as she opened the package.

"It is."

"Then here." She split the snack cake in two and held one half of it out for him. "Go on, you know you want it."

He mock-gasped as he took it from her. "Geez, Cat, really?"

Her face burned with embarrassment as she realized the crudeness of his joke, but she laughed anyway.

And it felt good.

It felt right.

"You know…" He wiped his mouth with his sleeve, in case there were any residual chocolate crumbs. "…a few weeks ago, you would have totally called me a jerk for that one."

She smirked at him, her eyebrow raised. "Totally?"

He motioned between the two of them, a smirk of his own touching his lips. "This is the part where if I was a total dick… oh, I meant jerk—"

"Of course."

"—I would wink at you or something equally as douche-like and say 'totally'. But since I'm not…" His voice trailed off as he opened the door, her laughter spilling out into the parking lot. "C'mon, birthday girl, before we're late."

She shrugged off her inner voice telling her to run, run like hell, and with another laugh joined Brody as he walked towards the front doors of Davis High.

She should have known that something was up, that something wasn't quite right. Even when she would ignore her feelings, her intuition, it had always been right.

She had blamed her stomach cramping on that half of a chocolate snack cake that she'd shared with Brody in her car.

She had told Brody at lunch that she was fine, in spite of being pale, in spite of sweating, in spite of wanting to curl up until the pain went away.

But when she felt a familiar trickle as she sat down in her car to drive Brody home, she knew.

"Brody." Her eyes wide, her face pale, she stared at him as she felt her tears well up. The alarm in his face confirmed she must have looked as bad as she felt.

"You need me to drive?" he asked, and she was out the door without even nodding in approval. She rushed to the passenger side as quickly as she could, her adrenaline kicking in and deadening the pain. Brody was hanging up her phone as she placed her coat over her seat before sitting down, choking back a sob as she did.

And another.

And another.

Until she let her tears fall while Brody drove her to the ER, letting her know that Greta would meet them there.

With Greta in the waiting room, Brody back at home with his brother and sister, her mother out at some function with Frank, her father over an hour away in his new home with his new life, she sat alone behind the curtain in the emergency room.

Where the attending physician coldly told her that she had lost her baby.

On her birthday.

The nurse was equally as distant as she explained follow up procedures with her own physician, along with the recommendation for birth control. If Catherine were to judge by her condescending tone, she would guess that the nurse felt it was better off for that baby to not be brought into this world, to be cared for by her.

With shaking hands, she dressed herself in the clean outfit that Greta had brought with her. When they pulled up in front of the big house on the hill, Frank's car was still missing. That didn't stop Catherine from pulling her sleeve down to hide the identification bracelet from the hospital before her housekeeper—the one she'd dismissed so often—dropped her off at home with a sympathetic pat on her knee.

Without a word, without looking around her, without regard for anything or anyone else, Catherine walked into that house, turning towards the right instead of the left, walking down the stairs into the basement.

Into Brody's waiting arms.

And she let him hold her as she cried.

CHAPTER 38

Pink

"I'm being punished, you know?" Catherine sniffled slightly, not protesting as Brody adjusted their positions on the couch so that her head rested on his shoulder.

"You don't honestly believe that, do you?"

His voice resonated through her, comforting her even through her crushing grief. She shifted, lifting her head to look up at him through her tear-dampened lashes. "Why else would this be happening? And please… please don't say something about 'meant to be', because I think that's just… well, it's a copout." Even through her grief, when she could see just a hint of his dimple when he gave her his half-grin, her stomach took a dive.

"No copouts, got it." He was playing with the edges of her hair, perhaps without realizing he was doing so, and kept his gaze locked with hers. "You were going through with it, then? With having the baby?"

She huffed out a sigh as she turned, placing her head back on his chest so he couldn't see the fresh tears brimming. "I don't know. I never got the chance to make that decision."

While her statement was true in a way, she knew it wasn't

entirely accurate. She'd been browsing through websites, tracking her unborn child's progress, reading through chat rooms of others who were close to her due date. She'd told herself it was strictly for research, even as her heart hurt for the mothers who one by one would announce their pregnancies hadn't 'stuck'.

Now she was among them.

"Hey, Cat?"

She sniffled quietly, hoping he wouldn't notice. "Yeah?"

"You would have been a great mom."

She squeezed her eyes tightly and bit the inside of her lip, unable to thank him at that moment.

"And some day it will happen, you know?"

Her frown deepened, fresh tears again threatening to fall. "You mean when I'm not in high school. And when I'm not with some guy who's just..."

"A jerk?"

Catherine smiled at Brody's teasing tone. "That word's too nice for him."

A silence fell over the room, and she found herself listening to Brody's heart beating steadily beneath her ear. She inhaled deeply, recognizing the distinct scent of him, one that she now associated with feelings of warmth, security, and an unmistakable hint of... extreme like? She didn't know how else to pinpoint it. There was no heavy cologne as Mitch had worn, no abundance of sweat like some of the other boys at school. Instead she could smell a hint of his body wash, the clean scent that was distinctly him.

And she liked it a little too much.

Until he ruined the moment by asking one simple question. "When are you going to tell Mitch?"

She sat up, wrapping her arms around herself as she did, and looked over at Brody. "Why should I tell him anything?"

His gaze never wavered from hers as he answered. "Because it's the right thing to do."

She raised her eyebrows and blinked several times, trying to form a decent, witty comeback. When one didn't cross her mind, she countered with, "So?"

His dimple appeared again. "Even though he's a jerk,"

"That's putting it mildly."

"He still needs to know."

Her eyes narrowed as she again racked her brain for some reason why she shouldn't. "Maybe I just want to see him suffer for a little bit."

"Cat—"

"All right, all right, I am going to tell him." She sunk back, her arms still crossed, her bottom lip still pouting. "Couldn't you at least let me pretend for five seconds that I wasn't going to?"

She thought for a moment she heard him chuckling. "Maybe I like getting you riled up."

She let out a half-snort. "Most people avoid it at all costs."

"Well, I'm not most people."

It was her turn to smile, even if it was only a fraction of one. "Good." She uncrossed her arms, her hands falling to her sides. The move was innocent enough, but left her fingertips brushing his.

Neither of them pulled away.

"I'm sorry your birthday ended up sucking."

She almost laughed but was afraid with her volatile emotions she would end up crying. "I guess both of ours sucked this year."

"Kind of?"

She turned her face in his direction, one eyebrow raised. "Kind of?" He didn't reply, and she nudged him. "What do you mean kind of?"

"You know." He glanced over at her, his expression a little playful, a lot shy. "Kind of."

Her own expression softened as the meaning behind his words sunk in. So much had changed that night, not only her perception of the world as she knew it, but the dynamic between the two of them. That night had been the beginning of this, of them, of their bond that she was certain was her only saving grace of the moment.

"Do you want me with you?"

She blinked a couple of times as her mind registered his words, but not the meaning behind them. "I'm sorry?"

"When you tell Mitch."

She turned her face away to hide the blush that she could feel creeping into her cheeks. "No, that isn't necessary. But thank you," she added. She felt his pinky finger lock around hers for a brief moment before he pulled away.

"If you're sure."

She nodded once, still not facing him. "I know you think I won't tell him."

"I didn't say that."

"You didn't have to." She inhaled deeply before she continued. "But I will tell him. Eventually. You know, because it's the right thing to do."

"Of course."

She nudged him again, this time a little harder. "I mean it."

When he was silent for a beat longer than she was comfortable with, she turned her gaze towards him once more. Her breath caught in her throat as she was met with Brody's intense stare, his blue eyes causing her heart to falter momentarily before it began to race.

They remained silent, even as their breaths fell into unison, even as their shoulders brushed, their fingertips barely touching between them. She watched as he swallowed, feeling her own throat clench, her chest ache, her stomach turn over. And when his eyes fell to her lips, they suddenly felt dry, cold. For a moment—one that stretched on and yet ended too soon—she was sure he was going to close that distance, kiss her the way she wanted.

Until she realized… that was what she wanted.

She pulled back just as they heard the door close one floor above. Her eyes widened in panic at the sound of Frank's voice, though she didn't pay attention to what he was saying. One silent nod from Brody had her scrambling for the shadows, just in case he came down the stairs. Closing her eyes tightly, she listened to every footstep, every creak, every hum, her entire body—though tired and sore—ready to run.

Or fight.

She jumped as she heard a distant door slam and opened her eyes to the now-darkened basement. Still afraid to speak, she waited in silence for her eyes to adjust to the dim lighting. After a couple of minutes, she could see just the outline of Brody's form lying on the couch, without having pulled the bed out.

"It's okay." His voice was a whisper, one that she could still hear in the deafening silence that now surrounded them.

She didn't answer him, didn't even wave in his direction before she stealthily made her way up the stairs to the main floor of the house, her heart still beating at an uncomfortable pace. After getting a glass of water from the kitchen—a reminder that she needed to replace the bottled water in her room—she made her way up to her room. Out of habit, she checked her door knob before retrieving her keys from her pocket, only this evening she noticed that it hadn't been locked. She shook her head once as she entered her room, hoping soon to regain control of her memory so she would quit making such careless mistakes.

Four days had passed, and with each one Catherine felt physically stronger than the last. She was remembering more, ensuring her door was locked when it needed to be, paying attention to subtle changes in Theresa and Frank's moods. She was doing this more so with Frank, of course, as Theresa would chase her mother's helper with her cocktail the moment she returned home from whatever function her appearance was required at. The relative quietness of Frank, however, was a welcome reprieve from his usual rants and bursts of rage. Even the younger children were beginning to relax more, at least when Frank escorted Theresa to whatever meeting or function she had going on in the evening. Catherine could only imagine what would happen if Theresa had been forced to drive herself.

Without the burden of wondering what she was going to do, who she was going to tell, school became much less stressful for Catherine, also. That didn't mean there were any fewer whispers, stares, or any less blatant disregard for her; it simply meant she was free from worrying about giving them any more gossip fodder than they'd already accumulated. The rumor mill was alive and well, as always, and the fact that Brody rode to school with her and ate lunch by her side every day only fanned the flames. She was sure, though, that soon some other crisis or great story would come along, freeing her from such intense scrutiny.

She was running a bit behind that afternoon, having convinced her guidance counselor that all was well, and she certainly saw no reason to speak to anyone about her personal life.

Late pass in hand, she walked swiftly towards her locker to retrieve her book for her next class, one that had started nearly ten minutes before.

"You won't get away with it, you know."

She jumped at the sound of Mitch's voice behind her, glancing over her shoulder on reflex only. She rolled her eyes and continued spinning the combination. "Get away with what?"

"Telling everyone it's mine. I know that's what you told that trash you've hooked up with."

She stiffened involuntarily, her anger roused by Mitch's words.

"I'm certainly not going around telling people you're knocked up, but—"

"*Was*, Mitch." Her book in hand, she slammed her locker door shut before she turned in his direction. "Was. Of course you wouldn't tell anyone, because we both know that child was yours. And now that my baby is dead, that gets you off the hook."

"At least you—"

"I said my baby was dead," she cut him off, taking a step forward. "I didn't say I was the one that killed it. So, again… you're off the hook, and I can resume my life as well starting with forgetting about any supposed feelings I may have lied to myself about having for someone like you."

What looked similar to a sneer crossed Mitch's face for the briefest moment before he muttered some incoherent reply and walked off, leaving Catherine alone in the middle of the hallway.

And she smiled.

Her smile continued throughout the day as she aced a test, ignored Bethany's dirty looks, and walked with her head held high as she approached her custom painted Mustang, where Brody awaited her arrival.

And as the sun hit her vehicle just right, she stopped.

She covered her mouth before she let out her first laugh, which was quickly followed by another, until she stood there in the parking lot, people eying her strangely, and Brody approaching her giggling form with caution.

"Are you all right there?"

With her hand still over her mouth and tears forming in the corners of her eyes, she could only nod. The look of concern on Brody's face faded as he realized that she was, most definitely, amused by something.

He began looking around, looking down at his clothing, wiping his face, trying to decipher what now had Catherine doubled over with infectious laughter. "You mind telling me what we're laughing about?" he asked, chuckling now himself.

She could only point at her car. "Look!"

"What?" He squinted. "Did a bird shit on it or something—ow! That didn't warrant you elbowing me, you know."

"Just look." She gestured in her vehicle's direction even as she gathered her bearings and began walking towards it.

"Looking." Brody was beside her, walking back in the direction he'd come from. "Still don't get it."

"Brody." She stopped beside it and placed her bag down, gesturing at her vehicle with both hands. "Look at it!"

His eyes looked over her vehicle, then back over to her. He shrugged once, letting her know he was apparently still clueless over what she found so hilarious that afternoon. "Are your hormones still out of… I'm moving away from you before you hit me again."

She was still grinning, still giggling as she unlocked and opened her door. "Brody," she said, and he glanced at her from across the hood. "It's pink."

His expression deadpanned, which caused her to laugh even harder even as they slid into their seats. "You're just now noticing this, Cat?"

Her eyes were sparkling, her cheeks aching from smiling as she looked over at him. "Shut up," was all she said.

And they both continued smiling all the way home.

CHAPTER 39

He Shouldn't Have To

The sun had already set while Catherine had been finishing up her homework. One glance at the clock let her know it was just after 8, and she shook her head in wonder. Where had time gone? Hadn't it just been summer, where the sun would have still been hanging on to its last bits of life for the day? For that matter, hadn't she just woken up and faced her dreaded adversaries at school, counting down the hours until they were no longer scrutinizing her every move?

With a sigh, she put her books in her designer bag, overlooking the small tear in it that would have sent her straight to the mall to get a new one just months before. With Frank and Theresa being home, she would be relegated to staying in her room for the evening, just as the other children opted to stay out of sight. Life would remain relatively quiet if they all did so, walking on proverbial egg shells as to not set off Frank's temper.

This also meant that Catherine would have to forgo her near-nightly excursions down two flights of stairs to the basement, where Brody would most likely be reading. There would be no retreating to the shadows, no whispered questions and answers, no sitting in silence enjoying the comfort the other's presence brings. Instead, they would be holed up in their respective rooms, awaiting the next event that would drag Theresa away, who would always take Frank with her.

"Maybe Mother should slip him some of her pills," Catherine muttered while she pulled out her pajamas. "Maybe I should." There was no need to stay dressed, no need to keep her makeup on, no need to be 'appearance ready' as she had been. With a sigh, she recalled the first night that Frank and his children had been at the house. She had been so self-absorbed, so angry, so bitter that she'd been downright rude to each of them. But then again, that's the way she had been with everyone in her life, without caring whether or not her actions hurt anyone else.

She stared at the door that she'd slammed so many times she was unsure how it had stayed on its hinges. Then again, any damage she may have inflicted on that door would have been repaired right away, at any cost, just as she had demanded about everything in her life.

The way that Frank did with his children.

That chilling revelation caused her to pause, to stare at that door as if it would magically open and show her a new life on the other side.

Instead, she was snapped out of her internal reflection by a loud bang resonating from the floor below, which was quickly followed up by the excited shouts of children, the pounding of feet on the stairs.

And Frank.

Always Frank.

His bellow could probably be heard clear down at the bottom of the hill, far away from where the 'perfect house' stood. "What the hell is going on?"

Unwilling to allow Brody, Tyler, or Sam to endure Frank's wrath, she quickly opened her door and followed the excited shouts to the entryway of the home, ready to step in with any threat she could think of. She was sure she'd come up with the perfect warning to remind him of his place, at least where she and her grandfather were concerned.

Threaten him with money, or the lack thereof.

Threaten him with his place in this house he so obviously coveted.

She counted down the many ways she could do so as she bounded down the steps towards whatever was causing the commotion. What could anyone have possibly done to illicit such a loud, angry response from him? Then again, when had anything they'd done warranted his reaction? All she would need to do was get down there, get into his line of vision, drop her grandfather's name, and pray it would do the trick.

Until she saw what the commotion was all about.

She stopped, her hands on the railing, her mouth slightly opened as she witnessed a frail woman embracing Tyler and Sam, her dark head bowed as she left kisses on their tear-dampened cheeks and whispered words meant for their ears only. There was no questioning who this woman was, even if she barely resembled the pictures Catherine had seen of her online.

Their mother had come for them.

"Leave."

That one word from Frank was spoken with so much force even Catherine took a step back, watching from the shadows as the woman raised her eyes in his direction. In spite of the fear, in spite of her trembling lower lip, Catherine knew the resolve and bravery this woman had to have to stand there still, her arms around her youngest children.

"I can take care of them," she said, her voice shaking. Had Catherine not been so shocked by her presence she may have intervened, spoken up. Their mother had to know she had to speak with much more power in her voice to stand up to the likes of Frank Harris. Judging by the few events Catherine knew of, their mother had tried before.

And failed.

"I've come to take them with me."

Sandra... wasn't that her name? Catherine couldn't quite recall, even though she'd sent the Facebook message.

"The Facebook message." Catherine whispered those words, then closed her eyes and winced. She hadn't even bothered to reactivate her account, having long given up that their mother would ever see the message. Still, Catherine stood in the shadows, shaking her head so slightly that the children's mother couldn't have seen it. Even she knew this wasn't the way to stand up to the monster known as Frank Harris; she would have to be forceful, demanding. She would need to...

"Mom?"

Brody's broken voice caused Catherine's chest to constrict, to ache in a way that nearly brought her to her knees. She brought her hand to her chest, rubbing it as if she could stop her heart from hurting. From the shadows she watched as he walked slowly towards his mother—the woman who could save him from the hell he was living in.

"Go on." Frank gave Brody's shoulder a shove, pushing him towards his mother. Brody caught himself before he stumbled, but he reached out just the same, withdrawing slightly when he finally touched his mother's shoulder.

As if he was afraid he'd been imagining her standing there.

"She's here to take you."

Catherine covered her mouth to stifle her gasp, silently cursing the unshed tears that stung beneath her eyelids. She was torn, so very torn, wishing he would say yes.

And knowing that he wouldn't.

He couldn't.

Tyler and Sam were cheering, jumping up and down, chattering excitedly about getting their things. Their joy was palpable, forcing a small but inaudible sob to escape from Catherine's lips. Her eyes once again rested on Brody, who remained still, stiffened, as if he knew exactly what Frank's next words would be.

"Not them. Just him."

She could see Brody swallow hard, see how he set his jaw to keep from lashing out.

Just as she could see their mother's resolve begin to crack.

"Frank, please."

"Take the bastard," Frank cut her off. "But they stay."

The silence that followed was punctuated only by Sam's tiny sobs as their reality came back to them. And while Sandra pleaded to the man who must only be doing this out of spite, Catherine's eyes stayed on Brody.

His eyes were closed, his breathing deep and slow, his jaw and fists clenched. She couldn't comprehend what must have been going through his head at the time. Sure, he could leave; he could get out of this hell, never have to watch his back, never have to worry about when Frank would strike next. He could play baseball this spring, go out with his friends, have a normal life without that monster breathing down his neck.

But he would have to leave Tyler and Sam behind.

Tyler and Sam, whom he loved dearly… who would have to face Frank alone.

"It's okay," Tyler said to Brody, squaring his shoulders as he looked up at his big brother. "You can go."

Just as Catherine knew he would, Brody shook his head 'no'.

Was that fear, pity, or relief that Catherine felt as Brody insisted to his mother that he would stay? She couldn't quite tell. All she knew was she couldn't continue to watch another moment, couldn't stay eavesdropping on something that was causing her own heart to ache. She turned and silently made her way back up the stairs and to her room, pausing only when she heard her mother's door open.

"What's going on out there?" Theresa's words were slurred, and Catherine leveled her narrowed eyes in her mother's direction.

"Their mother came for them."

"Oh?"

Catherine's eyes widened for a moment at her mother's nonchalant response and bit back her acidic reply, choosing to quietly go into her own room instead. There, in private, she began pacing back and forth, running her fingers through her already disheveled hair, trying to think of something, anything, she could do to help. But she'd already done that, hadn't she? She'd sent a message to Sandra, she'd let their mother know where they could be found in case she hadn't known already.

And for what?

For nothing, apparently, as she heard Tyler trying to console a still-sobbing Sam when they finally made their way back upstairs. Catherine sat on her bed with a huff, crossing her arms and chewing on the inside of her lip. Why had Frank not let them go? She'd done enough research—because it was definitely research and not spying—to know that he hadn't come from money, and that if Sandra had any, it was hidden away from the public eye.

What was it then?

Did it make Frank feel like a badass when he had so much power over…

Her eyes widened as she realized she only heard the children.

Not Frank.

Not Brody.

"Oh no…" The words were barely a whisper as she stood, her heart pounding in her chest. If Frank had gone after Brody, accusing him of telling his mother where to find him…

She took a couple of deep cleansing breaths before she opened her door as silently as possible. The hallway was darkened, the chattering of the children ceased, and their doors closed. One glance over her shoulder let her know that the door to Theresa and Frank's room was closed as well. As long as she remained as stealthy as she knew she was capable of, she could make it down the stairs without detection. She'd been able to do it this long, hadn't she?

But it shouldn't be silent. It was still fairly early, and she hadn't heard Frank's retreat to his room.

The fear threatened to consume her as her imagination began working overdrive, each scenario making her take her footsteps more quickly than the last. She would find them, tell Frank she was the one who'd sent the message, deal with whatever consequences on her own.

Moonlight peered through the parted curtains in the entry way, silhouetting a lone figure standing beside the window. Catherine paused as her eyes adjusted to the lighting, as she realized it was Brody standing before her, his forehead pressed against the glass, his eyes cast downward. His right hand let go of the curtain and raised slowly to the glass, his fingertips grazing the molding around the window as his shoulders began to shake.

"Brody?" Catherine didn't dare speak above a whisper, as she had no idea where Frank was. If Brody heard her, he didn't acknowledge it. His shoulders sank and curled inward as his quiet sobs continued to consume him. Not wasting any more time, Catherine closed the space between them, meaning to let him know she was here for him.

Just as he'd been there for her.

She gently placed her hand on his shoulder, her fingertips brushing his soft, dark hair. Was that a shiver or another sob that passed through him? She couldn't tell. All she knew was the way her stomach dipped when he leaned his head towards her hand, and she turned it palm up, cradling the side of his tear-dampened face. As another tear fell, she wiped it away with her thumb, and her eyes could finally see the pain etched in his features.

"Oh god, Cat," he managed to say before turning to her, pulling her to him, burying his face in the crook of her neck.

And he cried.

He cried tears of grief, tears of pain, tears of longing for all the lost moments he should have had. She knew he cried over his mother, but he had to be crying for himself as well. He was 17, just a boy, forced to care for and raise his brother and sister, forced to hide from the monster that should be protecting them all, beaten to submission, left bleeding on the floor so many times…

But any time was one too many.

Catherine held him to her, her hands stealing through his soft hair of their own volition as she whispered her apologies over and over.

He shouldn't have to go through this.

He shouldn't have to be afraid.

She shouldn't have contacted his mother, causing even more

pain to come to him.

"I'm so sorry."

"You didn't do this," he whispered in return, and she felt him leave a kiss in her hair before he shook his head. "Cat, you didn't do this."

But she had.

She had.

His movements were subtle, each one eliciting another response from deep within her.

His hands dropping to her waist made her inhale sharply.

The scruff from the small amount of unshaved stubble on his face brought chills to the surface of her skin as he brushed his damp cheek against hers before stopping, forehead to forehead.

His eyes—the pain, the intensity, the emotion she just didn't comprehend—held her captive in the small stream of moonlight that surrounded them.

His shortened breaths that fell across her face caused her breathing to match his own.

His lips, mere centimeters from hers, erased the thoughts of impropriety, replacing them with the shock, the acceptance that what she wanted right at that moment was for him to kiss her.

Did his lips brush hers?

The sensation was so brief, so soft, causing her to inhale sharply through parted lips.

And she watched as his gaze dropped to her lips and stayed there.

She felt his fingertips dig into the flesh above her waistline when she licked her lips, not realizing she'd done so until after.

He was going to kiss her; she was sure of it.

Until the clicking of a shutting door one floor above cut through the silence, breaking them from their spell, causing him to blink his eyes and raise them to hers.

But he didn't back away.

"Go to your room, Cat," he whispered, the sound of her nickname making her shiver in his arms.

"I'm sorry."

He pulled back slightly and shook his head. "You didn't do anything."

Of course he would say that; he didn't know.

"Brody, I…"

He covered her lips with one finger, indicating with his head that he heard more movement upstairs. He withdrew from her, his eyes locked with hers as long as he could before he turned and made his way down the other flight of stairs, to the basement below.

The same basement she knew she'd be visiting as soon as she could.

She touched her lips gingerly, still feeling the ghost of a kiss she was now sure he'd left there, along with one lone tear drop that had fallen.

Had that come from his eyes, or hers?

Without taking the time to decipher what had just passed between them, she retreated once more to her room, where she would wait for the stirring down the hall to subside. She closed her eyes for one brief moment, the heaviness in her chest overwhelming her, consuming her just as much as his grief had so obviously consumed him.

She'd meant to stay awake, meant to go back down the stairs when she was sure the coast was clear. Instead, she opened her eyes to her alarm the next morning, indicating another school day.

And when she went downstairs to drive herself and Brody to school, he was already gone.

CHAPTER 40

The Same Way

The last thing Catherine expected was for Brody to take his usual seat beside her at lunch. They were still on the bench outside, in spite of the cold weather and impending snowfall. He handed her a banana, which she accepted without a single word passing between them, only the stirring of the leaves that were scattered on the ground keeping them company. There weren't many other students out in the courtyard that day, aside from those hurrying to get inside and out of the chilled weather. She was hyper-aware of the boy beside her, though, long before he began to speak.

"She wasn't the same, after Brian died."

She glanced over at Brody, who was staring at the stirring leaves, watching the wind whip them up only to set them back down again. They hadn't spoken of his brother much, nor of his home life after his brother's death. He had told her he'd cared for Tyler and Sam, but hadn't gone into any great detail. She hadn't approached the subject since, figuring he would talk about it when he was ready.

And it seemed he was.

"She took it the hardest. Harder than me, even." He let out a short, humorless laugh. "He'd always been there with me. Obviously, you know, being twins. But Mom, she… I guess they really mean it when they say you're never prepared to lose a child. Especially not… like that. Not like that."

Catherine turned towards him, giving him her full attention. It took everything in her to keep from reaching out and taking his hand, but after his abrupt departure that morning she wasn't sure how he would react to it. Instead, she remained silent as he continued his story.

"Frank was even more… Frank back then. Hard to imagine, huh? But Mom was just losing it, and Frank kept pushing, and pushing, and just pushing her, until she broke." Brody took a deep breath, his voice softer than before when he added, "Like he did. Except different, because… because Brian had always been exalted, and Mom was just there. I didn't love her any less, before or after, because there is just… it's better. It's just better."

Although Brody failed to elaborate how or when that had occurred when his mother had attempted to take her own life, she knew the final outcome before he continued on.

"So, Frank, he had her committed." With a sigh, he placed his can of soda to the side, unwanted now. "And that was fine and all, because she needed it. And the divorce thing? That's fine, too. That is more than fine."

The divorce that was happening because of Catherine's mother. Because Frank had found his meal ticket at last and wasn't afraid to throw his former life away. Brody didn't need to say as much, and Catherine didn't need to offer it up either.

"To an extent, anyhow, because there is this slight complication in his plans." Brody was picking at a string in the seam of his jeans, ones that Catherine hadn't recognized. She came to the conclusion he must have taken them from one of his brother's boxes. Her mind suddenly drifted back to that day in the gym, to when Sam told her how Brody would pick at strings in his clothes, too. Nervous habits of a boy forced to grow up far too soon.

And here he was, still having to be the adult.

"Frank's never been big on the fatherly thing, and I would rather he not start. What would happen if one of them pissed Frank off? Without me there, I mean."

"I could help." The sentence was small, simple, and brought the exact reaction she was sure would occur, as Brody was shaking his head before she'd even finished.

"No. No, there's no way." He glanced over for a brief moment, before he turned his eyes away again. "He wouldn't care that you're a girl, Cat. It wouldn't matter. And no offense, but I think I'm a little more equipped at fighting him off."

Her eyebrows jumped involuntarily as she thought of the muscles she'd seen—and felt—in his lean arms. "I am just saying,"

"I'm not going to leave them. Hell, I—" He shoved his hand through his windblown hair, only to have it fall back into his eyes. "I have no idea how she found us. I suppose it wasn't that difficult, but… I don't know where she lives, if she's really okay, how she got there, if she could, you know… take care of us."

Catherine could feel her face growing hot as guilt consumed her. "Did Frank—"

"No." Brody was again picking at the string in the seam of his jeans. "No, he just retreated, probably to scour the internet and see if I'd gone against his demands, and…" His voice trailed off, after leaving another clue why Catherine couldn't find him online. He'd probably been forced to delete his profiles, erase his existence, or at least try to mask it.

"I'm not on, either. Anymore, I mean," she added when he

cast an unreadable look in her direction. "I don't look at Twitter, I deactivated my Facebook. There just wasn't much of a point in it, I suppose." She wasn't sure why she offered the information, or why it mattered when he was finally being so open with her. Before she could retract her statement, or minimalize it, his soft smile caught her off guard erasing her thoughts.

"I rode to school with Bethany this morning."

Catherine's eyes widened a fraction, a flash of jealousy surging through her veins. Quickly ignoring it as much as she could, she tried to sound as nonchalant as possible. "Oh?" She cringed inwardly, hating how much she sounded like her own mother in that moment. "Did you…" She didn't know how to word her question—had he called Bethany? Had he asked for a ride to avoid Catherine?

"She just showed up."

Catherine nodded, inhaling sharply as a gust of wind chilled her to the bone.

Until she felt Brody's hand on her leg.

The heat that coursed through her was sudden, yet no longer unexpected.

"Maybe we should go inside, Cat."

She lifted her eyes to his, felt the gravitational pull towards him that made her pulse race. Her voice was small, breathless when she said, "Are you sure we should?"

His nod was slight but noticeable. "We need to." His eyes were on her lips.

Again.

Even a snide comment from Chelsea as she and Laura passed didn't stop the smile that tugged at the corners of Catherine's mouth. In spite of the threats, in spite of Frank, in spite of everyone in this school she was now 100 percent certain.

Brody felt the same way.

Frank's presence in the home that evening was only part of the cause of Catherine's tension. He'd been on his phone periodically, peering out the windows any time he heard a vehicle in the distance. The younger children hid in their rooms upstairs, Brody was down below in the basement after again adamantly denying he'd contacted their mother, and each moment that passed riled Catherine's ire just a little more.

Why hadn't Frank just let them go?

And Theresa hadn't been much help, in spite of her earlier promise to Catherine that it was only temporary.

Catherine's eyes shot down the hall, to her mother's shut bedroom door. Frank obviously had her mother completely snowed, or kept her well supplied in whatever she needed to not give a damn. There was one thing that Frank kept forgetting, though.

When it came to manipulation, no one was better at it than Catherine Garner.

She took a couple deep breaths, conjuring up her best annoyed look before she marched down that hallway, her hands in fists by her sides. She ignored the tremor in her hand before she knocked, pushing it down before Theresa could see any urgency or nervousness in her demeanor.

She had to play this one just right.

Theresa was dressed impeccably when she opened the door, still on the more-sober side. "What is it, Catherine? I do have somewhere to be soon."

"We need to talk." Catherine crossed her arms and raised her eyebrow in her mother's direction. "And I don't think you want this conversation to take place out here."

Theresa's expression didn't change, bordering on indifference with a hint of boredom, as she stepped back and allowed Catherine to enter her suite. If Catherine had expected this room to have so much as one item out of place, she would have been sorely disappointed. Perhaps her mother didn't wallow away drunk and sloppy behind her closed door; no, perhaps she simply wanted nothing to do with other occupants of the house.

With a sickening lurch, Catherine realized that included herself.

Swallowing the bile that crept into her throat, Catherine turned towards the woman who taught her the great art of being a cold-hearted bitch. "Why are they still here?"

"Frank is—"

"I don't give a damn about what Frank is or isn't," Catherine cut her off, keeping her voice low. The fact that she'd cursed, even a word as slight as it was, had Theresa's attention, just as Catherine knew it would. "You said it was temporary."

It was Theresa's turn to raise an eyebrow. "It is."

"Let me bring you up to speed here, Mother." Catherine took a step forward, ignoring her racing pulse. "Frank isn't the one who cares for those brats; that job belongs to Brody. Brody, the same person who he almost sent packing when their mother showed up."

"It's called teaching responsibility, Catherine. You should try it sometime."

Catherine inhaled sharply, stopping just short of telling her how responsible she'd had to be in the few short months that Frank and his children had lived in their home. "I will not be the one looking after those brats if he sends that boy packing." Which was a lie; she absolutely would. She knew she would guard them with her own life. "So, since you claim it's only temporary, should the opportunity arise again you just may want to stand your ground instead of letting your boyfriend walk all over you."

Theresa's nostrils flared. "He does no such thing."

The short laugh that left Catherine was cold, bitter.

And absolutely genuine.

"Trust me, he does. So, unless you want to be stuck raising two more children that you don't want..." Catherine's voice trailed off as she waited for her mother to disagree.

And luckily, she hadn't expected her to.

"Are you done now?" was all Theresa said. "I have to finish getting ready."

Catherine stepped just a little closer to her mother, her eyes narrowed, meaning her words with everything in her. "Yes, I am done."

She stepped past her mother and opened the door, stomped her way down the hall to her own room where she slammed the door for good measure.

A sad smile touched her lips. The seed was planted, and Theresa would definitely not stand for having to be the one to raise Tyler and Sam. So, if Brody left, Theresa would now make sure the younger children went with him.

She placed a hand over her heart, trying to calm it from beating so fast, even as she contemplated her next move.

She didn't have to contemplate for long.

She knew exactly what to do.

It was just a matter of when.

And a prayer that Brody would forgive her.

CHAPTER 41

Different

With the holidays officially upon them, Theresa's charity schedule was in full swing. Flashing a diamond on her hand that was most obviously bought with Catherine's grandfather's money, Theresa also demanded Frank's presence at said functions. One was on Thanksgiving Day, a day that one would think she'd reserve for her own child even if Frank wouldn't do the same for his. Instead, the children were feasting on leftovers from a large lunch that Greta had prepared before leaving and enjoying a house far less tense than they'd been subjected to.

"I still can't believe he didn't demand that we go with him or some stupid shit like that." Brody once again glanced at the windows as he passed them, his eyes quickly darting away from them when he would see that his mother still hadn't returned.

Catherine's smile was soft and hinted of sadness. "I'm sorry you're not with her today, Brody."

When he turned his blue eyes her way, she welcomed the jolt it gave her, the dip in her stomach. "We'll be with her soon," he said.

And if Catherine had her way, it would be sooner than he

thought.

"I figured you'd be with your dad today." He was walking down the stairs to the basement, and Catherine followed close behind. "With your mom being gone, I mean."

"Well, I was supposed to be with her today. My father made other plans." She shrugged, even though Brody's back was turned and he couldn't see it. "I did promise him I'd go out there tomorrow."

"And you will." Brody peered over his shoulder, one eyebrow raised. "No choosing to stick around here instead."

More than once Catherine had opted out of proposed visits with her father in his new, less-than-stellar home simply because she was too afraid to leave her own. Now, though, with her thoughts and plans, she knew that it was necessary to go see him, to figure if her gut instinct was correct or not. The more her eyes were opened to her surroundings, the more they also opened up to other things.

Her father's consistent questioning of her life, her choices, her well-being.

Her father's struggle to make sure she had everything she needed, and sometimes things she only wanted but could honestly do without.

Her father's hope that she was happy.

And she'd pushed it all aside, ignoring the things he'd done that had annoyed her, for what? The house on the hill? Her wonderful boyfriend? Her social status, and reigning supreme?

Look how well they'd all turned out for her.

"What about your grandfather?" Brody asked as he turned and flopped back on the couch, landing perfectly so that he sat at a comfortable angle. Catherine opted to sit close to him, easing herself onto the cushions as she answered.

"He will probably be at the downtown luncheon with Mother." She tucked her feet over to the side, leaning just a little more Brody's way. "Why, are you trying to get rid of me?"

As if he were acting on autopilot, Brody reached out and lifted a section of Catherine's hair, running his fingers through it, twisting it around a time or two before he tucked it behind her ear. His smile was almost shy when his eyes met hers again. "What are you doing, Cat?"

She lifted one shoulder in a half-shrug. "Just the usual."

He leaned his head to the side, studying her expression. "Which is?"

"Whatever I want to."

His laugh was genuine and infectious, his blue eyes lighting up with his smile. "Now that I can believe." He pulled out the book he'd been reading and shifted slightly until she was tucked up against him. Although he inhaled sharply, he didn't push her away.

"Back to that one, huh?" She eyeballed his worn copy of Catcher in the Rye that he held in his left hand, even as his right arm settled half on the couch behind her, half around her shoulders.

"What can I say? It holds a special place in my heart now."

Catherine didn't have to look up at his face to know he was smiling; she could hear it in his teasing tone. With a smile of her own, she settled in, placing her head on his chest. "So hold it down so I can read it, too."

"Why, so you can come after me with a pickaxe in my sleep?"

The giggle that left her after he referenced a private blog she'd written about him—one that he'd spied on when he'd held her phone hostage—was responded to with what she could have sworn was a kiss in her hair. Unwilling to break the spell by questioning it, she simply reached up and angled the book so that she could see it, too.

"You're insufferable."

Her smile widened. "You wouldn't have me any other way."

She could almost swear she heard his heart rate increase just a fraction. "No, Catherine, I would not," was all he said, and they spent the next hour reading in silence.

Following the directions on her phone's GPS app did little to dispel Catherine's nerves the following day as she drove to her father's new home. Sure, she wasn't afraid of losing her way now, but everything else—the neighborhood, the implications of what she was planning to do—was weighing equally heavy on her mind. She wondered as she parked in front of the modest, small, and clearly rundown house that her father now lived in how he could stand to go from the lap of luxury to this.

Until she saw his smile as he stepped out to greet her.

In this home, in this neighborhood, with this new job, her father was genuinely happy.

Taking a deep breath before she walked up to him, Catherine painted on a smile of her own. Somehow it felt even more disingenuous of her to say how happy she was for him, but not for the reasons one would think. It wasn't that she wasn't happy, she simply felt…

Jealous.

Over this.

Over the small, cramped space with its second-hand furniture and a much smaller television in the living room.

Over the stained hallway carpeting, the single bathroom in need of a fresh coat of paint and perhaps new internal parts for the constantly-running toilet.

Over the small master bedroom, and even smaller room to its side which was still filled with boxes that had yet to be unpacked.

"Sorry about that, Princess." Her father chuckled more to himself as he scratched the back of his head, something she only now noticed that he did quite often. "I wasn't expecting you to be staying here tonight."

"I couldn't." She shook her head once as she followed him back to the combined kitchen and dining room area, where a scarred table and four mismatched chairs sat. "Not because of…" She gestured back towards the hallway.

"Yeah, you probably wouldn't want to leave your car overnight. Not out there." He was still smiling, though, as he sat down to the plates of leftovers that Catherine had brought with her. "Mmm, Greta's cooking. There's one thing I miss from that house."

Catherine blinked back unexpected tears as she looked down at her own plate, at the food she was so accustomed to. "Just Greta's cooking, huh?" The words left Catherine before she could stop them, and her eyes grew wide as she looked back up at her father. "I'm sorry, I didn't mean—"

"It's okay, Princess." He placed his hand on her arm, his smile warming all the more when she didn't pull away. "I miss you most of all."

She raised her eyebrow in response but didn't answer. She found it difficult to think of how he could say he missed her, when she looked back at the way she'd acted. For as long as she could remember, she'd been completely self-absorbed.

She'd been raised to be.

But had her father had anything to do with that, or did all of the pushing come from her mother? She couldn't quite recall, and it bothered her even as she sat at her father's modest table picking at the plate of food in front of her.

"Okay, spill." Her father nudged her gently with his knee, and Catherine looked up at him.

"Was I always difficult?"

Catherine noticed the deep dimples in Colin's cheeks when he smiled at his daughter. "I would say more along the lines of strong-willed."

"How very diplomatic of you," she teased back with a roll of her eyes, wanting to keep the conversation as light as possible. "It's okay, you know. You can admit it."

"You're not easily led. How's that?" He was still smiling even as he picked up another forkful of mashed potatoes, but this time Catherine wasn't smiling in return. While what he said was essentially true—she was more the leader than the follower—she'd still allowed herself to be herded in under the mentality that everything connected to being the best, being the top, being the Queen of the School was more important than true happiness. As far as she'd been concerned, it was true happiness.

Now she knew better.

"Are you going to tell me what's wrong?"

For a moment she contemplated it, thought about how she could confide in her father, hoping he could make everything okay. Frank, of course, knew Sandra's whereabouts, but was keeping that information to himself. Unfortunately, without Catherine knowing where his mother was or how to get in touch with her would only lead to the possibility of Brody and the kids heading off to foster care, being separated.

Or worse.

They could be left there, with Frank, with him knowing that authorities were involved. The implications of what this could mean for Brody, and for the younger children, were far too great for Catherine to fathom at the moment.

"Catherine,"

"I'm fine." She flashed him a fake smile, one that had dazzled many a person who couldn't see past it. "Just tired."

"Anything you want to tell me?"

There was an abundance of things she wanted to say.

She and Mitch had broken up. She'd lost his grandchild. Her mother's boyfriend was a monster who hurt his children.

She was pretty sure she was falling in love for the first time.

Almost as sure as when she accomplished what she set out to do, she'd probably never see him again.

"Nothing of importance." The lie almost stuck in her throat, but she'd forced it out anyway.

Colin's eyes narrowed as he took a closer look at her. "You seem different."

She was different. She was an entirely different person on the inside than she had been just a few short months before. "Is that a bad thing?"

Again, he was scratching the back of his neck, slowly this time. His eyes were still narrowed when he lowered his hand. "I'm not sure yet."

She took a deep breath and sat up straighter, looking her father in the eye. "I'm doing well in my classes, should still graduate with honors. Not quite Valedictorian, but I am close to the top of the class. I've been in my gym more lately, enjoying gymnastics again."

"But you're sticking with cheerleading."

She could feel the heat creep into her cheeks under his close scrutiny. "I'm not sure." She was better than the rest of them, by far, but with the politics within the team there was no way she'd make captain the following year. Did she honestly want to be under Chelsea's thumb after everything that had transpired this year? No, she most definitely did not.

"It could lead to great scholarships."

She nodded, trying to keep her expression neutral. "I know this; I just want to keep my options open."

Colin picked up his roll, turning it over in his hand a couple of times. "So, what does Mitch think of you being unsure of cheerleading next year?"

The lump in her throat as the sound of Mitch's name brought up memories she'd much rather keep buried kept her from taking another bite of her food. "We broke up."

Colin nodded, his attention now on his roll as he tore a piece of it off. "I'm sorry to hear that, Princess."

"Don't be." Their breakup was hardly what had hurt her, but again she wasn't ready to confide in her father just yet.

The rest of the meal was mostly silent, both father and daughter lost in their own thoughts. Catherine was grateful for the silence, though; it kept her from saying too much, revealing things she just wasn't ready to. She did know that her father was in no shape financially, or space wise even, for her to come stay with him. That was fine, though; Frank wasn't concerned with her, she wasn't his problem. Her father did assure her, though, that in time that second bedroom would be cleared out as much as he could, and he would have at least a daybed in there for her should she want to stay overnight.

That alone meant more to Catherine than she could convey.

While her father cleaned up the paper plates and washed the few dishes they had used, Catherine again looked around his home. Noticing a stack of bills, she picked them up, thumbing through them until she saw what she was looking for.

The car payment, for the custom painted pearl white Mustang that was parked on the street out front.

He'd kept up with the payments, just as he'd agreed to when he'd gone round and round with Catherine's grandfather. But the amount of that payment, what it was taking from him each month, caused her eyes to widen with shock.

He couldn't afford this.

There was no way he could.

She quickly placed the bills to the side when her father came back out to the living room, either none the wiser that she'd been snooping or too kind to call her out on it in their short time together. Instead he smiled at her—a smile that seemed a touch sad, an emotion she was becoming all too familiar with.

"It's getting close to that time."

She'd told him she'd wanted to leave by 8 that evening, with it being an hour and a half away. She nodded as she looked down at her hands, then back up at him. "Thank you for having me over today."

Just a couple of strides and he was beside her, putting his arm around her shoulders. "Thank you for coming, Princess."

She looked up at the man she barely knew, feeling the genuine warmth and happiness coming from him. Here he was struggling to make ends meet, but still went out of his way for her.

And she never once heard him complain about it.

She tilted her head slightly to see his expression better. "If I didn't have the car, would you come and get me?"

He pulled back slightly, confusion in his features. "Anytime. Is something wrong with it? Do you need to get it serviced? I'm sure the warranty is—"

"Anytime you could?" she asked, cutting him off. He was still smiling, even as he pushed her hair back out of her eyes.

"Anytime, Catherine. Anytime."

"Sell it."

His eyes widened a fraction, but before he could speak, she continued.

"I heard Grandfather talking, and… and I know that you're the one paying for it, and that you had to finance it. I don't…" She shook her head and shrugged slightly. "It's just a car, Daddy. It's just a car. As long as you can come get me, sell it."

She watched her father blink several times, his eyes shining the way she noticed Brody's did whenever he was on the verge of being far too emotional for his own liking. She expected some words about the car, the one he'd fought so hard to get for her when she now felt she'd hardly deserved it. Instead, when he reached out and cupped the side of her face in his hand he said, "You haven't called me that in a long while."

She was able to control her own emotions, able to keep her own tears from welling up, the resolve in her far too strong to let up. "So, it's a yes, then?"

Her eyelids fluttered shut when her father leaned down and placed a kiss on her forehead. "If you're sure."

She looked up at the man she'd taken for granted for far too long, and this time her smile was genuine. "I'm positive."

The only reservations on her mind that evening when she headed back towards that house on the hill was how she would escape if she needed to. Where else could she possibly go, though? Her father's house was out, her friends were non-existent. Once Brody and the other children left, all she would have was that house on the hill.

Would it be enough?

CHAPTER 42

To Love Somebody

With a glance at her phone letting her know the time, Catherine took a deep breath and stared in the mirror. The girl staring back at her barely resembled the one who had torn apart her closet looking for that perfect outfit for her date with Mitch, only to have it ruined by spilled red Kool-Aid. Back then her scowl was more prominent, her smile the epitome of faked perfection.

Tonight, the smile that touched her lips was far from faked.

Her eyes showed a touch of hope tinged with fear that she would do her best to mask.

And while her resolve ran just as deep, this time it was for completely selfless reasons.

She ran her hands through her slightly tousled hair, gazed at her soft but perfectly applied makeup and shrugged. Her clothing was still expensive, but she opted for a simple spaghetti strap top and a thin black hoodie with her favorite pair of pajama bottoms. While she was indeed more comfortable this way, she rationalized her clothing choice by reminding herself that if she walked down the two flights of stairs to the basement all dolled up, Brody would definitely know she was up to something.

She closed her eyes as she took another calming breath, whispering to herself that she could do this.

Of course she could.

Then she set out on the short walk through the house on the hill, past the closed doors of Brody's sleeping siblings, past the quieted kitchen, darkened on this Saturday evening, and finally past the entryway and down the last flight of stairs.

It was time.

Brody was in his usual spot on the couch, stretched out as he continued reading his favorite book. His own appearance was disheveled, with his unruly dark hair looking as if he'd been taking a nap, his shirt a bit wrinkled, his well-worn pajama bottoms low on his hips, and his feet bare. There was a small bit of scruff adorning his cheeks as well, showing that he hadn't bothered to shave since the previous morning. While it seemed to her that he had changed dramatically since the moment she'd first laid eyes on him, perhaps he hadn't changed much at all. Maybe… just maybe… her perception of him was the only thing that had altered.

The basement wasn't silent this time; Catherine had lent him an old portable radio with a cd player on top, and Brody had wasted no time pulling out his music that he'd had buried in one of the many boxes behind the couch. This evening the music was soft, a soothing male voice that Catherine didn't recognize but rather enjoyed played in the background as she walked closer. Brody didn't look up from his book—he rarely did—but she knew he was just as aware of her presence as she was of his by the way his breathing picked up ever so slightly.

Just as hers had at the sight of him.

"Who is this?" she asked, and she watched one side of his lips twist up in a half-smile.

"Ray LaMontagne." Brody briefly glanced away from his book to look up at her. "Heard of him?"

She shook her head as she walked closer, settling on the opposite arm of the couch. "I like him, though." She ran her slightly damp palms on her pajama bottoms, mentally chastising herself for being so nervous. She'd been down in this basement with him so many times, sat beside him, held his hand, even.

But tonight was different.

She tried her best to sound nonchalant when she spoke again. "So… heard the latest gossip?"

Brody's eyebrows rose even as he kept his eyes on his book. "Oh, you mean where we were all over each other on the dance floor at Homecoming, and Mitch threatened to kick my ass over it?" His cheeky grin was in place when he finally caught and held her gaze. "Nope, haven't heard it."

Her eyes zeroed in on his dimple for the briefest moment, a smile adorning her lips as well. When she averted her gaze, glancing around the room, she felt her heart rate increase. 'Now or never,' she repeated in her own mind before she took a deep breath and let out a sigh.

"What was that for?"

She returned her gaze to him, her earlier nerves dissipating and being replaced with something far more complex. "I feel cheated."

Even though his eyes were back on his book, his raised eyebrow showed she had his attention as well. "How so?"

With one more dramatic, over exaggerated sigh she threw her head back and opened her arms wide. "I feel so cheated!"

His chuckle showed that he got her joke, although not quite all of it. "Why's that, Catherine?"

She crossed her arms, a mock pout on her lips that he was now staring at. "I never even got one dance."

His eyes widened a fraction before he recovered, turning to place his book to the side, face down and opened to the page he'd been reading. Catherine watched as he stood, his lean muscles contracting with every move, his walk towards her slow, each step surer than the last as if he had come to the conclusion that this—whatever he was about to do—was what was meant to be. Her eyes were on his bare feet when he stopped in front of her and she looked up slowly, taking in every inch, her breath hitching as she did so. His legs were long, his pajama bottoms resting low on his narrow hips. His shirt had rose a fraction, and she saw just a dusting of hair trailing down his toned abdomen before he adjusted his clothing, drawing her attention to his hands. They were strong, she knew, and the lean, corded muscles in his arms were even more defined than she'd noticed before. His shoulders were squared, back, not hunched the way they'd been the first day she'd seen him. His Adam's apple moved as he swallowed, and she looked up further, at the dark dusting of scruff along his jawline, around his perfectly shaped lips. His blue eyes were piercing, their pupils dilated, framed by long dark lashes that were lowered as he looked down at her. His dark hair was in disarray, calling for her hands to run through it, feel its softness as she first had the night she'd helped him.

The night that had changed everything between the two of them.

Just as tonight would.

He held his hand out to her, palm up, and did a slight bow, more teasing than mocking. "Dance with me?"

Her smile was almost sad for a moment as it hit her how in sync they truly were, how he'd read her mind and she hadn't had to make that move. She recovered, though, her smile one of genuine happiness and she slipped her small hand in his and stood, and she moved with grace into his arms as the next song began to play. The acoustic guitars resonating through the small speakers surrounded them as his free hand gripped her hip, sending a jolt of electricity through her, before he slid it along her lower back, pulling her closer to him. Their joined hands were between them, pressed up against his chest where she could feel his heart beating, its rate increasing as she tangled the fingers of her other hand in the hair at the nape of his neck. Her own heart was beating erratically as he pulled her even closer, flush up against him, her head resting on his chest as they began to move.

Slowly.

So slowly.

His fingers were moving against her lower back, drawing her into him just a little more. The smell of his body wash—light, but completely Brody—permeated her senses, causing her stomach to dip, her mouth to water, heat to pool in her lower abdomen in a way she was unfamiliar with. Every sense was heightened, every touch felt to the core, every sound resonating in her soul. She felt a sensation in her hair that felt as if he'd left a kiss there, a sensation she'd felt on more than one occasion, and she shivered ever so slightly. His arm tightened around her then, his responding soft sigh telling her everything she needed to know.

He felt it, too.

The overwhelming gravitational pull, the attraction, the kindling of desire—an emotion, a sensation unfamiliar, uninvited into Catherine's soul—that led her to this boy.

This plain, ordinary boy who was anything but.

This boy who held her heart as surely as he held her in his arms.

So afraid of the emotions, the sensations, she thought maybe talking would help ease the burgeoning feelings threatening to take over. Her voice was barely above a whisper, though, when she finally asked, "What's this song?"

His own voice was low, his lips against her temple as he replied, "*To Love Somebody*."

She smiled against his chest, thinking to herself… how appropriate.

And she felt him smile as well.

She closed her eyes as they moved together, the basement transforming itself in her mind to the decorated gym, its lights soft and twinkling, the strumming of an acoustic guitar and the melding of voices surrounding them. Without a care in the world, without the onlookers giving a damn, she danced with the boy who made her heart sing, who shook up her entire world only to make everything so perfectly, painfully clear.

The boy she would do anything to protect.

All she had to do was stay there, in his arms, their actions innocent with a hint of something more for just a little bit longer.

But it was the something more that pushed her forward.

It was the something more that made her wonder, made that wonder turn to determination.

Made her pull away slightly… just slightly…and gaze up at his lips, filling her entire being with sweet anticipation. This hadn't been her intention when she'd come down the stairs, but with time growing so short, she had to know.

She had to.

They'd stopped moving, though their breathing was labored, their hearts pounding a single rhythm as Catherine raised up on her toes slowly, their bodies brushing together as she did, their heightened senses responding. A feather-light touch of her lips to his had them both gasping softly at the feel, hands applying more pressure, lips parting as they brushed together again.

And again.

"Oh god, Cat..."

Those words whispered against her lips elicited a sound from her—soft, breathy, releasing as she melted into him.

And she kissed him.

Full, lush, yet soft, tender. More than lust, more than heat, more than passion... this kiss was overflowing with emotion, each touch of lips meaning more than the last.

Soft... his lips were soft, just as she'd imagined.

These kisses, so full of promise, were exactly what she'd wanted, what she'd longed for.

She whimpered as his hands began to move, exploring her with a reverence she'd only thought she'd experienced before. There was nothing rushed, nothing pushed past any limits she may have imposed, nothing forced upon her as his hands traced her lines, her curves, her face with such adoration while their mouths worked a magic she hadn't imagined possible before.

And then his tongue touched hers.

And the Earth stood still.

With his fingertips on her cheeks, her hands fisted in his shirt, they deepened their kiss. Breaths mingling, teeth gently tugging on bottom lips, tongues exploring, hearts soaring, crashing, and soaring once more.

Until he pulled away.

"Cat..." His breathing was heavy, his chest rising and falling as he stepped out of her embrace and ran his hands through his hair, fisting them in and pulling. Was he trying to stop or will himself forward? There was no way for her to tell.

She tried taking a step forward, but he stepped further away, shaking his head once, causing her heart to splinter. The ache in her chest manifested immediately in unshed tears, brimming in her eyes, blurring her vision as she tried to find the words to say, the way to apologize.

But she wasn't sorry, so the words wouldn't come.

Instead, one lone tear trailed down her cheek, capturing his attention, crumbling his resolve.

And as he closed the distance between them, their names were whispered in adoration before one slight touch set them in motion again. There was no timidity, no holding back as their mouths met, over and over, their hands moving beneath clothing, tossing his shirt and her jacket aside, the forgotten book falling to the floor as they tumbled together onto the couch, first with her atop him, then turning as one, he pressed her farther into the cushions, gripping her hip as her leg wrapped around him.

His hands began to trace her slight curves with more urgency, his fingertips sliding beneath the hem of her shirt, her prompted sigh of 'yes' urging him onward.

Yes.

The word she'd never gotten to use before, the word she'd all but convinced herself she'd never say to something like this.

The word she repeated when his lips met her neck, his teeth lightly grazing where her pulse hammered beneath.

The word that hung in the air as the music was joined with sighs, soft whimpers, breaths mingling, and one brief moment of silence.

Then the radio hit the wall with a loud bang, shattering into pieces that fell to the carpet below it.

Frank Harris was home.

CHAPTER 43

Fight Back

Brody was quick to move up and away from Catherine, his demand that she run left hanging in the air as Frank wrapped one large hand around the boy's throat and began to squeeze. Did she scream? She wasn't sure… all she could focus on was the scene unfolding before her.

Frank's anger, so prominent that a vein in his temple could be seen pulsating.

Brody's resolve—if this was his fate, so be it.

Her heart racing, her limbs trembling as she scrambled off the couch, she ran to Brody's side, her hands instinctively reaching for Frank's arm. "Frank, stop!" Catherine's shout resonated throughout the basement, her voice shaking. "Just stop!" She ignored Brody pulling on her clothing, his slight shake of his head to her.

She wasn't about to leave.

Frank didn't acknowledge her words, or her attempts to pull him away from Brody. Instead of distracting him, it only seemed to egg him on, and he began to taunt the boy who refused to show fear. "Look at you, playing house while we're away. You play the protector for them." He sneered as he gestured towards the stairs, obviously referring to Tyler and Sam, and doing so with the same contempt he seemed to have for the boy standing before him. "You play your little game, you get people to feel sorry for your punk ass when you can't do any damn thing right, and look at you! Look at you now!"

Brody's gaze never wavered; instead, his eyes narrowed at his less-than-loving mention of the brother and sister that Brody cared for so deeply. He stayed silent, though, in spite of Catherine's pleading from his side to fight back.

Just fight back.

If Brody wasn't going to, then Catherine would.

"You're the monster here, Frank!" she yelled at him. "Stop! Just… let him go! Mother!" Her scream up the stairs for Theresa's attention resonated through the basement. As much as she wanted to run up the stairs, drag her mother down to witness what was happening in her own house, she didn't dare.

She was too afraid of what would happen while she was gone.

Frank's short laugh was cold, biting. "She isn't in here, Lady Catherine."

Catherine could feel the blood draining from her face, her stomach dipping uncomfortably, her heart momentarily stopping before taking off soaring, making her feel lightheaded.

No… no, this wasn't what was supposed to happen.

Not at all.

She'd planned everything so carefully, each move meticulously calculated, timed almost to the minute. How… *how* was it all falling apart?

This wasn't supposed to happen.

She was Catherine Garner. Everything she demanded came to be.

So why... *why* had this... this stroke of brilliance that she'd masterminded fallen apart?

But she already knew the answer to that, as the thud of fist on skin, the dotting of blood against her shirt were reminding her of the reality of her life now.

The reality of her life ever since Brody Harris had entered it.

Her mind was a whirlwind, thinking up something...anything to get this under control, to get the end result that had to happen.

It had to.

Frank was still sneering, his eyes locked on Brody's face—Brody, who wouldn't fight back, who knew what he would get if he did. "That bitch had you fooled, boy, so fucking fooled. And you just couldn't keep your hands off that whore, could you? Didn't matter to you how many pricks she was spreading her legs for."

Frank never saw Brody's left hook coming. It all happened so fast—the left, followed by the right, and another left.

The guttural scream that left Catherine when Frank's large fist contacted with Brody's face, sending blood splattering across her exposed skin as she pushed her way between them.

"No... no more! No more." She knelt in front of Brody, who instinctively moved to place her behind him as he stood to face Frank once more.

Frank, who was smirking as Brody wiped the blood off his face with the back of his hand, shaking the excess onto the carpet.

And with a sickening lurch, Catherine realized she'd seen spots such as this everywhere, all throughout the house.

"You leave her out of this." Brody's voice was low, controlled, his body positioned to shield her. As Frank made a subtle shift to move towards them, Catherine called out for her mother again. She had to be there, she had to come down those stairs.

Not because she needed her mother's protection.

It was because she needed her mother to see… to finally see.

"Save your breath, Lady Catherine." Frank spoke to her, but kept his eyes on Brody. "Theresa is taking care of some business, kind of like the two of you failed to do."

She opened her mouth to ask what he meant, ignoring Brody's hand squeezing hers.

But she never got the chance.

She involuntarily flinched as Frank pulled folded papers from the back pocket of his dress slacks. "Exactly what do the two of you think you're going to do, huh? Raise that bastard kid here, in this house?"

Papers from the doctor's office, regarding her pregnancy.

Papers she'd kept in a dresser drawer, even after she'd lost her baby.

In her peripheral vision, she saw Brody swallow, his eyes widened for only a fraction of a moment before he recovered his calm demeanor.

Catherine, however, felt her anger boil to the surface, spilling over before she could contain herself. With a rage she hadn't felt inside in months, she pushed Brody out of her way, brushing his hand off her arm as she stood in front of Frank. "You went through my things?"

"Cat…"

"You think a locked door will stop me from finding what I need to know?"

Catherine's eyes widened, though not from fear. The mere thought of this monster crossing the threshold into her room, going through her drawers, her personal belongings made her angrier than she'd ever known possible. She thought of everything she'd had hidden, though most was on her phone.

What else could he know? What had she printed out, what had she…

"Go upstairs, Cat."

The tone of Brody's voice should have been a warning, but what would Frank possibly do to her? If he touched her, her grandfather…

Her grandfather.

"Go ahead, Frank, pull all the papers out you want." She crossed her arms in front of her and raised her eyebrow in challenge. Frank wouldn't dare lay a hand on her. "Let's pull them all out, and let's make a phone call, shall we? Let's call my grandfather, let's tell him how his precious granddaughter got knocked up. And let's tell him who the father is."

She stopped short of lying, but the implication was there.

Her grandfather had warned them all in his own way, hadn't he?

Brody's deep intake of breath wasn't as subtle as he'd wanted it to be, but Frank's attention was now on Catherine, just as she'd hoped for. He was opening up the folded papers, one side of his mouth lifted in a sardonic grin, one that let Catherine know he thought he was going to win.

But there was no way she would let him.

"That's right, Frank, pull out those papers. Do it, and prepare to…"

Catherine and Brody both stiffened as Frank thrust his hand forward, the opened paper pointed towards them, its printing small and insignificant to the enraged girl.

"…to give up your control over them, Frank. Do you hear me? Let's call Grandfather. Now."

"Cat?"

Brody's voice was soft, his tone questioning.

And Frank's sneer grew.

Catherine didn't turn towards Brody, unwilling to take her eyes off the monster who'd turned the house on the hill into a hell she would never have imagined living. "Would you like to make the call, or shall I?"

Brody had taken the papers from Frank, had begun to back away, but she stood still. She lifted her chin defiantly, her hands on her hips as she stared Frank down.

Frank was calm.

Far too calm.

"So, this was all your plan, then." This time he pulled a handkerchief from his pocket, wiping what blood hadn't already dried onto it, the rust colored stain smearing across the stark white fabric. "Let's set this up. Let's get this ignorant boy to fall for everything you say, let's get him to fall into your trap that you so elaborately set."

"Hey!" She stepped forward, her finger pointed at him, jabbing his chest for effect. "You watch what you…"

"And let's get these kids out of your hair, out of your space, out of your rooms. Let's put Lady Catherine back at the top of the heap, right?"

She shook her head ever so slightly, refusing to fall into his entrapment. "This isn't about…"

"It's always about you, Lady Catherine." Frank's hand on her wrist as he moved her arm away held just enough pressure to let her know he meant business.

"Let go of me!"

"Cat?"

"What?" she snapped as she finally turned towards Brody, then she took a breath to calm herself. "I'm sor—"

The paper he was holding wasn't anything from the doctor,

though.

It was a print out of the Facebook message she'd sent to Sandra, the message she'd never told him about, the message that had led their mother to them.

"So you contact their mother," Frank continued, stuffing the soiled handkerchief back into his pocket as he spoke. "You coax him into your bed, conveniently show up pregnant, and set up this elaborate... scheme." He gestured around the basement, the fragments of the broken cd player scattered across the floor.

Catherine couldn't bear to look at the hurt expression that Brody was trying—trying, and failing—to hide from Frank, from her. She couldn't take the time to correct Frank, couldn't console Brody at that moment, not when so much was at stake.

"How many times has Greta had to clean up after you, Frank?" she asked, her eyes narrowed at her adversary. His smirk widened as he took a step towards her, undeterred by her unspoken threat to bring the housekeeper into this.

"Not nearly as many times as she's cleaned up after you."

Catherine opened her mouth for another reply, one that was sure to bring Frank to his knees, but was interrupted by her mother's voice as she slowly descended the stairs into the basement. "Greta is gone, dismissed." Catherine's eyes shot to her mother, her heart equally pounding in anger and aching for the loss of someone she'd only recently learned the value of. "And her severance pay will be more than enough to keep her quiet about this mess you've gotten this family into, Catherine."

"Me?!" Catherine gestured around the room. "Look, Mother... look around you. You think I did this?"

Theresa let out a tired sigh as her eyes briefly rested on Brody. "It's time, Frank. It's time for him to go."

"All of them," Catherine interjected quickly. "All of them,

Mother, just as we discussed."

"I'll handle this," Frank said with a sneer, which Theresa dismissed with a wave of her hand.

"It was temporary anyway, you said so yourself. It's time."

The relief flooded through Catherine, but she was careful to not let it show in front of Frank. No weakness, wasn't that what she'd learned throughout all of this? Don't show him weakness, and he would have nothing to use against her. But still… still, they would all be safe—Brody, Ty, and Sam. Catherine let a small smile touch her lips as she turned towards Brody.

And she stopped.

She stopped as he stared at her with a guarded expression, his jaw set, the papers still in his hand. His eyes so blue, so hardened were more of a shock to her than the last dried blood that remained, or his swollen eyelid, the edges of the skin around it turning shades of black and purple already.

"Pack."

The one gruff word from Frank that should have made Brody elated, should have had him smiling and thanking her had no effect on him. He stood still, motionless, his eyes boring holes into Catherine's soul, holes that she couldn't explain with Frank still standing there.

"I said pack." Frank emphasized his words with a shove, one that barely moved Brody at all. His hand gripped the paper tighter, the crinkling noise being disrupted by Theresa's demand that Catherine follow her up the stairs.

"He goes, too," Catherine said, gesturing in Frank's direction.

"He's not leaving." Theresa's tone was clipped, and Catherine bit back her more hateful reply to the mother who should have put her child's needs and safety first.

"Of course not, Mother, but he's leaving the basement. No

more of this."

"You think you rule things around here?" Frank began, and it was Catherine's turn to scoff.

"I know I do."

But that was so far from true.

"Frank, make the arrangements." Theresa could have been talking to her hired help with as little regard she gave to the man she planned to marry. Catherine noted how little it must matter to him, at least in comparison with the monetary payout, as he followed Theresa up the stairs.

Catherine turned to Brody as her mother called out to her, hoping to tell him, to show him she'd done all of this for him, for the kids. With Frank gone, he would be free to show her how he felt, how she knew he felt for her.

But his eyes were dead, cold.

He finished crumpling up the paper in his hand and tossed it in her direction, purposefully missing her but not by much. "Go on, Lady Catherine," was all he said.

And in that moment, she couldn't tell which of them was better at the game—her with Frank, or Brody with her.

Perhaps she didn't want to know.

Without a word, she turned towards the stairway and left him behind, pieces of her broken heart falling away with every step.

CHAPTER 44

A Gift

"Catherine."

Theresa's tone was sharp, demanding her daughter's attention the moment she ascended the stairs. Catherine didn't bother to sigh, didn't show an ounce of emotion as she followed her mother down the hallway to the master suite. Her heart was still stinging from Brody's rejection, Brody's failure to listen, to see.

How could he not see what she'd done… or why?

"Close the door behind you."

The Catherine of old would have snapped a response in Theresa's direction, perhaps even slam the door behind her. No… no, the Catherine of old would have refused to follow Theresa so blindly down the hall. She would have stopped at her own room and demanded her mother speak with her there, if she wanted to speak at all. Or maybe she would have simply refused until such time as she felt necessary, which would probably be never.

But the Catherine of old would never have been so selfless as she'd become.

"We need to discuss how we're going to handle this… situation."

Theresa spoke the last word with a dismissive wave of her hand showing how little the child she believed Catherine to be carrying meant to her.

The truth should have been devastating.

Instead it was expected.

"That situation," Catherine interjected, "was your grandchild."

"Was?" Of course that was the word that Theresa would hone in on. "Well, past tense is a good thing. I hardly think your grandfather would welcome the news." She picked up a glass, its barely melted ice cubes showing she'd felt it more important to procure a beverage than to stop Frank from inflicting any more harm.

"Seriously?" Catherine snatched the glass from her mother's hand, the distinct scent of gin wafting through the air as she did so. "Put down the booze and pills for five minutes, mother, and look at the hell you brought into this home."

The smack across Catherine's cheek came so suddenly she didn't have time to react, to stop her mother from striking her. The glass slipped from her fingers, falling with a thud to the floor below, its contents splashing her feet and leaving a dark puddle that she watched seep into the carpeting.

She wouldn't cry.

She wouldn't give Theresa the pleasure of watching her break.

"You," Theresa said, her voice shaking slightly, "are going to learn your place."

"I'm fairly certain I know it already." Catherine raised her head slightly, her eyes piercing as she stared her mother down. "The apple of grandfather's eye, the reason he insists on this home, on you having the best of everything. The pawn in your game against my father, whom you discarded the moment grandfather told you to. The ticket to your lifestyle, in spite of being unwanted by you."

"I was your age." Theresa was calm as she retrieved more ice from her bucket, more alcohol from her crystal dispenser. "I had the world at my feet, and no intentions of giving any of it up. Your father destroyed my plans for myself when he announced the pregnancy." She took a sip and turned her cold eyes in her daughter's direction. "He had nothing, could give me nothing, but my father was gracious. This house, everything in it, he arranged for you. I was forced into a marriage I didn't want—and lucky for me, eventually my father agreed. At least on that point."

"Dad loved you, you know." Catherine wasn't sure why she felt the need to point out that simple fact, or why her father could have loved such a calculating human being to begin with. She knew it to be true, though; now that she could remember with this new perspective, she knew how much love her father had in him.

"Your father was a fool, thinking love is all you needed. You think he's doing as well in a job that he 'loves', Catherine? You think that love could have given you everything you've demanded over the years?"

"It would have made me a better person." She answered without hesitation, knowing now from experience it was the truth.

"And instead here you are." Theresa crossed her arms, a sardonic smile on her lips. "As cold and as calculating as I've taught you to be. With one minor flaw, of course… the same flaw I had at your age." She took another sip then barked out a short laugh. "But we both know the price to be paid for sleeping with someone beneath us, don't we?"

Catherine didn't correct her regarding her personal relationship with Brody; doing so would jeopardize Frank's willingness to give up his control, to let the children leave. She also refused to acknowledge—at least to Theresa—that Brody was far from beneath her. Doing so would give Theresa leverage, an advantage.

It was something she'd taught Catherine from a very early age.

So instead, she stood her ground, her eyes narrowing ever so slightly. "There is a difference between you and me, though."

Theresa huffed out an almost bored sigh. "Which is?"

"Aside from the obvious." With a roll of her eyes, Catherine gestured to the drink in Theresa's hand. "Which I will never need to function, so have fun with that." She stood a touch taller, with the grace and poise that had been instilled in her. "I will make a kickass mother, and I will love my children with everything in me. One of these days, Theresa." Her mother's eyes widened just a fraction at Catherine's use of her name. "One of these days when you look at me, you'll see what you should have been." She turned to leave, her hand on the doorknob as she looked over her shoulder. "And we both know it's already too late for you."

Without another word—not from her nor her mother—Catherine left the suite and walked with her head held high down the hallway, her face holding no trace of the pain in her heart of her mother's rejection.

Catherine's heart was heavy, even with the sound of the children's excited chatter. Even within the confines of her own room, its door shut to the bustling in the hallway, she wasn't immune to the children's elation.

Just a couple short hours—perhaps even less—and the house on the hill would be silent of all the joy it had held.

And it had held joy, and hope, and even a bit of…

No, there couldn't have been love. Catherine was certain of it.

Wasn't she?

"And… and we'll be with Mommy for Christmas!"

"I know, Sammi. I know."

Catherine's heart stilled momentarily at the sound of Brody's voice so close to her doorway. If she'd expected him to knock, or even speak through said doorway, she would have been disappointed. Instead, she listened as his voice trailed away, his apologies of having to get his own belongings together fading.

"I'll make sure we have everything."

That was Tyler, of course, stepping up to take over the big brother role. As Catherine moved about her room, straightening up, gathering a few items together herself, she smiled fondly as she remembered Brody hitting the baseball in his direction, coaching him on catching. In spite of her embarrassment over her own behavior, so much had changed that she rarely thought of the Catherine of old.

Lady Catherine.

Queen of Davis High.

Ruler of this household.

Former cheerleader.

Ex-girlfriend.

She looked at the various items gathered in the middle of her bed and smiled softly, even though there was a touch of sadness behind it. Once upon a time she'd placed so much importance on the things laid out before her.

Today she knew better.

Although she knew, without a shadow of a doubt, who would appreciate them.

She took a deep breath and opened her door, her smile in place as she stepped into the hallway. The younger children were running back and forth between the rooms they'd occupied for a few short months, forever making them theirs in Catherine's eyes.

She had her arms behind her as she crossed the hallway to Sam's room. She had never questioned the lack of toys, although Sam was more preoccupied with gymnastics as Catherine had been at her age. Sam's eyes were bright as she turned towards Catherine, her smile infectious as she grabbed the few articles of clothing she had and laid them on the bed. "Did… did you hear, Catherine? Mommy's coming! She's coming tonight!"

Catherine blinked back tears, tears she hadn't expected. "I heard," she managed to say softly.

"And… and we all get to go!"

"Just us, Sammi." Tyler was entering the room, his worn catcher's mitt in his hand.

"And Brody," Sam added, and her smile suddenly dimmed. "Where is Catherine going to stay?"

"Here." Catherine was surprised at the strength in her voice. "I'll stay here. This is my home." Yet even as she said the words, she didn't feel them to be true. It was the house she resided in, the one that held her 'things'.

If home was where the heart was, hers was preparing to walk out the door.

"Don't forget anything," Tyler said as he stepped out of the room again.

"We didn't bring much," Sam continued chattering while Catherine stepped closer. "We're only supposed to leave with what we brought, but…" She eyed her clothes on the bed, the ones that Brody had chosen that day he'd forced Catherine to spend her money on them.

She wished now she'd done so much more.

"Those are yours," Catherine said to her. "They're a gift, and whenever someone gives you a gift it's yours to keep."

Sam was silent for a moment, her fingers tracing a pattern on the shirt before her. "I'm sorry I ruined your jeans, Catherine."

Sam's voice was small, wavering, and threatened to break the small bit of control Catherine had over her emotions. She held herself in check, though, even managing another smile as she approached the young girl. "I'm sorry for how I reacted." Sam looked up at her then, with gray eyes full of curiosity. "It was wrong of me to be so angry over a silly little accident."

And Catherine was certain had she known what this child—what all three of the children—had seen, she never would have acted that way towards them.

With a shake of her head, Catherine shifted the focus from an unpleasant memory to the bag she held in her hand. "I didn't get a chance to go Christmas shopping," she began, "but I know how much you really liked all the…"

"These are your new… your new…" Sam took the bag from Catherine, a small giggle escaping as she pulled out the first full bottle of sweet-smelling lotion, followed by the matching body wash. Her glee was short lived, though, and she replaced the items in the bag. "I used all…"

"Which is how I knew you like them," Catherine cut her off. She sat on the bed, patting the spot beside her. "I knew you would appreciate them more than anyone else here."

Sam took the seat that Catherine offered, her gray eyes wide. "More than you?"

Catherine nodded, but resisted the urge to reach over and push the girl's hair back out of her eyes. It was all she could do at this point to keep from crying. "Which is why they're my gift to you."

"Because you don't want them?"

"Nope." She watched the confusion cloud over Sam's face, and let out a short laugh. "It's because you want them more than I do. It isn't about me, Sam. This is about you."

Sam's mouth was shaped like an 'o' as she again looked through the bag, this time with pure joy. "This is my Christmas present from you?"

The words 'don't cry, don't cry' repeated through Catherine's head as she nodded.

Until Sam threw her arms around Catherine's neck and squeezed with all of her might, and two large tears escaped.

"But I didn't get anything for you," she heard Sam squeak out as she hugged the child back.

Catherine knew that statement couldn't be further from the truth.

This small child had given her more than she could possibly know.

"Brody, did you see my… oh." Tyler stopped as Catherine entered his room, another bag in her hand. "Hi, Catherine."

"Hello, Tyler." Of the three, he was still the wariest of her, the most distrustful. Perhaps he seemed a bit of an outsider looking in. Catherine had shared gymnastics with Sam, and had shared… what had she shared with Brody? There wasn't much interaction between herself and Tyler, though, and given their family history she could understand his caution.

"Have you seen my mitt?"

"Didn't you just have it?" Catherine asked. "In Sam's room?"

"Oh… right, maybe I left it there. I'll…"

"Could I talk to you for a minute first?" She knew if she didn't act fast, he would be out the door and away from her. He nodded once, shifting uncomfortably from foot to foot while he waited for her explanation.

And his eyes dropped to the bag she held out.

"I know you'd been talking about wanting to play this game." She smirked a little as she gave herself a mental pat on the back for rummaging through the shopping bags Greta had hidden before her untimely dismissal. This was a game she'd mentioned in passing, and while she was interested in playing it, she knew who the owner should be.

"But… but we're getting ready to leave, and…" Tyler took the unopened game from the bag, turning it over and over in his hand, a wistful expression on his face. "I don't have time."

Catherine shrugged with a smile. "It's yours, Ty. Take it with you."

He began to smile, but it faltered for a moment. "Maybe we'll be moving close to where we used to be. I… I think Brad has…" He didn't finish his sentence, but stood up a little taller and looked Catherine in the eye. "Thank you, Catherine."

At that moment she knew without a doubt this young man would never follow in his father's footsteps. He was gracious, kind, and humble without any of the cruelty that Frank Harris possessed. She could also tell he was too proud to tell her that he wouldn't be able to play the game in his own home, that they didn't have the system he and his little sister had spent countless hours on while they'd lived in that house on the hill.

And she knew exactly what to do.

"C'mere." She walked over to the small television cart and began fiddling with the wires. "This will fit in your bag, won't it?"

"I'm not going to steal…"

"You're not stealing, silly." Catherine smiled over her shoulder. "This is for all of you, so you have to share." She unhooked the console, ensuring all of the wires and controllers were present before she handed it over to Tyler. "And don't forget the games, okay? I know Sam's favorites are in there, too."

"Are you serious?" Tyler said the words with a half laugh, trying to contain the smile as if he was afraid this was just a joke.

But it wasn't.

It couldn't have been further from.

Catherine placed her arms around him, giving him a close hug to hide her own tears. "Merry Christmas, Tyler," she said, then she walked back to the safety of her own room to cry.

The sun was still a good hour away from rising when the excited shouts from the children let Catherine know the time had come.

Sandra Harris had arrived to pick up her children.

As the shouting became muffled, and footsteps shuffled down the hallway—probably carrying bags—Catherine took one last look in the mirror.

Her makeup was barely there, her eyes showing the tears she'd shed over the thought of them leaving.

Of her being stuck here, alone.

Of Brody walking out of her life thinking the worst of her, refusing to speak to her, demanding that she stay away from him.

And in just a few short minutes, he'd be driving away from this house on the hill—and from her life—forever.

She looked down at the object in her hand, the object she'd retrieved from its hiding spot in the basement when she'd tried to speak with Brody less than an hour before, and knew she wasn't going to let him leave without it.

One last deep breath and she opened her door, walking

quickly to the staircase, taking the empty steps two at a time as fast as her feet would carry her. Theresa had already gone back to her room leaving just Frank standing at the doorway, his arms crossed, his eyes narrowed as she passed by him.

"Where do you think…"

"Fuck off, Frank," she muttered as she pushed her way through the door and sprinted towards the older green station wagon, its back end already loaded, the small children in the back seat waving excitedly.

And Brody.

His back was to her, stiffened as if he could sense her approach.

"Brody!"

He shook his head and opened the front passenger door just as she reached him.

"Brody, wait."

He shook her hand off, staring down at her with cold eyes. "Go back into your precious house, Lady… Cath…"

His words died off as she placed her nearly new, barely used, professional grade digital camera in his hands. She pulled her hands away quickly, knowing he would grab onto the camera, keep it from falling.

"It's her Christmas, Brody!" Sam called from the backseat.

"Take it," Brody said, holding it out, and Catherine shook her head.

"It's yours."

"I don't want your charity," he snapped, his mouth closing in a thin line at the tears that sprung up in her eyes.

"And you don't have it."

Before he could move, before he could protest, she quickly wrapped her arms around his neck, whispering softly in his ear before she pulled away.

"Now you'll be safe."

One last look at him, watching him swallow, his hands clutching the camera as he stared at her was all she allowed herself before she turned and made her way back into the house on the hill.

The prison she would have to endure for days on end without him.

Without love.

"I've got a few things to set straight with you, Lady Catherine," Frank was saying as she walked up the stairs towards her bedroom. She paused, turning to face him, feeling nothing but disgust.

"My name is Catherine," she corrected him. "Just Catherine. And from here on out, you will refer to me as nothing but Catherine, do you understand?"

Without waiting for his reply, she bounded the rest of the way to her room, slamming her door with a bang. She not only locked it, but also pushed her desk chair in front, lodging it beneath the knob before dramatically flinging herself onto her bed.

Next to her laptop, opened up to her Twitter account, where she longed to post that her life was now over.

But she didn't.

She didn't because not a single person remaining on her so-called 'friends' list gave an actual damn about her.

And the only person she wanted to give a damn would never see it.

CHAPTER 45

The House on the Hill

The silence that permeated the house on the hill on the days following the children's departure was nearly more than Catherine could take. She'd stayed in her room for the most part, venturing out only when she knew that Frank had left either for work or for a function that Theresa would demand his presence at. Catherine even opted out of dinner with her grandfather, feigning illness when Greta's replacement had come to her door.

She hadn't even bothered to find out the new housekeeper's name.

When she could no longer stand the confines of her room, she stuffed a few essentials into a duffel bag and ran straight for her gym. Seeking refuge there, though, was futile at best. Her one attempt at practicing gymnastics on that cold and rainy afternoon had Catherine's heart hurting, longing for the companionship that she had grown so fond of.

She missed Sam and Tyler's laughter.

She missed the chaos surrounding her as they would play, free from the worry of Frank in this sanctuary that she'd welcomed them into.

But most of all… most of all Catherine missed Brody.

And this gym, with its high windows and wall of mirrors, was the place her whole outlook, her entire world had changed. There was no returning to her old way of thinking, her old way of being. Truth be told, in spite of it all, she had zero desire to ever go back.

With a heavy sigh, she retrieved her duffel bag—why had she even brought it out with her in the first place?—and opened the large door leading to the sprawling back yard. She looked wistfully over her shoulder towards the open grassy area, wishing for one more afternoon of Brody hitting baseballs towards Tyler to catch.

But it wasn't coming.

"Catherine."

She startled a bit but recovered quickly, turning towards her uninvited guest that stood in her back yard. Unwilling to feel uncomfortable, or at least unwilling to show it in front of someone who had so willingly participated in her downfall, she stood taller, her expression as even as she could get it, and sighed as she adjusted her bag on her shoulder. "Brody is gone, Bethany."

"I know. Or I was told, anyhow." Bethany eyed Catherine's state of disheveled mess up and down. "I see you're not taking it well."

Catherine shook her head, a smirk touching her lips. "That's the problem; you're looking with your eyes. They can only see so much, you know."

Bethany moved to take a step forward, then stopped herself. With her eyes narrowed, she assessed Catherine again. "No, I'm actually not. Perhaps to the outside world you look the same. A bit unkempt, but that's only because you didn't know I was coming."

Catherine half-scoffed. "I'd hardly go out of my way."

"I suppose you wouldn't anymore." Bethany shifted her weight to one foot, her arms crossed in front of her. "I don't want to be here; I was asked to."

"Oh really?" Catherine let out a short laugh as she looked around. "So, which one of the goon squad sent you? And... and where are they hiding out? When are they going to come bombard me, spewing their hatred? Because that's what you do. That's what you all do. And I would know." She faced Bethany, her eyes narrowed. "Because I used to be one of you."

"Used to be," Bethany reiterated, then shook her head again. "Never mind, why I'm here doesn't matter to you. But this?" She gestured towards the duffel bag, still on Catherine's shoulder. "Where are you going to run to, Catherine? Don't you have everything you wanted now? Your house back, all of your rooms, your..."

"Leave."

"Fine, I'll go. Just be sure to check,"

"Leave."

Catherine spoke that one syllable through clenched teeth, her hands fisted at her sides to keep from nervously fidgeting.

Bethany didn't need to know how desperately Catherine missed the chaos her life had become.

Bethany merely nodded before she turned, her hips swaying as she walked back to the house where Frank held the door open for her. To the untrained eye, Frank's smile was genuine as he spoke to the girl, out of earshot from where Catherine could hear him spew lie after lie.

She didn't want to hear any of it. Not what Frank had to say, not why Bethany had come, not who had put her up to it.

Instead, she pulled her duffel bag higher onto her shoulder and retreated to her gym hoping to work herself to the point of exhaustion.

And maybe... just maybe... she could chase the memories away.

Perhaps the silence was getting to Catherine. She'd once been the consummate social butterfly, after all, with so many people clamoring for her attention it was almost embarrassing. With no one to talk to, though, and no school to lose herself in, her world was closing in around her. Her waking hours all ran together, with no clear beginning or end. And now... now her dreams were haunting her, chasing her, waking her with fright.

And they were silent, too.

Always silent.

She would be in the room with Mitch, who wouldn't take his hands off of her no matter how many times she tried to push him off. Her attempts at screaming would be nothing, the dread as he would force her down suffocating her as she fought against him.

And she would see Brody.

He would be passing by the room.

He would glance at her with hate in his eyes.

And he would walk away.

They would all walk away.

Catherine would wake up with a start every time, her breathing labored, a sweat across her brow. The initial relief when she realized she was in her own bed alone would soon fade, leaving the crushing realization that her dream wasn't all that far from the truth.

They had all walked away.

Catherine was completely alone.

Christmas morning arrived with no fanfare, no screeches of excitement, no bustling within the house, no smells of food being prepared in the kitchen. Catherine hadn't even woken up early, only opening her eyes when her phone chimed with a text from her father.

Merry Christmas, Princess

She hardly felt like a princess as she stretched her sore muscles, overworked from her countless hours in her gym. Theresa and Frank had gone on some holiday getaway, one that Catherine would have declined to attend had she even been invited, so that left her in that huge house on the hill alone. Luckily, she'd reminded Theresa that she was to visit her father, otherwise the keys to her car that she'd been forbidden to drive would have remained in their hiding place.

She didn't bother to tell Theresa that she'd be returning the car to her father, who had found a potential buyer for it.

With no one there to impress, Catherine wasn't quite sure why she showered, why she put just a touch of makeup on. She didn't even have plans to go to her father's until the following day, when she would drop the car off, have a small dinner, sleep on the futon he had placed in the spare bedroom that she would share with unpacked boxes. This day—this lone, solitary day—was supposed to be one of celebration.

Wasn't it?

She paused for a moment as she stood before her mirror, assessing herself in her long-sleeved t-shirt and yoga pants, her hair in the perfect messy bun, her makeup soft but flawless.

Her fingertips traced across her beating heart that ached for all that would never be.

She wouldn't be welcoming her child into this world in a few months.

Her phone wasn't flooded with well-wishes and Merry Christmas greetings the way it had been the year before.

Even her Facebook was bare of notifications, partly from her settings change to keep the hate off of her page and partly due to her dwindling friends list. There was no reason to go through her newsfeed, to see how happy everyone else was, who was having the latest party, what the 'in' crowd was doing. There was no reason to open up her messages to read the latest hate mail, nor to check who the lone friend request was coming from. She'd long since turned off notifications for any of it, refusing to be pulled in, to be hurt any more than she already was.

Her growling stomach reminded Catherine there was no need to stay holed up in her room all day. The kitchen would be empty, leaving her free to whip up whatever she chose. Her usual fruit and juice would suffice, but that morning she wanted something a little special.

Like a bowl of Sam and Tyler's favorite cereal.

Cradling that bowl in her hand, she walked into the living room to do the forbidden—eat outside of the dining room or kitchen area. Why not? She'd already been doing it for months, only in the confines of her room or the gym. She curled up on the end of the couch, savoring every bite, wondering how their day was going.

If they were happy.

If they were around a tree together, as a family, enjoying themselves.

If they were mourning the loss of Brian one year to the day that he took his own life.

And her appetite vanished.

Catherine set the bowl down on the coffee table and looked

around her, honestly taking in her surroundings. The furniture was the same it had been—expensive, pristine, pieces that were the envy of anyone who had visited the home. The Christmas tree in the bay window of the living room was decorated impeccably, breathtakingly beautiful even without its lights turned on. Presents were aligned just so underneath, no clashing papers or unkempt bows. She hadn't bothered to go through to check the names; she knew they were all hers, each one of them bought out of necessity or obligation rather than out of love.

She didn't want a single one of them.

Leaving her cereal bowl behind, she took the stairs down to the basement, the number of boxes dwindling daily as Frank either shipped or discarded them. The remnants of the broken cd player had been cleaned up, the scuff on the wall painted over, the dots of blood soaked up from the carpeting. Still, a flash of light caught on an object that rested mostly beneath the couch, drawing Catherine's attention to it. She knelt down and retrieved the disc, unscratched, unharmed in spite of the violent end of the last player it had been in. Her fingertips traced over Brody's slanted handwriting on the front, her heart aching to hear the song they'd danced to.

But not here.

Not in this house.

She moved with purpose up two flights of stairs, straight to her room… her room that held all the luxuries that she had demanded before. So many clothes, dozens of shoes, the latest and greatest gadgets.

She retrieved her duffel bag and began to fill it… slowly at first, her speed increasing with every movement, every article of clothing, everything she deemed necessary. She grabbed a second bag for the bathroom, grabbing the assorted bottles, her toothbrush, all of her makeup, her hands shaking as she zipped it closed.

She didn't know what time it was, didn't bother with the presents beneath the tree, didn't think twice when she dropped three bags into the trunk of her car.

And she didn't look back as she drove away from the house on the hill for the last time.

CHAPTER 46

Hope

Traffic was light on nearly every road that Catherine drove down. The parking lot of Davis High was empty, devoid of any stray vehicles the students hadn't been able to start the last day of school before winter break. The shops were deserted, their windows darkened, leaving all last-minute gift shoppers to hit up the few convenience stores that had remained opened for the holiday.

Still, Catherine drove.

She left the town behind her, hitting the highway without fear of a traffic jam, her fingers tapping on the steering wheel to the music from the alternative rock station that Brody had left her radio on. She didn't bother lying to herself; she wasn't listening simply because it was one of the only stations not playing Christmas music. Instead she was allowing memories of the boy, of the rides they'd shared to and from school, of the cupcake she'd forced herself to eat with him the morning of her birthday. She thought of the lake party, her panic to get him home in time. She thought of the late-night talks hidden in the shadows of the basement, fingers laced together.

She allowed herself to miss him.

The first of the snow flurries began fluttering to the ground, not quite sticking but not entirely disappearing. This left slivers of white among the dying grass of the lawn in front of the small house she pulled her car up to. What was it that she and her former friends had called these? She couldn't quite recall, although the term 'crackerjack box' was sticking out in her mind. This one in particular was in a state of disrepair, its gutter hanging low on one side, shutters in need of a coat of paint, different colored shingles on the roof where a makeshift patch job had been done in lieu of replacing everything. The front door was a garish shade of red, its paint peeling to show the gray beneath, its doorknob faded from its original luster, had it ever truly shown to begin with.

With a soft sigh, Catherine picked up her purse from the passenger seat and timidly walked up to that front door. She wasn't quite sure what she would say, how she would say it, whether or not her presence would even be welcome.

But when her father opened that door, smiling with joy and surprise no words were needed.

He welcomed her into his open arms, holding her closer as her tears began to fall, as she clung tighter than she had since she'd been a small child.

Catherine Garner was home.

"Here."

Catherine looked up from her spot on the lumpy threadbare couch to see her father holding out a steaming cup of hot chocolate. She smiled through her tears, sniffling a bit as she thanked him and carefully took the cup from him. Her eyes drifted back to the miniature Christmas tree, its white lights barely illuminating the few plastic ornaments haphazardly placed. Her father had never been one for style; he'd always hired decorators or personal shoppers to handle that side for him.

"Not much, I know," he commented as he sat beside her, leaving a little room between them.

Catherine shook her head. "It's beautiful."

Colin's laugh was loud, genuine. "Nothing about that tree is beautiful."

"Of course it is," she replied. "It was done with love." Her voice caught on the last word and she drew in a shaky breath.

"Ah."

She glanced over at her father, who was nodding slowly. "What?"

"That's what this is about." He reached over, gently wiping away a stray tear with the pad of his thumb. "A broken heart."

Her words were soft as her gaze returned to the mug in her hands. "You have no idea." She felt his hand brush her hair back, the gesture more comforting than she ever remembered feeling from her mother.

"I wouldn't be so sure about that, Catherine." There was no scolding in his tone, only a sadness reminding her of how much her father had truly loved her mother, and perhaps even her. "So… I know he's a lot bigger than I am, but I'm sure I can find some way to intimidate… Mitch? Was that his name?"

Catherine shuddered involuntarily. "No… no, he's… well, no we're not together anymore, thank god." She set her mug down on the table and drew her knees up to her chest, wrapping her arms around them. "He was not a nice boy, by the way. And that's all I ever heard… 'that nice young man'. Money doesn't make someone nice. I'm a shining example of that."

"Catherine,"

"No, I know I have done some… some horribly cruel things to others, and… and that they all enjoyed reciprocating." She focused on the sparsely decorated tree, a sad smile tugging at one corner of her mouth. "I can hardly blame them, though. But Brody…" Her voice trailed off as she struggled against the tears, the overwhelming emotion bombarding her senses. "He was…" Kind. He'd been kind to her, until he'd felt he'd been betrayed.

"Brody." It was more of a statement coming from her father, and she nodded before burying her face in her knees to collect herself.

"He was…" She sighed then, unable to finish her thought out loud.

"And this… Brody. Does he have a last name?"

"Hmm?" She looked over at her father, his eyes narrowed in concern as he took in her expression. "Harris. He's… he's…" She stopped short of calling him Frank's son, even though by law he was. "Mom's boyfriend, when he moved in, he brought his kids with him."

It was Colin's turn to hurt, although he recovered far more quickly than Catherine had. "I see."

Catherine's expression softened, her heart hurting for her father. "I'm sorry, that… I thought you knew."

Colin sighed, a wry smile touching his lips. "I'm fine, Catherine. I was hardly holding out hopes of going back to that pr… house."

"Prison. You were going to say prison."

"Which isn't fair to say with you here."

"It's accurate." Catherine could especially attest to that fact since Brody, Tyler, and Sam had left. "With Frank there, it's only gotten worse."

"Frank?"

"Harris, Mom's... whatever he is." She couldn't hide the disgust from her voice or her expression, not that she wanted to. "He's a monster, Dad. I'd never really seen a monster up close before him." And Mitch her subconscious added, but she didn't say it out loud.

"What did he do to you, Catherine?"

She shook her head, unwilling to look over at her father as she willed her tears to stop.

They began to flow again anyway.

"Hey... hey, look at me. What did he do to you?"

"Not me, Dad. Brody." She sniffled again but decided against stopping her tears. They were going to come regardless. "You just... you just don't know what he did to him, Daddy. The bruises he would leave, the... the stitches he should have had, the... the cracked ribs. I know they were cracked, I know, because of when I injured myself before. And... and he would always hit him where no one could see, but not this time." She shuddered again as she remembered Brody's face—the face she'd mistakenly seen as plain—with blood streaking down it, a swollen eye, bruising beginning to form. "And I don't know if he's okay."

She heard rustling and didn't need to look over to see that her father had pulled out his cell phone. "I need to know what you saw."

"Everything, and... you don't have to call anyone, Dad. Not right now. Their mother came to get them." She choked back another sob and wiped a few falling tears away. "I made sure of that. It was... it was the least I could do, and I don't know if it's enough, and... oh... oh, Dad, I have to go." Her eyes were wide as she looked up, a realization dawning on her. "I have to... I have to go back, because... because what if he goes to get them again?"

"You're not going anywhere." Those words from Colin were spoken with as much love as they were conviction.

"You don't understand, he's… he'll bring them back, and… and he won't touch Ty or Sam if Brody's there, so Brody won't leave."

"Catherine, listen to me. We need to call…"

"Not the police, Dad. Please, he… I don't know what will happen, and Brody doesn't want the kids to get split up, and… and what if their mom still isn't well? Oh… what have I… no, it was right. It was right." She shook her head, knowing she couldn't possibly be making much sense to her father. "As long as Frank doesn't bring them back, they'll be okay. Brody was the one taking care of them anyway, and… and I have to make sure that…"

"Catherine, if we involve the police then Frank can't bring them back."

Catherine's eyes were pleading as she looked over at her father. "And say what? I can't prove anything. Everything was always cleaned up, and Greta… Dad, Mom got rid of Greta after… after she helped. And I don't even know where Brody is. Without him, it's just my word. No pictures, no… no video. I mean I did, but… or I tried to, and it was on the memory card of the camera that I gave to him when he was leaving. I didn't tell him though, Daddy, and he wouldn't talk to me. I just… I just want them to be safe."

"Brody Harris… he has your camera."

"I gave it to him," Catherine clarified. "I… well, I would have given him the camera anyway, but I didn't get a chance to tell him about the memory card, and… and I don't even know what's on it, if you can see anything." She choked back another sob, wondering if their dance, their kisses, any of it was on there. She hadn't planned on everything that had occurred, never thinking it would go so far.

And not thinking ahead of time how this really must look to Brody, if he only watched the beginning.

Without explanation from her, it would be so easy to misinterpret her intention.

"I don't have a way to tell him why." She drew in a shaky breath, her tears causing the Christmas tree before her to blur. "I hope he would know, but…" She shook her head again, sobs shaking her slender shoulders. "I want to stay, Daddy. I want to stay here, I want to… I'll get a job to help, and… and you found someone to buy the car. I'll help around the house, and… I want to stay, but what if I can't? What if Frank—"

"Princess, I want you to listen to me, okay?" Colin turned his daughter's tear-streaked face in his direction, forcing her to look at him. "You're not going back. You're not going back, I don't give a damn how much money your grandfather throws at the courts, as long as Frank Harris is there, you're not going to be subjected to that."

"But… Brody, and—"

"I need to make a couple of phone calls." Colin wiped her still-falling tears away. "I have failed you, Catherine."

"You didn't." She took in a shaky, but steadying, breath. "You didn't know what was going on."

"But I should have. I should have demanded to know, should have pushed to be more involved, and maybe… maybe someday you'll forgive me. And when you have children of your own,"

He didn't finish his sentence as the remainder of Catherine's resolve crumbled.

"Oh… oh no." He gathered her close, rocking her as she cried into his shirt front. "It's going to be okay, sweetheart. You have a big decision to make, and…"

"I'm not… not anymore, and… I just can't right now."

"Brody?"

She was quiet for a moment, wondering if she should keep up the ruse, just in case.

But she knew better.

She knew she was safe.

"No. Not Brody."

She felt the kiss her father left in her hair. "Do you want to talk about it?" Catherine shook her head, but remained there, tucked up against her father's chest. "Some day?"

She thought for a moment… one brief moment, and that was all it took to have her nodding. "Someday. I promise."

"Listen." He left another kiss in her hair before he pulled back, tilting her face up to his. "I have a couple of phone calls to make, okay?"

"I'm sorry, I… I didn't mean to interrupt any plans you…"

"Nothing like that." He placed a kiss on her forehead and ruffled her hair, invoking memories from years before. "Then you and I are going to endure some sort of concoction that I'm sure I can find ingredients for, and we are going to celebrate."

She smiled through her tears, but it faded just as quickly. "I keep forgetting it's Christmas. I didn't even go shopping or anything."

"What you've given me today can't be bought in a store, Catherine." He leaned over, kissing her forehead once more. "It's going to be all right. You'll see."

While the side of her that questioned everything, that had been questioning it for months, had problems believing in what her father said, the child that still resided within her relaxed, albeit slightly, at his words.

It was all going to be all right.

And for the first time since Brody had left that house on the hill, she allowed herself to hope.

CHAPTER 47

Just Cat

Three weeks was a relatively short time in the great span of life, but to Catherine those weeks had seemed endless. There were phone calls to be made, though, and legal issues to be sorted out. Theresa had scoffed when she'd been told of Catherine's intentions to remain with her father in the valley, telling her ex-husband that in less than a week's time once she was 'over her tantrum', she would be back.

Catherine assured everyone who would listen that wasn't the case.

Instead she acclimated herself to her new town, her new routine, with no mention of what she had gone through. Her father had tried, of course, but would merely nod when she would tell him she would talk to him when she was ready.

She wasn't ready yet.

With her car gone, she learned her way around by walking, or in the evenings borrowing her father's car to run errands. She found the small town to be quaint, so much within walking distance of the house or even close to the bus lines that navigating her way wasn't an issue. Her father was more than a little concerned in the evenings, though, insisting that Catherine didn't know the area well enough to walk around with little to no sunlight.

Just six blocks from the home she shared with her father, she found exactly what she'd been looking for—a gymnastics studio with a well-respected instructor. A little bit of negotiating had Catherine 'volunteering' to help out with the classes, with a potential position once she'd proven herself. With no doubt in her mind that she would, Catherine had accepted the position, penciling in her classes on the calendar that hung in the cramped kitchen area.

This date, though… this date that morning was the one circled on the calendar, not by herself but by her father. All of the paperwork was in place, all semester finals made up so that grades could be transferred.

Catherine Garner, no longer Queen of Davis High, was merely another student starting her first day at Valley High School.

That January day was cold and snowy, so she opted for more sensible shoes rather than an expensive pair of designer footwear that was sure to be ruined. With her jeans slightly looser than they had been—she hadn't had much of an appetite—and a comfortable black sweater, she was sure she would blend right in. Gone was her desire to stand out, to have the best of everything that money could buy. All the money she'd had before had never filled her with as much joy as her father peeking in her room as he passed by her open door that morning.

"I can give you a ride in, if you'd like. I have to stay later, though, so you'll need to take the bus home."

The school bus stop was only a block away, but with Catherine not knowing anyone she opted to ride that morning with her father instead. Without the extra time to get ready, she pulled her hair into a high ponytail and kept her makeup to a minimum. It wasn't as if she had an agenda to impress anyone; if they were going to like her, it was going to be on her own terms.

"You're quiet this morning," her father remarked as they drove the short distance to Valley High, a school Catherine had once looked down upon for its neighborhood alone. Glancing around that the few students arriving as early as they were, she noted that they seemed no different than those at any other school. Perhaps their clothing wasn't just so, or their cars top of the line. The students, though, walked around the school campus the same—with a purpose, either to learn or to socialize, or perhaps with no purpose other than their attendance was required. Each one had their own struggles, each one their own triumphs.

"It's just first day jitters," she finally said as he parked the car in the staff's lot. "They'll have my schedule for me in the office, right?"

Colin smiled over at her, a smile that she'd never seen on him when he'd be heading in to work at his former job. "Of course. I did look over it, made sure they had you in the classes you'd requested. In order to get your elective, though, a few things had to be switched around."

Catherine was puzzled as they exited the car. "I thought that was the hardest class to get into. Even the guidance counselor had said so. She'd said I probably couldn't take it until next year." She walked alongside her father, speaking to him as any other student would, no one paying her any mind as they passed.

"Let's just say I know people."

"Hey, Coach," a boy in the hallway said to her father as he passed, and Colin acknowledged him with a nod and a smile.

"Coach?" Catherine asked.

"I'll be taking over as the baseball coach this spring." He pulled open the heavy glass door leading to the office where a frazzled but friendly older woman was bustling through papers. "Good morning, Rita."

"And a good morning to you, Mr. Garner." She then turned her smile in Catherine's direction. "And how may I help you, dear?"

After a reassuring smile from her father, Catherine stepped up to the counter. "I'm Catherine Garner, and I'm here for my schedule."

"Ah, Catherine." Rita smiled knowingly, and Catherine didn't know if she should be concerned or amused. "Any relation to you, Mr. Garner?"

"You know better than to ask," Colin said as he pulled papers from what Catherine was assumed was his mailbox. "I have to get to the classroom."

"Oh, we'll make sure she finds her way around."

Catherine had to stifle a giggle. The woman was clearly flirting with her father, right in front of her no less. She did see the subtle shake of her father's head in her direction letting her know that no, nothing of that nature was going on, before he headed out of the office. Catherine's attention was again drawn to Rita, scurrying about behind the tall counter, muttering to herself about where she could have placed that copy that she'd printed off.

"Is that what you're holding?" Catherine finally asked, causing Rita to pause and glance at her left hand.

"Oh… oh, of course." She said this with a laugh, one that was infectious and had Catherine smiling as she took the paper from Rita's hand.

Sure enough, her schedule had changed, even if it was only a slight one. The elective she'd wanted—photography—was her first class, even. She declined Rita's offer of help finding the classroom more so because she was certain the woman would have had her lost. Instead, she set out on her own, figuring she'd arrived early enough to find it.

She was definitely mistaken.

Students were milling about, walking past and around her as if she wasn't even there, staring at the numbers above the doorways on both sides of the hall. Thinking her schedule had a misprint on it, Catherine sighed and walked back towards the office, hoping that Rita maybe had a map of some kind. She paused mid-stride and turned towards a side hall, almost swearing she'd seen a familiar head of dark hair with an even more familiar walk. Disappointment settled in when she realized it had to have been her imagination, since the boy was nowhere to be found.

And neither was room 138.

With a sigh, she turned back around, colliding with another student who hadn't been watching where they were going. The other girl's books scattered across the floor as she mumbled her apology to Catherine.

"Let me help," Catherine said as she stooped down, picking up two of the heavier books and handing them to the girl. "I was the one just standing in the hallway anyhow. I'm Catherine."

The girl looked a bit skittish as she glanced at Catherine over her glasses, her brown curly hair falling across her forehead. "Hi," was all she said.

"Are you new here, too?" Catherine asked, and the girl shook her head.

"Nope. Sorry, I know I come across as rude. Well, I kind of am, but… hi." She stuck out her hand, which Catherine shook. "I'm Jen, and I'm guessing you're lost. But not lost in thought, like

I was."

Catherine smiled, liking this girl already. "Lost, definitely" With the sound of a bell, she cringed. "And apparently late as well."

"Nah, that's just first bell." Jen took Catherine's schedule from her hand without asking and glanced down at it. "Ah, that's why. The photography lab's actually through this class here. Its door is on the other side of the room. It's normally marked, but..." Her voice trailed off and she shrugged. "They think us photographers are nothing but nerds, so they'll do things like take signs for our classes."

"You're in this one?" Catherine asked as she took her schedule back.

"Yes and no. Photography yes, but not this period. Fear not, there are some badasses in there that are even better at it than I am. But I'll see you in chemistry, fourth period. Believe it or not, that door is still marked. Bye."

Catherine stared at Jen as she walked away, wondering if maybe she'd just made a friend. With the second bell looming, though, she had no more time to ponder. With her head held high, she walked into the classroom that Jen had pointed to, noticing the door on the opposite side, clearly marked 138.

Not that she could have seen that from the hallway.

She kept her eyes focused on the instructor behind the desk of the photography lab, his glasses perched on the end of his nose as he glanced over the paper before him. "Excuse me... I'm..."

"Ah, our new student. Welcome, Catherine Garner."

This time there was no mistaking the movement from the corner of her eye.

At the mention of her name, a dark-haired boy had looked up, his blue eyes wide as they locked with hers, his expression one of shock.

One that mirrored her own.

Then realization.

As it hit him—and her—that they really were in the same room together.

And finally… *finally* the beginnings of a smile.

A smile that sent her heart racing, the butterflies in her stomach taking flight, the blush in her cheeks that she couldn't keep from happening.

She could only smile—just a slight one, just the corners of her mouth tipping upwards as they always seemed to do whenever she made eye contact with him.

"Mr. Harris, I asked if you would show Catherine where to sign out the school equipment. Any day now."

"Yes, sir."

Brody's voice was sure as he stood, each step towards Catherine making her feel lightheaded.

Elated.

The bruises were gone, and apparently so was his razor that morning as he had just the slightest bit of stubble across his jaw. He looked older this way, and yet… yet in his eyes, he looked so young.

Carefree.

Happy.

His familiar scent as he stood beside her had chills breaking out across her skin, and her fingers tingled as she fought the urge to reach up and run her fingers through his unruly hair. She barely registered what the instructor was saying, or even Brody's words when his hand rested on the small of her back, leading her to yet another door, one that was tucked away in the corner, far away from other students and even blocked from the instructor himself. Her hands were shaking when Brody reached around her and opened the door, his hand on her back urging her forward.

One step.

Then two.

Then another.

And his hands turned her suddenly, pinning her back to the wall, their foreheads resting together, their eyes locked as his fingertips pressed into the flesh of her hip.

One whispered word from him.

"Cat…"

One lush kiss, unspoken apology and forgiveness passing between them as lips parted, tongues caressed, fingertips tracing unseen patterns across slivers of bare skin.

One smile that lingered as he pulled away, handing her a camera and a clipboard to sign.

"Where do I.."

"Here."

She placed the camera on the shelf and took the pen from his hand, their eyes meeting as their fingers touched.

"I didn't know your number."

He'd wanted to call her.

"And I tried emailing, and it kept getting sent back."

"Why would… oh." A shy smile touched her trembling lips. "I blocked your email after you went through my phone."

Their laughter was soft, the memory of their former animosity softer.

"I even got back on Facebook, sent you a friend request."

He was so close she could feel the words against her skin.

"I haven't really… not after…"

"I know."

Her eyelids fluttered closed as his fingertips brushed her hair back from her face.

"I even asked Bethany to tell you to go online, check Facebook. I swear the friend request is there."

And the spell was broken.

"You asked your ex-girlfriend to come to my house?"

His head tilted back as his laughter filled the room. "I've missed you."

"That is so wrong, and what,"

He silenced her words with another kiss.

"I've missed you, too," she whispered.

"Our story's not over."

She smiled as his words washed over her, filling her soul. "No, it's not."

"Excuse me, lovebirds." A grinning redheaded boy leaned into the room. "I've been sent to remind you we still have class."

"Right." Brody's eyes never left Catherine's. "Sign for the camera."

Her hand was still trembling as she signed her name on the designated line.

"What about you?" she managed to ask as they left the room.

He glanced over his shoulder as he led her to her seat—one beside a girl who was chatting animatedly with the redheaded boy who sat beside Brody—and he smiled. "Santa was good to me this year."

Catherine's laugh was soft, as to not draw attention to herself, although the boy next to Brody wasn't about to let that happen.

"So… Lady Catherine… you do exist."

Catherine's eyes widened in surprise.

Brody had mentioned her.

Not just mentioned her, but with *that* nickname.

"Shut it, Max." Brody had no animosity in his tone, but kept his eyes averted, focusing on the papers before him. He pulled out a couple of sheets, writing a short note on one before passing it forward. "You'll need these for later."

Catherine nodded, holding the papers slightly open so only she could read them. They were class notes, but over to the side in his familiar slanted writing he'd printed *Frank's locked up. THANK YOU, Lady Catherine.*

Frank was locked up… those words alone made her smile. Brody had found the memory card, he must have.

But the nickname.

Again, he had used it.

She raised her eyebrow as she looked back at him. "That's not my name, you know."

"You're not Lady Catherine?" Max asked, still having his own conversation, oblivious that Catherine wasn't participating. "So, you're a figment of our imagination, too? Man, I need to quit drinking."

"There's so much you need to quit doing, you have no idea," the girl sitting beside Catherine spoke up. "Since they're rude, hi. I'm Sarah, your new lab partner in this lovely little photography class, and I'm so glad to have some estrogen in this mix back here."

"Because, you know, we're the badasses," Max continued. "Me especially. Brody here's my wingman."

"Keep telling yourself that," Brody muttered, nudging Max to keep him quiet as the instructor stood to give out the instructions.

Max, apparently, wasn't going to listen.

"So, if you're not Lady Catherine, then who are you?"

"Catherine," she replied softly, a smile on her lips. "Just Catherine."

"Well, Just Catherine," Max said, ignoring the instructor

altogether, "welcome to Valley High."

"Yes, welcome Just Catherine," Sarah added, and when Catherine felt a nudge to the back of her chair, she glanced over her shoulder.

And she met Brody's smile with one of her own.

"Cat," he whispered, causing her to blush.

And so began her first day at Valley High. No longer a cheerleader, no longer driving a custom painted pink convertible, no longer Queen.

She was Just Catherine.

Just… Cat.

Just a girl who lived in a small, rundown suburban home full of love and promise.

Just a girl in a school where those who spoke to her were friendly without an agenda.

Just a girl in love with a not-so-ordinary boy whose presence made her feel as light as air.

And Catherine Denise Garner wouldn't have it any other way.

Authors (especially indie!) rely on your reviews. Please take a moment to review this novel on the platform that it was purchased from. It is appreciated more than you will ever know!

ABOUT THE AUTHOR

Carlie Yates (That One Writer Chick) has been writing stories since she was in the fifth grade, convinced that if she didn't get her thoughts and characters down on paper, her head would 'plode; it could be ex- or im-, but either way, it wouldn't be pretty. Inspired by S.E. Hinton, she always said when she grew up that she would be a published author. She is currently renouncing her pledge to grow up. This Midwest mom of boys has addictions to reading, road trips, hair dye, and the Oxford comma, and is thoroughly convinced at any given time the theme track to *My Three Sons* will start playing in the background of her home.

STALK ME

(Honestly, just follow, but hey… that was catchy)

www.thatonewriterchick.com

https://www.facebook.com/thatonewriterchickakacarlie

https://www.instagram.com/thatonewriterchickakacarlie

https://www.goodreads.com/thatonewriterchickakacarlie

RESOURCES

This book is a work of fiction. In no way do I condone any of the acts within. They are, however, important issues that many people face, no matter their age, gender, or social status. If you or someone you love has dealt or are dealing with any of them, please reach out. Help is available. You can look for local resources or contact one of the national centers below.

National Suicide Hotline

1-800-273-8255

https://suicidepreventionlife.org/

https://www.crisistextline.org

Text HOME to 741741

National Sexual Assault Hotline

1-800-656-4673

https://www.rainn.org/get-help

National Domestic Violence Hotline

1-800-799-7233

https://www.thehotline.org

ACKNOWLEDGEMENTS and THANKS
(in no particular order)

My Fifth-grade teacher, Mrs. Cheryl Doblar - When I said that someday I would be a published author, you told me to follow that dream. Thank you from the bottom of my heart.

Rose I can't put into words how grateful I am that you are a part of my life. Thank you for accepting me when I didn't know how to accept myself. Love and monsters all the way!

Christa for EVERYTHING! And also your belief in me and in this story, which started this ball rolling.

Becky for sitting beside me that first day of kindergarten and announcing that you were my new best friend. Girl, the stories that we can tell… although we probably shouldn't. So, if they ever end up in a book, we won't acknowledge them… or will we?

Stephanie – I would be so lost without you. Thank you for being you and allowing me to be me. And a HUGE thank you for sticking beside me from my horrid younger years to now. I love you always!

Courtney – My soul sister, my spirit animal. I see so much of me in you. I love you to the moon and back, and I promise we will get US time soon!

Amy DeNapoli- My forever girl crush, I am SO proud of you!!! You are truly an inspiration, and someday I hope someone will say to me that I am #AmyStrong

Cody Bailey – not only for the amazing book cover, but also for always interrupting my irrational emotional outbursts with things like facts and logic and reason. I'm still on this earth, and my minions still have their mom. THANK YOU.

Nicole Bellare – My editor extraordinaire! My missed Oxford commas, dreaded 'teh's, and I are forever grateful for you.

Amber my writing partner, I love you SO much!! Thank you for asking "when." Had you not pushed for that answer, I wouldn't be writing this thank you in my debut novel.

Scoot- we sure do make awesome babies, don't we? I'm grateful for them every day. And look at us adulting! Thank you for working on you.

Tami- my preview baby. You're the T to my J always.

Nellie Corriveau and all of Magical Mentorship 2019… Thank you for the support, the accountability, and the love that I carry with me every day. Believe in the magic, loves, and let's climb that mountain!!!

Vera- my V, I love you with my whole heart.

Tina- You are a true warrior! Let's do that Outsiders House Museum trip, for serious!

Food food FOOD and Books- the best book club EVER!!! What an incredible, diverse, intelligent, and FUN tribe. Thank you for your support, thank you for beta reading for me, and THANK YOU for accepting me as one of your own. I will do my best to have a food theme in future books.

My Visions babies – This thank you is for every alpha reader in the online reading world, whichever board you were a member of. You gave me a chance to spread my writing wings and believed in me when I didn't believe in myself. I love you all, forever!

My family and my tribe Where would I be without all of you?

I've been blessed, and I count those blessings every day.

My readers Yes, that's you! Find your tribe. Love them hard. Lean on them when you need to.

And finally…

Typos – to any that have made it past writing, revising, alpha readers, beta readers, editing, and proofreading… Kudos to you. You're the real MVP.

Entrapped

Book 2 of the *Entangled* series

Releasing October 28, 2019

It's the summer before senior year, and now that Brody's dark secret has been exposed, he's left with too many wounds that just won't heal.

He fell for Catherine—*hard.* And even though their love is the brightest part of his life, it can't chase away the shadows of his past. Years of torment still plague him, and it's a constant battle between old, haunting memories and trying to make new ones with Catherine.

Brody soon realizes that the only way he'll be able to let go of the past is to find the truth hidden behind a life filled with lies. But as he discovers who he truly is, it becomes painfully clear that the road he's currently on will turn him into the devil he fears the most.

Now Brody is faced with the daunting decision that will change his life forever. Does he stay and risk becoming a monster himself? Or should he save his soul by leaving behind the girl he loves?

www.ingramcontent.com/pod-product-compliance
Lightning Source LLC
Chambersburg PA
CBHW021213260626
47172CB00002B/406

* 9 7 8 1 7 3 3 2 6 4 9 0 7 *